OX
in the
CULVERT

GERALD BRENCE

QUIPPY
QUILL

PART I

CHAPTER 1

CULLUMAR VALLEY OF CALIFORNIA
JANUARY 1848

The sign nailed to the top of the building read Sutter's Sawmill. James I Marshall saw it every day. The old man who owned the mill, John Sutter, wasn't around much. He and James had been arguing a lot lately. Captain Sutter, as they called him, made sure Marshall knew that one dollar per day meant ten hours of work at ten cents an hour. That didn't count taking time for lunch or supper.

Marshall had no choice but to adhere to the captain. It was the only work he could find. Late in the afternoon, fog was blowing in from the Northern California range. Marshall was having trouble with rocks and chunks of dirt getting into the saw apparatus's wooden trough. The trash was slowing everything down. The saws would clog and force Marshall to keep shutting the mill down. He had an idea to dig a trench at the front of the mill's runway. As the logs came to the mill, he could stand there and redirect the rocks and dirt with a shovel. He believed the trench current would carry the debris all the way down to the river. Marshall believed it would work, and he had been working on it all day.

Marshall was worn out from a rough day's work, and he was in a foul mood. All of a sudden, Captain Sutter showed up. It was just before dark. Sutter had on a big plantation hat. He was fat, and he was smoking a big agar.

He used a five-foot-tall walking stick that had a brass handle.

"Marshall, what are you doing down there? Why aren't you in the mill?" he barked.

Marshall and Sutter's relationship had become strained. The captain was very impatient with the mill's progress.

"I'm digging this trench away from the mill," Marshall told him. "I think it'll flush the rocks and clods out."

"That's a stupid idea, boy," bellowed the captain. "Get back up here and do your job. Quit worrying about rocks."

The old man's tone insulted Marshall and put him into a rage. He knew what he was doing, and he also knew Sutter wouldn't fire him. Nobody else knew how to run the mill. Marshall had built it himself, and he knew every inch of the operation. He was determined to get the job done, so he decided to spite the captain.

Marshall started digging the trench like his livelihood depended on it, because maybe it did. Feverishly, he pushed the dirt with his shovel in an almost perfect groove. He dug a little over two feet deep and another three feet wide. Pretty soon, the trench ran all the way down into the river. Captain Sutter owned the land for miles around, but he didn't own the river itself.

Marshall continued digging. In all, he figured he had dug at least forty yards. He looked back up the hill where the mill stood. Captain Sutter was gone. It crossed his mind that the old man might actually fire him for being so disrespectful. The thought would keep him up all night long.

Captain Sutter expected Marshall to sleep at the mill every night. He was afraid of leaving it unattended for any length of time. Sutter never thought of paying him to sleep there though. That was just part of the job.

It didn't matter. Marshall didn't have anywhere to go anyway. He was just trying to save up enough money to get away from the old man. His bed was on the mill floor. Cotton twill sacks served as his covers. The de livery men would show up early in the morning to haul the lumber back to town. Only twelve planks had been cut today. Marshall had shut the mill down because he was too busy digging the trench. Captain Sutter wouldn't be happy with only twelve boards. He was used to at least twenty-five to thirty per day.

Marshall got up at daybreak and walked down to look at his trench. He walked all the way down to the riverbed. When he got there, he looked back up through the trench to the mill.

That was when he first saw it. A shining streak lit up the trench. Marshall didn't understand it at first, but it didn't take him long to figure it out. He grabbed his shovel and started slicing the dirt. The glistening amber metal was plentiful, and it stretched all the way through the trench. It was a fine substance, almost like sand. Marshall looked closer. His senses came alive. As he was trying to figure out what to do, he heard the sawmill delivery men arrive. One man was on a horse. The other man was driving a team of horses that pulled a wagon. Marshall ran fifty yards to meet them. He needed to block them from the mill.

"I got no lumber for you today!" Marshall yelled. "You can go on your way."

The man driving the wagon got angry.

"The trip is too far to make without trading goods. I can wait for you to produce if you need more time."

However, James Marshall wanted no part of any visitors.

"Go on your way," Marshall ordered the men. "I have nothing for you today."

Ten minutes later, the men turned the wagon around and left the valley.

Marshall watched them until they were out of sight. When he thought it was safe, he ran back to the trench. By then, four of Sutter's hired hands had showed up for work. They ran to him. James Marshall knelt down and cupped the dirt into his hands. He looked up at them and calmly said, "Boys, by God, I believe I've found a gold mine!"

CHAPTER 2

MELBOURNE, AUSTRALIA JUNE 1851

*F*ew people in the Port Phillip District knew that Lt. Governor Charles La Trobe was battling severe depression. He had been thrust into power very unwillingly. Traveling the world was his passion, yet he was stuck in the port area of a chaotic township, trying to govern. His district was a wreck. Australia had a gold rush in action similar to what was going on in California. Everyone, it seemed, was dropping all business and heading off to the fields in search of treasure.

Of course, only a few were so lucky. However, that didn't stop the throngs of people from leaving the day-to-day duties of city life to head for the search of gold. La Trobe was a tall, good-looking man. He had impeccable character, but his moral values were being tested. Educated back in England, he never thought of being assigned the mundane task of trying to organize a city. He wanted to travel and write books. He didn't want to deal with unruly citizens and outlaws. La Trobe came from an established family back in the old country. It was his duty to serve. That was why he was in Melbourne.

What was so disheartening to La Trobe was how much his township had fallen into ruins. It seemed that he couldn't count on anyone to stay in the city and finish any job. The local economy was in a tailspin. Basic services were left undone. Law enforcement personnel was scattered, and crime was at an all-time high.

La Trobe had taken it upon himself to police the city. Housing criminals was very expensive and time consuming. To keep the peace, he had to haul the lawbreakers into the jails to keep them off the streets. He learned quickly that a large sum of money was the only reason a beefy Australian man would serve as a peacemaker. But that was what he had to do, and he did it. The process was costing a fortune. He knew something drastic had to be done to keep the city from going bankrupt, so he made a difficult decision. He decided to deport all criminals from the city jail right into the Pacific Ocean.

La Trobe made a deal with one of the most unsavory characters in the region, Cyrus Welch. Welch had lived his entire life in Southern Australia. The son of a sharecropper, he had no taste for the farm life. He migrated to the city when he was fifteen years old. His goal was to break away from the drudgery of farm work and his father's vicious temper.

Welch's first job was as a hand on a cargo ship out of Port Phillip Bay. It was there that he saw he could either be a weak pauper or a wealthy entrepreneur. It was his choice to make. He just had to figure out how mean he needed to be to get what he wanted. He also had to figure out what his moral spirit would allow him to do.

That question was answered on his eighteenth birthday. Welch was working on the dock, loading wheat onto a ship. The foreman, an unfriendly man named Thomas McMahon, decided to slap Welch around a little bit. McMahon, it seemed, thought since he was the boss that he had the power to bully any worker he chose. He carried a whip with him everywhere he went.

Welch was in a good mood. It was a Saturday, and he was planning on doing a good bit of drinking that night. He sensed McMahon's attitude as he approached from the far side of the dock. Welch noticed that only the two of them were on sight. There were no witnesses around.

"Work harder, you scum," McMahon chided Welch. "You worthless as far as me concerned."

Welch kept his composure until McMahon pulled out the whip and yelled at him.

"I say harder, boy," McMahon yelled.

Then the foreman snapped the whip at Welch's feet. Welch immediately pulled his knife, lurched at McMahon, and stabbed him repeatedly up and under the ribcage. McMahon was dead in ten minutes. Welch gathered his body and deposited it into one of the large grain sacks. He shoveled grain into the sack until it was full. Then he dragged the sack and placed it with the rest of the cargo. The ship would depart later that after-noon. The entire episode took place in less than thirty minutes. Nobody ever heard from Thomas McMahon again.

After Welch had tasted murder, he no longer cared so much about the value of human life. Eventually, he worked his way up to foreman. Then he became the company man for a ship owner. Before he knew it, he was in position to buy a ship that had been abandoned in the harbor.

One day, La Trobe approached Welch down on the dock.

"Mate, would ye be 'trested in free labor should I be able to provide?" La Trobe asked.

Welch raised his eyebrows.

"Yay, I think I would," he answered.

That was the day that Cyrus Welch got involved with slave labor.

Lieutenant Governor La Trobe had gotten to the point that he didn't care so much about ethics. He and Cyrus Welch made their deal secretly in the lieutenant governor's office. La Trobe just wanted to get rid of the outlaws that haunted the port. He had heard of other government leaders in the region that had made similar deals with ship owners. The plan was simple. Shackle the prisoners and take them down to the docks. Tell them they had two options. They could go back to jail, or they could get on the ship. If they chose the ship, they would be released to Cyrus Welch. They just could never come back to Melbourne.

The prisoners really didn't have the option of going back to jail. The offer of staying was just a way to pacify La Trobe's conscious. Life in Southern Australia was moving too fast to know much about a shipping cargo owner, so Cyrus Welch got a pass on his background. La Trobe wanted as many people as possible to see the prisoners, so he walked them from the jail down to the dock. The shackles on their ankles and wrists scared the bystanders. He knew the value of a strong deterrent penalty.

La Trobe had leaked the news to the public, and a crowd had gathered to watch. It was similar to a public hanging. Welch loved the feeling of power that he had over the prisoners, but he knew not to abuse them. He remembered the incident with Thomas McMahon. He would take a different approach. His method would be to treat the men fairly until one of them rebelled. If they threatened his comfort level, the solution to the problem was simple. The prisoner would be thrown off the ship.

Welch had knives, shotguns, and handguns. He also had sixteen paid men on his ship. The slaves would bring a new dimension to the environment. Welch knew he had to keep both the paid hands and the prisoners down. If they gathered any power, there could be a mutiny. Welch knew the risks, but he was excited about the rewards. Labor was his biggest expense. Now he had a way to work around it. He would turn the prisoners into sailors. He would train them on the voyage.

The prisoners were loaded onto the ship. La Trobe felt very uncomfortable about the whole thing, but he stuck with the plan.

Suddenly, one of the prisoners realized that he might be on his death walk, and he started to rebel. Welch, the savvy business person that he was, stepped into action.

"We have no reason to harm ye," he said. "Work hard, do what ye told, and we let ye go in America."

Cyrus had a way of calming everyone down. The shackled man got on the ship, and it sailed away.

Things went well the first two days. There was nothing close to a mutiny. Slowly, Welch trained the prisoners to sail, but his plan didn't work well. On the second day, the prisoners got very hungry. He had done a poor job planning how to feed them. Welch didn't think of what might happen when one of the prisoners passed out from hunger or exhaustion. There were other problems. The paid men didn't like the situation, and it got testy on the ship. Finally, Welch gave up on training the prisoners and decided to hold them down below. He cuffed them to chains attached to the wall.

Welch also realized that he had too many slaves for the trip, so it was then that Cyrus Welch decided to throw twenty of them off the ship and into the ocean. The Melba Lee was five hundred miles east of Melbourne.

Cyrus Welch needed to get to America as quickly as possible. He had to figure out how to put the pieces together. Captured slave labor was the way to go. He just had to think it all through. He had heard of the great gold rush in Northern California. People were getting rich there. He had to get to San Francisco as fast as he could.

CHAPTER 3

SOUTHWEST TEXAS

As usual, it had been a long, hot summer in Texas, Capt. Ray Andrews was thinking about his future like he had done a hundred times before. He couldn't help but to wonder what was going on out in California with all this gold rush business. Ray had been poor his entire life. He had ten one-dollar coins to his name. The coins were kept on his body. He kept one coin in his pocket. The other nine coins were in small bags tucked into his boots. He had been good about saving his money. The ten coins amounted to the most money he had ever put together at one time in his entire life. He was intrigued by fortune, but he was a very conservative person by nature.

Maybe the rumor of people getting rich in California was just cheap talk, but Ray couldn't resist the temptation to at least listen. His best friend and fellow Texas Ranger, Tom Jenkins, wouldn't stop talking about it.

"They say all ya gotta do is ride down into the valley and start digging. We can do that better 'n anybody, Ray," he said repeatedly.

However, Ray knew he was going to have to give Tom the bad news. He wasn't going on any great adventure to California, but they could talk about that later. Right now, he had more serious business. He and Tom, along with eight other Rangers, were on a mission to protect a payroll wagon to Camp Stockton. There had been some ruthless Indian raids in the area. The Rangers believed the Indians were

Apache, but they weren't sure. They could be Comanche. The renegade leader of the band had been identified as one of the most savage Indian leaders in the southwest. The Rangers didn't know what to call him, so they gave him the surname of Empty Heart.

The scouts knew very little about him, and the Rangers were worried about his legend growing too quickly in far Southwest Texas. The only intelligence that the advanced scouts had offered was vague information about an Indian leader who wore a red feather. He did use guns, and he was a savage in his raids. A month ago, a friendly Indian scout made mention of a small group of what he thought were Apache. He had never seen them before. They looked to be dangerous. When pressed for information, he remembered the leader was wearing a red feather in his hair That was why the Rangers figured Empty Heart was in the general area.

Empty Heart, it seemed, was a master at hiding, planning, and executing his crimes. He was especially brutal. He not only killed his victims; he also dismembered them. He was a cold-blooded killer that could care less about the value of life. After surveying the carnage of one particular slaughter, an officer made the statement that, "Whoever did this has an empty heart." That was the story of why the Rangers gave Empty Heart his name.

Ray took a drink from his canteen. It was almost empty. He knew he wouldn't be able to fill it for a while. He and Tom were on top of what the locals called Rosary Hill. The hill was right at 120 miles west of Aus-tin. The Rangers strategically picked Rosary Hill because it would allow the small group of men to see from all sides. They felt it was a relatively safe place to camp. Ray and Tom had always competed against each other in their ability to shoot guns. Samuel Colt, the shrewd entrepreneur, had just developed a new handgun. It was a lighter, sleeker version of his four-pound, nine-ounce 44-caliber Colt Walker revolver that had changed everything in the Indian wars.

Colt's new version was a smaller 36-caliber revolver that weighed less than three pounds. On the cylinder, he had elegantly roll-engraved a depiction of an 1843 Texas naval battle with Mexico. He thought he could sell it to the navy. However, they didn't seem interested. His next target was the Rangers. The gun's accuracy was exceptional and could be aimed to fire at two hundred yards.

Colt was not only a great gunsmith, but he was shrewd at marketing his goods. A catchy name for his new creation would help sales. He tried a few different names, but his favorite was always the Colt Navy. He needed to test it, so he developed a contest. Both Ray and Tom were at the front of the line to sign up to compete. One of Colt's salesmen brought the revolver to Austin. The ten best shooters in the contest got one of the guns. They also got an assignment to guard a payroll wagon headed to Camp Stockton. None of the Rangers knew about the Camp Stockton trip when they signed up to win the revolver.

The contest was simple. Each Ranger got an opportunity to empty the six shots in the chamber at a board that was set up fifty yards away. Ray Andrews took first place by hitting all six of his shots inside a circle. Tom finished fourth.

"Ray, this is a waste of time," Tom Jenkins sneered. "I bet they're just building this Injun's name up to scare us. Don't you think?"

Tom was looking through his saddlebags for whiskey.

"Well," Ray replied, "I don't know 'bout that, but I've been thinking about this gold trip. I'm gonna re-up for another year with the Rangers. I'm not going to California."

The news jolted Tom Jenkins to the core. He sank his head, and then he rose to his feet.

"Well, you go ahead," he said, "I'm goin' on out there. You can stay here in Texas and starve the rest of your life if you want. All they're gonna do is use you until you get killed out in the middle of nowhere. You disgust me, Ray Andrews."

Ray had heard it before. Tom never mixed words when it came to emotion.

"You don't mean that, Tom," Ray replied.

"Yes, I do," said Tom. "I thought we were in this together. You're just a suck-up company man. The Rangers own you and always will. My old man was right. You won't ever amount to nothin'."

Tom Jenkins's father, William I., owned two full sections of land just south of Austin. He was one of the wealthiest men in Central Texas. Tom could go back and live a safe life if he wanted. Ray, on the other hand, didn't have anything. His parents never married. The story Ray had always heard was that his father died in a jail cell after being beaten up in a drunken brawl. Supposedly, that had happened somewhere in Central Texas. At the time, Ray was just eight years old. His mother, Della, left him with her mother, Ruth Anne Andrews, in Austin. Ruth Anne was in her seventies when she took in Ray. Tom and Ray met one day when they were kids and had been best friends ever since.

William T. Jenkins never liked Ray. He always viewed him as a low-class vagrant. But if the truth were told, it was just the opposite. Tom was the one who always got the two of them in trouble. One of his ideas led to the both of them signing up for Ranger duty at age eighteen. That did it. He always blamed Ray that Tom was a Ranger and not a farmer.

"We can talk about it later," Ray scolded Tom. "Empty Heart could be out there."

Tom snorted. "He ain't out there. Nobody is gonna bother us, and you know it."

Ray was thinking the same thing, but he wouldn't admit it. This was the third night of the escort duty. They had seen or heard nothing. Ray was worried that some of the Rangers would start taking things for granted. That was a serious mistake when dealing with Indians. He bounced down the hill to check on the men. Strategically, he had placed two men in dugout holes on each of the four sides of the hill. Hopefully, if Empty Heart attacked, he wouldn't know the Rangers were hiding below ground level. Ray and Tom were at the top of the hill. All ten Rangers had the new Colt Navy revolvers. Each one could get off six shots before having to reload. Placed in pairs, one could load the gun while the other was shooting. Hopefully, any battle would be a huge mismatch in favor of the Rangers.

Ray scrambled as low as possible to the north foot of the hill. Billy Terry and Big Scaley Johnson were down in a foxhole. Ray immediately noticed their foxhole wasn't deep enough.

"We better dig this hole a little deeper," he said as he jumped down with the men. "Give me your shovel."

Nobody in the Texas Ranger organization could push a shovel like Ray Andrews. He mastered the skill as a young Ranger out in the Texas fields. In less than ten minutes, he had dug the trench down another foot. He crawled out onto the prairie and grabbed three thistles. By the time he made it back to the hole, Billy and Big Scaley were digging again them-selves.

"Here, use these thistles to hide your heads. Don't take anything for granted. Take more pride in your cover," Ray said.

Ray always believed in leading by example. He never thought twice about doing physical labor. Now he needed to make it to the other three foxholes to make sure the men were ready.

It was right at dusk, and the weather was threatening. A sharp south wind had escalated. Lightning bolts sparked the skies. The smell of rain acted as a fragrance in the air. Everyone on the hill knew that Indians usually didn't attack at night. Most of them thought that it was against their honor, but this band was different. All the men knew it was at night that they were the most exposed. That was why Ray had set things up like he did. One Ranger could sleep while the other watched for Indians. The hill was surrounded with men in foxholes, and Ray was confident they had a huge firearm advantage.

Ray had gone to the trouble of ordering all the men to Carly huge body shields to protect themselves from arrows. The shields were just round pieces of wood that had been used as trash can lids. Ray had ordered one of the men to attach handles on one side. He had tried to think of everything. The plan was to create an image of four men traveling the route. Two men traveled on the wagon, usually Ray and Tom. The wagon was pulled by a team of four horses. Two other men traveled on horseback with rifles. Six men rode inside the covered wagon. It was tough duty staying inside the wagon all day in the Texas sun. The Rangers didn't want the convoy to look too heavily armed. If so, Empty Heart would know they had the money. Ray thought the whole mission was a gamble. Nobody knew what might happen, but the payroll had to get to Camp Stockton somehow.

Ray fought his way over to the west side of the hill. There was the first sergeant Cletus Smith. In Ray's opinion, Cletus was the best Kanger on the mission. He had the weakest Ranger, Sonny McGraw, with him.

There were plenty of big rocks to help establish cover on the west side, 50 it was easy for Smith and McGraw to set up their post. Cletus had formed a hole in the rock pile to shoot at anyone who threatened. Ray sure hoped any attack would come from the west because that was obviously the most fortified position.

Tom Jenkins had already started drinking whiskey. He had a bad attitude about the mission and was taking things for granted. Ray was very frustrated with his best friend, but he knew it wouldn't do much good to argue with him. Being on top of Rosary Hill was the last place in the world Tom wanted to be, and he let everyone know about it. Tom was a talented Ranger, but his attitude had gotten the best of him. The California Gold Rush was on his mind, and he had a tough time thinking about anything else. Tom was supposed to check on the south and east flank, but Ray took nothing for granted. He made it all the way around the hill.

The south flank was the most exposed. Ray would back it up from the top of the hill himself. Tom was supposed to back up the north flank, but he was wandering all over the hill, drinking and talking.

John Wilder, a veteran Ranger, was dug in deep. Wilder, it seemed, never slept. He was a family man with two kids at home. Ray tried as hard as he could to get Wilder out of the mission. He was the only Ranger on the hill who had a family. Wilder's droopy eyes made him look twenty years older than he really was. He realized the danger of a renegade Indian like Empty Heart taking over the territory. With every attack and victory, Empty Heart gained more power. Wilder realized that he had to be eliminated, so he convinced Ray that he needed to go on the trip.

Wilder's partner was a young Ranger named Will Johnson. Johnson was the second-best shooter in the group only behind Ray. If Johnson got his chance with the new Colt Navy revolver, Empty Heart's tribe could be decimated.

Wilder was on edge.

"I haven't seen nothing, but I got a feeling somebody's out there," he said as he tore off a piece of beef jerky. "You better get everybody ready, Ray."

Ray took anything Wilder said very seriously. Suddenly, his mood be? came much more intense. The trip had already been long. If anyone was watching, it wasn't hard to figure out that they had something valuable. They probably would be a target for someone. It could be the Indians or Mexican outlaws.

The Rangers reputation had become a bit of a hindrance. If it became known that a group of them was in the area, problems would often scat-ter. Usually, Rangers went on the offensive chasing villains. Guarding money was not what they were interested in doing.

The east side of the hill should be secure. The convoy had traveled from that direction. They had passed an old broken-down barn on the way. It could be a perfect staging area for someone to hide and then attack. The barn had concerned all the men when they passed it in the wagon.

Stuttering Henry Jones, the oldest man on the mission, was looking for any sign of life. Stuttering Henry didn't talk much because he hated being the butt of jokes. He had always been the victim of a terrible speech impediment. Often, he used hand signals to communicate. He was not fond of the new Colt Navy even though he was very good with it. A shotgun was his preference. He had two with him in the foxhole plus the revolver. His partner, Leo Wilson, made up for both of them with his talking. He wouldn't shut up. As soon as he heard the rock hit in front of him, he knew it was the captain. That was how Ray signaled to the men that he was coming around to check on them.

"Ray, is that you?" Wilson whispered.

"Yea, it's me. Do you see anything?" Ray responded.

Leo and Stuttering Henry had their eyes transfixed on the direction of the old barn, which was about five miles out. If anyone was following them, the men knew that was where they would hide. It was completely dark now, and the Texas sky was not kind to the Rangers. Lightning bolts seared sideways and provided brief glimpses of open prairie land. The clouds blocked the light that was put out by the stars. That gave away the advantage of being on top of the hill. The darkness was very scary to Leo Wilson. He was sweating profusely.

"Ray," Wilson said in a half whisper, "keep your gun pointed right over my head. If we get in trouble, I'm gonna just slip under this shield."

At the very moment he said it, lightning lit up the sky. "What do you think, Stut?" Ray whispered to Henry Jones. "C-C-Concerned," answered Henry. "D-Don't like that b-barn out there."

Ray stood up and looked in all four directions. "Well," he said. "If anything happens, use your best judgment."

Ray realized that the men were worried. All of the men except one, Tom Jenkins.

CHAPTER 4

*E*mpty Heart's real name was Sores Aguilar. His mother, Cincilla, was captured after a raid on her home Apache tribe by a band of Mexican outlaws years ago. She was sold as a slave to a much-despised man in the Big Bend country named Pinney Aguilar Cruz. Pinney was a noted criminal. His main source of income was in moving stolen horses from Texas into Mexico. He was also known as a thief that was accused of three murders in which he was never officially charged.

Cincilla was a very beautiful woman. That was the main reason that Pinney had bought her. He used her as a sex slave along with many other duties. A son was conceived the year after Cincilla was purchased. Pinney was fond of the young boy at first, but he quickly became bored. They named the boy Sores. Cincilla raised him pretty much alone. She wanted her son to find a way out of the rough life of outlaw living. Sores learned how to speak both English and Spanish. He also learned to communicate well with his Indian mother. Everyone who ever spent any time with him noticed that he was very smart.

Sores also had a good demeanor, but he also had a quick temper like his father. One night, Pinney rode into Cincilla and Sores camp with his men. He started drinking tequila. One thing led to another. When he slapped Sores, Cincilla charged him. She tried to knock him to the ground. Pinney pushed her aside and picked up an axe handle with his right hand. Then he hit her over the head with it. He went back to drinking and left her to die right there on the ground.

After he gave his mother a proper Indian burial, Sores began to realize what he was: a bastard child of both Apache and Mexican blood. He took only one thing from his mother. Cincilla loved the feathers of a bird that was native in the area called the Summer Tanager. After it became fully grown, the Summer Tanager's feathers were completely red. She wore the Tanager's feathers every day. Sores took every red feather but one. He left that one woven into his mother's hair. He then took one of the feathers and wove it into his own long, black hair. The feather draped across his right shoulder. It looked subtle, but it was very easy for others to see. He would wear the red feather in honor of his mother for the rest of his life.

Even though he hated the old man, Sores was forced to ride with him and his unsavory entourage. As the years went by, the younger Aguilar began to pick up some of his father's unsavory habits. Both Pinney and Sores liked money, women, and power over others. They argued often, but they tolerated each other. Pinney taught Sores how to take advantage of uneducated traders, and he taught him how to intimidate the men who traveled with them. He had already taught him how to kill.

Sores never talked much. He didn't trust anyone, especially his father. But unlike Pinney, Sores rarely drank, and he was always aware of what was going on around him. He realized by watching the bad example of his boisterous father that blending into the countryside and staying low-key would be a huge advantage. Somewhere along the way, Sores realized that it would be smart to commit his crimes as an Indian. Then he would slip back into his appearance as a Mexican. It was a perfect cover.

One night, the gang stopped at a saloon in Juarez. Pinney got into an argument with the bartender. All of a sudden, a bouncer came through a door behind the bar carrying a shotgun. Pinney immediately became the savvy politician. He explained that everything was fine, and everyone should just calm down. Finally, the bouncer lowered the shotgun and pointed it to the ground. As soon as he did that, Pinney pulled his gun and shot the bouncer right between the eyes.

"Nobody pulls a gun on me and gets away alive," he shouted to everyone in the bar.

Then he did something that Sores would never forget. Pinney walked over to the bouncer and took out his knife. Then he cut the tongue right out of the dead man's mouth.

Suddenly, Sores realized why Cincilla was missing a finger at her buri-al. Pinney must have cut it off. Pinney Aguilar believed that he had to dismember any murder victim in some way to keep the body's spirit from following him. It was an old superstition that he had picked up somewhere. Sores thought it was odd, but it made quite an impression on him.

The Aguilars continued to travel through the deep Southwest for a few more years. Sores grew into quite a bitter man, but most of his differences with people were about money. He, Pinney, and the men began to look for caravans to raid and loot. The first-person Sores ever killed was an old cowboy that couldn't get a shot off at him from thirty yards away. If the old cowboy's gun would have fired, Sores would have been a dead man. He couldn't do it, so Sores slammed the butt of his rifle against his head. He was dead in an instant. Sores didn't want to waste any ammunition.

After his first killing, Sores Aguilar didn't think twice if he had to murder to get what he wanted. However, he was skillful in hiding his reputation. He was smart enough to know that outlaws were tracked by bounty hunters, Rangers, and even the army. He often scolded the old man when he got sloppy. Sores believed in operating in secrecy. He once shot one of his own men because he felt that he was too dangerous. He wasn't a threat to Sores physically. It was that he talked too much. Sores felt he would say something to someone who might figure out how ruthless the Aguilars really were.

One day, Pinney and Sores came across three Apache brothers named Muraco, Kele, and Elsu. Sores could communicate with them easily. He and the old man needed manpower. They knew they were probably in for bigger fights ahead. Sores offered the three brothers a one-dollar coin to ride along with him. He had already noticed that they were carrying firearms. Two of the brothers, Kele and Elsu, had Colt Paterson revolvers. The oldest brother, Muraco, had a shotgun. All three carried bows. Sores really liked that. He knew the devastation that arrows caused. All raids were to be split five ways. It was a fair deal for all, Sores explained.

Muraco, the oldest of the brothers, was skeptical of Sore's skin color. He looked Indian, but his Mexican tone was obvious. It was the way Sores wore his hair that was so confusing. He dressed like a Mexican, but he wore his hair long with a feather like an Indian. The other two brothers would do whatever Muraco told them to do. Sores picked up on that quickly. If he controlled Muraco, then he would also control Kele and Elsu. Since the first day they met, Sores had wondered what it would be like if Muraco wasn't around.

Sores could be quite convincing if he needed to be. Quickly, he convinced the brothers that he could lead them to more money and guns. That was what they wanted to hear even though they didn't really know what to do with the money. They figured they could learn that later.

The rocky relationship between the Aguilars came to a head over a woman. The gang had stopped at a small saloon in El Paso. Pinney was harassing a prostitute who was showing him no interest. Pinney wasn't used to that, and it made him mad. Between the tequila and his rage, it was evident that something bad was going to happen. Sores told the old man to back off the woman, but Pinney wouldn't stop.

The physical violence started. It was more than what Sores could take. He threw the old man off the woman. Pinney pulled his gun. Sores knew he wouldn't hesitate to kill his own son, so he dived behind a table and pulled his knife. Pinney started firing away. Sores rolled to his right. He jumped to his feet and threw the knife right into Pinney's chest. Sores didn't even try to save him. He just sat there and watched him die. It was a cruel reminder of the day he lost his mother.

When Sores was sure Pinney was dead, his instincts took over. He pulled the hatchet off his belt. A hammer stroke sliced his father's right arm off at the elbow. He had used the hatchet that way before. Sores picked the arm up off the ground and ordered Muraco to load the body onto his horse. Sores and the three Indian brothers rode away quickly, leaving little evidence of what had just happened. They stopped on the side of a canyon about five miles from town. There Sores covered Pinney's body with rocks. They got back on their horses and rode another five miles to a small canyon. Sores instructed Kele to dig a small, shallow grave. That was where they buried the old man's right arm.

CHAPTER 5

*S*ores Aguilar had no idea that the Texas Rangers had given him the name of Empty Heart. A month ago, roughly a hundred miles southeast of El Paso, he had organized a raid on a small group of traveling homesteaders. The attack was so well executed, the settlers had no chance. Sores made sure that Muraco, Kele, and Elsu knew that there would be no survivors. That wasn't just an order from the boss; it was part of the plan. He was smart enough to know not to leave any kind of witness behind.

Ranger investigators had observed that arrow marks looked like they had been fired from all four directions at the caravan. Seven of the twelve settlers had been hit with extremely sharp arrows. The other five had been shot at close range. Every one of the twelve settlers, ten men and two women, had a body part cut off their torso. Mainly it was a hand or a couple of fingers. One man had his forearm chopped off at the elbow. The separated body parts were nowhere to be found.

It was a gruesome scene, one that couldn't be explained. The Ranger brass believed the attack was based on treasure. There was no money to be found anywhere. Often, Indians left money behind after an attack.

Here it was obvious that the killers searched the bodies for every coin.

That was the extent of the intelligence that Capt. Ray Andrews knew, and it was the reason that he set up the camp the way he did.

Ray figured that Empty Heart had access to both bows and firearms, but what worried him the most was the organization of the attack. If and when Empty Heart attacked, what would be his strategy? What did he know? How long would he stalk them? He didn't realize how close he was to receiving the answers to his questions.

Sores had practiced long and hard to compete with the three brothers as an archer. He had become almost as good as the young Elsu, but he was far behind the other two brothers, Muraco and Kele. He positioned himself on the south side of the camp, thinking it would be the least fortified and the easiest to attack on foot. Muraco came in from the west. He was the best archer in the crew. He would have to fire over the rocks. Kele attacked from the north, Elsu from the east. All four had forty arrows. Sores instructed them to fire half of their arrows in the first wave of the attack. Then they were to take their guns and fire directly into the camp. Sores had figured out the angles. He knew how to position the three brothers and himself without shooting each other. They had gone over the raid many times.

The first arrows hit the campsite right about three o'clock in the morning. Sores, Muraco, Kele, and Elsu used the lightning in the sky to help zero in on the target. Ray had made a big deal about keeping the shields close at all times. However, the shields were heavy and awkward. It didn't take long for the Rangers to lose interest in them. That would prove to be a grave mistake.

Most of the arrows landed on top of the hill. Ray was under the wagon, taking his break. However, he was wide awake. Tom was supposed to be watching, but he had wandered off somewhere. Suddenly, two of the horses were hit and screamed wildly. It started raining arrows at a slow, deadly pace. Ray drew his Colt Navy, but he could see nothing. Then the gunfire started. It came from four directions. There were different types of firepower. Shotgun sprays, rifle shots, and handgun fire pierced the campsite. Every horse was hit in the savage crossfire. Then, as quickly as it started, it all stopped. Capt. Ray Andrews felt like a sitting duck, so he scrambled on all fours to a rock pile thirty yards away.

"Tom," he yelled. "Where are you?"

There was no answer.

The silence was the worst part. The only sounds came from loud thunderclaps. Ray had accumulated several rocks so he could throw them at the foxholes before approaching. As he was getting ready to throw a rock at the first sergeant's foxhole, he heard Sonny McGraw's voice.

"Captain, Sergeant Smith's been hit."

Ray scrambled on all fours down to the rock ledge. There he found his great friend and fellow Ranger, Cletus Smith, with an arrow right through the middle of his back. He was dead.

It took everything Ray had to fight off the shock. He not only lost one of his best friends, but he also lost his best soldier.

McGraw was in a panic.

"Quiet down," Ray hissed at McGraw, but it was too late. Another wave of arrows started. This time the trajectory was flat, and one of the arrows hit McGraw right in the face. Suddenly, the arrow barrage ceased. A minute later, the gunfire started again. It was chaos. Five minutes later, the firing ceased.

The west flank was now completely decimated. Both Smith and McGraw were dead. Ray grabbed the Ranger pistols off their bodies. He realized that he shouldn't leave the west flank open to attack. He had cover with the rocks. He also had a lot of firepower. He settled into the rocks the best he could and checked the revolvers. Not a shot had been fired.

Once again, the arrows started coming in on the camp. It was a short barrage this time. Ray knew the shooting would start again right after the arrows stopped. When it did start, the fire was much lighter, but he was trapped in the rocks not knowing what would come next. He sensed the shooting would stop soon, and then it would be quiet again. He was right.

Ray decided to run to the top to the hill. A huge lightning bolt ripped through the sky and forced him to duck for cover. When he looked up, he saw some kind of shadow down on the edge of the south flank. He aimed the Colt Navy, and he fired every bullet from one gun. He put the gun down and grabbed another one. Something, man or animal, was running south. He was pretty sure that it was a human being. He aimed, and he fired. It was unclear if he had hit anything or not. Finally, he stopped shooting.

The terror of the silence was almost too much for Ray. He ran back to the wagon and crawled underneath it. He was sure another barrage of arrows was coming. He waited. He waited some more. There were no more arrows or fire.

It was very quiet. All six horses were dead. They were full of arrows and bullets. Ray crawled around the wagon. He jumped into the back and pulled up the plank from the floorboard. His heart sank. The brown saddlebags that were hidden underneath the floorboard were gone. They contained $3,000 worth of paper money and coins for the payroll. Somebody had stolen it all.

Ray was so upset that he forgot about being scared. "Wilder, Terry, Stut, where are you?" he yelled.

Stuttering Henry Jones popped his head out from the foxhole. "Ray," he said. "I'm here."

Billy Terry came crawling up the hill on all fours. "Here," he screamed at Ray. "Where's Wilder and Cletus?"

The three men met at the wagon.

"Sergeant Smith is dead, so is McGraw," whispered Ray.

"Big Scaley is down on lookout," responded Terry.

"He's okay." Ray was already looking around the hill for Tom Jenkins.

"What about Leo?" he asked Stuttering Henry.

"He-he's all right," responded Henry. "Down in the hole."

Ray called to the men, "Everybody, come to the wagon."

Big Scaley and Leo Wilson got up quickly and met the rest of the men.

"Where's Wilder and Johnson?" Ray asked in a panic.

He ran to the south side of the hill. There he saw John Wilder and Will Johnson both lying in the foxhole. Both men had taken a bullet to the head. Ray looked to his left, and he saw an even more horrifying sight. Tom Jenkins was on his knees. An arrow had gone right through his torso. His body was leaning against a rock pile. His gun belt was missing. He had also been shot multiple times. His boot had been chopped above the ankle, but it wasn't separated from the rest of the body. Whoever was trying to cut it off had failed to finish the job.

CHAPTER 6

*F*ive men were dead, three thousand dollars had been stolen, and the five surviving men were stranded out in the Texas sun. Ray Andrews was inconsolable. His best friend, Tom Jenkins, was a butchered mess. The last words they shared were very cross. First Sergeant Cletus Smith and Ranger Sonny McGraw had been killed with arrows. John Wilder, a family man that should not have been on the mission, was dead from a close-range gunshot wound to the head. His left hand had been cut off his body. Will Johnson was also shot at close range. He was missing a thumb.

At first, Ray wanted to go on the attack. He wanted to take out on foot and try to find the men who inflicted the slaughter. But he quickly came to the realization that he had to deal with five dead bodies and six dead horses. Then he realized that he had another problem. What about the Colt Navy revolvers? A quick count of the guns brought attention to the fact that whoever attacked the camp also had taken three of them. That just made things worse.

Captain Andrews decided to bury the bodies on top of Rosary Hill. He led the digging himself as the other Rangers took turns watching out for trouble. Ray decided to dig at least seven feet deep before burying the bodies. There was no way he was going to let animals get to his men. He would use rocks to mark the graves. That way, they could be easily found. The five Rangers dragged the horses to the opposite side of the hill. It was gruesome work, but it had to be done. The physical labor in the hot sun brought a seemingly simple attitude of disbelief to everyone. They knew this kind of a day might come. They were just struggling to accept it. All five of the surviving Rangers were wrestling with the same questions: Are we being watched? Will they attack again tonight? How did they pull this off so easily?

The difficult job had taken the entire day. Burying Tom was the worst part. Ray cried right in front of the men. There was no way the men were going to stay on Rosary Hill another night. They started walking back to Austin. That was the direction the image of the man was running when Ray tried to shoot him. Ray insisted that every man carry a shield with him. Never before had he seen such a devastating arrow attack. He wanted to make sure nobody else got killed. Ray's pride had received a tremendous blow, but he had to keep going or things could get worse. Now he had to get everyone back to town.

The walk back to headquarters was very quiet. Stuttering Henry broke the silence. "I-I'm gonna kill Empty Heart. I-I don-don't know-know how, but I-I'm gonna do-do it."

After Henry broke the silence, it seemed everyone had something to say.

Billy Terry chimed in, "I ain't never seen nothing like that. I was just trying to keep from getting hit by one of them arrows. When it quieted down, everybody was gone. I only fired two shots. I didn't even see nothing to shoot at. I just fired anyway."

Big Scaley Johnson didn't say anything. Everybody knew that Leo Wilson probably never even came up from underneath his shield, but he spoke anyway.

"I really don't know what happened. There were so many arrows and gunshots. I never saw anybody."

Every step Ray took as he walked back to Austin haunted him. He had to report the deaths, the stolen money, and the failure. He also knew that he was going to have to face William T. Jenkins. That was the worst part of all.

Sores Aguilar didn't think the robbery would go as well as it did. His plan worked almost perfectly. Only a few things didn't go right. Muraco, the oldest of the three brothers, survived the raid. Sores had planned to kill him in the firefight, but he never got the chance. Another thing that bothered Sores was that he couldn't separate the spirit from one of his victims. He tried to chop off the foot with his hatchet, but the victim was stuck onto a rock pile at an odd angle. Sores had two bags full of money and three extra handguns. He had used an original Colt Paterson revolver that he bought in Mexico to execute the two men in the foxhole. He skillfully crawled up the hill when the arrows and the shooting were terrorizing the Rangers. He saw the foxhole as he got close. It was easy for him to sneak up on them from behind, so he shot both of them in the back of the head.

He killed the two men. Then he dismembered them and ran to the wagon to steal the money. On his way back down the hill, he saw Tom Jenkins's body lying up against the rock pile. After taking Tom's gun belt, Sores pulled his hatchet. He attempted to chop off Tom's foot, but then the shooting from the top of the hill started. Sores couldn't risk waiting any longer. He had to run.

Sores knew the money was in the wagon because he got information from a state worker in Camp Stockton.

Conversation started in a bar about how the state was transporting payroll. Sores kept the tequila flowing and the talk easy. Before long, the drunken employee spilled the beans. Treasury was brought in by the wagonload, and the money was hidden in the baseboard. It was a simple system -keep a low profile, plan every detail, execute with precision, and bring in the money.

Sores had watched one delivery to the Camp Stockton post personally as he stood disguised as a friendly Mexican. He refined his plan over and over until he had it down pat. He would create complete havoc from four sides in the middle of the night. He would start with launching arrows into the campsite, and he would follow the arrows with gunfire. He knew the victims would be in shock. He would wait a few minutes and repeat the same attack at just the right moment, and then he would personally sneak up the easiest route to the wagon. Muraco was on the other side. He knew when to shoot and when to stop. Kele and Elsu followed his lead. Sores would kill anybody that got in his way. He would get to the wagon and steal the money himself, at least all he could carry. The four bandits would then flee the scene and meet up the next day.

But Sores Aguilar had never pulled off a heist like this one. This fortune was bigger than he was expecting. A big man of over six feet, he could move and run better than anyone he knew. When it was time to leave the scene, he had few peers. By the time the Rangers knew what was happening, he would be long gone. Ray's shots at him with the Colt Navy revolver came a little too close for comfort, but they were never a real threat.

Sores tried to break the money down before the brothers found him the next day. He was going to separate a huge chunk of the cash before he divided it four ways. He also had three new guns to hide from the brothers. Sores had heard of the gold rush. He now had more than enough money to make the trip and re-establish himself. He didn't care about mining gold. He would just take advantage of those who did. Though he left few clues to his identity, he knew he was now an extremely wanted man. It was time to leave the territory, but first he had to deal with the three Apache brothers.

All along Sores thought if he could kill Muraco, the oldest and most seasoned brother, he would spare the two younger siblings, Kele and Elsu. He thought he could bring the both of them into his own fold. That way, he would have more manpower. He would not worry about a revolt from either of the two. However, Muraco would always pose as a threat. Muraco was savvy and calculating. He was a lot like Sores himself. The fact that he was alive meant that all three had to go.

Sores had three of the new Colt Navy revolvers. They were all loaded with six shots. He had eighteen bullets to kill three men. If he needed more firepower, he also had his Colt Paterson revolver. Immediately, he had realized how outdated it had become. After retrieving their horses, the four outlaws were to meet up at the canyon where they had camped prior to the robbery. Sores had instructed the men to come into the camp separately, but he knew Muraco would find a way to meet up with his brothers. Muraco knew better than to trust Sores. He made a big mistake in letting Sores be the only one to make the run to the wagon.

CHAPTER 7

*S*ores Aguilar had set up a sniper's perch at the top of the canyon wall. She had never been a particularly good shot. He had questionable eyesight, and he really had never taken much to guns. Now he was in a precarious position. Would he try to shoot all three brothers from long range? Would he wait on them to get up close? Would he drop the whole idea and wait on another chance later on down the road?

He was a calm man, and his calculated ways had always been his best friend. It was bothering him that he didn't dismember the Ranger that was staked into the rock pile. He kept replaying it over and over in his mind that he didn't get the job done. The spiritual belief of dismemberment bothered Sores more than anything. He felt that it made him weak, but he had never gone against it. He was a conflicted man. His half-Mexican, half-Apache blood had always played havoc with his psyche. Being as shrewd and mean as a man could be did little to help his insecure self-image.

Another problem started when one of the guards started shooting from the top of the hill. Sores had two huge bags draped over his shoulders. One was full of coins. The other was full of paper money. He hammered Tom Jenkins's ankle. The boot was a mess. However, it wasn't close to being separated from his foot. He took off down the hill to a ridge he had planned for cover. Circling back around on Muraco was too farfetched. That was where he had planned to shoot him. He would then blame it on the Rangers. But it was not to be.

There was no way to get to Muraco. Somebody in the camp started shooting at him in the dark. Sores foot speed got him down the hill and over to the ridge. He regrouped the bags and composed himself. After a quick look for trouble, he took off for the small mountain range close to the Rio Grande.

There was one more thing that really bothered Sores. Somewhere along the way, the red Tanager feather had come out of his hair. He had other feathers, but he valued every one of them greatly. He wasn't worried about anyone actually finding the feather and putting the whole story together. It just bothered him that he lost it.

It helped that the brothers were so unschooled. Their heritage was important to them. They hadn't done much business with any white man. Sores looked different. Most of the Apache's hated Mexicans, but Sores could speak their language. He knew the culture. Muraco struggled with the relationship at first, but he knew he needed to hook up with someone from outside his own world. His people were starting to thin out. He knew he needed knowledge and contacts to survive. He quickly saw how clever Sores really could be. Sores was respectful to them. He knew how to translate their names. Kele, the talented one, was "Sparrow." The youngest, Elsu, was "the Flying Falcon."

He referred to the two younger brothers by both of their names. He was trying to educate them, but he only referred to the oldest brother as Muraco. Only once, when the brothers asked if he knew, did he refer to the oldest sibling as "White Moon."

Ironically, there was no white moon the night of the payroll raid. Sores was planning on the light from the moon to help him find Muraco. But dark, overcast skies made it nearly impossible to see anything. It was good for the raid, but it was bad for Sores's plot to kill Muraco.

The three Apache brothers met five miles away from their meeting point with Sores. All they had to do was find the Bison herd. Muraco knew a small Apache tribe that rode the Rio Grande Valley. It was easy for the three brothers to find them. Muraco viewed Sores as somewhat of a men-tor. He liked him, but he was scared of him. Sores taught him to plan, to think, and to focus on execution of the plan.

But Muraco was worried that he was leading his two brothers into a trap. He wondered aloud to Kele and Elsu about it.

"Was the money worth it?"

They didn't even really know what to do with the money. What if they rode into an ambush?

He had learned. Why couldn't they pull off the same crime without Sores? Muraco was trying to influence his two brothers only a little more than he was trying to convince himself.

"Let's ride and separate from the crossbreed," White Moon said.

Kele and Elsu didn't care about the money. They only wanted to make their big brother proud. They would do whatever he told them to do. So, they rode off into the valley and left Sores Aguilar on top of the cliff with all the money.

Sores waited on them for a day and a half. He knew they weren't lost. Muraco was too good of a navigator for that.

"It is time to leave Texas," he said to himself. He had plenty of money. Now he needed to figure out how to travel with it. It was bulky, and Sores liked to travel light. He knew he had to keep it close to his body. If he didn't, the money could get away from him in an instant. Any common outlaw could tell that the huge bags were odd looking and probably very valuable. The bag with the paper money was enough trouble, but the bag with the coins was really a problem. The coins chimed as his horse walked. It was obvious what was in the bag to anyone who had any sense.

So, Sores made a strategic decision. He dispersed the paper money all around his body and throughout his saddlebags. He even lined some bills into his hat. He accounted for every dollar. He also kept as many coins as possible. However, he decided to bury the rest of the coins in a makeshift grave at the top of the hill. He dug the grave and filled it with rocks. He put a stone and wood marker at the base of the fake grave. Then he took a red feather and tied it into the wood marker with thread he pulled off his shirt.

Surely, Muraco would figure out that it was for the brothers. They could dig it up and get their share. If they couldn't figure it out, then that was too bad. Maybe he would come back through the country and dig it up himself some other day. It was a good plan, he thought. He was just

interested in one thing now. How would he get to San
Francisco?

CHAPTER 8

William T. Jenkins got up every morning and went downtown to Ranger headquarters. Sometimes he would stay around for the entire morning, awaiting word on the mission to Camp Stockton. Other days, he would only stay an hour or so. On this day, he sensed that something was wrong.

It was ten o'clock in the morning when Ray Andrews and the rest of the Rangers walked into town. William T. was one of the first people to see them. He ran straight to the men.

"Where's my boy?" he screamed at Ray.

Ray didn't have a chance to talk. William T. ran to each Ranger. He grabbed them and shook them. Frantically, he looked for his son.

"Where is he?" he screamed.

Finally, he realized that his son wasn't with them. William T. dropped to his knees and started crying like a child. It was a horrible scene.

The Rangers were led by Colonel John Buckner. He ran to William T. and tried to console him. People started gathering in the early morning Texas sun to see what was happening. The colonel handed William T. off to a junior officer and went straight to Ray.

"How many men did we lose?" he asked him.

Ray was in shock. He couldn't speak. Things were bad enough before he saw William T. break down. He could barely keep his wits intact.

"How many men?" screamed Buckner into Ray's ear.

"Five men," chirped Stuttering Henry. "Five men."

"What about the money? Is it gone too?" shouted the colonel. "Money's gone too," spitted Henry.

By then, Ray had found a chair in the shade of the front porch at the Ranger headquarters. All of a sudden, he was really sick to his stomach. He wondered if he was dreaming. "This can't be true," he said to himself. But it was true. Empty Heart had not only robbed them of the money, but he had murdered five men.

William T. broke away from the Ranger who was trying to comfort him and ran straight to Ray.

"You son of a bitch!" he screamed.

Then he started flailing away. He clubbed Ray upside the head two or three times.

"It's your fault, Andrews. It's your fault."

Ray just sat there and took it. He didn't know what to say or do. Suddenly, his memory flashed back to the first time he and Tom got into some alcohol. They were just kids. Tom drank so much he could barely walk. Ray dragged him home to the south side of Austin. He knocked on the front door of the Jenkins's house. William T. answered. All of a sudden, Tom woke up. Right in front of the old man, he blamed everything on Ray.

"I told you we shouldn't do it, Ray," he said. "I knew Pop would kill us."

It wasn't the first or the last time that Tom would put blame off on Ray.

Colonel Buckner pulled William I. away. "Mr. Jenkins, Mr. Jenkins! You have to calm down. You can't attack another man like that."

But the damage was done. A man couldn't be lower than Ray Andrews. He crawled on his hands and knees around the corner of the building and started dry heaving. There was nothing in his stomach to vomit.

The heavily armed envoy that went to Rosary Hill to retrieve the bodies was without Ray Andrews. The mission went without any conflict at all. Ray attended every funeral but one. He was not permitted to step foot on the grounds of the First Christian Church in Austin during Tom Jenkins's service. He waited around the block and tried to watch everything he could. Then he followed well behind the family on the trip to the cemetery. It was on the east side of town.

Colonel Buckner, at the demand of William T. Jenkins, was preparing to court-martial Ray Andrews for neglect of duty. He didn't want to do it, but William T. had a lot of political clout in Austin. He threatened the colonel behind closed doors that Ray Andrews was to get a dishonorable discharge. If that didn't happen, he warned, the colonel himself would be on the chopping block. It turned out that the governor and William I. were childhood friends.

William T. also wanted jail time for Ray, but that wasn't in the cards. Colonel Buckner fought back on that. If the truth were actually told, it was Colonel Buckner who deserved most of the blame. He had the intelligence on Empty Heart. He sent the men on the mission knowing full well the risk. Colonel Buckner simply didn't know the best way to haul the payroll through the depths of Southwest Texas.

In the end, Ray Andrews was simply discharged from the organization that he loved, the Texas Rangers. He was welcome no more. The colonel wouldn't give in to a dishonorable discharge, but he knew that Ray had to go. William I. hit the roof when he found out the results, but he knew deep down that was as far as it would go. He had successfully run Ray Andrews out of the Rangers. Now he wanted to run him out of Austin.

It didn't take much. William T. sent a message to Ray through Colonel Buckner.

"You need to leave town," it said. "Nobody wants you around here. You have done enough damage already."

Ray still had the ten coins that were stuffed into his boots. He decided to walk over to the funeral home that had buried Tom Jenkins. He asked the owner if William T. had paid the bill.

"No, not yet," the undertaker answered. "It isn't customary to pay for at least a week or so."

Ray looked into the undertaker's eyes. "How much does he owe you?" He stared back at Ray. "Well, that would be about fifteen dollars," he whispered.

"I'll pay you eight dollars to clear the bill right now," Ray said sternly. "I would appreciate you working with me."

The undertaker looked down at the ground. "Okay, son," he said. "I'll take the eight dollars."

Ray pulled the coins out of his boots.

"Another thing," Ray grumbled to the undertaker. "You don't tell Mr. Jenkins about this. You tell him that the bill was paid by the Texas Rangers."

CHAPTER 9

Stuttering Henry Jones had spoken more words in the last week than she had in the last year. All of his life, he was the butt of jokes because of his speech impediment. For years, he had decided just not to talk instead of taking the ridicule. But after the attack on Rosary Hill, he didn't care anymore. In his mind, he had all the evidence that he needed to hold Empty Heart accountable for killing his fellow Rangers. He had a fire burning inside him now that had never existed before. In the past, he was just a regular soldier. He did what he was told. He never made waves about anything. But now things were different. He had a different outlook on everything. He was determined to see Empty Heart pay for what he did.

Jones had never married. Born in Cleary, Mississippi, he came to Texas with his widowed father when he was just a boy. What little schooling he had was not of high quality. His father never even recognized his speech problem much less try to get him any help. After his father died when he was sixteen, Henry started working as a farm and ranch hand in the Austin area. Neither profession appealed to him.

In 1823, Stephen F. Austin needed men to protect seven hundred newly settled families in Texas after the Mexican War of Independence. Henry tried to sign up but was not accepted as worthy of the challenge. Things got tough. The Rangers needed men. Henry was finally accepted into the Rangers in 1827. The pay was terrible. The job was worse, but Henry Jones had an identity for the first time in his life. He was part of something special. He was a Ranger. In 1835, the Rangers were formally recognized by the state. By then, Henry was an eight-year veteran.

He was never paid much attention until an officer needed a man he could count on in a tough spot. Henry never complained. He lived in a boarding house that cost seventy-five cents a month. He ate when he could eat. He saved almost every dollar he ever earned. He was great with a shotgun and better than average with a revolver. But there was one thing for sure. He was a great Ranger.

He and Ray were close friends. Their relationship was cemented at the hip years ago by a disturbing incident. One day, Henry was hanging around outside headquarters when a fellow Ranger, Sam Reed, decided to make fun of him.

"Hey, Jones," Reed said. "Sing us a song. We're bored."

All the men laughed. Things started escalating from there. "Come on, Jones," Reed pried. "We want to hear you talk. We need a laugh. You got the brains of a sow."

Henry tried to stay calm, but his pride wouldn't let him. "To-to-to-to-to hell with you," he sneered.

Reed jumped on Stuttering Henry and had him on the ground in an instant. He punched him in the face and kidneys several times.

A young Ranger named Ray Andrews was in the building. When he heard the commotion, he came out the front door. He barely knew Stuttering Henry's name, but that didn't stop him from stepping in.

"Knock it off, Reed. Let him go!" he yelled.

"Stay out of this, Andrews," barked Reed.

Ray didn't hesitate. He shoved his right arm around the front of Reed's neck and pried him off Henry. Reed rolled over on top of Ray and tried to punch him. But Ray knew exactly how to get away. He locked his legs inside of Reed's and started squeezing his shoulders upward. He flipped his body right out of Reed's hold. Just like that, he was free. All the men howled with laughter. Reed charged Ray. Ray responded by decking Reed with a right-handed punch. Ray had never done anything like that before.

Reed got up and stared at Ray Andrews.

"Who do you think you are?" he shouted.

Ray wasn't cordial.

"Don't ever do that again," he scolded Reed.

Ray looked at the six other Rangers who were watching. "You should all be ashamed of yourselves," he said.

By then, Henry Jones was standing beside Ray Andrews. "Are you okay?" Ray asked. Henry just nodded.

"Come on, I'll buy you a drink," Ray said calmly.

The two of them walked away from Ranger headquarters together. Stuttering Henry Jones would never forget it. He would be loyal to Ray Andrews for the rest of his life.

Henry had an idea. It seemed that everyone was interested in heading to the California Gold Rush. There was just this big problem. How do you get there? What's the best route? There were several theories. People argued every day about it. Should you go north, or should you go straight west? Nobody knew the real answer. Henry had never been west of El Paso. He didn't know much about the desert territory, but he wasn't interested in going north. The mountainous terrain he had heard about scared him about as much as the cold, snowy weather. Those were two reasons to travel west.

There was a man in town that had this idea to haul people to San Francisco for a fee. His name was Sawyer Crenshaw. Few people took him seriously. He was a lot like Henry. He was sort of a lonely person who didn't socialize much. But he was good with horses. He was also a good mechanic if he needed to be, and he was very handy with a shotgun. Crenshaw just wanted to make some money and be his own boss.

So Stuttering Henry thought he would go over and talk to this Sawyer Crenshaw. Surely, Crenshaw would need a couple of guards. If so, Henry was ready to resign his job as a Ranger and recruit Ray Andrews to go with him to California. On the way, maybe, just maybe, they would cross paths with Empty Heart.

Henry approached Crenshaw during the middle of the day. Crenshaw had been asleep underneath his rig. He had just awakened.

"Ca-a-n I talk t-t-to ya, sir?" Spat out Stuttering Henry. "Sure, you can," answered Crenshaw.

"Well, I-I hear ya-ya might need a couple guards," Henry said. Crenshaw stood up and rubbed his eyes. It was obvious he was a little disoriented.

He spat down on the ground and said, "Who told you that?

I don't need no guards."

Selling anything was not in Henry's skill set. He was easily intimidated by the verbal word, and he almost left the scene. But he gathered his composure and kept on.

"You-you gonna take this outfit to Cal-Cal-California?" he asked.

"Well, yes I am," bellowed Crenshaw. "I have six paying customers."

"Well, s-s-sir, I c-can tell you fr-f-from from experience. You bet-better get you some g-g-guards."

Henry knew from the look on Crenshaw's face that he had made an im-pression. Crenshaw wanted to hear Henry's story, so Henry told him all about Empty Heart, the robbery, the arrows, the gunshots, everything. It took him almost thirty minutes. But when he was finished, Sawyer Crenshaw had a whole new impression of the trip west.

"I hope you don't mind," Crenshaw finally said. "But I want to confirm your story."

Henry was impressed with himself.

"G-go down to ra-Ranger headquarters," he told Crenshaw. "Ask around. I-I'll come back t-to tomorrow."

Henry Jones could barely write, but he scribbled out his resignation on a piece of paper and gave it to Colonel Buckner. The colonel was dumbfounded.

"Why are you doing this?" he asked Henry.

"I-I got a better j-job," explained Henry. "I'm g-gonna be a-a g-guard."

Colonel Buckner knew he had now lost two of his best men, Ray Andrews and Henry Jones. He had also lost the five in Southwest Texas. He was not happy. Henry didn't get much respect on the surface, but deep down, most of the Rangers thought a lot of him. Buckner knew that pinning the blame on Ray was wrong. He also knew that he should have stood up for him. But he didn't. He gave in to the political pressure from William T. Jenkins.

Ray had picked up a job as a carpenter north of Austin. He spent most of his money for the burial of his best friend. He had gone out to Tom's gravesite in East Austin twice. Both times he broke down and cried. When he made his way to the other four men's burial sites, he would always break down.

He worked as many hours in the day as he possibly could because it helped keep his mind off what had happened in Southwest Texas. His future was not his biggest concern.

Every night, Ray made his bed on the floor where he was working. He had become a vagabond. It was easy for Henry to find him, but it was a gamble to set everything up with the Crenshaw stage line before approaching Ray about the job. Henry just figured Ray would be up for it.

Henry found Ray hauling trash away from a worksite. Ray saw him coming from a distance.

"Hey, Stut," he said. "How ya been doing?"

He could still see the pain on Ray's face. Henry tugged at his handlebar mustache.

"G-got us a j-job," he said proudly.

Ray was perplexed. "What do you mean a job?" he asked. "Well, I-I talked t-t-to that Crenshaw feller. He's-s-s the man that is get-t-t-t' in paid to haul p-people to C-California," Henry answered. "Told him we-we would guard for him. Pay is t-ten dollars up front and t-ten dollars whe-when we get there."

All the talking Henry had done the past few days had made him exhausted. He was hoping Ray would take over from here so he could just be quiet and work. The thought of going to California had given him a vigor that he hadn't had since his first years of Rangering.

"I don' know, Stut," whispered Ray. "I don' know."

Stuttering Henry replied in a confident tone.

"Leave S-Sunday from the courthouse at s-seven," he answered. "S-See ya there."

CHAPTER 10

SAN FRANCISCO

*C*yrus Welch ailed across the Pacific Ocean from Melbourne to San Francisco in seventy-two days. He was disappointed that it took that long. Had he been more organized, meaner, and better supplied, he could have cut the trip substantially. He had learned a lot. Only once did he lose his way, and he figured it out quickly when the cold weather told his instincts that he was too far north. He waited for a sunny day to check for an accurate position of the ship. He used his sextant to change the path and get back on course.

Welch had named his clipper ship the Melba Lee. She was cut tight as all clippers were to slip through the sea at a high rate of speed. Welch liked the clipper over bigger, heavier ships because he was always a little worried about needing to get away fast. He was a businessman, and he was proud of it. Now he just needed to get on with making some money.

Like everyone else, Cyrus had heard of the boisterous section of San Francisco they called Aussie Town. That was where the Aussies congregated. It was located over on the east side of downtown at the foot of a small mountain. Telegraph Hill, as it was known, was one of the highest points in town. At the bottom of the hill was where Aussie Town was located

Several streets made up the original part of town that was famous for its ill repute. Saloons, prostitution houses, gambling halls, and dope shacks were side by side. The area was a huge attraction. Sailors from everywhere in the world passed through town. Almost all of them came to see Aussie Town. They were joined by gamblers, petty crooks, prostitutes, and bums. The romantic view of the bay area enhanced the excitement. Cyrus quickly noticed all the Aussies that he saw walking the streets. They were everywhere he looked. He might as well be back in Melbourne.

But Cyrus Welch was only there to party for a little while. He was looking for a way to use the Melba Lee to make his fortune. Maybe he had never been to Aussie Town, but he was no stranger to the dangers of a place like this. He decided to walk the streets and survey the landscape. At night, he went back to the Melba Lee to sleep. He had released all his prisoners when the ship docked just like he said he would. He didn't care. It was in his best interest to get rid of them. His paid help was instructed to check back with him in a few days. Right now, there was no haul, so there was no work for anybody. It was up to Cyrus to come up with a plan. It only took a few days.

On a Saturday afternoon, Welch was walking through town. He saw a bar that caught his eye called the Lonely Sailor. The bar was on two levels. There was an upstairs and a downstairs. A makeshift staircase led to the front door of the bar. The second story had a small balcony. There was a big hand-painted sign on the top story window that read Enter Here. The bottom of the building was some sort of a house. It looked like someone lived there.

That was odd, Welch thought to himself. Why wouldn't it be the opposite? You would think the owner would live on the top, not the bot-tom.

He climbed the staircase on the outside of the place and walked into the bar. There he sat down and bought some whiskey. Welch had been there about an hour when he saw an odd-looking character walk through the back door and take his place behind the bar. He was a big man, easily six foot tall with an odd color to his dark skin. His hair was long and very black. The style of his clothes was peculiar. He didn't seem American or Aussie. He was dressed in all black with a vest that had some kind of stones woven into it. Welch had never seen anyone before who looked like this mate. He peered closer. He noticed something the color of red attached to the bottom strands of his hair. Welch figured the man owned the bar. After all, he did walk in from the back door. There was something about this fellow that intrigued him. Welch was not a shy man. He got up and walked to the bar.

"How ya doing, mate?" Cyrus asked.

The big, dark-skinned man behind the bar didn't seem to be in the mood to talk.

"This is quite the place here, this Aussie Town. I come from Melbourne, but I do say I like it here." Welch kept trying, but he couldn't get much out of the man behind the bar.

"I'm looking for some work, mate," Welch said. He got nothing but silence.

"I've got a clipper docked down at the port. She's a beauty. I call her the Melba Lee. Named her after me mum." Welch kept pressing the issue.

"Made it over from Melbourne in less than 2 months," he said. "The Melba Lee was flying, mate. Hauled tea, linen, and tobacco. Figure I can get back over even faster. I got a crew of mates that can sail all day and all night. That's me biggest expense ye know, manpower. Got some ide-as, mate. Me just need a partner. Know some mate that might be of interest in the cargo business?"

It seemed that the subject of the shipping trade suddenly awoke the man behind the bar.

"Me name's Welch. Cyrus Welch." Welch stuck out his hand to shake. Finally, the dark-skinned man spoke. He stretched out his arm and offered his hand. "Aguilar," he said. "Sores Aguilar."

CHAPTER 11

The lonely Sailor was never intended to be a business location. It was just a big, two-story house that was built on Montgomery Street back in the forties. There was a For Sale sign on the front door when Sores Aguilar walked by one day. He knocked on the door, but nobody answered. He started staking out the house every day.

It would be perfect, he thought. He had been talking to some businessmen down on the docks. Ideas in his head had gotten him excited about the possibility of turning the money he had into a fortune.

He made his way down to the city headquarters, which was nothing but a shack. Aguilar asked a city official about the address, Fourteenth Montgomery Street, San Francisco. It turned out that the property had been abandoned for over a year. Sores spoke quickly.

"How can I purchase it?"

The city official tugged at his cap. "Let me go back and find the deed," he answered.

The city official went to the back and started scurrying through some files. Sores waited patiently at the counter. Thirty minutes went by before he came back to the front.

"Got it right here," he shouted. "Deserted property, no deed. Says here that the value is $500. You want it?" he asked.

The big man dressed in black was almost in shock. He had never bought any property before. He couldn't believe how easy it was. The property was right in the middle of the most sordid place he had ever seen. It was worse than the streets of Juarez back on the Texas-Mexican border. Drunks, crooks, drug addicts, and prostitutes walked the streets. Sailors and Aussies fought regularly in the back alleys. It was a terrible place, but it was perfect for him.

"I'll be back tomorrow," Sores answered.

He went back down to the docks where he was sleeping at night. He had been carrying over $3,000 on his body. He was looking for a place where he could settle down a little bit, but he also wanted a place to start a business. The house at Fourteenth Montgomery Street provided both.

He wrestled for a short while about giving up $500 for the property. It was a large part of his loot from the robbery. If he bought the house, it would take a huge bite out of his cash. He entertained thoughts of going back to Texas for the coins he had buried

Sores's biggest strength was the diligence that he put into every decision he made. He stayed up the entire night, thinking about whether he should buy the house. Ironically enough, what appealed to him the most was the fact that he would have a home. He had not had anything like that since his mother was alive. Even then, it wasn't much. His mother did everything she could, but raising a child with Pinney Aguilar was a pretty tough job.

Sores awoke the next morning and counted his money before anyone else could see what he was doing. The sun had barely peeked over the mountains east of the bay when he had $500 together in his pocket. The rest of the money was evenly distributed in his boots, vest, and hat.

He walked down to the city headquarters and summoned the officer.

"I want to purchase the property at Fourteenth Montgomery Street," he stated plainly.

The city officer went to the back and produced a deed. He stamped Paid in Full on the deed when Sores put the money on the counter.

"Sign here," said the city officer.

Sores had only signed his name a handful of times in his life. He was a very intelligent man, but he had only limited schooling. He took great pride in how he printed his name. He looked up just in time to see the city official put the money into his pocket. The deed gave him a feeling of pride that he had never experienced before. He was now a property owner.

Fourteenth Montgomery Street now had a brand-new identity. There were no keys exchanged, so the first order of business was to put locks on all the doors. Sores did everything himself. He went completely around the house and secured every door, window, and loose board he could find.

After securing the house, he went back to the hardware store and bought a long, flat board, some red paint, and a brush. He was going to open a bar right there on Montgomery Street. He didn't know what to call it, so he went back to his Indian instincts and traditions. He walked out in front of the house and watched the people. It didn't take long for a poor soul to walk right up to him and beg for money.

"I'm just a lonely sailor," the man bellowed. "Can you spare me a coin?"

Normally, Sores Aguilar would not give a vagrant like him the time of day. However, this was a special occasion.

"I'll give you a coin," he said. "You just helped me name my saloon." Sores grabbed the board and started painting. In big block letters, he wrote the Lonely Sailor.

The saloon business was pretty good on Montgomery Street. There was a lot of competition, so Sores started small. He served whiskey and beer that he could buy cheap at the docks. A small surcharge was priced into every drink. At first, he only made a modest profit. He closed the place early every night. He bought a bed for the downstairs and took pride in being an established man for the first time in his life. Strategically, he hid his money. Under each lamp, he took up the wooden planks of the floor and buried gold. That way he could always remember where to find his money. If he was robbed, it would be almost impossible to steal all of his fortune. Sores was happy. He was settled. He was also living right on the edge of Aussie Town.

People came into the bar and told all kinds of stories. Some tales were tall, but some were believable. Sores heard several stories about the opium trade. The city didn't seem to care much about it even though it was obvious that the drug was evil. Sores was smart enough not to try the stuff himself. He already had witnessed what it did to people. Addicts would get so high they couldn't remember their own names. It made them easy targets for vandals. Sores noticed everything. He wondered how he could do two things. First, he needed to find a contact in the opium trade. Second, he needed to figure out how to market the drug.

He solved his problems by walking the docks. What little city government and police force the city had was too busy dealing with other is-sues. They didn't have time to worry about opium. They didn't even know much about it. Sores walked the docks and the city by day, and he sold alcohol in his bar at night. He noticed that it was the Chinese who seemed to have access to the opium. He started asking around about how to obtain the drug. He found that he could buy it down at the docks if he talked to the right people. It was smart, he thought, not to buy and sell opium at the Lonely Sailor. There was no reason to invite trouble, and the opium trade had trouble written all over it. Besides that, Sores had no interest in being a small-time drug dealer. He was interested in the big picture.

Sores wanted to meet the man who was in charge of the distribution. To do that, he figured he should start attempting to buy the drug himself. It didn't take long for him to learn that opium was used as a weapon as much as it was used to make money. Opium was so addictive that it only took a couple of highs to capture a prisoner. Sores saw it immediately. He could not believe that it was going so unnoticed in the city. He was tempted to try it, but he never gave in to using it himself, not one time.

It took a couple of weeks of communicating with the small-time pushers down at the docks to find out who was the big fish in town. He was a man named Min Cho Fat. Sores wasn't familiar with Chinese custom, so he didn't know exactly how to approach him. He played it cool and watched things closely. He gathered as much information as he could every day, and he made his own contacts down at the waterfront.

One morning, he got up early to stake out the small-time dealers he knew. He followed one of them all the way back to Chinatown. The dealer he followed entered and then exited a house.

This must be it, he thought to himself. This must be where Min Cho Fat does business. It was only a few miles from the Lonely Sailor.

Sores recognized the Chinese drug dealer was an easy mark. This Min Cho Fat wasn't much on keeping things secret.

If I wanted to rob him, Sores thought to himself, it would be so easy. It just wouldn't be the best move to make right now.

Sores staked the house out every day for a week. He saw people come and go. He waited for someone to walk out who he thought might be Min Cho Fat. Finally, one day around the noon hour, a small, frail Chinese man with a ragged goatee walked out the front door. He headed in the direction of the docks. Sores followed.

It would be so easy to kill him, Sores thought to himself.

He followed Fat to the docks and watched as he met with another Chinese man. This man was even smaller than Fat. Sores watched as the two men talked. Suddenly, the conversation turned sour. Fat started waving his arms and yelling at the other man in Chinese verbiage. There was obviously some kind of problem. Fat turned and walked away. That was it. He scurried back to the house as quickly as possible. Sores followed him. the entire way. He waited across the street for about an hour before going back to the Lonely Sailor. He thought about Min Cho Fat all the way back to his own place. He opened the door, sat down, and started thinking. He knew it was time to make a plan. Later on, that very night, he met Cyrus Welch.

CHAPTER 12

It took two weeks for Sores Aguilar to figure out his plan. He knew Cyrus Welch would be on board, but he didn't know about Min Cho Fat. It was time to approach the drug boss. Sores decided to do it alone. Welch, he figured, might scare the little Chinese man away.

He staked out Fat's small house for three days. Finally, early one Thursday morning, Fat opened the door, and he looked both ways down the street. He started walking toward the docks. Sores followed him, but he stayed a good distance behind. He wanted to watch a little more. The next morning, he followed him all the way down to the docks again. Fat met with the same smallish Chinese man both days. Once again, they seemed to start arguing.

Suddenly, Fat started walking back toward China Town. This is it, thought Sores. I need to approach him now.

He followed him all the way to within about a half mile of Fat's house. Sores picked up his pace and got within thirty yards. "Min Cho Fat," bellowed Sores in a strong voice. "I want to talk to you."

Fat looked back at Sores. Then he turned and started running.

But it was impossible for Min Cho Fat to outrun Sores Aguilar.

"I come in peace," shouted Sores. "I have a business proposition."

Sores followed Fat to his house without any trouble. Fat slammed the door behind him. Sores waited across the street.

An hour passed. Finally, the front door opened, and Min Cho Fat stepped a few feet into the street.

"What you want?" spouted Fat.

"I have a business proposition," returned Sores. "We can meet somewhere in public if you want. I mean no harm to you."

Fat's insecurity intrigued Sores.

"I'm going down to the corner," Sores said. "You follow me. Stop when you feel safe."

After saying that, Sores started walking west. He hoped that Fat would follow. After about a quarter mile, he heard Fat yell.

"Stop here!" Min Cho Fat was standing directly in front of a Chinese market.

Min Cho Fat would not meet with Sores Aguilar and Cyrus Welch anywhere but in his own house. Two bodyguards searched Sores and Welch for weapons before they walked in the door. Fat's paranoia was obvious. He was a very small man who had migrated from the old country just a year ago. He was skeptical of everyone, and that included his own people. Now he was meeting with an Aussie and some kind of a crossbreed Indian. It wasn't difficult to detect his fear, but Sores had the business opportunity figured out. He had a plan that would make all three of them rich. There would have to be trust involved, but Sores had figured out how to ensure that too.

The three men sat down at a table in Fat's home. The guards were told to wait in the next room. Of course, Sores opened the meeting

"We're all businessmen," he said. "We're all looking for an opportunity.

I propose a plan to the two of you. If you are interested, we can talk further. If you are not interested, we can go our separate ways. I do think that we each need the other two to make this plan a success."

Cyrus Welch was in already. It was Min Cho Fat who had to be convinced. Sores had already prepared Welch on how to conduct himself. He was to stay quiet and let Sores do the talking. Welch was to confirm his commitment to the project when the time was right.

Sores's plan was simple. It was the execution that would be difficult. Fat would produce the opium contacts. Welch would provide the transportation. Sores would plan the project. He would also finance it. He was also willing to work with Welch on supplying free labor for the clipper ship.

Sores had found out through his reconnaissance that the opium was coming from Hong Kong. He also had suspected that there were a lot of problems involved in Fat's operation.

"My proposal is this," he started. "I fund the operation with my own money. I'm taking the biggest risk. We will also supply some free sailors for the operation of the ship. That will cut the expenses down. Cyrus captains the voyage to Hong Kong. Fat, you make the first trip, of you send someone we can trust to ensure the connection. Welch also buys tea and linen to cover up the opium. The round-trip should take sixty to eighty days. When the Melba Lee returns to San Francisco, I will distribute the goods. All the profits will be divided between the three of us."

Sores gathered himself and leaned back in his chair. He knew the value of silence. Fat kept his head down. He was thinking. Welch finally spoke up.

"Will work on my end, mate. Not a problem. Just need to know who to find in Hong Kong. That's the only problem for me." Sores knew there was no way Min Cho Fat would get on a boat with Cyrus Welch. He had been following Fat almost every day. He knew he had someone he could send on the trip. The value that Fat brought to the operation was the opium connection in Hong Kong. Sores figured he would obviously help in San Francisco, but he wasn't a necessity.

Sores had his eye on a bodyguard they called Suk Too. That was who he really wanted to make the trip with Welch. Sores had never seen Suk Too utter a word. That was good. Suk Too was the biggest Chinese man Sores had ever seen. He was at least six foot two, and he obviously weighed over three hundred pounds. His slick, bald head scared everyone.

As always, Sores had a backup plan. If someone other than Fat made the trip to Hong Kong, then Fat's value to the operation would be eroded. Sores could then eliminate him. It wasn't obvious to Sores that Fat had figured that out yet.

Min Cho Fat finally spoke up.

"I have question," he said. "After we get dope, why we need you?" he asked. "How you know we come back?"

Sores looked at Welch.

"Show him," he uttered.

Welch reached into his pocket and produced a diamond ring

He had stolen it back in Melbourne.

"You understand collateral?" Sores asked. "Cyrus leaves the ring with me. You don't come back, I keep it. It's worth the money I have invested in the trip."

Fat looked at both of them. He had been waiting on such a deal. His people were incompetent. His business was floundering. It was obvious that Sores knew it.

"How I protected?" he asked. "What you steal my contact?" Sores was impressed.

"You can tell your contacts in Hong Kong that they only do business with your people," he answered. "That's your protection. No contact with your people, no business."

Fat understood the deal.

"I not go Hong Kong. I send Suk Too," he said.

That was exactly what Sores wanted to hear. But Fat wasn't finished.

"How you get free sailors?" he asked.

Sores looked over at Welch.

"You don't have to worry about that," he said. "Just leave it up to me."

CHAPTER 13

Austin, Texas

*St*uttering Henry Jones was getting a little worried. It was 6:40 a.m. The boss, Sawyer Crenshaw, was getting fidgety. The stagecoach was leaving at seven. There was no sign of the second guard.

"What if he don't show?" Henry spoke to himself. "What have I got myself into?"

Henry was checking every piece of equipment because he had always been a worrier. He packed almost everything in his possession for the trip. Certainly, every weapon that he owned was on his horse, Buster. He had been practicing with the Colt Navy and was getting better every time he used it. He and Ray had mastered the art of molding lead balls in a grate over a campfire. They had more ammunition than they would ever use. Though he had little schooling, Henry was a smart man. He was especially smart when it came to survival. He knew the Colt Navy was going to be a difference maker somewhere down the line.

"Where's your friend?" yelled Crenshaw.

Henry looked up at him in disbelief. Crenshaw was up on the stagecoach and ready to go.

"There will be no more pay for you if he doesn't show," he whined.

Crenshaw was a heavyset man. His long, thick sideburns blended into his overcoat. He preferred a different type of hat than most other people. It had a wide, curled brim that protected him from the sun. Crenshaw's fair skin was something that everyone who met him noticed. Heading into the west desert, it could be a problem. Henry had never heard anyone say anything about it, but it was a concern.

The stagecoach was in great shape. It was only a couple of years old. It was painted a dark burgundy color. That way, it would blend into the prairie better. There were six paying passengers. They were to ride inside the coach during the trip. Two were from New York. Tom McLemore and his wife, Mara, seemed to have both money and sophistication. Both looked to be in their mid to late forties. How in the world they had made it to Austin was beyond everyone's imagination. Another couple named John and Lovie Kitchens were from East Texas. They seemed to be a little older, maybe their early fifties.

The third couple was very odd. They didn't seem to go with each other at all. The woman did not look like a married lady. She wore trousers and a vest. Henry noticed that she was carrying a Colt Walker in her holster just like a man.

The man was a snappy dresser. He looked like a card player and carried a Colt Paterson in his holster. He was very friendly.

"Say there, sir," he said to Henry. "When do you think we will make it to the first town?"

Henry just looked at him.

"I-I dunno," he replied. "Camp Stockton, I guess. It ain't really a town. It's just a p-p-post."

Henry was amazed that these people were willing to go on this trip. He wrestled with the notion that he should tell them how crazy they were. He knew better than to say anything though because this was his new livelihood.

"They play poker in Camp Stockton?" the card player asked.

"I-I reckon," answered Henry. "Bunch of Rangers. They play cards, I ga-ga-guess."

The card player wasn't too impressed. "Well, that's good, my man. The name is Fields. Ben Fields. Pleasure to make your acquaintance."

Fields stuck out his hand. Henry Jones shook it politely.

"I'm sure we're gonna have a good trip. I didn't catch your name."

Henry wasn't used to fancy introductions.

"Jones," he said without any stutter. "Henry Jones."

Henry looked at the stagecoach.

"I n-need to get back to-to work," he said to Fields. "Will visit la-a-a-later."

Suddenly, the woman in trousers walked up to the two men. "We close to starting out?" she asked. "I'm ready to get this show on the road."

Fields couldn't help himself but to introduce her to Henry. "Mr. Jones, I want to introduce you to my companion. This is Junior Hoskins."

Henry tipped his hat and responded, "Nice to to meet you, Miss Hoskins."

Henry turned his attention back to the stagecoach. He had always been the mechanic on duty during his Ranger hitch. He enjoyed moving vehicles. Crenshaw had been watching his every move and was impressed. It was obvious that Henry knew what he was talking about because of the way he paid attention to detail. He had talked Crenshaw into strapping two spare wheels underneath the coach. It was a long way through some rough countryside to California. Henry Jones didn't want to be caught out in the open with these people on foot. He had gathered every spare part he could find and found a way to get it onto the coach.

Henry fell in love with the stagecoach the very first time he saw it. Crenshaw had bought it in Austin. If it wasn't in such good shape, Henry would have never been enthusiastic about the trip.

The coach sat six people on the inside comfortably. There was ample room for storage on top. Each passenger was allowed one suitcase. All the other room would be for food and supplies. Crenshaw had figured they could travel fifty miles per day. He had figured in stops for both the passengers and the horses. They would stop at night for camp. Henry Jones would be in charge of security, but Crenshaw had hedged his bet. He made deals with both Ben Fields and Junior Hoskins. Both would pay only half of the fare that the McLemore's and the Kitchens paid. In return, they would both act as hired guns. That part of the deal would be a secret kept between the two of them and Crenshaw. He never completely bought in to Henry Jones.

There was also the issue of the horses. Four horses pulled the stagecoach. Crenshaw would be the driver. The two guards would ride and strap a spare horse to them for a total of eight. The horses could eat grass along the trail, but water would no doubt be a problem somewhere along the way.

Rations were a different issue. Crenshaw had hired a cook named Willie Foster. Willie had been sitting on the stagecoach driver's seat all morning long. He was asleep. It seemed that he got snot slinging drunk the night before. Crenshaw never bothered him. He knew that Foster would take care of everyone's appetite. Foster could make rations last as long as needed. He also knew Foster could handle a shotgun. On top of all that, Foster was the kind of guy that made things bearable on the long trail. He drank often, and he drank a lot. He was usually the life of the party everywhere he went. Pushing fifty years old, Foster had lived his life on the road. He traveled from town to town, doing whatever work he could find. He and Crenshaw had been friends for years.

It seemed that everything was packed. Henry had been trying his best to control every word he spoke. He wanted a new start in more ways than one. It was obvious to Crenshaw that Henry was looking for ways to stall.

"What time is it?' Henry asked no one in particular.

"Ten 'til seven," a voice rang out.

Henry spun around to find the timekeeper.

"Morning, Stut," bellowed Ray Andrews. "Everything ready to go?"

CHAPTER 14

It was taking a while for Ray to get back into the swing of things. His self-worth was gone, and he felt like a total failure. But as friends often do, his buddy had picked him up. The most important thing to him was that Stuttering Henry cared about what had happened. There was no way Ray was going to let him down.

Ray had eyeballed every character on the trip. He didn't mince words when he and Henry got out front to lead the convoy out of town.

"Stut, do you know how much money is on board between all these people?" he asked.

"Don't know, don't care," Henry answered.

Ray glanced back at Henry and said, "You know we'll be an easy target for the Apaches, don't you?"

Henry had just started a new chew. He had already talked more than he wanted today.

"Figure so," he said. "Empty Heart might try to raid us again."

Ray noticed that Henry wasn't stuttering as much as he usually did.

"Well," he said. "We need a better plan this time. I've been thinking about it. I got some ideas."

"Told Crenshaw I wouldn-n-n't go north," Henry said. "Don't like cold weather. Never been that way before. Besides, E-Empty Heart is this way."

Ray hadn't given Stuttering Henry Jones his due. It hadn't dawned on him until this moment that this was a hunting trip as much as it was a job. All of a sudden, Ray felt energized.

"What you got in mind?" Henry asked.

"We got to be ready for those arrows," Ray answered. "Did you pack those shields?"

Henry was amazed at how the two of them were on the same page.

"Eight. P-Put 'em under the coach. Ain't enough, but we have to m-make do," he answered.

Ray picked up the tempo in his speech.

"I figure we have a couple of options. We can put the two sophisticated women in the coach at night. The rest of us have got to keep those shields close. I'm more scared of the arrows than I am the gunfire. If they attack like last time, we can all just get down on the ground and wait it out."

Henry felt some good from Ray's confidence.

"Th-think we-we should lure 'em in?" he asked.

Ray had thought about a lot of things since the attack on Rosary Hill. The main thing he thought about was how to defend another attack from four directions. How do you position the men? How do you get rest but still be ready to fight in the middle of the night? How do you shoot into the darkness? How do you keep everyone from a panic? Ray hadn't figured it all out yet, but he had some theories. He also had the Colt Navy revolvers.

"I think we sleep in a tight circle," Ray said softly. "We stay together. We wait on them to come to us. Then we shoot together from a circle. We'll kill 'em all."

"We could also approach it another way," Ray continued talking as he looked out at the open range. "We can set up a trap. We leave the coach at camp with a fire.

Then we sneak everybody out with the horses and set up a second camp. We try to draw their fire. We wait 'em out 'til they attack the camp on foot. Then we try to ambush 'em."

It sounded simple to Henry. He decided not to respond. He was tired from all the talking anyway. It was time to ride and knock out some mileage. Henry was concerned about the cook, Willie Foster. He hadn't made a peep of a noise. He had been asleep the entire morning. Henry handed Ray the reign of his spare horse and circled back to the stagecoach. As he circled around the coach, he peeked over at Foster. He noticed Crenshaw sneering at him. Henry kicked his horse, Buster, and galloped a couple of hundred yards behind the coach. He and Ray would continue to rotate around the stage coach for the duration of the trip. There would be no sneaking up on the convoy from behind.

Crenshaw didn't stop for lunch all day. He did take one break for the passengers to relieve themselves. He found a small tree line for the women to hide behind. When he stopped the coach, he almost threw foster right off the front. Crenshaw got down off the driver's seat and walked around to the back of the coach. Then he grabbed the open-ended wooden box that was to be used as a commode. The passengers slowly climbed out of the coach. Obviously, it was a painful day for all of them. However, they didn't complain.

Suddenly, the cook, Willie Foster, spoke.

"Go ahead ladies," he said in a comedic tone. "By the time we get to California, we'll all know each other good. There ain't gonna be no secrets. Go on out there and do you a good grunt. Besides, after you eat them beans, I'm gonna fix up tonight, you ain't gonna be shy about using that crapper."

Foster started laughing. He sounded like a hyena.

"Now, Mr. Foster, that comes off a little crude, don't you think," chimed in the gambler, Ben Fields. "These ladies are sophisticated. We need to show a little more respect."

Junior Hoskins, the lady who dressed and acted like a man, wasn't embarrassed at all. "Give me that thing. I've been holding back all day."

With that, she grabbed the wooden toilet and headed off to the tree line. The other two women, Mara McLemore and Lovie Kitchens, watched her. It got quiet and awkward, and then Lovie Kitchens burst out in laughter.

"Well," she said. "Like Mr. Foster said, I guess we're going to get to know each other really well."

The first evening went as well as it could. Everyone had figured out why Sawyer Crenshaw would put up with a drunk like Willie Foster. Supper was delicious. Foster cooked chili beans and cornbread. There was plenty to eat, and it was tasty. The plan was to eat twice a day, breakfast and supper. There wasn't a plan for lunch. Crenshaw wanted to move and gain ground. According to his calculations, the coach had traveled about forty-two miles. It was really just a rough guess, but somehow, he convinced everyone that he had some type of system for gauging mileage. If they stayed on this pace, it would take about forty days to get to San Francisco. Crenshaw's confidence was reassuring to the passengers. However, Ray and Henry knew things were going to get more complicated down the road.

Ben Fields, the gambler, pulled out a deck of cards. "Anybody up for a quick game of poker?" he asked. Everyone looked at him with a little disdain. There was no way any of the people on the trip would take on Fields in a card game except maybe Foster. Everyone already knew he was crazy. But Fields put everyone at ease quickly.

"I don't want to play for money now," he said. That eased everyone's tension.

"I just enjoy the gamesmanship," he added. "We can use rocks for money."

Fields was a first-class politician. He was also way too smart to take any of the other passenger's money. He just needed to stay sharp. The only way he could do that was to practice. He also knew how to get people to let their guard down. He looked at Ray.

"Sir," he said. "I never had the pleasure of meeting you. I'm Ben Fields. I come out of St. Louis."

Ray got up off the ground and walked over to Fields.

"My name's Andrews, Ray Andrews. Pleasure to meet you." Lovie Kitchens once again broke the tension.

"I have always wanted to learn to play poker, Mr. Fields.

Would you teach me to play?"

Her husband, John Kitchens, interrupted the conversation. "Lovie," he lectured. "It isn't proper for a lady to play poker." "The hell it ain't," spoke up Junior Hoskins. "I can play poker.

Don't tell me a woman can't do it. Come on, Lovie Kitchen, I'll teach you."

With that interaction, the games began.

"Well, Ray, let's gather up some pebbles that we can use for chips and get started,"

Fields said with enthusiasm.

It turned out that everyone was really interested in learning to play poker. Both Ray and Henry had played before, but they had never played enough to learn much. It was an intimidating game. Ben Fields had done his job. He had created an environment where the passengers would have some fun. Things lightened up a little. This was the first of many nightly card games.

"Let's see here. What do the cards have in store for you tonight?" Fields said as he dealt the cards.

Willie Foster pulled out his flask and took a drink. He handed it to Junior Hoskins who also took a drink. John Kitchens did play cards, but he passed on drinking. He handed it right over Lovie to Tom McLemore.

"Come on, Lovie Kitchen, take a shot of whiskey," Hoskins spouted.

"No, no, I'll pass, thank you," she said.

Tom McLemore took a swig and looked at his wife, Mara. Everyone noticed that she shook her head.

McLemore handed the flask to Crenshaw who took a drink and handed it to Fields. Fields took a small swig, and he gargled the brew in his mouth. Then he swallowed.

"That's a mighty strong brew," he whispered.

Fields handed the flask to Stuttering Henry Jones who declined a drink. He had never touched alcohol in his life. Henry handed the flask to Ray Andrews. Ray looked at the flask, and then he looked up at the rest of the passengers. They were all watching him. He turned to face Henry Jones.

"To Cletus, Sonny, John, Leo, and Tom," he said.

He took a big gulp of whiskey out of the flask. He handed the flask back to Willie Foster. As the card game began, the passengers talked and laughed. Ray watched them all. The whiskey gave him a quick shock. He was tense, and he couldn't help himself from worrying.

He thought to himself, how in the world are we gonna get these people to California alive?

CHAPTER 15

*B*oth Ray and Henry wondered how they would approach the subject of Rosary Hill with the passengers. They both knew that by the end of the second day, they would be within reasonable distance of the barn that had spooked all the Rangers. Both of them wondered if that was where Empty Heart had been hiding before the attack on Rosary Hill.

Sawyer Crenshaw had been briefed on the attack by Henry. The two of them agreed to camp early on the second day of travel to avoid Rosary Hill at night. Hopefully, they could just pass right on by in the middle of the third day. It was the barn that had Ray worked up so much. He couldn't just pass by it again without at least checking it out. However, there were bigger problems to address. What if the Indians were in the barn? What would he do if he just rode up on them? What was the strategy on the approach? A simple scouting mission could turn into a deathtrap.

Ray had been thinking about what to do.

"Stut," he said. "I've got an idea. What if we ride on by the barn? Then we set up a camp just late in the day enough that they know where we are. But we set a trap. We take those shields and rope 'em on me and my horse for protection from arrows. I will ride right up to the barn. Either they will come out or, at least, we will know they aren't in there. If they chase me, I will lead them right into an ambush."

The plan sounded primitive to Henry.

"Su-Su-Su-Surely, they're s-s-s-smart 'nough ta know what they're doing, d-d-don't you think?"

Ray wasn't sure about anything, but he did know he wasn't just gonna ride by that barn again without some kind of a plan.

"I don't know, Stut. I just haven't got a better idea than that. They always told us when we were Rangering to take the fight to them. The officers told us not to let 'em take the fight to us. We didn't do that on top of the hill. We let 'em bring it to us."

It was an odd situation that night when Ray decided to tell everyone about his plan. Right in the middle of a card game, he broke the news.

"I need to tell everybody something," he said. "You knew when you signed on that this trip could get a little rough. Well, old Henry over there and me have been on this route before. We had some bad luck. There are some bad Indians out this way."

Ray looked at Henry.

"Tomorrow about noon, we're gonna pass by a barn. It'll be 'bout a mile north of us. Be looking for it. We think they might be in there. It's far enough away from the trail that if somebody went out there to scout, they could run and hide."

Ray looked directly at each of the three women. He could sense the terror in Mara McLemore's eyes. Lovie Kitchens was scared, but she was calm. Junior Hoskins looked like she was enjoying the story.

"Our plan is to ride right on by the barn. We will get past it far enough to be pretty much out of sight. We'll eat supper really quick. Then we're gonna leave and set up another camp away from the stagecoach. If there is an attack, you should be safe. Stut and I will ride down close to the barn and watch for 'em. If an attack is in the works, we'll be waiting."

Everything went silent for about a minute, and then Ben Fields spoke up.

"I'll go with you. You're gonna need firepower."

Ray smiled when he heard from Fields.

"I was hoping you would volunteer. Three of us will be enough.

Sawyer, you, Willie, Tom, and John stay back with the women." "What about me?" Junior Hoskins smirked. Ray looked over at Henry. He nodded and said, "Okay, you come with us."

There was no question that Ray Andrews had bounced around a bit on his plan to deal with the Indians. It was quite the serious situation, life and death. The calamity of all the new characters in the situation clouded Ray's sense of urgency. But this was no game. He realized it, and he made some adjustments.

"Listen," he told the entire group. "Everybody needs to settle down. Check your ammunition. We're not going down there without full firepower."

Junior Hoskins was starting to really worry Stuttering Henry.

"Have you ever sh-sh-shot that thing at anybody?" he asked her.

"Never killed anybody if that's what you're asking," she responded. "But I can shoot better than most men. Don't worry 'bout me. You just worry 'bout yourself."

Henry started checking his weapons. He had two Colt Navy revolvers. One was his own. The other had belonged to Cletus Smith. He pulled it out of a bag he had with his belongings and loaded it. He didn't like carrying a loaded weapon around like that. However, there would be no time to load it if trouble showed. He would have to pull it and shoot. There was plenty of ammunition. Ray and Henry loved to mold lead into bullets over a fire at night.

Henry tied a knife to his knee-high boots. He had never used it in any kind of battle. The weapon that separated Henry Jones from others was his use of a shotgun. He had two of them that he was ready to carry down to the barn. It would slow him down a little bit, but attacking him would be like attacking a cannon. If he got within a close range, he could kill two or maybe even three Indians with one shot.

Ray traveled much lighter. He also had two Colt Navy revolvers. He still had possession of Sonny McGraw's weapon. Ray also carried a shotgun that he rarely used. He was not particularity good with it. It was the revolvers that he excelled in shooting. Ben Fields carried an old Colt Paterson. Both Ray and Henry eyeballed it. It looked to them that he wasn't gonna be much help.

It was Junior Hoskins who pulled out the hardware. She had two .44-caliber Colt Walker revolvers. The Colt Walker was the revolver that was designed to shoot like a rifle. They weighed over four pounds each, but Junior was big enough to carry them. It was obvious from the start that she knew how to carry, load, and fire the gun. She wasn't shy either.

"I'm ready," she said. "I can hit 'em at about forty to fifty yards easy."

The men were both jealous and intrigued. Ray was the first one to speak up about her proficiency with weapons.

"I ain't never seen a woman who could handle a gun. Where did you learn all that?"

Junior was just getting warmed up.

"Been shooting in shows for years. Never have had the chance to be in a real fight. I'll be okay. You don't have to worry 'bout me."

Ray was losing his patience.

"Okay, let's go," he said.

The party made their way down to the barn. Crenshaw, Foster, the Kitchens, and the McLemore's hid about one hundred yards north of the stagecoach. All money aboard the stagecoach was with them. If there was an attack, the villains would have to find two different parties.

It only took about forty-five minutes for Ray to get everyone where he wanted them. There was a rock ledge that would be a perfect cover. Ray had walked his horse down with Henry, Ben Fields, and Junior Hoskins. Everything was set for an ambush. Ray tied the shields to his back, chest, and one on each leg. He had to get help from Henry to get up on his horse, Salty.

"You'll be okay if they fire arrows, but you might be a dead man if they fire bullets," said Junior.

"I know," Ray replied. "That's why you guys better be ready if they are in there. I ain't staying around long."

Ray slowly walked Salty toward the barn. Henry Jones hadn't said a word since the group left the camp. He was up in front of Ben Fields and Junior Hoskins. He had worked his way over about thirty yards to the north flank. If there was an ambush tonight, Henry was going to put the Indians into crossfire. There was brush everywhere. It was very dark, and it was also very scary.

Ray got to within twenty yards of the barn. He looked back at the others or at least where he thought they were hidden. He took out his Colt Navy. He aimed, and he fired into the barn. Nothing happened, not a sound. Everything went stone quiet. Then out of nowhere, something shook in the bushes to the south of Ray. It sounded like a horse. Junior Hoskins decided to react. She opened fire right into the bushes. Henry followed her with a shotgun blast. He only fired once.

Ray was only about twenty yards short of being caught right in the middle of everything. He took off to the north to avoid fire. Junior Hoskins kept firing until every bullet in her two guns was gone. Everything went quiet again. Stuttering Henry Jones snuck up a little closer to the bush where the firing was aimed. He was careful not to get in Junior's firing lane.

"Come out!" he screamed.

There was no response. He dropped to one knee, aimed his second shotgun at the bushes, and fired again. Then he dropped the shotgun and pulled his Colt Navy.

"Hold your fire," he called out to the others.

Ben Fields put his arm over the top of Junior's guns. He still hadn't fired a shot.

Henry walked into the bushes. It got real quiet again. Finally, Henry yelled to the others, "I'm coming out."

He came out of the brush, pulling the horns of a four-point buck deer. The poor deer had been blown to bits.

Ray circled down to the barn. For some reason, he wasn't scared at all now. The barn was empty, so he didn't wait around very long. He and Salty galloped back up to the others.

"Let's get out of here," he said.

With that, the group headed back to camp. Not a word was said, but a lot of thoughts were going through everyone's mind.

On top of a bluff about a quarter mile away, three Apache Indians—Muraco, Elsu, and Kele—watched the four traveling companions make their way back to camp. The three ran to the bluff to hide immediately after seeing the stagecoach back around noon. They had been using the barn for scouting just like they had done in the past. This night, however, there would be no raid. All three were at least a little bit surprised to see what had happened down below.

It never occurred to any of them that someone might think or even know that they were in that barn. After all, Sores had told them that it was the perfect hideout to scout oncoming convoys. They could simply pick and choose which one to attack. That was how they had been doing it all along.

Muraco was savvy enough to start thinking things through a little bit more. Unfortunately, Kele and Elsu were the ultimate followers. They relied on Muraco to tell them what to do and when to do it. It had started worrying Muraco that he had no one else to help him evaluate the situations they were being dealt. He was not that confident, but he was smart enough not to show it to his brothers.

Muraco had been both the oldest brother and makeshift father since he was fifteen years old. That was when his mother and father were butchered in a raid by the Mexicans. For some reason, the young were spared. Muraco had led his two brothers through the Mexican-Texas territory ever since trying to find food and clothing. He had run into Sores Aguilar down on the river just before his twentieth birthday. Sores could speak his language. He was friendly. He was somebody Muraco could trust, at least he thought.

The main thing that Muraco liked about Sores Aguilar was the way he conducted himself. He liked his confidence, his swagger. That was why he wanted to be like him. It was easy for Sores to tell him and the other two brothers into riding with him and Pinney.

Muraco had never led a raid. He was not surprised that Sores Aguilar had totally disappeared. Muraco had pegged it correctly. Sores could not be trusted in the end. However, all three of the brothers had learned from him. Now it was time to prove himself to his brothers. It was also time to prove something to himself.

CHAPTER 16

The walk back to the campsite was very quiet. Everyone was a little embarrassed about what had happened. Finally, just before Ray, Henry, Ben Fields, and Junior Hoskins made it to the spot where they had hidden the other passengers, Junior just couldn't help herself.

"You're an idiot, Andrews," she said sarcastically. "You could have gotten us all killed."

Stuttering Henry was astonished. He had already heard enough from the boisterous woman who acted like a man.

"We should have n-n-n-never taken you d-d-down to that b-b-barn," he bellowed back to her. "Why'd you f-fire like that? Nobody gave you the go ahead to fire."

Junior was unimpressed.

"You followed right behind me, you old fool. Why'd you decide to blow a hole in that buck? There's no telling what lies ahead for us with you two idiots guarding the stagecoach."

Ray was trying to be civil. However, before he could respond, Ben Fields broke into the conversation.

"Now, now, everybody calms down. Nobody got hurt. Plus, we know those Indians aren't in that barn, don't we?"

"I'm still not so sure about that," Ray answered.

I didn't get a chance to really look in there. There was too much shootin' going on. I'll tell you what, lady. You can call me whatever you want, but I'm not going on another scouting mission with you. We need to get back to camp. We've had enough excitement for one night."

Everything was fine back at the makeshift camp. Junior Hoskins kept hammering away to the other passengers about how inept Ray and Stuttering Henry were performing their jobs.

"You better be careful girls. ol' stuttering man will blow you away if you make any noise," she told everyone.

Ray, Henry, and Ben Fields all knew she was just trying to cover up the fact that she panicked out in the field. They all three realized that she was a very shallow person. It was going to be a long trip to San Francisco with her in the fold. More importantly than that, what would she do next? She was the wild card that nobody had expected.

Ray tried to reason with her at breakfast the next morning. "Miss Hoskins, can I talk to you privately?" he asked her.

She was not too friendly to him at all.

"What do you want, some shooting lessons?" she responded sarcastically.

"No, ma'am, I just want to talk privately," he answered.

The two of them walked over to a small rock pile about twenty yards away.

"Miss Hoskins, we have a long way to go on this trip. We've all got to get along. I don't mean you no harm. I wasn't even mad about you firing away like that last night. I just don't know why you had to say those things about me and Stut. We're trying to protect everyone, that's all. You wanted to go along. We let you go, but we're not going to let you go again."

Junior had calmed herself down overnight, but now she was getting mad again.

"You do what you have to do," she said. "I'll just tell you one thing. I ain't waiting around on a couple of two-bit losers. I'm gonna protect myself."

With that, she turned around and walked back to camp. Ray just watched her. His self-image was now at an all-time low, and it made him very depressed. Now he had a wild woman to contend with that was sabotaging his confidence in the troops.

But he had a much bigger problem. He wasn't even aware that the three Apache brothers were tracking the stagecoach. Muraco, the oldest brother, was looking for a way to make his mark. He was a proud man of only twenty-three years old. He knew he was responsible for his two younger brothers who were not made up of high intelligence.

Muraco had his own demons that he was fighting inside his soul. It was obvious to him that the way of the Apache was in grave danger. More and more of these white faces were streaming into the great chambers of the lower Rio Grande. The Apaches were used to the Mexicans. They had dealt with them all their lives. However, the white man was a shrewder foe. He had better weapons. He was in many cases much smarter. Often, he had better horses. The firearm was the white man's best friend. Most Apaches used second handguns they took from raids. There was very little ammunition. There was no training. Most of the time, the Apaches went back to their use of arrows and knives. Muraco knew this would not be sufficient for his people very much longer.

A bigger dilemma kept Muraco up at night. He knew that he and his brothers had a choice. They could either try to communicate with the white man in a similar way they did with Sores Aguilar, or they could continue to fight him. Sores was different than the white man. He was intriguing. He spoke the Apache language. He knew the customs. His mix of the Mexican heritage with Apache customs was perplexing, but Muraco never viewed him as a threat until after the payroll robbery. It was then that he scared Muraco, and it was then they parted ways.

Muraco had a decision to make that would change the course for him and his brothers. What would he do? Would he attack the stagecoach, or would he try to communicate with the white men? What if he just left them alone? There was one factor that overruled everything else. It was his Apache pride. He felt that he needed to show his two brothers, Kele and Elsu, that he was a great leader and warrior. He wanted to be like Sores Aguilar. So, the decision was made. The three brothers would attack, kill, and take whatever money and goods they could get. They would discourage the white man from coming into this territory. It was not the white man's land. It was Apache land.

The next day was very quiet on the trail. Junior Hoskins wanted nothing to do with anyone. At least Ray and Henry could get on their horses and get away from her during the ride. The others were stuck with her all day in the stagecoach.

The sense of urgency that had enveloped the group the day before had vanished. All of a sudden, everyone was solemn, but they weren't nervous. It only took three hours to come upon Rosary Hill. Ray and Henry got out in front of the coach and rode to the top. Their plan was to let the others pass right on by them.

Ray rode to the gravesites of the Rangers. Of course, they were empty. The Rangers had made sure of that. However, there was an odd-looking scene at the top of the hill. The Rangers had done little to mask what had happened. The empty graves were still visible. Some of the arrows were still at the battle site. Ray looked at Henry. He couldn't help himself.

"We need to clean this place up a bit, don't you think?" he said.

Henry looked back at the stagecoach. It was about a mile behind them.

"Better n-n-not leave them alone," he spat. Obviously, he was stuttering again.

"You go back," Ray told him. "I'll clean this up. It isn't a proper place for the men." It was all Ray could do to hold back his emotions.

Henry took off back down to the coach. Ray pulled his shovel and went to work. He picked up every arrow. It only took about an hour to cover everything up to his liking. He built the biggest, nicest rock pile he could at the gravesite. There were no bodies, but it didn't matter to him. He did not want the site to go unnoticed in the future. He walked down to the side of the hill and found the exact site where his best friend, Tom Jenkins, had died. He knew exactly where to go. He decided to mark it by building another rock pile. By then, the stagecoach had passed Rosary Hill. Ray knew he needed to hurry, so he worked feverishly to gather rocks.

The shrine to his fallen friend was almost finished. It was only a rock pile, but it was important to Ray. He was only going to make one more run to gather more rocks. He was looking for the most attractive stones he could find. He walked about five yards over to his right to grab a particular rock. When he reached down to pick it up, he noticed something out of the corner of his eye. At first it didn't even faze him, but then he looked closer. He dropped the rocks he was holding and bent down on a knee. Knarled up into a thistle and trapped by a couple of rocks was a red feather. Ray's heart sank into his stomach. He stood up and looked around to make sure Empty Heart wasn't standing somewhere in the area.

After gaining his composure, Ray knelt back down and dug the feather out of the thistle. It was torn and battered. He stared at it like it was some kind of valuable coin. He carefully put it in the front pocket of his shirt. It was what a lawyer would call circumstantial evidence. It wasn't concrete, but it was good enough for him. He was sure now. The Indian the Rangers called Empty Heart was the person responsible for killing his fellow Rangers.

CHAPTER 17

*R*ay Andrew's mind was racing as he rode to catch up with the stagecoach. The sense of urgency, the edge or whatever it was that had always motivated him was suddenly back. A simple feather had sparked his soul. It seemed like he was alive again. He pushed his horse, Salty, on a slow gallop right past the stagecoach. Henry was fifty yards out front. When Henry looked back to see what was happening, he turned his horse around. Ray pulled up to him and stopped. He didn't say a word. The wind was howling, and it almost blew the hat right off his head. He opened his coat and reached into his shirt to pull out the feather. He handed it to Henry.

"I don't n-n-need no proof," Henry responded. He handed the feather back to Ray. "We'll get him," Henry said.

Ray Andrews continued to be impressed by his new best friend, Stuttering Henry Jones. It was his confidence in the mission that he liked the most. That was encouraging to Ray. It was inspiring.

He had all but forgotten the day that he stood up for Henry in Austin. It was nothing to him. But to Henry, the incident formed a bond that would last a lifetime. Now it was all coming together in Ray's mind.

Why did Henry come after him to go on this trip to San Francisco? Why did he care so much about me? he thought to himself.

All of a sudden, he had figured it out.

"What ya thinking, Ray?" Henry asked. "I-I mean about these Ind-Indians. What you thinking?"

Ray rode straight ahead.

"Well, I wish I knew," he responded. "I've been counting the guns we have. I don't know what to think about Fields. I don't know if he will be any count when it gets hot. Crenshaw can shoot, but I don't know if he can hit anything from a distance. Foster's the same. Junior's crazy, but I think we're gonna have to use her. The Kitchens and the McLemores, well, we're gonna have to just hide them."

That was about the same thing that Henry had been thinking. He just wanted to hear it from Ray. He had already developed a strong dislike for Junior Hoskins, but he knew she could at least shoot. It was common for Rangers to worry about being outmanned and outgunned in the field.

"Everybody knows the plan, so let's stick to it. If any of them don't want to go along, they can stay at the campsite and fend for themselves. We'll move everybody else out away from camp. We take all the horses with us. The only thing that stays at camp is the coach and a fire. You and me, we hide and hope to see them fire their guns. When we see them fire, we sneak up on 'em and kill 'em. We probably won't get 'em all, but we will get most of 'em. What do you think?"

"W-w-what if we're way outnumbered?" Henry asked.

Ray had already worried about that since the beginning of the trip.

"Use your best judgment," he responded. "That's the best I can tell ya."

At supper, Ray told the entire group his plan. As he had expected, Junior Hoskins was the only malcontent.

"I'm staying here by the coach," she bellowed. "There ain't no Indians out there that are gonna attack at night."

Her new buddy, Lovie Kitchens, tried to persuade her to go along with the group.

"Junior, please come with us. These men know what they are doing. They have been out here before. I would feel much safer if you were with us."

Everyone in the group appreciated Lovie's effort to get Junior Hoskins back into the fold. It amazed everyone how quickly such a bond between the two women had developed.

"You really think these two idiots know what they're doing?" she asked.

"Yes, I do," Lovie spouted back.

It was the first time anyone had seen much spunk out of her. Junior took a long look at everyone.

"Love Kitchen," she said. "I'll go for you, but I think these two guys are fools. I just hope they don't get us killed."

Sawyer Crenshaw had been noticeably quiet through all the hoopla. He was the boss, but he had given total control of the trip to Ray and Henry. He finally spoke up.

"Andrews, I hope you know what you're doing. We could all get killed out there in the brush."

Ray was very polite and respectful in his response.

"Yes, sir," he said. "You're right. We could get killed out there in the brush. But we could also get killed here at this campsite too. This is really dangerous country,

Mr. Crenshaw. You knew that when you decided to come out here."

Willie Foster broke the tension.

"Just don't forget to bring the crapper. It might get pretty tough out there."

Just about everybody laughed. Ben Fields chimed in at just the right time.

"I think Mr. Andrews and Mr. Jones are doing a fine job. They're just trying to stay a step ahead of the Indians."

Junior Hoskins jumped into the conversation. "If there are any Indians."

Ray looked over at Henry who was rolling his eyes. Ray had never seen him do that before.

That morning, Muraco told his brothers, Kele and Elsu, that tonight would be the night. They were having trouble keeping up with the stagecoach. Things were beginning to get a little bit out of Muraco's comfort zone. They would follow the same plan they used when attacking the payroll wagon. However, there were many problems with this raid. There were only three of them this time. They hadn't thought about the angles of the gunfire. They hadn't done near the job of scouting that Sores had done. And there was one huge difference. Muraco had decided that all three brothers would attack the camp on foot after the barrage of arrows and gunfire.

By midnight, Ray and Henry had everyone assembled in the makeshift camp about 150 yards from the stagecoach. Again, tonight, all money and horses were secured. It was tedious and tiresome work to get everything into place without causing a stir.

Just before Ray and Henry started out from the group to assume their positions, Ben Fields spoke up. "Fellows, don't you want me to go with you?" he asked.

"Mr. Fields," answered Ray. "I don't want to put you at risk. Why don't you wait here and watch. If there is any trouble, use your best judgment."

Henry had heard that line from Ray enough. "Use your best judgment."

"What about me?" Junior Hoskins asked.

"S-Same to you, la-la-lady," answered Stuttering Henry Jones. "Use your best ju-judgment."

Three o'clock in the morning rolled around. Everyone fell asleep at the alternate camp. Ray and Henry had both hidden about fifty yards from the stagecoach. They had their shields close and their guns loaded. Sure enough, here came the first wave of arrows. Both the former Rangers assumed their positions. The barrage of arrows wasn't near as intense as the last time they had experienced it. The gunfire came next. It was eerie how they knew exactly what to expect.

Ray and Henry waited out the next round of arrows and gunfire. Amazingly, the group back up the ridge was hanging tough. Ray had briefed them on what he thought might happen. Finally, the third round started. Ray and Henry waited patiently. After the gunfire stopped, they crept out from under their cover and moved closer toward the stagecoach. They were crawling like ants through the prairie. There was a high moon with no clouds in the sky. Visibility was good.

Suddenly, they saw the dark formation of two men creeping up on the stagecoach. Henry waited with two shotguns ready to go. Ray waited too. He wanted to get every one of the Indians that he could. He waited until they got all the way to within twenty yards of the stagecoach. Suddenly, another figure came running up to the camp. That was enough. It was time to fire.

Ray put his two Colt Navy revolvers on the ground just in front of his feet. He got on one knee and assumed a sniper's position. He started firing right into the stagecoach area. It was dark, but he could see. He emptied one of the Colt Navy revolvers and put it down on the ground. He picked up the other one. By then, Henry had assumed his position on the north flank. As soon as Ray ceased firing his Colt Navy, Henry fired his shotgun right into the intruders. He dropped it and grabbed the other one. At the same time, the two former Rangers approached the coach.

It was quiet. Ray and Henry looked around to see if any other intruders were on the site. They couldn't tell. Slowly, they made it all the way to the stagecoach. Three dead bodies were lying within fifteen yards of the coach. All three had multiple gunshot wounds to the torso. Two had been shot in the head. The other body had been almost blown into two pieces by the shotgun blast. It was over.

"We can't leave 'em here," Ray whispered to Henry. "It'll upset the women. We need to drag 'em away from camp."

That was exactly what they did. It took a couple of hours to clean up the area. They stayed there the rest of the night. When the sun rose, Ray and Henry searched the bodies for every clue they could find. They were frustrated. There was no red feather anywhere to be found.

CHAPTER 18

Camp Stockton, Texas

It took three more days of hard riding to get to Camp Stockton. The group finally arrived early on a Sunday afternoon. Every night, Ray and Henry had used the same tactic to secure the passengers. They stopped and ate dinner and gathered their belongings. When things calmed down, they went out to hide in the brush. They had seen no trouble since the attempted raid. Crenshaw, Foster, and the passengers had a much different opinion of both Ray and Stuttering Henry now. Even Junior Hoskins kept her mouth shut and didn't say anything. Not a soul on the stagecoach convoy could think of anything else but the raid.

They had watched the entire battle from a distance, safely tucked away. There was no reason to draw their guns. Ray and Henry had taken care of everything. When the group returned to the campsite early in the morning, all the men and Junior Hoskins went down to look at the three Indians. They didn't know the names of the dead men. They didn't even know what type of Indians lay there dead. But Ray and Henry knew. They identified them as Apaches because of the way their hair was cut.

Muraco had long hair on one side of his head. The other side was shaved clean. He had been shot twice in the torso and once in the head. Kelsu had the same haircut. He had three gunshot wounds, one to the face. Kele had never had a haircut in his life. The group agreed that he couldn't be older than fifteen or sixteen years old. His head was untouched, but his torso had been blown apart by Henry Jones's shotgun blast.

All the men participated in the burials. Even though they were outlaws who would have killed every one of the passengers, they were treated with great respect. Ray made sure of that. He ended up digging almost every grave himself. All three graves were dug an extra foot deep, just like the last grave he dug. The dirt was smoothed out on top by hand. Rocks were scattered over the gravesites. These were graves that were not meant to be recognized.

Camp Stockton was a welcome sight. It was just an old army outpost that the Rangers had taken for a postwar station. Crenshaw and Foster had done a pretty good job of gauging the water and food supply. Both were low and needed to be replenished They would spend one night in Camp Stockton. There were quarters that could be used by travelers. The women were very happy to be able to bathe. The men wanted to relax. Ben Fields wanted to play poker.

Ray and Henry started looking for somebody to talk to about the road ahead. They needed information. Ray walked straight to Ranger headquarters. As soon as he got there, he noticed a big argument had gotten started across the street.

He walked over to get a better look. As he got closer, he saw the conflict. A covered wagon's axle was propped up on blocks. The left rear wheel was broken. A young woman was trying to put a new wheel on the wagon. She was tall with long black hair. She wore a wide, flat-brimmed hat. Ray couldn't get a good look at her. He did notice that she had quite an attractive looking body. She was arguing with a man. He was short with a long robe and a long white beard. His hat was pressing down on his glasses. She towered above him, but he was screaming at her.

"You cannot work on the Sabbath, young lady!" the short man screamed. "It is totally unacceptable to God. You must stop this instant."

But she argued right back at him.

"Listen," she said. "Luke fourteen five says that if your ox falls into a culvert on the Sabbath, you've got to push him out! That comes straight from the Bible. Now leave me alone."

The little man in the long robe didn't waver. He kept right on scolding her.

Ray walked over to the wagon. "What's the problem here?" he asked the both of them.

"This woman is breaking God's law," the elder man said to Ray. "It is unforgivable. She must stop."

Ray looked at the young woman. It was the first time that he could get up close enough to see what she looked like. His instincts were correct. She had an ivory tone to her skin and shoulder-length black hair. It didn't matter that dirt was smudged on her face, and she was drenched in sweat. She was beautiful.

"Sir, you need to go on your way," Ray said to the man in the long coat. "Leave her alone. She has work that she needs to do."

He turned and looked at her. "My name is Ray, Ray Andrews. I'll help you with this."

The little man in the cape went into a furious rant.

"You will both go to hell," he screamed. "You will both go to hell."

Ray had heard enough. "If you don't get out of here right now, I'm gonna deck you. Now get," he said.

The little man started backpedaling. "You are both sinners in the eyes of God," he said. "Now you threaten me with physical violence. Pitiful you, pitiful you!" With that, he walked away.

The two new friends looked at each other. Ray immediately tried to figure out how old she was. He was twenty-six. It looked like she was close to the same. Neither could figure out what to say. Finally, the young woman broke the ice.

"I'm sorry," she said in a flux. "My name is Sarah Thomas. My father is over there buying supplies. We're going to San Francisco." Ray was just a little bit stunned. He couldn't spit out anything worthy to say, so he just stood there and looked at her.

"Do you know how to put a wheel on this wagon?" she asked him.

Just then, a very ironic thought hit Ray. He had all kinds of Ranger skills, but he didn't know how to change the wheel on a wagon. He tried to gather himself before he said anything. Then it came to him.

"Go over there in the shade and sit down, ma'am. I'll get that wheel fixed real soon, be back in a few minutes."

Ray shuffled across the street to Ranger headquarters. Henry was inside, looking at a map.

"Stut," Ray whispered. "Can you come over here and help me put a wheel on a wagon?"

Henry never even flinched.

"Sure," he answered. "Where is it?"

The two of them walked across the street. Henry saw the problem and walked straight to it.

"Let me get my tools off the coach," he yelled.

He took off down the street. Ray walked over to the wagon, bent down, and looked at the wheel. He wanted it to look like he knew exactly what to do.

"Where ya headed?" the young woman asked.

"Well," Ray answered. "We're heading to San Francisco too. At least, we're headed to that area. We haven't even talked about where we're gonna stop."

He realized that he needed to be on his best manners. He was careful about everything he said. Suddenly, the thought hit him that he hadn't taken a bath in over a week.

"Why are you going to San Francisco?" he asked her.

She leaned back and removed her hat. She exhaled and focused her eyes out on the street.

"My father wants to set up a church there. He's a Methodist preacher. He says that's where God's calling him to go. I think he's crazy, but I couldn't let him come out here alone."

Ray got up under the wagon and acted like he knew what he was doing. It got quiet, so he jumped out and walked over to her.

"Where you from?" he asked her.

She shifted her eyes to him without moving her face. "Mississippi," she answered. "All over the state. My dad preached in several towns. We've moved around my whole life." Ray couldn't help but ask the next question. "Where's your mom?"

However, Sarah Thomas didn't seem to like that question.

Before she could answer, Stuttering Henry Jones came walking up with a bag full of tools.

"Captain, can you help me get this wheel lined up straight?" he asked.

Ray broke away and dove into the chore.

The two Rangers had the wheel on in ten minutes. Of course, Henry didn't stop there. He walked all the way around the wagon to check every bolt, nut, hinge, and anything else that needed attention. He didn't like the bench on the wagon, so he took his mallet and started banging on it. He reached into his bag and pulled out some kind of apparatus. Before you knew it, the bench was fixed.

Sarah Thomas was in awe.

"There ya go, nice lady," said Henry without the glimpse of a stutter.

She looked at Ray and said, "Thank the both of you."

Henry was happy to answer. "Nothing to it, ma'am," he said. Then he asked Ray, "Captain Andrews, permission to return to headquarters?"

He smiled and winked at Ray as he said it. Ray had never seen him smile like that. There were two big gaps in his teeth.

"Thank you so much, Stut," Ray answered.

Ray walked over to Sarah who was sitting on the bench. He turned around and looked at the wagon.

"Is it just you and your dad on that wagon?" he asked.

Sarah looked at him like he just asked her something a little too personal. "Yes," she answered. "That's it. We haven't had any trouble until this wheel snapped."

Before Ray could get out any more questions, a man hollered from across the street.

"Sarah," he yelled loudly. "Are you all right? Is that man bothering you?"

Ray stepped back and away from her instantly.

"No, Pop," she explained. "He fixed the wagon wheel, look." The older man stared at Ray. There was a time when Ray might have cowered down to an older man, but he had gone through quite a bit in the last few months. Besides that, he just fixed the man's wagon.

"My name is Ray Andrews. I'm a guard for Sawyer Crenshaw's stagecoach."

Ray stuck out his hand to shake. The older man held both arms around big bags of supplies he had bought across the street. Finally, he put them down on the ground and stuck his hand out to Ray.

"Reverend William Thomas," he said to Ray. "Call me William. Thank you for fixing the wheel. What do I owe you?"

Ray was almost insulted. "William, huh," he asked. "I think I'll just call you reverend."

Ray eyeballed the reverend from head to toe. His hat had a round top and a flat brim. His shirt was clean. His overalls were fitted nicely around his athletic frame. The reverend had just bought some new boots yesterday. They were the lace-up kind. Probably better, he thought, for a preacher to wear. He had also just gotten a haircut and a shave. It was obvious that he took pride in his appearance.

"I'm sorry to be on the defensive, but there are a lot of bad men out here. I have to look out for my daughter."

Ray had always admired people who took regular baths and dressed nice. He just didn't know very many of them. He looked over at Sarah. He had already noticed how nice she looked.

"It's okay, sir," Ray answered. "Which way are you heading? I believe we're going to the same direction."

Reverend Thomas was slow to warm up to Ray, but he needed all the help he could get on his navigation skills.

"We're just heading straight west until we hit the ocean. Then we're turning north. We hear that will take us straight into San Francisco."

The three of them talked for another two hours. The time went by so fast that none of them noticed how late it was getting. Ray knew there would be no way that Sarah and the reverend could stay up with the stagecoach. They were on a two-horse wagon while the Crenshaw entourage was riding on a four-horse carriage built for speed. Crenshaw wanted to travel fifty miles per day. The Thomases would be lucky to travel twenty.

"We've been leaving a trail behind us," Ray explained to Sarah and the reverend. "It's easy to follow. Just stay in our tracks. If there is trouble, I will figure out how to stay behind to help you." Sarah Thomas was a little worried that she had already fallen with this Ray Andrews. She had never met anybody like him. It was obvious that he was concerned about both her and her dad. It wasn't like her to be so infatuated with someone like that. She had heard of love at first sight, but she didn't think it would be like this.

"Thank you," she said. "Will you try to find us in San Francisco?" The reverend quickly scolded her. "Sarah!" he said. "Don't be so forward."

Sarah wasn't flustered at all.

Ray just smiled and said, "Sure, I will. But just where exactly will you be?" Ray and Sarah spent the next ten minutes trying to figure it out.

Everybody on the coach found out about the preacher's daughter the next morning. The women were mad they didn't get to meet her. While Ray was riding out in front of the coach, he noticed that he was the center of conversation. The dynamics of the trip had just changed, and they knew it. Ray was such a likeable young man. Everyone respected his dedication to duty and how he looked after them. After the run-in with the Indians, no one even thought to challenge what he said.

Stuttering Henry Jones had earned the respect he deserved too. He was happy that they had met Sarah and the reverend. He knew Ray had met his match, and he was happy for him. At the same time, he felt sad. He had never met a woman to care for. He was a little jealous. This girl would probably take away his best friend someday. But for now, that wasn't important. It was time to get back to work.

Ray and Henry had been discussing whether or not it was still necessary to use the alternate campsite. Ray said yes. Henry said no. He was tired of dragging everybody and everything out to the boonies late at night. But as usual, Ray won out.

"It's the safe move, Stut. I just feel like we need to stay on the edge of things. They won't like it, but they know it's the right thing to do."

Henry wasn't so sure, but he relented easily to the captain. The conversation turned to other things.

"How-how we gonna keep an eye on that girl and the preacher?" Henry asked.

"I'm not sure," Ray answered. "Thought about asking Crenshaw to just let 'em ride with us, but I didn't."

Henry stared straight out into the desert. "Thought about as-asking myself. Didn't know how you felt 'bout it though."

The two men rode on the rest of the morning without saying another word to each other.

Junior Hoskins brought up the subject of moving to the alternate camp at supper.

"Hey, Andrews," she said in a scolding tone, "you gonna make us go out in the desert and hide tonight?"

She immediately got everybody's attention. They were all thinking about it too. Ray had just poured himself a cup of hot coffee. He was gently blowing into it to cool it down.

"I know you guys don't want to go out there," he said in a quiet tone. "But I think we need to. I don't know this country very well. Henry and me can keep a better watch that way."

Everyone was disappointed. However, deep down inside, they knew that Ray was right. Ben Fields was the first to speak up.

"Well, I think it's a good idea," he said. "I trust Mr. Andrews. If he thinks we need to do it, then I say we do what he says. It sure saved our tails before."

Ray was appreciative that Fields backed him. He knew it wasn't a popular choice. John Kitchens chimed in.

"I agree," he said. "I know it's uncomfortable, but I feel like we all know the plan."

Tom McLemore also agreed. Willie Foster just wanted to make a joke about the whole situation.

"It ain't so bad," he said. "I stink so bad won't nobody bother us. Besides, if somebody tries to rob us, we'll get to watch Ray and Henry kill 'em." Everybody laughed, even Junior Hoskins.

CHAPTER 19

San Francisco

Sores Aguilar had moved quickly to establish and execute his plan to import opium from Hong Kong and sell it on the streets of San Francisco. He worked hard to ensure that Cyrus Welch, Min Cho Fat, and Suk Too trusted him. It was a tough job. Sores didn't look the part of a man who could be trusted. He was a half breed who had no formal education. His unique dark skin seemed to overshadow his natural good looks. His big, physical stature was also a factor. Sores had begun to slowly shorten his long, jet-black hair, but he still kept it at just above shoulder length. He thought long and hard about taking the red feathers of the Summer Tanager and putting them away. He thought that might help him look a little bit more normal. But he just couldn't get himself to do it. Every morning, he carefully weaved a red feather into the locks of his hair down by the collar. The look was subtle, but it was an obvious trademark. It helped that many of the characters of the San Francisco streets looked so odd. After all, it was not a normal community. The streets were filled with Aussie sailors, gold seekers, outlaws, gamblers, and vagrants. There were very few women in town. Sores had already decided that prostitution would be his next project after he got his opium business off the ground. He had already begun dabbling in it. He knew not to spread himself too thin though. Not only was he extremely intelligent, but he was also very disciplined. He knew how to focus on what needed to get done. His father, Pinney, was a ruthless drunk, but he knew how to think through his business affairs. Sores learned early on how to plan for what he wanted to get done, but he realized that he had to be ready for when problems occurred. His insecurity and fear of what would happen if he failed drove him hard.

Sores knew he needed to kidnap sailors for the trip to and from Hong Kong. His plan was to capture them and work them as slave labor on Cyrus Welch's clipper ship. Welch would eliminate them close to their return to San Francisco. He didn't want many people knowing about the drug operation. He knew he couldn't risk any sailor walking around the streets of San Francisco talking. The law was very crude and unorganized, but it would improve over time.

The one man that Sores knew he had to count on was Cyrus Welch. He was even more critical than Min Cho Fat. Sores figured that he could find another drug contact, but it would be difficult to find an expert sailor who was willing to transport contraband across the Pacific Ocean. He also knew that Welch would have to be on board about his dastardly approach to the sailors.

The two men sat down one late afternoon at the Lonely Sailor to drink whiskey. It was time, Sores thought, to explain his plan. Welch liked everything he heard, but he struggled with one part. According to Sores, slaves had to be threatened at gunpoint on the ship during sailing time. Welch and Suk Too would be outnumbered, and they must establish leverage. If a mutiny happened, then it would be them who would be thrown overboard to the sharks.

Sores Aguilar had an idea.

"What if we cut Suk Too in on the deal?" he asked.

Welch didn't know exactly what Aguilar meant.

"Don't understand, mate. Ye going to have to explain," he responded.

Sores went into detail teaching Welch about the complexities of loyalty and partnership. Suk Too could turn on the two of them any time he wanted. They needed some way to keep him accountable 'til the end. They needed a way to secure his loyalty. Sores mentioned the idea to Welch to cut him in on the deal with the two of them and Fat.

"In other words," Sores explained. "There will be four partners. If we don't have the muscle to handle the slaves on the ship, the whole trip will be in danger. This way, you worry about sailing the Melba Lee and let Suk Too worry about guarding the sailors."

Welch liked what he was hearing. "Ya sure Fat will go along, mate?" Welch asked.

Aguilar looked out the window of the Lonely Sailor. He saw what he estimated to be two or three hundred people walking the streets below.

"Leave that to me," he answered. "Once the ship leaves for Hong Kong, he won't have a choice."

Sores was now very close to starting the execution of his grand scheme. He had helped Cyrus stock the Melba Lee with supplies. Underneath in the cargo area, the two of them had bolted chain cuffs to house the sailors at night and during meals. There were chains on the cuffs to allow the sailors to move just enough to get food and water. Sores even thought to build a small latrine in the belly of the ship for the slaves. Suk Too would be in charge of guarding the slaves. He was so big that it would be foolish for one of them to challenge him. On top of that, he would be heavily armed at all times.

The plan was to feed the sailors just enough to keep them strong enough to sail the ship. It was important not to feed them too much. Otherwise, they might have the energy to try a mutiny.

If serious trouble ensued, Suk Too would simply walk them to the plank or shoot them on sight. Then the other sailors would just throw the troublemaker overboard. Cyrus needed sixteen men to crew the ship, two sets of eight. He had ten paid sailors and seven kidnapped sailors. One extra slave had been added for the first day.

Sores was convinced that on the first day of the trip, Suk Too would need to throw one of the captured sailors overboard. That would terrorize them, and it would discourage any mutiny. But Cyrus Welch didn't like the idea.

"Still don't see why we need to throw a sailor off the ship the first day, mate," he said. "Seems like a waste to me."

Cyrus gulped down a long drink of whiskey. The fact that he didn't appreciate that part of the plan bothered Aguilar.

Sores pulled himself up close to Cyrus Welch.

"Listen, brother," he whispered. "You are going to have to kill one of those sailors on the first day. You can shoot him, you can hang him, or you can just throw him overboard. I don't care how you do it, but you have to do it the first day. If you don't, they won't fear you. This plan is based on those sailors being scared to death of you and Suk Too. You tell 'em that if they are good sailors, you will let them go free when you get back to San Francisco. You can tell them that you are going to pay them. Just don't lose control of them."

Welch saw a sense of urgency in Sores Aguilar's eyes that he had never seen before. He looked down at the floor. Suddenly, Sores snapped at him.

"Welch," he barked. "Look at me. You have to understand this part of the plan. You must control the labor. Make sure they fear that you will kill them at any minute, but make sure they think they will be released when you return."

Welch was beginning to fear Sores Aguilar himself. "I understand, mate," he responded.

"One more thing," Sores said with a serious tone. "You must eliminate them from the voyage before you come back into the docks here in the city. Nobody survives the trip but you and Suk Too. We can't afford any witness."

Welch was now sweating profusely. He was obviously intimidated. Sores continued explaining the plan. Welch and Suk Too would stay on the deck of the ship. Welch had built a small cabin in the center of the ship for bad weather. There would be no need for either of them to go down below unless they were getting food or going to the head. The conditions were going to be tough, but the payoff would be worth it.

Everything was set. Welch had been studying the route. He was confident. The ship was ready. The gold to be used to buy the opium was hidden in a place that only Welch and Sores knew existed. It was now time to find the sailors for the trip.

CHAPTER 20

*S*ores Aguilar had been scouting the docks, streets, and saloons of the San Francisco Bay area. He was looking for just the right fit. It really didn't matter to him whether or not the victims were sailors. Welch had already told him that it wasn't that important. They just needed to be big and strong enough to do what they were told to do. After all, slave labor was just that, labor.

But Sores was even more acutely aware of what he was looking for than Welch thought. Once he spotted a potential victim, he zeroed in for the capture. He was looking for the strong, silent type. He didn't want a leader. It was an unnecessary risk. Someone like that might lead a rebellion. Making this judgment about anyone was just a guess, but he tried to hedge his bet the best he could. Welch needed physically powerful men, but he didn't need emotionally powerful men. Sores was the only judge on who was to be taken. Welch was not even consulted.

Sores had made his deal with Suk Too. Their relationship was an odd one, but it was working. Sores did all the talking. Suk Too almost never spoke. Somehow Sores could communicate with Suk Too on another level. They understood each other. Sores probed to find how he could reward the giant hulk of a man from the East. He found that Suk Too liked money, but he loved beautiful, young Asian women. Sores was already using the bottom story of the Lonely Sailor for prostitution. He was careful when he brought women in the building and how he housed them. They were not plentiful. There were very few women in the city at all. Sores had already figured out how to find them and keep them happy. The women became a drug that Suk Too could not resist. There was no way he could have the pleasure of company with these women without his new business partner. Sores had brought Suk Too into the palm of his hand.

On a cold and windy Sunday evening, Sores Aguilar made his move. Suk Too was waiting back in the Lonely Sailor, and Cyrus Welch was waiting at the docks on the Melba Lee.

The plan was set. Sores was nervous. When he got nervous, he never talked. The tension was a double-edged sword. He loved it, but he also hated it. There was one thing for sure though. He couldn't live without it. The thrill of the risk was the one thing that drove him so hard. The thrill was also always buffered by a financial opportunity.

Even San Francisco slowed down a little bit on Sunday night. Sores wanted as few people around as possible. He walked down to the docks and approached an area that he had been scouting for days. There he spotted his prey. A medium-sized sailor who had a strong-looking torso had caught Sores's eye. Sores knew where the sailor stayed. It was right at eight o'clock in the evening.

Sores walked over to the small shipping vessel and offered the sailor a smoke.

"Who do you work for?" he asked the young man.

The young sailor looked at him with just a little bit of sharpness. "I'm waiting on a job," he shouted. "I was supposed to be outta here a week ago, but my boss says we have to wait."

Sores was ready to pounce, so he asked, "Well, what is he waiting for?"

"I don't know," replied the sailor. "I'm not in the loop on that."

Sores looked around to see if anyone was watching.

"I'm looking for some men for a job," he said. "You interested?" The young sailor looked at him with just a little hesitation. "Yeah, I'm interested. What are you talking about?"

Sores had him in his grasp.

"Let's walk over to my headquarters. It's about two miles from here."

At first, the young sailor didn't buy it. "Naw, not interested," he said.

Sores looked him straight in the eyes.

"That's fine," he said. "Your loss, not mine. I'll find someone else."

With that, he turned around and started walking back home.

After he had walked close to a mile, he stopped and looked back. The sailor was following him.

"Come on." Sores rolled his shoulder toward the young sailor. Then he turned around and started walking again. The young man followed him all the way to the Lonely Sailor. Sores walked up the stairs on the outside of the house and into the bar. About thirty minutes later, the young sailor walked in the door. There were six men in the bar, drinking. Sores declared that the bar was closed. He sent his hired help away for the night and escorted all the paying customers out the door except the young sailor. Now it was only the two of them alone in the upstairs story of the house.

Sores took out a key from his pocket and opened a drawer that had a lock on it. He pulled out a bottle and held it up for the sailor to see. The young man walked over and stood across from Sores who was standing behind the bar.

"What's your name?' Sores asked.

"Billy Lambert," the kid belted out.

"Well, Billy Lambert, I'll buy you a drink," Sores replied. With that, Sores poured a long draw into a tall glass.

"What's this?" asked Lambert.

"My best beer," Sores replied.

The young man, Billy Lambert, looked around the room and then took a big gulp. Before he knew it, he had drunk the entire glass of beer. Sores filled the glass again. Lambert felt an immediate high. He had never felt that way before. He lost his balance while he was standing at the bar. Everything seemed to be moving.

He reached for his mug and asked Sores, "What kind of job are you talking about?

CHAPTER 21

Sawyer Crenshaw's stagecoach was moving along quite well. Since the dustup with the Apaches, there had not been any dangerous excitement. Ray Andrews and Stuttering Henry Jones were feeling a little better about things. That worried Ray. He had always been a worrier, and he was starting to feel uncomfortable that he was feeling so comfortable.

Henry had a question that was nagging at him, so on the trail, he just flat out asked Ray about it.

"How in the world," Henry asked, "d-d-did that p-p-preacher and his daughter make it all the way out here by th-th-themselves?" "I asked 'em 'bout that," Ray reported. "They said they haven't seen one Indian. They came through Waco on a trail called the West Pass."

Sarah said the reverend wanted her to stay in Waco to go to school. They have a new college there called Baylor. But the reverend is hell bent on going to San Francisco, and she wouldn't let him go alone. The West Pass ran right into Camp Stockton. They heard there were a lot of soldiers there that would discourage the Indians.

"That's amazin'," Henry said as he shook his head. "Hope they stay out of trouble."

Ray put the brakes on Salty and looked at the beautiful afternoon sunset.

"We've been so busy we haven't even talked about some things," he said to Henry. "Do you think we got all those Indians?" Henry stopped and backpedaled his horse, so he could talk to Ray.

"No," he said without hesitation. "They weren't n-n-near as re-ready. That first time they a-a-attacked, they kn-kn-knew what they was doing. That last time, they wa-wasn't ready."

"What about the feather?" Ray asked.

Henry shrugged his shoulders, took off his hat and sighed. "D-D-Don't know 'bout th-the feathers," he answered. "You got me on that. D-Don't know what to think."

Ray needed to talk. He had been keeping busy on the trip to San Francisco. It was good that his mind was occupied. But deep down inside, he was still grieving. He felt a deep-seeded guilt that he was responsible for the deaths of five men. One of them was his lifelong best friend, Tom Jenkins. It also didn't help that he was sure Tom's dad was telling everybody back in Austin that he was at fault. He had been thinking that he might never be able to go back there again. The pain was just too deep.

"Something in my gut's telling me that Empty Heart is still out there," Ray finally said to Henry. "But I don't even know what he looks like. He might be dead, but I don't think so. He's like a ghost."

Henry didn't like the way Ray was talking. He never viewed Ray as a weak person. The first attack by the Indians was planned perfectly. Then it was executed perfectly. The Rangers, on the other hand, had done a terrible job of planning. They ended up putting their own men in a ridiculous situation.

Nobody had ever said it out loud, but the Rangers that were on the trip all felt the same way. The whole mission was a setup for failure. It was all about money. The payroll was the only thing that mattered. There should have been three times the men on the trip to Camp Stockton to guard that much money. Headquarters thought they could just slip it through without any bandit noticing anything. Then on top of that, Ray Andrews was tagged as the scapegoat. The entire event was disgusting to Henry. That was the main reason he quit the Rangers and took the job as a guard for Sawyer Crenshaw.

A thought ran through Henry's mind. He never was much for planning anything. That was for other people to do. He just went with the flow. All of a sudden, it hit him hard that he was out in Far West Texas without thinking about his future. He asked himself a question, "What if I die out here in the middle of nowhere?"

The trail to California was simple. Scouts had told Crenshaw and Henry to just travel straight toward the west sun. There were light tracks that would disappear sometimes along the way. Then they would be visible again. It was obvious that this route hadn't been traveled by very many people. Moving toward the sun would lead to a wide river. That river, called the Rio Grande, would turn north and take the coach right into El Paso. Before they hit the Rio Grande, there would be smaller rivers, creeks, and streams for water. It was about as uneducated an assessment as any Ranger could imagine. But that was the route they were taking.

Traveling fifty miles a day was quite a chore. The women were getting tired. The men were getting edgy. There were some advantages to the West Texas climate though. There seemed to be little humidity, and there were no bugs. The weather had been very warm but not unbearably hot. It was now October, the prettiest weather of the year for Texas. Things were going well. Crenshaw wanted Henry and Ray to make a hard push to El Paso. He thought maybe they could pick up an extra eight to ten miles per day.

Everyone had plenty of time to think. Ray was having a tough time getting his mind off the preacher's daughter. He couldn't quit thinking about her. Never before had he seen a more beautiful girl. He liked the preacher too. He wondered aloud about any trouble back behind the coach. The preacher and his daughter could only travel about half as fast as the coach, and now Crenshaw was pushing the both of them to pick up the pace.

The coach had made it to the third day since stopping in Camp Stockton. The terrain was starting to look different. A mountainous background was appearing to the northwest. Could it be the Rio Grande? Everyone noticed the beauty as the sun slowly settled behind the mountains. It seemed so peaceful. Ray Andrews tried to focus his eyes as far out as possible. It was close to time to set up camp for the night. He decided to kick Salty and sprint on up a few hundred yards before the evening sunset.

Salty galloped at three quarters speed. Both he and Ray felt great. The beauty of West Texas was breathtaking. The weather was charming. The sunset was an awesome sight. Ray pulled on Salty and slowly came to a stop. He glared out into the low-lying mountains. Out of the corner of his eye, he caught a glimpse of something. He did a quick double take. Maybe he was just seeing things.

He peered closer. Sure enough, men on horses were traveling in a row a few miles ahead. Ray Andrews was not an educated man, but he was very smart. His instincts were his biggest strength. He didn't like what he saw, and he sensed danger.

Ray decided to sit tight and watch. He did not want to go any closer. On a whim, he had decided to ride up ahead for a quick scouting trip. Something told him to do it. He didn't understand why, but on impulse, he rode ahead.

After another twenty minutes or so, he decided to slowly walk backward. The coach was catching up to him. Finally, he turned around and kicked Salty in the ribs. They had gone far enough for the day. They were close enough to the mountains for now.

Ray rode back into camp and tried to keep a calm look on his face, but Henry picked up on things quickly. He was already on edge. Things just looked dangerous, and he could sense trouble. Ray went about his nightly chores, trying to get the horses and the passengers ready to make an alternate camp for the night. He was very quiet. It was too quiet for Henry, so he approached Ray.

"Is something bothering ya?" he asked.

Ray looked over his shoulder at Henry as he pulled the saddle off Salty.

"Stut," he said. "You can read me like a book, can't you?" Henry didn't smile at all. He just kept on prying for information. "D-d-did ya see sumpthin'?"

Ray was hesitant to say anything because he wasn't sure what he saw. There was one thing for sure though. This was no time to keep any secret from Stuttering Henry.

"Let's walk these horses over to that ridge," Ray replied.

Henry grabbed the reigns of his horse, Buster. Slowly, he followed Ray to the ridge.

Ray sat down at the top of the small hill.

"I knew everything was going too good," he finally said. "I barely saw 'em, but they were there. I counted eight men on horses up in the pass area. I'm sure they saw me too. Don't know who they are."

Henry was standing five feet from Ray. He was using his shotgun as a cane. The barrel was pointed straight down into the dirt.

"Makes sense," he answered. "It-t-t-t's a perfect t-t-trap. Where exactly d-d-did you see 'em?" Ray tried to pinpoint the exact area from the ridge. It was almost dark now, but Ray and Henry were glued to the mountain pass like eagles. It would be a long night.

At that very moment, Ray went into leader mode.

"All right," he said with enthusiasm. "Let's get a plan together."

He rubbed his hands together and covered his eyes as if that would give him some kind of wisdom.

"We have to figure out what we're gonna tell everybody. They don't have a clue right now."

Henry was thinking hard too. Working with Ray on the guard detail was the first time he had ever been in a leadership role. He was enjoying it. It was especially gratifying to him working with Ray. He wanted to contribute, but he was careful not to say anything until it made sense.

"Do you want to st-st-stall for some time?" he asked.

Ray looked up at him. "Maybe," he replied.

"The biggest problem is that they have the high ground," Ray said. "They will have us pinned down when we get to 'em. I'm sure they want all our money. They might want the women too. The first thing we need to do is inventory all our guns and ammo. We have to tell everybody what's happening. You're right. We might have to stall for a while 'til we figure out what we're gonna do."

Ray was in battle mode.

"Let's set up camp tonight like we always do," he said. "Think this through the best you can. Act like everything is okay for now. Don't let 'em know anything is wrong. We can talk again later."

With that, Ray and Henry walked the horses back to camp. Everybody was going about their normal duties and habits. Sawyer Crenshaw was checking the coach for any problems. He was not in a good mood. It seemed to him that they were way behind schedule. Willie Foster was busy cooking beans and cornbread for supper. He didn't seem to be happy either. Ben Fields and Junior Hoskins were playing cards. Ray had noticed that they seemed to be playing a lot lately. Lovie Kitchens was watching them play, but she was not participating. John Kitchens stood over to the side. He looked like he was bored to death. Tom and Mara McLemore had pulled their luggage down off the top of the coach and seemed to be looking for something.

Ray walked up to Willie Foster and started a conversation.

"What's for supper tonight, Willie?"

Foster was quick to respond. "Beans and cornbread," he answered. "I got some coffee going for you too."

Ray was always polite and thankful to the cook.

"You're doing a good job," he told Foster. "I really appreciate you."

Foster didn't seem to notice the compliment.

"How much further to El Paso?" he asked.

"Pretty sure it's just over those mountains," Ray replied. "Well, let's get over them mountains then," Foster barked. "I don't like this territory. It's spooky to me."

Ray looked down at his boots for a second. He decided to move on to someone else for conversation. John Kitchens approached him.

"How are things going, Captain?" Kitchens asked with obvious respect.

Ray was caught a little off guard. He and Kitchens had never really had much conversation before.

"Just trying to get ready for tonight," Ray answered. He walked right on by Kitchens as if all were good.

Tom and Mara McLemore seemed to be in a flux. Ray walked up and spoke to them.

"Everything okay?" he asked.

Mara looked up at him. "We're okay, Ray. We just can't seem to find a piece of jewelry. It was my daughter's brooch. I thought for sure I packed it." Ray noticed the worrisome look on her face.

"Can I help," he asked.

"No, it's okay. I'll find it," she answered.

The card game that Ben Fields and Junior Hoskins were playing was very serious. Ray overheard Fields gently chastising Junior. "No, you can't do it like that. That draws too much attention to yourself. Do it like this, Junior."

Fields shuffled the cards and began to deal. Card games bored Ray, but he watched a little longer along with

Lovie. Fields was throwing cards around like they were pebbles. Every card seemed to land perfectly. He was dealing to Junior, but he was also dealing to phantom players just like a real game. Junior was glued to the makeshift card table that was actually just the ground.

Ray tried to initiate a little conversation.

"Are you guys, okay?" he asked.

Not a single one of them acknowledged him. Finally, he walked away. That was enough conversation for now.

CHAPTER 22

*E*veryone on the trip was sick of the alternate campsite. It was hard to sleep and very inconvenient. They traveled all day long with only a couple of breaks. After that, it was time for supper. Then Ray and Henry led the way to an alternate campsite. Even though the alternate site had saved them once before, it was very unpopular.

It seemed that neither Ray nor Henry ever slept much. They worked a system out between the two of them to alternate watches. At most, they were getting three or four hours of sleep per night. It was starting to take a toll on the both of them.

Junior Hoskins was difficult to deal with all the time, but at night, she would be especially nasty. That night, after the move to the alternate campsite, she decided to tear into Ray.

"Andrews," she said. "This is a waste of time and energy. We're a good hundred miles from those Indians. I don't know why you're so scared all the time. You're making us all miserable."

Ray knew she had a good point. He didn't want to go to the alternate site either. He was just playing it safe, but he never responded to Junior's whining. He was thinking about how he was going to use her in his plans to go through the mountain pass. After all, she was a trick-shooting specialist with handguns. They were going to need a sharpshooter if he was correct about the men on the horses.

Everyone was so tired it was easy for them to fall asleep. Ray took a short nap before he relieved Henry. His mind was racing. The Rangers didn't have any training on mountain warfare. This would be a different kind of battle. He looked over at Henry who was sawing logs.

It would be better to let him get a good rest, he thought to himself. He is older than me and needs the sleep.

The rest of the night, Ray sat there, looking at the coach about a half mile away. A small fire burned and lit the area. It was actually a beautiful sight. The horses were quiet. The passengers were sleeping. His eyes peered up into the mountains.

They're not that big, he thought. It didn't seem like it would be that difficult to ride through them. He had come up with a plan. After breakfast, he would tell the passengers about it. Henry would stall for him until he was ready. Nervous energy flowed through his body. A man of violence, he was not, but it was obvious to him at that moment how much he thrived on situations like this one.

At dawn, Henry tapped Ray on the shoulder. He had nodded off in the early morning.

"Get some rest, Captain," Henry told him. "I'll start getting things ready."

Ray grabbed his arm.

"Figure out some way to stall," he said as he tried to get comfortable sitting up against a big rock. "And wake me up in thirty minutes."

Henry started gathering the horses. He always tried to find somewhere for them to graze early in the morning. The time passed quickly. Ray didn't need any help waking up in the time he allowed himself. Like an alarm clock, he woke up right on time.

The rest of the passengers slowly awoke and began the slow walk back to the original camp. By the time they got there, Henry was already working on the left rear wheel of the coach. Crenshaw immediately noticed.

"What's wrong?" he shouted.

"I don't like the looks of this wheel," Henry answered. "I'm gonna change it out."

Crenshaw almost exploded.

"There isn't anything wrong with that wheel. You're gonna put us back two hours," he shouted.

Henry kept on working. The left rear wheel was already off the coach. The jack was stable, and Henry was going to change the wheel out no matter what Crenshaw said.

Ray walked up and calmed things down.

"Sawyer, we need to have a little meeting anyway," he said. "Why don't we gather everybody up?"

All of a sudden, it hit Crenshaw that something wasn't right.

"What's going on?" he said as he scowled at Ray. "You better know what you are doing."

Ray didn't yell, but he did raise his voice pretty loud.

"Everybody needs to come on over. I got something I need to go over with you."

Henry kept working on the wheel. The rest of the passengers slowly walked toward Ray. He was standing about ten yards from the coach.

Ray looked at everyone. He realized that they didn't understand what was happening. He began to speak softly, but he was very firm.

"We feel like there is trouble ahead. Last night, I saw eight men on horses up in the mountains. I 'spect they're Mexican bandits. Don't think they're Indians. I saw that they were wearing hats. They're probably waiting on us somewhere up in that mountain pass. We would be foolish not to have a plan. Maybe I'm wrong, and we will just ride right through there with no trouble. I don't want to chance it though."

Mara McLemore sighed and crumbled down to her knees. Tom McLemore grabbed her. She began to sob.

"Mara," Tom scolded her. "Come on, dear, it will be all right."

He dropped to a knee to comfort her, and then he looked up at the others.

"She had a long night. Somewhere, she lost the brooch we gave our daughter on her wedding day. She is really upset about it." Suddenly, everyone refocused on the story the McLemore's told one night at supper about their daughter, Harriett. She had died two years ago. She was an only child. It had upset Tom and Mara so much they decided to start a new life in California. Lovie Kitchens started crying when Mara was talking about the funeral. The story brought back hard memories to Ray and Henry. Even Willie Foster seemed to shed a tear.

Mara climbed back to her feet and waited for Ray to continue. He looked at her and saw the pain in her face. He figured that brooch was probably all she had left. Ray gathered himself together.

"Anyway," he continued. "We need every weapon to be inventoried. Please put everything in a circle right here. We need all ammunition too. Let's see what we've got."

It didn't take long. Sawyer Crenshaw had an old single-bolt arm rifle and a single-shot pistol. Willie Foster had a rifle and a shotgun. He also had two big knives. Ben Fields had a Colt Paterson revolver and the smallest handgun Ray had ever seen. Junior Hoskins had two .44-caliber Colt Walker revolvers. It was the revolver that was designed to shoot like a rifle. Neither the McLemore's nor the Kitchens even had a gun.

Henry had two shotguns and two Colt Navy revolvers. He also had three knives. Ray also had two Colt Navy revolvers and a shotgun. He also had a small knife.

Ray grouped all the weapons into separate categories, and then he placed all the bullets to the side. They had a lot of firepower and several knives. Ray didn't like knives. Deep down inside, he hoped they wouldn't be necessary.

Ray examined the weapons, wrote something down on a piece of paper, and he looked each person in the eye. Finally, he spoke, "Okay, this is what we're gonna do."

With that, Capt. Ray Andrews started explaining to everyone what role he or she was going to play on the route through the mountain pass. Nobody dared to interrupt him, and there was not a question asked.

CHAPTER 23

*S*awyer Crenshaw wasn't happy that the stagecoach would sit and not move for an entire day. However, he realized the reason it was necessary. There was a lot to do. The main reason Ray didn't want to travel for a day was simple. He wanted to make sure that everyone was very well rested and knew exactly what to do. The plan included a nonstop trip right into El Paso the next day.

The passengers did their duties and killed a lot of time. Ray repeated the plan over and over. Stuttering Henry Jones was trying to rest up the best he could. All the horses would be fed, watered, and rested. There would be no going to an alternate campsite tonight. An early breakfast before dawn would be served. After breakfast, it was time to go. Ray wondered if he might be wrong about what he was expecting. He wondered if the coach might not pass right on through without any trouble. He almost wanted some kind of a skirmish to occur just to prove that he was correct in his assessment. That kind of thinking was dangerous though, and he knew it.

Everyone was on edge all day, evening and night. It was difficult to sleep. Stuttering Henry left just after midnight. He would travel up the mountainside to the north flank. He was going to try to beat the bandits to the punch by outflanking them. The numbers would not be on his side, so he would have to use some trickery. Ray gave a quick thought about being the flank man himself, but he gave up on that quickly. It was important that he stayed with the passengers. That was just common sense. Everyone knew that he was the leader of the pack.

Ray and Henry were really gambling on one thing, the Colt Navy revolver. Both of them knew the gun as well as anyone. They were both winners at Samuel Colt's shooting contest in Austin. That event had led to the reason they were here today. Ray won the contest himself. Tom Jenkins finished fourth. Stuttering Henry finished fifth. They all won a new Colt Navy and an assignment to guard the payroll. The Mexicans, or whoever was up there, surely would not have access to the revolvers.

Ray led the way. He kept a good fifty-yard lead on the coach. They moved at a brisk pace. It only took two hours to hit the base of the mountains. Slowly, they turned to the north. The pass was easy to see, and Crenshaw drove the team firmly behind Ray. Everyone saw smoke high in the mountains. The smoke was a signal from Henry. He had spotted the outlaws. Ray felt an awkward sense of relief. At least, he was correct about what he saw.

Ray had the two extra horses tied to Salty. Both Henry and Ray had been pulling a spare horse. Ray had them both now. He kept them up close on each side of himself and Salty. That was how he could protect himself from gunfire. He spotted a turn about a half mile up the road.

"This is it," he said to himself. Slowly, he brought Salty and the other two horses to a halt. He turned around and put his right arm straight up in the air. Waving three times across his body was the signal to Crenshaw that the fight was getting close.

The coach started heading toward the turn in the pass. When it got within thirty yards of the turn, two

Mexicans on horseback came through from the other side. Ray stopped all three horses.

Immediately, he skillfully tucked the two horses tight up beside Salty's body. He looked for snipers but couldn't see any.

Ray and the Mexicans stared at each other for a couple of minutes. Finally, one of the Mexicans spoke, "Fifty dollar."

Ray waited about thirty seconds and responded, "We don't want any trouble. We just want to move on through."

Neither of the Mexicans changed expressions. The three men and the five horses stared at each other. Ray pulled out a bag and threw it up to the two Mexicans. One of the Mexicans got off his horse. When he reached down to pick it up, Ray started moving toward the turn in the pass. The two Mexicans quickly moved to block his course. That was what Ray needed to know. He had already decided that it was worth a try to see if they would let him go on through. There was nothing in the bag but rocks.

Ray took a quick look back at the coach. He did not believe in shooting first. In this case though, he might have to make an exception. Everyone involved just looked at each other. Finally, the same Mexican who had spoken earlier spoke again.

"Fifty dollars," he yelled.

"No! Can't do it!" Ray screamed back at him.

The fire grew bigger. Smoke was starting to circulate through the mountain valley pass. Suddenly, one of the Mexicans drew his gun. That was it. Junior Hoskins was on top of the coach, zeroing in on them with one of her

Colt Walkers. She was hidden between the luggage and was covered with blankets. If gunfire came in from the mountains, she could easily slide into protection. The first shot hit the Mexican who had drawn his gun right between the eyes. Ray had instructed her to wait until he was threatened. However, he figured she would shoot when she was ready. The second shot hit the other Mexican right in the chest. Both the men slumped over and fell off their horses. Ray hurried over to them. It only took a minute to take both of their gun belts. Quickly, he slapped both of their horses and cleared the turn. He looked back at the coach and waved it through the pass.

The fire was now burning hard, and there was a lot of smoke. Ray waited for the coach to get to him. He turned left into the pass, and then he kicked Salty in the sides. They were moving quickly. Suddenly, a shot rang out, and the horse on Ray's left collapsed. She screamed in terror. Ray dropped the reigns and kept moving. Crenshaw skillfully evaded the sprawling horse and veered through the pass.

More gunshots came from the left flank, but the smoke made it tough to hit a moving target. Sparks lit up as bullets bounced off the rocks in front and behind Ray. There was almost no visibility. Ray dropped the reigns of the second horse, and Salty sprinted up and over to the right side of the mountain. The coach flew right on through the pass.

Ray didn't wait. He jumped down off Salty and climbed into the mountainside. There he looked to establish a shooting position. He used the smoke to hide the best he could. As he crawled to higher ground, he found a great place for cover. The shots kept coming. When he looked down into the pass, it was easy for Ray to find the shooters.

Four men were behind a ledge. Two others were twenty feet higher behind a rock pile. Ray had two Colt Navy revolvers on his body. He unloaded the first one into the ledge. Before he could get hold of the second one, shots started firing from over his right shoulder. Three shots rang out. A couple of seconds later, three more shots were fired. Ray waited for the gunshots to come to an end, and then he looked up to find the shooter. It was Stuttering Henry Jones. Everything got quiet. Ray and Henry carefully walked down the mountainside. The job was done. It wasn't necessary to fire any more shots from the Colt Navy revolver.

CHAPTER 24

Hong Kong

It took Cyrus Welch thirty-two days to sail the Melba Lee seven thousand miles from San Francisco to Hong Kong. Things had gone surprisingly smooth. Suk Too was an excellent guard. He didn't flinch at the end of the very first day when Cyrus told him to walk one of the kidnapped sailors to the wooden steps on the north bow of the ship. It terrified the captured men just like Sores said it would. One of them was the young Billy Lambert. He was lucky he wasn't chosen at random to be executed on the first evening of the voyage. He had shown some attitude toward Welch and Suk Too, but he wasn't the most vocal slave.

Welch had pushed everyone on the voyage to travel at least 250 miles per day. They didn't do quite that well, but they came close. He was an expert sailor and a very good teacher. The slave labor was slow to come around on the first few days of the voyage. The Melba Lee only sailed about 100 miles the first day. Cyrus was patient but gruff to the young slave sailors. As he was instructed to do by Sores Aguilar, he was planning on getting their attention just before dark that night.

When the time came for the dirty deed to be done, Cyrus Welch and Suk Too picked out the weakest sailor on the ship, John Calhoun. Calhoun was also the laziest and the loudest. It was an easy choice. The hangover from the opium-based beer he had drunk the night before was just now wearing off. Nobody had much interest in conversation. Calhoun was belligerent and disrespectful.

Everyone was bitter once they figured out their fate. Calhoun was just the loudest to voice his displeasure.

At dusk, Cyrus walked over to him as he sat on a bench.

"Suk Too," Welch yelled. "Over here, throw this lazy mate overboard."

The men were exhausted and absolutely miserable. They had fought off a terrible hangover on the waving Pacific Ocean. They had been in the sun all day. All they had to eat was some stale bread and a couple of handfuls of rice.

Billy Lambert thought it was all just a bad dream. He had sailed all the way to the San Francisco docks from New York City. The son of Irish immigrants, he was a natural sailor who had just turned thirty years old a month ago. He never knew what hit him at the Lonely Sailor.

Lambert watched as Suk Too grabbed John Calhoun and started walking him to the plank.

"Let go of my shirt," yelled Calhoun. "Who do you think you are?"

Suk Too never said a word. Finally, he had heard enough from Calhoun, so he slapped him up the side of his head with the back of his right hand. The slap stunned Calhoun. Suk Too literally pushed him up the steps of the plank, and then he raised his shotgun to blast him into the water. Calhoun was probably dead before he ever hit the ocean. It certainly got everybody's attention.

Welch studied the landscape from the Melba Lee when they arrived in Hong Kong. Once he found the spot he liked, he secured the clipper. There were nineteen men on the ship. Welch and Suk Too were armed. The six prisoners were cuffed against the wall in the belly of the ship.

Cyrus Welch had never seen this land before, and it was making him very queasy. Suk Too, however, seemed quite at ease. This was his homeland. Welch would not leave the ship the first day. He used his time wisely plotting exactly where he and Suk Too would go. He studied to know just how long it would take them to get to their destination. Next, they had to execute the trade. Finally, they would bring the haul back to the clipper.

The opium had to be loaded first. Obviously, it needed to be done discreetly. After that, tea, linen, and rice would be added to the top of the cargo. If there was any trouble, the opium should be hidden.

Just before time to bed down for the night, Welch started quizzing Suk Too.

"You know exactly where to go, mate?" he asked him. "Know exactly what to say?"

Suk Too just looked at him and nodded.

"Mate, I sure wish ya would just talk!" Cyrus said in a frustrated tone. Suk Too didn't even blink. Finally, the giant, baldheaded ogre spoke.

"Know where to go. Need men to help carry back to boat."

Cyrus already knew that. With all his brilliant planning, Sores had forgotten one thing. How could two men carry all the goods by themselves back to the boat but still be secure from thieves? They would need two more men to help, and that would be dicey. Welch was scared to take the paid sailors to the drug deal. It could lead to a mutiny.

"Which two?" Welch asked Suk Too.

The giant Chinaman turned and looked down into the belly of the ship. He pointed at Billy Lambert. Then he pointed at another slave named Homer Pell.

"Them," he blurted.

Lambert thought at first that he was going to be the next sacrifice. He had done everything he could to stay in the good graces of Suk Too and Cyrus Welch after watching Charlie Calhoun be blown into the water.

"Agreed," Welch said as he looked down at Lambert.

The young Irishman went into a frenzy.

"No, no, no," he wailed as Suk Too walked down to him and unshackled his cuffs.

"I'll co-operate with ya," he yelled desperately.

Suk Too never said a word. He literally picked Lambert up by the arm and pulled him above onto the deck. By then, Lambert was inconsolable. He twisted and squirmed to get away from the Chinaman's grip. Finally, Suk Too squared Lambert's body up and punched him right in the face. Lambert collapsed and almost passed out.

"We not gonna kill ye," Welch snorted. "At least not if ye do as we say."

Lambert was literally punch drunk from the smack of Suk Too. He looked up at them. They were out of focus. Suk Too pointed his shotgun right at Lambert's head.

"I kill you, you don't do what I say," he said with authority.

Lambert wiped his forehead and tried to get up off the deck. It took him a couple of tries before he was successful. He decided to speak.

"What?" he asked.

Suk Too rudely interrupted him.

"Shut up!" he said. Then he pointed the shotgun at Lambert's head. Lambert put his hands up and did what he was told. Welch handed Lambert a shotgun. Of course, it had no shells in the chambers. Lambert was simply a show of firepower and would supply the muscle to haul the opium back to the ship.

Welch wasn't through with him.

"You try to run, and I will kill ye on sight," he scowled.

The four men left the docks. Suk Too led the way. Lambert stayed in front of Cyrus Welch. They walked for over an hour. Finally, they arrived in what looked to be the worst ghetto either Welch or Lambert had ever seen, but they both felt confident with Suk Too. Once they got into the bowels of the ghetto, they continued to walk another thirty minutes through pathways and alleys. Finally, Suk Too stopped and knocked on a door. There was no answer. Suk Too knocked again. There was no answer. Suk Too knocked a third time. Welch was close to telling Suk Too that it was time to go. He had been in some rough areas before but never anywhere as scary as this place.

All of a sudden, the door slowly opened. A very small Chinese woman stepped out and looked both ways down the downtrodden alley. She and Suk Too began speaking to each other in Asian dialect. Neither Welch nor Lambert had a clue what they were saying. The little Chinese woman turned and walked into the house. Suk Too followed her, so Lambert and Welch walked in behind them. They walked over to the far side of the room. A blanket was strung over a string, creating a makeshift bedroom behind it. Suk Too raised his hand to Welch as if to say, This is far enough for you.

The little woman and Suk Too walked behind the blanket. Welch and Lambert listened. Chairs were scooted across the room. Boxes were being moved. The sound of some kind of a door opening was clear. A few minutes later, Suk Too walked around the blanket, carrying a huge suitcase. He put it on the floor and went back behind the curtain again. He brought another suitcase out and put it in front of Lambert.

All along, Lambert had looked at Suk Too as a monster. All of a sudden, he realized that he was wrong. Suk Too knew exactly what he was doing the entire trip.

Welch spoke up, "Do we need to inspect it, Mate?"

Suk Too looked as if he was insulted by the question. "Pay her," he ordered Welch.

Welch pulled the bag out from the crotch of his pants. He handed it to the old woman. She sat down and inspected every piece of gold. Neither side would agree to deal in any other currency. The thought hit Welch that Sores Aguilar was probably the smartest person he had ever met. Everything had been planned almost perfectly.

The old lady looked up at Suk Too and nodded. He said something in a short, terse way and motioned Lambert and Pell to pick up the two cases. Away they went back through the ghettos of Hong Kong in the middle of the night.

It was easy for Pell to haul the cases, but Lambert was struggling. He had to stop every fifty yards or so and gather himself. However, he was working hard. The realization had come to him that his best chance out of this situation was to cooperate and help Welch and Suk Too. The men continued their journey back to the boat.

They finally made it back to the street. Welch was careful. He looked both ways and motioned Lambert and Suk Too to move forward. It seemed like it took forever to get back to the docks. When the three of them saw the Melba Lee's Aussie flags, they felt victory. It was overwhelming. Even Suk Too showed more energy. Welch boarded the clipper first. Suddenly, he realized that he wasn't even paying much attention to Lambert anymore. He pulled his pistol and pointed it at the young Irishman.

"Don't be getting no ideas, mate," he said with a growl. "Put those cases down below."

Suk Too ordered them to continue with the labor. When they had things in place down below, Welch ordered them to stack everything in sight around the cases for cover.

When Cyrus was satisfied, he pointed to Lambert and Pell. They were to walk back over to the chained cuffs on the side of the wall. The other slaves were awake and watching. Suk Too walked over and slammed the cuffs shut on both of them.

"I need water!" Billy Lambert pleaded to his captors.

Welch and Suk Too looked at each other. Finally, Welch walked up on the deck. A couple of minutes later, he came back down into the belly of the ship carrying a wooden bowl that was filled with water. He put it on the floor in front of Lambert. Slowly, he took his boot and pushed the bowl toward the captured slave. Lambert didn't hesitate. He got down on his hands and knees and slurped the water out of the bowl like a dog.

PART II

CHAPTER 25

East of El Paso, Texas

*S*arah Thomas and her father, Rev. William Thomas, had been arguing since they left Camp Stockton. The argument started over biblical philosophy. It gravitated into a sharpness that neither of them had ever experienced. Sarah was bitter that the disease had taken her mother and soul mate, Abigail, about a year ago. Both Sarah and the reverend agreed that Abigail had always been the rock of the family. She also was the strongest of faith. That was the only thing they had agreed on lately. It had always been just the three of them. Abigail and the reverend always wanted to have more kids, but it just was not in God's plan. At least, that was always how it was explained to Sarah. She wanted a brother or a sister so bad that she would spend entire days praying about it when she was a child, but it was never to be.

Since losing her mother, Sarah had started having doubts about the Almighty. That really upset the reverend. Sarah had never been any trouble. Arguing with her was just not natural to him. She had always been the light of his life, but she was changing both visibly and emotionally right in front of his eyes.

She was committed to him, but it didn't seem that she was committed to the cause. It was the cause, after all, that mattered most to Rev. William Thomas. God's work must be put first and foremost, and that work was in San Francisco.

The days had been long on this journey. It was all either one of them could do to coexist with the other. It was a most unhappy time. The reverend was in no mood to argue, but it had to be done when Sarah started questioning the written word. Tempers flared. The reverend raised his voice as he drove the team of horses.

"I don't know what your mother would think of you right now!" he yelled in a way that was intended to cut to the core. Sarah was in no mood to give any ground.

"Yeah," she answered. "You've bought into it your entire life. What's it gotten you? We have no money, we have no place to live, and we're out here in some godforsaken land where we could get killed. You're the one she would be questioning, not me!"

The reverend pulled on the reigns and stopped the wagon in its tracks. He got down off the carriage seat and threw his hat on the ground. Stuttering Henry had bolted some brackets on the side of the wagon to place a shovel. The reverend took the shovel and started slamming it against the side of the wagon. He didn't stop for three minutes. Sarah refused to watch him. Finally, he threw the shovel on the ground and started in again.

"I tried my best to give you and your mother everything you wanted. I can't help who I am. I've made mistakes, yes, but I provided for you and Abigail."

But Sarah was full of venom, which was very uncharacteristic of her. She was known for her politeness, poise, and sincerity. However, she was about to boil over with frustration and anger.

She stood up and looked down on the reverend.

"I'll tell you something else, you old hoot. If you would have taken Momma to that doctor I told you about, she still might be here. You always have all the answers though, don't you? Nobody can ever tell you anything. God will always take care of us. Well, he didn't take care of Momma, did he? Now we're out here in the middle of nowhere. We're going to a town where we don't know anybody if we make it. All because God told you to drop everything and go there. What a bunch of hogwash!"

The reverend came right back at her.

"And you're mad because you're here. I tried to tell you to stay in Waco and go to school. I had a good arrangement for you. You say I don't have any money, but I had you taken care of forever. They were going to honor my ministry by putting you through school. But no, you had to come with me. I wasn't strong enough to make it without you. Well, I will tell you this. I don't need your smart mouth. When we get to El Paso, you can do whatever you want."

Sarah jumped down off the wagon, put her hat on tight, and then she started walking straight ahead. The reverend decided he needed some time to pray. Her pace was very fast. After all, she was almost six feet tall. That was another thing that made her mad.

All her life, she had been unusually tall for a girl. She learned years ago to bundle her hair and put it up underneath her hat. Blessed with a sturdy frame, she could stand up tall, and she would pass for a man. At least she could pass for a man at a distance. When anyone got close enough to see her face, it was obvious that she was a woman. There was no mistake about that. Not only was she a woman, but she was the most beautiful woman that most men would ever see in their lifetime.

When she was just a girl, she began attracting attention just by walking into a room. She learned to act gruff and tough to any man who approached her. It was her safety mechanism.

As the years went by, she would change her appearance from a beautiful woman to a young tomboy more and more often. It relieved the pressure. The reverend pretended not to notice, but he did.

Unbeknownst to him, she had been approached in a general store in East Texas earlier on the trip by a drunken rancher. The reverend was trying to buy a horse down the street. Sarah was in the store shopping for supplies. The rancher grabbed her by the arm and got right up in her face. She shoved her knee right into his crotch. When he released his grip, she punched him square in the nose. The punch knocked him into the squash and green bean racks. The vegetables and the drunken rancher crashed to the floor. She had read about what to do in a book. Sarah never told her father about the incident. After that, she always carried a small, round rock in her pocket. If she sensed trouble, she would put it in the palm of her hand. It would give her a more powerful punch. So far, she hadn't needed to use the rock.

Sarah walked the rest of the day. The reverend finally gathered himself from prayer and followed after her in the wagon. Sarah had noticed the opening between two small mountains up ahead. It was obviously the best way to get through. She kept a fast pace as she walked straight to it. It was late in the afternoon, but there was still plenty of sun. She was only about a mile from the opening in the mountains. That was when she first saw the Indians.

Her heart jumped, and then it started racing. She looked back for her father. He was about half a mile behind her. The Indians started walking toward her. She froze in her tracks. Something told her there was no reason to run. The Indians didn't seem to have weapons. As they got closer, she realized that they were women.

"Sarah, be careful!" the reverend cried out to her.

She looked back at him with a tense look on her face.

Three Indian women walked right up to her. They didn't say a word. The oldest woman, probably fifty years old or so, waved for her to follow them. The four of them started walking toward the gap in the mountains. When they reached the opening, the old woman stopped. She pointed up to the side of one of the small mountains. Sarah slowly turned her head and shoulders and looked.

The scene startled her. Her body snapped back, and she bumped into one of the Indian women. After she gathered herself, she looked again. Eight dead bodies were propped up against the mountainside by rocks. Vultures were feeding on the carcasses. For some reason, Sarah had just noticed the smell when she saw the bodies. It was disgusting. She stood a good forty or fifty yards away, but the odor was stifling. She covered her face with her hands as if it would help. The Indian women didn't flinch.

The old Indian woman pulled out an envelope and handed it to her. In beautiful handwriting was written the name Sarah Thomas. The reverend walked up beside her just as she received it. They looked at each other in bewilderment.

She slowly opened the envelope. It contained one page of high-quality writing paper. Before she read what it said, she noticed how neat it looked. Whoever wrote it was obviously well educated. It read:

Sarah,

Don't be afraid. These men tried to rob the stagecoach, but they were not successful. It is custom to make examples out of bad men. Other outlaws need to see them. The custom is to treat Indians differently. They are buried with no grave markers. There is no reason to anger them.

These Indian women have been waiting for you. They will assist you with anything you need. You will have to use hand signals to communicate with them. I know you will treat them with great respect. They were very grateful that we cleared the pass for them.

Keep following our tracks. You are close to El Paso. I will leave another letter there for you at the city mail office. Tell Reverend Thomas I said hello. I look forward to seeing you further up the road.

Yours truly,
Ray Andrews

Sarah raised her eyes and looked at the Indian women. They were staring at her. Her first thought was that Ray must have known they couldn't speak or read English. Surely, he wouldn't have written about burying Indians without grave markers if they could read. She handed the letter to the reverend.

"I bet he didn't write it," she said with a sharp tone. "That letter was written by someone with an education."

The reverend read the letter carefully. After he finished, he gently folded it and put it back into the envelope. As he handed it to Sarah, he started speaking in his preacher voice.

"There are different kinds of education, Sarah," he said. "He might not have written it, but he was the one who spoke it. This letter encourages me. We do know people on this journey. You say you have doubts about God. Well, you better think about that real hard, because we're here for a reason."

Sarah Thomas took the letter and put it in her back pocket. Suddenly, the boyish cowboy with the smooth face was on her mind again. She remembered his politeness, his sincerity, and his friendly demeanor. A wave of comfort came upon her. For the first time on the trip, she felt hope.

CHAPTER 26

Yuma, Arizona

*I*t took every passenger's best effort to talk Sawyer Crenshaw into stopping at Yuma for a break. According to Crenshaw, the trip was behind schedule. He was nervous all the time, always complaining about Ray and Stuttering Henry slowing down the trip. However, though things had not been perfect, so far the trip had gone very well. Twice, the two former Texas Rangers had not only evaded trouble but had eliminated the villains.

It was Lovie Kitchens who made the lasting impression on Crenshaw to break the trip for a two-day rest in Yuma. She was worried about Mara McLemore. Mara, it seemed, had gone into a stage of depression. She wouldn't talk, and she would barely eat. Lovie had tried everything to pull her out of the sadness.

The coach pulled into town around two o'clock on Friday afternoon. The streets were bustling, and it was very hot. Lovie asked Crenshaw to stay in town through Saturday night. For some reason, he couldn't tell her no. Deep down inside, he knew everyone was exhausted. Two nights in a hotel bed would make a big difference for everyone. Also, it was wonderful just to see a little bit of human sophistication. He relented to Lovie. Everyone on the trip hooped and hollered when she broke the news.

When everyone settled down, Ben Fields made his way over to Ray.

"You mind if I have a word with you?" he asked. The two of them walked over to the shade of a local bank.

"Ray, I've been watching you the entire trip," Fields said. "You're quite a guy. I was wondering if you would be interested in a job tomorrow night."

Ray was a little perplexed, but he was interested.

"What kind of a job?" he asked.

"Well," replied Fields. "Tonight, I'm gonna wander over there to that saloon and find out who plays cards. Tomorrow night, I figure I'll get into a game. Now, I'm not one to get into trouble, you know, but I was wondering if you would cover my back just in case things got a little ornery."

Ray clenched his teeth. "Why do you need a guard?" he asked.

"Well, I've never played cards in these parts. It's just a policy of mine when I play somewhere new," Fields explained. "It's an easy job. Just keep a low profile and watch. If any trouble breaks out, just use your best judgment. Isn't that what you always say? Use your best judgment."

Ray was intrigued. He needed every penny he could put in his pocket. He did have a dilemma though.

"Henry and me are partners," he said. "I don't do anything for money on this trip without him."

Fields took a deep breath. "Okay," he said. "Two men are better than one, but I can only pay for one. You will have to split it."

Ray looked out into the streets of Yuma. He thought about the job offer for a couple of minutes. Finally, he responded.

"Okay, you have a deal. What time do I meet you?"

"Make sure you're at the saloon tomorrow night at nine o'clock sharp. You'll see me come in the door. Don't you want to know the wages I pay?" he asked.

Ray nodded his head.

"I'll pay you three dollars for your trouble," Fields continued. "You can give whatever you want to Henry. I only want to pay you though. Now, if you are willing to take a chance, I'll pay you a commission out of anything I win. What do you think about that?"

Ray was confused.

"I don't really understand," he answered.

Fields was ready to explain.

"Well, I'm a pretty good card player. I might win quite a bit of money. Of course, I might lose everything. If you choose to gamble with me and I win, you will make a lot more than three dollars. But if I lose, you lose too. I don't pay you anything."

Ray smiled at Ben Fields.

"What would you do if you were in my place?" Ray asked the slick-dressed man.

"Well now, Ray"—Fields smiled— "I'm a gambling man. I would always take the odds when they were in my favor."

Fields winked at Ray and began to walk away. After he walked ten yards, he turned around and asked Ray, "Well, what will it be, salary or commission?"

Ray took off his hat and held it in the air. "Commission," he yelled.

Fields leaned back and smiled. He started walking back toward Ray.

"Wise choice, my man," he responded. "Oh, one other thing," he said as he walked up close to his new employee. "Anything that happens tomorrow night stays between you, me, and Henry, now you hear? I don't want to talk about this with anybody else on the trip, especially Crenshaw. That a deal?"

Ray nodded back in agreement.

Ray made his way over to Henry who was inspecting the horses. "I got us a job tomorrow night, Stut," he said with enthusiasm.

Henry wasn't in the mood to hear about another job. He was exhausted with the one he already had.

"What k-kind of job?" he asked.

Ray couldn't wait to answer. "Ben Fields wants us to watch his back tomorrow night while he plays cards."

Henry was a lot more street smart than people gave him credit. He sensed trouble and told Ray about it.

"I-I think I'll s-s-sit this one out," he said. "You b-better be careful about what you're g-getting into. Y-you haven't been involved in very many of them c-c-card games, have you?"

The truth was that Ray had never been involved in a card game ever.

"Well, we still split any money I make," Ray spouted.

"N-no, we don't," answered Henry. "I-I-I don't take money if I I-I don't work for it. Don't you even off-off-offer it to me, cause it will make me m-m-mad if you do. I've got to get some rest. I plan on being in b-b-bed both nights by nine o'clock. Y-You listen, now. Be careful, you don't get yourself k-k-killed."

Henry went on with caring for the horses. Ray jumped in to help. It was obvious to him that Henry was really tired. When he got tired, he really stuttered a lot. All of a sudden, his happiness in being back to civilization turned a little sour. He wondered to himself, what did I just get myself into?

Saturday evening rolled around quickly. The break helped everyone. Mara McLemore slept almost the entire time. Lovie Kitchens and her husband walked the streets and shopped, but they never bought anything. Henry and Ray worked all day Saturday, getting the stagecoach ready for a 7:00 a.m. start on Sunday. Sawyer Crenshaw fretted, Willie Foster drank himself silly, and Junior Hoskins barhopped all over town.

Ray took a bath and put on the cleanest clothes he could find. He walked over to the saloon an hour early at 8:00 p.m. Just before he got to the front door, a salesman walked up and addressed him.

"Sir," the salesman said. "I've got just what you need right here, London Nightingale Syrup. This syrup will clear up any ailment you got. Only costs one dollar per bottle. How 'bout it, sir? You look like you could use it."

Ray growled at the salesman. It didn't stop him from continuing the pitch though.

"What is it that ails you, sir? I can tell something is wrong with ya. Do ya have a fever? Is it a headache? Ya look sick to me." Ray tried to walk straight ahead, but the salesman wouldn't leave him alone. Finally, Ray snapped.

"Leave me alone or I'll deck you!"

"Go ahead and do it," cried the salesman. "Yeah, just go ahead and do it."

Ray realized the salesman was baiting him. He gathered himself and walked to the front door. The salesman didn't flinch. "You go right ahead," he yelled at Ray. "I'll be here waiting on ya when ya come out of there."

The saloon had no name on the door, but it was rocking with action. Ray walked over to the bar.

"What'll ya have?" the bartender asked.

"What do you call this place?" Ray screamed.

The bartender changed facial expressions and scowled at him.

"If you're not drinking, then get the hell out of here," he yelled. "Okay, okay,"

Ray replied. "Shoot me a beer. I don't mean no trouble."

As soon as he said it, a frothy beer sailed down the bar right at him. He barely saw it in time to stop it from flying off the counter. Ray all but threw a nickel at the bartender.

"You never answered my question," Ray shouted. "What do you call this place?"

The bartender didn't look back, but he did answer.

"Bill's Pawn and Drink," he yelled as he poured more beers for other patrons. "Oldest bar in town."

Ray looked around the room. It was as wild and raucous as Austin on a Saturday night. He still needed some more information from the bartender.

"Where do they play cards?" he yelled.

"You're sure full of questions!" the bartender responded. "Over there."

He pointed to a door in the far back corner of the saloon. Ray walked over and grabbed the last chair in the house that was unclaimed. He placed it at the table close to the card game room. He figured that would be his station for the rest of the evening.

Sure enough, right at nine o'clock, Ben Fields walked in the door. Ray didn't notice him at first. It wasn't until Fields walked right up next to him that he noticed him at all. He was smoking a cigarette. That was odd because Fields had never smoked before.

Fields didn't acknowledge Ray. He just made sure they made a connection. Fields was dressed completely different than Ray had ever seen him before. He looked more like a farmer than a gambler. He wore scuffed boots and regular jeans. His shirt was acceptable for the evening, but it wasn't anything as fine as what he had been wearing during the trip. A simple vest draped his upper body, and he wore a worn, rugged cowboy hat. He was not wearing a gun belt. That seemed odd to Ray. Fields had always worn his shiny, black belt that sported a Paterson revolver. Nobody ever saw him draw it, but they did notice it.

There was a banker sitting at the card table, selling chips. There would be no fighting over currency in the card room. It was acceptable, however, to trade items such as jewelry, watches, or handguns for poker chips. The banker who dealt out the chips owned the bar. He was the sole appraiser. Negotiating was subject to how many men needed chips. If there was no wait, there was more time to bargain.

Fields strolled back through the saloon. A few minutes later, he made his way back to the card room. He knocked before he entered.

"You fellows mind if I take one of those seats?" he asked politely.

There were four men playing cards. Only one player acknowledged him. He was dressed in a suit and was smoking a cigar. He looked like a refined man, a doctor, banker, or something. Two other men were also at the table with the banker. One was some kind of a cowboy or rancher. The other man looked more like a gambler. The five of them sat at the circular table.

Fields bought one hundred dollars in chips. He fumbled all of them as he tried to place them in stacks on the table. Ray could hear the banker talking. The game they would play was called Five Card Draw. The first hand didn't go too well for Fields. He called when he wasn't supposed to call. The other players all jumped him immediately. He apologized fervently. For a second, Ray thought they were going to kick him out of the game.

Things got worse. After losing three hands in a row, Fields thought he had a straight flush. He put his cards down on the table and laughed. As he was attempting to rake in the chips, the rancher, who went by the name of Bob Steadman, stopped him.

"You have two diamonds and three hearts. That isn't a straight flush!"

The businessman, Horace Johnson, just laughed.

Fields sat back down and took his humiliation. Ray thought for sure they would kick him out this time, but they didn't. The group just kept right on playing. Finally, Fields won a hand with a pair of kings and a pair of eights. He was so giddy that he decided to buy a round for everyone at the table.

"I have to go to the John anyway," he said with victory. "I'll be right back."

He returned in ten minutes with four whiskeys. As he walked around the room, putting the drinks in front of the other gamblers, Ray noticed something odd. Every time Fields put a drink down, it seemed that he nudged an ashtray over a little, or he would move someone's glass to a different spot.

They played for over two hours. Ray was getting bored. The crowd in the saloon was getting bigger. Ray went to the bathroom and lost his chair. That was okay. He could hold his attention better standing up anyway. He also had a better sightline into the card room. Ray watched Fields paying the banker again. That was the third time he had seen him buy chips.

What is he doing? Ray wondered to himself. He's gonna lose every one of those chips.

Ray looked at his timepiece. It was five minutes until midnight. He was tired and ready to go back to the hotel. He wondered to himself how long the game would last. He noticed that every player had a big pile of chips.

"We're gonna be here all night," he grumbled under his breath.

Suddenly, a big commotion hit the door. Ray peered across the room to see what was happening. He couldn't believe it. Junior Hoskins had just entered the saloon. It looked like she was as drunk as a skunk. She stumbled straight toward him, but she never acknowledged him. She went right to the card room, but she didn't knock.

"I wanna play cards!" she yelled at the banker.

Ray positioned himself closer to the room for a better view. Fields immediately rose out of his chair.

"You can't play. You're drunk!" he said sarcastically.

"The hell with you," she replied.

She wandered over to one of the empty chairs and sat down.

Fields was fit to be tied.

"I object to her playing," he scowled at the banker. "She's in no condition!"

Before he could finish his sentence, the banker interrupted him. "Do you have any money for chips?" he asked Junior.

She reached into her pocket and pulled out a wad of bills. "Yea, I got money."

The banker looked up at Fields.

"She's got money, she can play. You can leave if you want." With that, the banker started doling out chips to Junior. Ray could sense Ben Field's anger. Fields sat down in a huff. It was obvious that he was much more motivated than he was before. The banker started dealing the next game. Junior was so drunk that she almost fell out of her chair. She picked up her cards, but she fumbled them back onto the table. Everyone saw her hand. She didn't seem to care. She lost that game and three more in a row.

Fields had already seen enough.

"Lady," he said. "This is no place for you. Why don't you move along?"

That was like pouring gas on a fire to Junior Hoskins.

"Shut the hell up, cutie boy!" she answered.

The tension at the table was thick as lye soap. Fields was ready to pounce on her, but she was a woman. She was just a pathetic symbol of one. The jabs kept coming from both sides. Finally, the banker told Fields and Junior to knock it off. They quieted down enough to continue playing poker.

Fields started betting big. He lost one huge pile of chips to the other gambler, Benny Hicks. Hicks smiled as he retrieved his winnings. He lost another pile to the rancher, Steadman, who showed no emotion when he won the hand.

Ray was exhausted. He couldn't believe anybody would risk all that money on a card game. He looked at Junior. She was fishing through her coat for something. Finally, it looked like she found it. She pulled something out of her pocket that was wrapped in brown paper. She started opening it and called out to the banker, "I want to pawn this for some chips." She finally got the paper off the item. Ray peered in at the banker. He couldn't believe it. She was handing him Mara McLemore's brooch.

Ray almost broke into the room to stop the money exchange, but it was too late. The banker had one of those funny little one–eyed goggles. He was already examining it. Ray was furious, but he didn't interrupt the negotiation.

"It's real gold, Mel," she said in a slurred speech.

Nobody knew why she called the banker Mel. The banker kept looking closely at the brooch.

"I believe you are correct, ma'am," he replied. "What do you want for it?"

"I'll take a thousand dollars," she answered.

"Can't go that high," the banker countered. "How 'bout $500?" Junior was wobbling in her chair.

"I just want to pawn it. I need some money for the game. Give me seven hundred."

The banker looked at the brooch again.

"Okay," he said, "Seven hundred."

With that, the banker took out his notebook and documented the pawn. He gave Junior a ticket. Ray immediately zeroed in on where she put the ticket. It occurred to him that the banker probably hoped that she would lose it. After he gave her the ticket, he counted off seven hundred dollars in cash. She turned right around and bought seven hundred dollars in chips

"You're a fool," Fields smirked under his breath.

Junior got up from her chair. It looked like she was reaching for her gun. Steadman and Hicks both jumped up from each side and stopped her. Everybody got quiet for a minute, and then Steadman spoke.

"It looks like the stakes have gone a little higher."

He pulled out his wallet and asked the banker for more chips. Horace Johnson decided that he would do the same. Benny Hicks just watched.

Everyone was conservative the next two hands. On the third hand, Fields seemed to

smile when he first picked up his cards. The bets started going around the table. Fields decided to push all his chips onto the middle of the table. To stay in the game, Steadman had to match him. Horace Johnson matched Fields with his bet as well. The banker didn't hesitate. He matched the bet too. Junior Hoskins looked at each player.

"What the hell!" she said in a loud tone. "You gotta take some chances in life."

She counted out the money she needed to stay in the game. It took almost every chip she had.

Ben Fields put his cards on the table. He had a queen, a jack, a nine, a three, and a two. All his cards were diamonds. That was a queen high flush. He leaned forward and folded his arms on the table. Bob Steadman confidently laid his cards down. He had three eights and a pair of queens. That was a full house. Horace Johnson eyeballed every player before he put his cards down. He had three aces and two tens. That was another full house. Benny Hicks just watched. He had already folded. The stakes were too high for him. The banker was shocked at all the strong hands.

"I've got four sixes," he mumbled as he placed his cards on the table.

Junior Hoskins closed her eyes and shook her head. Finally, she snapped her five cards down.

"Well, boys," she said. "Four kings with an ace kicker beats all of ya!"

Fields jumped to his feet. His face was as red as a fire. Junior howled with laughter as she took her arm and raked the chips toward her chest. Fields screamed at her.

"How did you do that? I know you're up to something." Junior shot right back at him.

"I ain't up to nothing. I'm just a better poker player than you, you old windbag." She turned to the banker.

"Cash me out, Mel. That's enough for the night."

Fields was about to tear into Junior. Ray decided that he had to intervene. He ran into the room and grabbed Fields.

"You can't leave now! You have to play some more!"

Fields screamed.

It didn't seem to occur to him that he was done for the night.

He didn't have any more money. The other players had grown tired of the whole scene. They began gathering their belongings.

A woman dressed like a man had just taken their money. It was embarrassing. On top of that, things were getting violent between Fields and Junior. Steadman got up to leave. Johnson followed behind him. Benny Hicks disappeared into the crowd. The banker paid Junior and decided to close up for the night. Before he could get out the door, Junior wanted something else.

"Hey, Mel, I want my brooch back."

She pulled the ticket out of her pocket. The banker came back over to her. She paid him the $700 plus another twenty-five dollars for the pawn interest. By then, Ray had wrestled Fields out of the card room, but he was still swearing at Junior.

"You crook," he scolded her. "I'll get you. I want my money back."

Ray kept struggling with Fields. Junior took the money and the brooch. Then she headed for the door. Fields made one more push toward her, but he couldn't get past Ray.

Fields smirked at Ray.

"You better go and guard her tonight. I'm gonna get drunk. Then I think I'm gonna go get my gun. I'm think I'm gonna kill her," Fields said.

Ray looked over at Junior. She was standing at the front door, looking back at them. She raised her right hand and showed them her middle finger.

Fields broke off and headed toward the bar. Ray did as he was told and followed Junior down the street. After all, she was carrying a small fortune on her body in one of the meanest towns in the West. He walked up to her as she headed for the hotel.

"Get away from me," she scolded Ray.

"Was that Mrs. McLemore's brooch?" he asked her. She wouldn't answer.

"It was her brooch, wasn't it?" He continued to badger her.

Junior never said another word. She went straight to the hotel. Ray followed her close behind. When they got there, Junior went straight to her room. She slammed the door after she entered. Ray didn't know what to do. His mind was racing. There were probably a hundred people who saw her walk out of the saloon with all that money. He figured he had better stay right there for the night. She had the brooch too. Ray knew he had to somehow get it back. Fields might show up to kill her. Some outlaw might try to rob her. He stood at her doorstep wide awake the rest of the night and into the morning.

Inside the room, Junior Hoskins had taken off her hat and coat. She had put her gun away for the night. She sat down at the desk and pulled out the money. Slowly, she started counting. She separated the money into two equal stacks. She estimated that each stack was worth around $2,000. One stack was for her. The other stack was for Ben Fields.

CHAPTER 27

San Francisco

*S*ores Aguilar was building his empire at a rapid pace. He had figured out that he was smarter than almost everyone else in town. On top of that, he planned and worked all of his waking hours. He was always thinking business, solving some problems that never occurred. Thinking on another level was a way of life for him.

The Lonely Sailor was doing a brisk business. Sores walked the streets every day and knew the prices charged at every bar. It was his standard practice to keep beer and whiskey deals the best in town. He scoured the streets to find the finest-looking women, and then he found a way to get them to his tavern. Cash flow was strong.

Secretly, Sores was preparing to begin the operation of his opium business. He was really looking forward to Cyrus Welch and Suk Too getting back to town. Min Cho Fat, though, was a nuisance. Since becoming partners, Fat showed up at the Lonely Sailor almost every day.

"When you man and Suk Too be back?" he would ask every time.

It was embarrassing to Sores. Not only did Fat not appreciate keeping things discreet, his annoying attitude was grating. However, he put up with the little, insecure, Chinese man. He needed him for now.

Sores had opened an account at the new Wells Fargo Bank. He was one of the first in town to do so. Having a place to put some of his money made him sleep well at night.

He wasn't completely sold on the bank's security, but it was better than hiding money at the Lonely Sailor. He was becoming quite a man about town now that he was a tavern owner and a local businessman. He upgraded his clothing and paid close attention to speaking like an educated man. Relationships with other citizens in town were now very important to him. But deep down inside, he was still the same Sores Aguilar who was a thief and a murderer. Now he would become a drug dealer.

That didn't mean that he didn't have problems. Fires would break out in San Francisco that were dangerous to property and livelihood. The street in front of the Lonely Sailor was still just a dirt road. It was a giant mess every time it rained, and that was often. Rats walked the streets that were as big as cats. It wasn't uncommon to see a sailor or a miner shoot one on sight. Sailors, vagrants, and thieves would constantly try to run up bar tabs in the Lonely Sailor, knowing full well they didn't have the money to pay. San Francisco was the type of town where a businessperson could lose control of his establishment with just a hint of apathy. Crime was rampant all over town. Prostitution houses were opening, and opium dens were plentiful. The law was pretty much a nonfactor.

But Sores had one problem that was really bothering him. One particular band of Aussies, led by a man named Big Jim Stuart, had become particularly dangerous. Big Jim's crew traveled in a pack. Twice, he and eight other men had visited the Lonely Sailor. They were all big men who carried weapons. Sores always had security, but Big Jim's men could easily overwhelm them.

The first time Stuart's gang walked in the door, Sores knew there would be trouble. When Sores asked the men to pay in advance for their liquor, Big Jim threatened to tear the place to shreds.

"How dare ye question me honor?" Big Jim cried.

Sores backed off and let the men drink. When it came time to pay, Stuart and his men started to walk out the door. Sores tried to stop them. He followed them down the stairs. "You owe six dollars for your tab," he explained. Big Jim and his gang just kept walking.

Three days later, Big Jim and his men came back. Sores met them at the door.

"You're not welcome here. Go away. Don't come back," he yelled.

Big Jim kept walking right in the door. When Sores signaled to his bartender not to serve the group, Big Jim exploded. He picked up a chair and threw it across the room.

"I want a drink, Injun!" he shouted at Sores.

"Pay in advance, and I'll serve you," Sores responded.

Big Jim pulled out a quarter and flipped it on the table. Sores walked around behind the bar and served two beers. As he was looking down to pour the beer, Big Jim reached over the bar and grabbed the red feather out of his hair. He ripped the feather and a handful of Sores's hair right out of the scalp.

"Never saw no man wear a feather in his hair that wasn't an Injun, mate," Big Jim said.

Sores was furious, but he knew that he and his bouncers were outnumbered. Big Jim Stuart pulled out his pistol. Sores didn't recognize it. It was some kind of an odd single shot. He must have brought it over from Australia. Big Jim pointed the gun right at Sores's forehead.

"Now get me men a round, Injun," he directed.

Sores had to comply. He thought of pulling out the beer that was spiked with opium, but he relented. He didn't have enough to poison all of Stuart's men. He made a decision to serve them. If he fought them now, he would lose, and he would probably get killed in the process. The gang ran up a bar tab over ten dollars. Everyone who was in the bar left quietly while Stuart and his men drank. Finally, Big Jim got up to leave. Before he walked out the door, he looked back at Sores.

"I'll be back, mate," he scowled. "When I return, ye might think 'bout what you will pay to keep me from burning ye 'stablishment."

With that, Big Jim Stuart and his men left the Lonely Sailor. Though he had been involved in many crimes, this was Sores Aguilar's first experience with extortion.

It was ironic that Sores was now someone who might need the police. Up until now, he viewed the weak security in San Francisco as a huge opportunity. He needed to make as much money as he could illegally before the city became more sophisticated. When it did, he would have other legitimate businesses established. The time to prosper was now, but everything changed when he met Big Jim Stuart.

Sores was expecting the Melba Lee to arrive any day. Very quietly, he had made three contacts to sell the opium the very day it arrived. All he had to do was deliver and collect. Then he would split up the money between himself, Min Cho Fat, Cyrus Welch, and Suk Too. He had estimated that each would earn somewhere around $3,000. That was big money. Sores had even gone so far as to influence each of the partners to open an account at Wells Fargo just to park the loot. It made sense because as soon as this deal was completed, another one was to be planned. He wasn't planning on taking all of the financial risk on the next trip to Hong Kong himself. He wanted to make sure the money didn't get away.

One thing was for sure. Sores Aguilar loved money and power. He also loved the game. Planning, manipulation, and execution were the components that challenged and motivated him. He was a physical man who loved to exercise. He had gotten to a point of rarely drinking alcohol, and he never used drugs. He realized the advantage of being sober when everyone around him was drunk. Every morning and many times in the evening, he would walk the streets of San Francisco. During his walks, he was polite to everyone. Quickly, he became well known for his caring and generous attitude toward the townspeople. The walks expanded his network and his power. He loved it. His most prized material possessions were his lace-up boots that fit perfectly. It was nothing for him to cover ten miles on a single walk.

Sores was trying to figure out the weak police force in the city. He had also noticed a sign at the end of Market Street that read "Vigilance Meeting Tuesday 7:00 p.m." He decided that it would be a smart move to close the Lonely

Sailor and attend the meeting. He needed to know everything that was going on in the city. The meeting was held in a meat-packing warehouse on Market Street. Sores arrived ten minutes early and sat at the very back of the room. At seven o'clock sharp, the meeting started.

A young-looking man in his thirties walked to the podium. His father owned the warehouse. He was balding and a little overweight, but he spoke with elegance and confidence. His name was John Griffith. The room was almost full. Griffith waited on everyone to settle down and be quiet. Then he began his message.

"I want to thank you for coming," he began. "I called this meeting because I am a concerned citizen. Crime is at an epidemic level in the city. I don't begrudge our police. They are doing the best they can. However, they do not have the resources to stop the growing problem. My reason to bring you together today is simple. We, as private citizens, need to help uphold the law. I propose that you join the Committee of Vigilance. This committee will seek power in numbers. We will band together against crime in San Francisco."

Griffith went on for another twenty minutes. Sores focused on every word. At the end of his speech, Griffith asked for volunteers to come forward and sign up for duty. Fifty people walked to the podium. A man was sitting at a table with paper and pen. Sores Aguilar never made a rash decision. He got up and walked back to the Lonely Sailor. He thought about the Vigilance Committee constantly. Every day, he planned his walk toward the meat-packing warehouse on Market Street. The warehouse sat at the end of the street just west of the bay. He would stop at the warehouse and think.

Almost exactly one week after attending his first Vigilance Committee meeting, Sores strolled back down to Market Street. It was four o'clock in the afternoon. He walked right into the warehouse and asked for John Griffith. Ten minutes later, Griffith appeared. He was wearing denim overalls that were stained with blood and sweat.

"What can I do for you?" he asked.

Sores held out his hand and introduced himself.

"My name is Aguilar, Sores Aguilar. I own a tavern down on Montgomery Street called the Lonely Sailor. I was at your meeting last week. I've given it a lot of thought. I want to volunteer to be on the Vigilance Committee."

Griffith smiled as he folded his handkerchief and put it in his back pocket.

"That's great," he said. "Our numbers are really up just in the last few days. I figure we need to get to at least 150 to be safe."

Sores understood the concept of literally taking the law into your own hands, but he didn't understand the details of what the Vigilance Committee was planning. He decided to ask.

"What exactly do you need me to do as a volunteer?" Griffith pulled out his notebook and sat down at a table. "Sign here," he said with authority. "My plan is actually pretty simple. We have power in numbers. A hundred or so of us can take any outlaw and his gang. We just need to know who to target. We go overwhelm them, and then bring them back here to the warehouse for trial."

Sores was stunned.

"What do you mean bring them back here to the warehouse for trial?" he asked. "Who are the judge and jury?"

Griffith looked up at him.

"I'll volunteer to be the judge. You can be on the jury if you want."

Sores still didn't understand.

"You mean we just capture 'em and bring 'em back here. Then we decide if they're guilty or not."

Griffith looked amused.

"What's so complicated about that?" he asked.

"What are the penalties?" Sores asked.

"Well," answered Griffith. "To me, there are certain penalties that can't be tolerated. You know like murder or pulling a gun during a robbery. That just can't be tolerated. If they are guilty, we hang 'em right after the trial."

Sores was astonished. That sounded like what the Texas Rangers would do.

"I already know a criminal like that," Sores answered.

"Who would that be?" Griffith asked.

"Man named Big Jim Stuart," Sores replied.

Griffith raised his head and looked Sores right in the eye. "Yeah, I've heard of him," he said as he looked through his notebook.

"Look, I have seven other complaints about him. One man says he killed his brother 'bout a month ago. Big Jim punched him in the face so hard he died on the spot. Big Jim was trying to shake his grocery store down. There are rumors that he's starting a lot of fires in town. He would be a good one to bring in for trial."

Sores Aguilar had never been on the right side of the law. This was a whole new experience for him. He knew one thing for sure though. Big Jim Stuart had to go, and this was the best idea to get rid of him he had heard of yet.

"What do we do next?" Sores asked.

The look on Griffith's face turned deadly serious.

"I'm trying to gather at least one hundred men here at seven o'clock Friday night," he said slowly. "That will be the best time to go find him. We go out in a committee to apprehend Big Jim. We bring him back here. Then we deliver justice."

Sores was eager to participate. It was Tuesday afternoon. The committee was to convene work on Friday. He had two days to find Big Jim.

"I'll make sure we know where to find him on Friday night," he told Griffith.

Sores was electrified when he left Griffith's meat-packing warehouse. On the walk home, he started planning. The Lonely Sailor would be closed for the next three nights. There was no way he was going to risk Big Jim walking into his saloon. Instead, he would walk the streets and find him. He would follow him home. He would know his every move. There would be no way Big Jim would be able to escape the Vigilance Committee come Friday night. Sores decided to go back to his strategy of changing his appearance. It was subtle this time. He didn't need to come off as an Indian. He just needed to make sure Big Jim didn't recognize him. He grabbed a hat that some Aussie sailor had left in the bar. He wore a long coat instead of his usual tight-fitting vest, and he put the red feather into his pocket.

Sores had no luck on Tuesday night. Big Jim was nowhere to be found. Sores started looking again at midday Wednesday. Finally, around six o'clock at night, he spotted Big Jim and his gang hanging out in Aussie town. He was three blocks from the Lonely Sailor. Sores made sure he wasn't noticed. Big Jim and his gang finally left the bar at three o'clock in the morning. Sores followed them at a safe distance. The men walked into an old boarding house four blocks away on Mimosa Street.

Easy mark, Sores thought to himself.

Sores went home that night. He returned the next day around two in the afternoon. Big Jim left the boarding house around 4:00 p.m. Sores followed him all over town. Big Jim decided to visit the Lonely Sailor that evening. He all but broke down the door, trying to enter the saloon. He did tear the closed sign off the entrance and threw it to the ground below. By Thursday evening, Sores could almost predict where Big Jim would be and when he would be there. He followed Big Jim again on Friday until time to head to the Vigilance Committee meeting. By then, Sores had gone back to his flat-brimmed, black hat and vest. He also had weaved the feather back into his hair. One of the Colt Navy revolvers that he had stolen on Rosary Hill was loaded and in his gun belt.

Sores arrived at the warehouse just before 6:30 p.m. There were already over a hundred men waiting in the streets. They held big sticks, guns, and knives. Sores simply blended into the crowd. He searched for Griffith, finding him standing at the front door of the warehouse. As he walked up to Griffith, the crowd started chanting, "Justice! Justice! Justice!" Griffith focused on Sores Aguilar.

"Do you know where he is right now?" he asked. Sores nodded his head.

"I know the general area. We will find him easily. Follow me."

With that statement, Griffith called on everyone to quiet down.

"We are gathered here tonight to seek justice," he said loudly. "We have eight witnesses ready to testify against one man. His name is James Stuart. He is the man we seek tonight. He has threatened many. He has murdered. He has burglarized, and he has started fires in our town. He will face justice tonight.

Are you with me?"

The crowd roared as Griffith pumped his fists in the air. "Lead the way!" Griffith yelled to Sores Aguilar.

Sores turned and led the group down Market Street. It was only ten blocks to Monroe Street. The group turned right and walked another three blocks. It took six stops before Sores spotted Big Jim and his entourage walking into a saloon called Society's Tavern. By then, Sores was just an observer. The mob took over the situation. As soon as they spotted Stuart, the maul was on. Sores and Griffith watched from across the street as the Vigilance Committee dragged Big Jim Stuart out of the bar. The mob let Big Jim's eight men go free. Griffith led the march back down to the warehouse.

The doors of the meat-packing warehouse were open when the mob arrived with Big Jim. Several committee members had stayed back and prepared the second-floor balcony for the trial. John Griffith took his seat to lead the proceedings. A ten-man jury took their place to his right.

As soon as Griffith sat down, he yelled, "Who is to be tried tonight?"

It took ten men to drag Big Jim Stuart to a chair six feet away from Griffith.

"This man, James Stuart," said one of the committee members. "What is the charge?" Griffith asked.

One of the members stepped up.

"This man killed my brother. He punched him out of the blue. He killed him instantly."

Another man stepped up beside the first witness.

"I witnessed it too," he added. "I was right there when it happened."

A third witness stepped forward.

"This man is in the business of extortion. He threatened to burn my business down if I did not pay him. I did not. He beat me up in front of my wife. The next day, my printing business burned down."

Sores was standing against the far wall. His job was done. He couldn't believe what he was seeing. Several witnesses came forward to testify. Big Jim just sat there in disbelief. He never uttered a word. It was as if he already knew his fate. Finally, Griffith called out to the crowd, "Does anyone else want to come forward and testify?"

Sores could have joined in, but it was obvious that his testimony wasn't needed.

Griffith looked at the jury.

"Let's vote," he ordered. "Raise your hand if you think James Stuart is innocent."

Not one person raised a hand.

"Raise your hand if you think he is guilty," Griffith ordered. Every juror raised his right hand.

"Guilty!" Griffith yelled. "I mandate that your penalty be death by hanging." Griffith pounded his open palm on the table. "Let's get on with it!" he cried out. The mob ascended upon Big Jim. The noose was around his neck in an instant. He started cursing the mob as they carried him to the window. Big Jim fought as hard as he could fight.

"Push him on out the window," someone yelled.

Stuart started screaming. Suddenly, Sores heard a roar from the street below. Big Jim Stuart was hanging by the neck from the second-floor window of the meat-packing warehouse.

Sores decided that it was time for him to leave the scene. Without saying good-bye to anyone, he made his way back down to the street. He walked inside the mob to the front of the warehouse. For some reason, he needed to see the sight of Big Jim hanging out of the window. Sores hadn't had a drink in over a month, but for some reason, the urge to celebrate hit him. His biggest nemesis had just been eliminated. Suddenly, it occurred to him that he didn't dismember Big Jim's body. He turned back and headed into the warehouse to find Griffith. An hour later, Big Jim's body was still hanging from the second floor. Sores pleaded with Griffith to bring the body back into the building. Finally, Griffith relented. Several volunteers pulled the body back into the building on the second floor. They put Big Jim's remains on a table. At that moment, Sores became the leader of the pack.

"This man is evil," he shouted to the others. "But even evil men deserve dignity. Please allow me to serve the last rights to this man in private."

The other men seemed a little stunned.

"Please," Sores asked. "It will only take a minute."

Sores ushered the men out of the room. It was just him and Big Jim Stuart alone. Sores grabbed Big Jim's left hand. He pulled out his hatchet. It was razor sharp. Slowly, Sores sawed off Big Jim's left little finger. When he was finished, he put the finger in his pocket. Then he pulled out a pair of gloves from his coat pocket. He put the gloves on both of Big Jim's hands. There was some blood but not much.

Sores secured the scene and went back over to the door. He opened it and let the crowd back into the room.

"Thank you," he said over and over to the men.

With that, Sores Aguilar disappeared into the foggy streets of San Francisco. He didn't touch alcohol much, but at this moment, he craved a drink. He couldn't get back to his residence and bar quickly enough. As he left the scene, many people still were enjoying what had happened.

He turned the corner on Montgomery Street and spotted the Lonely Sailor. The businessman inside him started thinking. Why not open up for business tonight? he thought to himself. He unlocked the door and entered. After lighting the lanterns, he unlocked the cabinets. He poured himself a drink of his best bourbon and sat down to enjoy it. He would enjoy a few minutes before opening the door for business. Just before he got settled, the door flew open, and two men walked into the Lonely Sailor. A familiar voice rang out.

"We back, Mate!" Cyrus Welch and Suk Too stood there, glaring at Sores. They had just arrived from Hong Kong.

CHAPTER 28

Los Angeles, California

*R*ay Andrews was in a hurry. He was trying to find the city post office. The owner of the stagecoach, Sawyer Crenshaw, had granted him two hours to try to find it. Ray had asked the local folks of the whereabouts of the mail center, but most of them didn't even know there was such a thing. It had only been open for about a year. Ray made his way downtown to what was called Temple Square on Spring Street. He had never seen a town this big. It swamped the size of both Austin and Yuma. Things were rowdy and busy.

Ray turned the corner at Temple Square and saw a sign on the front of a small building. United States Post Office was easy to spot. He entered the front door and stood in line for twenty minutes. When his time finally came due, he pulled a letter out of his back pocket. On the envelope was written Sarah Thomas in beautiful penmanship. This letter was two pages long. The only thing that could get Mara McLemore out of her depression was when she got to write letters for Ray. She was an old school teacher. It would pull her out of her downtrodden attitude every time Ray asked her to help him. He would talk, and she would write. She offered to teach him how to write himself, but he always said he just didn't want to do it.

Ray had not told Mara about the brooch yet. He was still trying to figure out how to do it. To his knowledge, Junior Hoskins still had the brooch in her possession. The drive had been hard since the coach had left Yuma. Ray hadn't really spoken to either Ben Fields or Junior. He was disgusted with the both of them. Ray hadn't told anyone about what had happened in Bill's Pawn and Drink. Nobody really cared anyway. It was all any of them could do just to deal with the trip.

The postmaster was a grubby old man who walked around hunchbacked. It didn't look to Ray like he had taken a bath in a month. He had muttonchops sideburns with little wire-rim glasses. A small hat with the top cut out of it lay on top of his head. Ray spoke first.

"Sir, my name is Ray Andrews, and I would like to leave this letter for a lady friend of mine. Her name is Sarah Thomas. She will be coming through here in a few days."

The postmaster took the envelope from Ray and examined it like it was a piece of gold. Without saying a word, he fumbled through a stack of letters on the table to his right. It was all he could do to unravel the string around one particular stack. Finally, he pulled out a letter and looked it over for a minute. Finally, he looked up at Ray.

"Your name again?" he asked softly.

"My name's Ray Andrews," Ray replied with a big smile. "Why do you need my name? "The postmaster handed the letter to Ray. He didn't know Ray couldn't read. Ray looked to the right and then to the left. He took the letter from the postmaster.

"You sure this is for me?" he asked.

"Got your name on it," replied the postmaster.

Ray Andrews had never received a piece of mail in his life.

He looked at the postmaster with a perplexed look on his face and pointed to the top-left corner of the envelope.

"What does this mean?" he asked.

The postmaster took it from Ray and held it up in the light. "Sarah Thomas is the name on it," he replied.

"Sarah Thomas!" Ray cried out. "How'd she knows how to do that?"

Sarah had beaten Ray to the punch. It was his idea to write her a letter so he could communicate. In return, she had sent a letter on past him to Los Angeles.

Ray ran all the way back to the street where the coach was parked. Everyone on the trip was doing whatever they needed to do. Nobody paid much attention to Ray. The trip had calmed down since the plains of West Texas. There had been no more Indian danger. There had been no more threats from bandits. The coach had met the West Coast, and it was headed for Northern California. Ray asked Crenshaw where Mara McLemore was staying.

"Her husband took her to the hotel over there," he responded.

Ray walked across the street to the Belton Hotel. He noticed that it was very clean when he walked in the door. The man at the desk seemed very uninterested in helping anyone.

"I'm looking for Mr. and Mrs. McLemore," Ray told the deskman. "Do you know what room they're in?"

The deskman wouldn't give Ray the number. "It is against hotel policy to give out information like that, sir. You need to leave."

Ray didn't know what to do.

Just at that moment, a man and a woman rushed into the hotel and approached the deskman.

"I'm Dr. Collins," the man told the deskman. "Where is this lady that is so ill?"

Ray knew exactly who they were talking about. Before he could say anything, John McLemore walked down the steps.

"Up here, room 205," he told the doctor and his lady nurse. McLemore looked at Ray.

"Come on up, Ray," he said solemnly.

When they walked into the room, Mara McLemore was lying in bed, gasping for air. Dr. Collins went right to her and did something. It seemed to help, and she settled down a bit. Since she and Ray had been working together on the letters he had been writing to Sarah Thomas, they had become good friends. After about ten minutes, Mara opened her eyes. She saw Ray. He immediately stood up and approached her. Mara held out her hand. Ray awkwardly grabbed it.

"Mrs. McLemore," he said. "You're not gonna believe this. Sarah wrote me a letter. I just picked it up at the post office."

He reached into his shirt pocket and lifted it out to show her. She smiled as Ray took the letter out of the envelope and handed it to her. She read silently to herself. There was a pleasant smile on her face the entire time she read.

After a few minutes, she closed her eyes. The letter softly fell from her fingers. "Mara! Mara!" her husband yelled. Dr. Collins tried to rescue her, but he couldn't do it. She was gone. Things finally quieted down after a few minutes. John McLemore and Ray sat quietly while Dr.

Collins and his nurse tended to Mara. Dr. Collins covered her face with a blanket and turned to John.

"I will notify the coroner," the doctor said with great respect. "I'm very sorry."

After a quick look at Ray, Dr. Collins and his nurse left the room.

Ray and John McLemore sat quietly for another five minutes. Finally, Ray broke the silence.

"I know who has the brooch. I can get it back for you," he said softly.

"What do you mean?" McLemore asked.

"I know who has the brooch," Ray answered. "They stole it from you. I should have said something. I'm so sorry."

John McLemore stood up and confronted Ray.

"Nobody stole the brooch," he said firmly. "I sold it to Fields for $300. My wife and I were out of money. I had no choice. I didn't have the heart to tell her what I did. I am the one who is sorry. I don't want it back." McLemore turned to his wife's bedside. "Would you mind giving me some privacy?"

Ray was in shock, and he was very confused. He got up and left the room. As he walked down the street, he started thinking about the card game in Yuma. If Fields bought the brooch from John McLemore, then how did Junior Hoskins get hold of it? Ray struggled on down the street.

Crenshaw and Stuttering Henry were working on the coach when Ray walked up to them.

"G-G-Gonna stay here tonight, Ray," said Henry. "G-Get an early start in the morning."

Crenshaw never looked up at Ray.

"Mara McLemore just died," Ray told them.

Stuttering Henry and Sawyer Crenshaw stopped what they were doing and looked at Ray. Neither spoke a word.

"At least she died in a nice bed," Ray said. "She didn't die out on the trail."

After an awkward, quiet moment, Ray gathered himself. "Do either of you know where Ben Fields is right now?" Ray said.

Henry spoke up first. "I-I just saw him go into that saloon a while ago," he said as he pointed down the street.

Ray turned and walked straight to the saloon. As soon as he walked in the door, he looked to his left and saw Ben Fields and Junior Hoskins sitting at a table playing cards. Ray immediately confronted them.

"Mara McLemore just died over in the hotel," he said passionately. "Mr. McLemore told me he sold the brooch to you?" Fields looked around the room. It was obvious that he didn't know what to say, but Junior Hoskins didn't care.

"You've got to be the dumbest Cowboy I ever saw, Andrews," she said sarcastically. "You're a good guard. You're just not very smart."

She pulled the brooch out of her coat pocket.

"We've been waiting for the right time to pay you for your work. I guess this is as good a time as any. Here, you keep this." Junior slid the brooch on the table toward Ray. "Not sure how much it's worth. You need to have it appraised. I almost left it in Yuma. The dealer gave me $700 for it, remember," Junior said.

Junior got up and walked toward the bar. After she got there, she leaned back toward Ray.

"You saved our ass twice," she said. "And you didn't even know there was a man that was about to rob me in Yuma. He left when he saw I had a guard."

Junior yelled at the bartender for a whiskey before she turned around again.

"Besides that," she continued, "old man McLemore says that brooch is bad luck."

The tension at the table was broken by the rowdy nature of the crowd in the saloon. It seemed that a fight was about to break out across the room. Ray picked up the brooch and stuffed it in his left boot. Fields still had not said a word. Ray was stunned. Junior Hoskins had never said anything nice to him before. She realized it herself, so she decided not to change the tone.

"Oh, don't be so high and mighty, Andrews," she said. "You ain't no saint yourself. There are a lot of ways to make a livin'."

Ray went over to the bar and sat down beside a very big sailor. Ray and the sailor made eye contact immediately. The sailor stunk. His stench almost knocked Ray away from the bar. The teeth he still had were brown and crooked. A lady bartender finally made her way over to Ray.

"What'll ya have?" she asked. "I'll have a beer," Ray responded.

"A beer?" she asked again.

"Yes, ma'am," Ray answered. "A beer."

The foul-smelling sailor couldn't help himself.

"Well, mates, we got us a 'yes, ma'am' boy here," he said.

His accent was unmistakable. Obviously, he was from Australia. Even people who didn't know Aussies would recognize it. Ray was in no mood to mess around with an Aussie. He paid for his beer and walked away from the bar. There was nobody there he knew but Fields and Hoskins. He didn't want anything to do with them at the moment. He walked over to the other side of the room, but he noticed that the Aussie sailor was following him, carrying a pool stick.

Ray sat down next to the wall. The Aussie walked right up to him and said, "We don't like strangers round here, mate. Why don't ye just leave?"

Ray raised his eyes and looked at the Aussie. Finally, Ray spoke, "If you don't leave me alone, I'm gonna take that pool stick and crack it over your head."

The Aussie grabbed Ray by the shirt and yanked him out of the chair. With one punch, the Aussie leveled him. Ray got right up and tried to tackle the Aussie, but he was half the size of his opponent. The Aussie slung him across the room and into a table. Ray was lying flat on his back. This time, the Aussie was ready to go in for the kill. Ray's eyes were wide open. The Aussie reared back his right arm. Suddenly, a loud sound like a lightning bolt, went off right in front of Ray. The giant Aussie fell to the ground. Ray was in a fog. He could barely focus on the man standing in front of him holding the bottom half of a pool stick. Sure enough, the Aussie got his head cracked open. But it wasn't Ray Andrews who did it. The deed was done by none other than Stuttering Henry Jones.

CHAPTER 29

YUMA, ARIZONA

*R*everend Thomas always took pride in being in great physical condition. Nobody he knew paid attention to good health like he did. The trip to California had been hard, but he was managing it quite well. His wife, Abigail, had not quite been so fortunate with her health. It broke both his and Sarah's heart when she died just over a year and a half ago. Sarah was also a physical specimen. She was tall, beautiful, and graceful with great posture and physical talent. It was nothing for her to outwork men, but she was always able to carry herself like a dignified woman. The reverend had never seen a woman who could put on a hat and a pair of gloves and carry herself like a man. She could then just as easily put on a dress and be very ladylike. That was a talent in itself, and it always amazed the reverend.

But truth be told, the reverend looked at Ray Andrews as the biggest blessing the good Lord had given him in years. If not for Ray, Sarah's attitude would be horrendous. He and Sarah were fighting like cats and dogs until Ray left the letter for Sarah at the pass south of El Paso. Since then, she had been reading and writing letters every day. The reverend could tell she was smitten with him. Writing became very therapeutic for her. She wanted to get a letter to Ray, and she figured out how to do it through the mail.

The reverend and Sarah had joined up with three other families to travel together. It was much safer and much less lonely. The reverend was concerned about Sarah falling in love with a young man that she didn't really know. However, the other option of not having hope for this trip to San Francisco made it worth it. He had made many a sermon about hope and faith. Back in Mississippi, Reverend Thomas was famous for his views on the definition of faith. He believed things would work out the way they were supposed to in the end.

The reverend noticed that Sarah was talking a lot more. She suddenly had become amiable. Yuma, Arizona, was the hottest, most desolate place that either Sarah or the reverend had ever seen. Neither could wait to get out of there and continue moving westward. First, however, they needed supplies, and Sarah wanted to go to the post office. She was sure Ray had left her a letter. The heat was blistering, and everyone was drained. Word was that there would be much cooler temperatures as the caravan got close to California and the ocean.

Sarah and her dad stopped into Smith's General Store in Yuma to get supplies. Money was getting a little bit low. Hopefully, the reverend had saved and managed his money so they could make it to San Francisco. While the reverend counted out the coins, Sarah struck up a conversation with Wilbur Smith, the man who owned the store.

"Sure, is hot around here," Sarah started the conversation.

Wilbur's frazzled hair was standing up and sweat was glistening on his forehead. He was not in a talkative mood.

"I like your store," she continued. "Did a stagecoach come through here a week or so ago?"

Wilbur Smith tried to keep his right eye on the receipt he was writing for the reverend. He lifted his left eye to look at Sarah.

"Saw that stagecoach come right through here. Hope that business gets going. Could use the traffic."

Sarah's enthusiasm was obvious.

"Did the men come in your store?" she asked.

Wilbur started paying closer attention to Sarah once he got a good look at her. She was startling, certainly the best-looking woman he had seen in years.

"Yeah, talked to the guards. Said they was headed to San Francisco," he responded. "Seemed like good boys."

Sarah peered in on Wilbur.

"Did they say which town they would pass through next?" she asked. Wilbur was starting to really enjoy the conversation. "Big town or little town?" he asked.

Sarah looked at her dad.

"Big town," said the reverend.

Wilbur tore the receipt off and handed it to him.

"That'd be San Diego. Hundred miles straight west. You'll like it. Nice and cool."

Sarah was feeling quite friendly. Just the thought of cooler weather felt good. Ray had told her and the reverend that once they hit the ocean, they should just turn north and go straight on to San Francisco. Sudden- ly, the trail seemed shorter.

"Where's the post office?" Sarah asked Wilbur.

"Don't have no post office here," he snorted. "Trying to get one. Don't know when we will."

That was not good news to Sarah. She was so looking forward to a letter from Ray.

"Told them boys, better watch their backs in that San Francisco," Wilbur said. "I went there once. Place is dangerous. They'll rob you blind. It's them Aussies. Told them boys they better watch out."

Sarah Thomas had heard a lot about San Francisco. Some of it was good, but most of it was bad. However, she didn't know much about robbery. The reverend was ready to go.

"Come along, daughter," he said as he gently pulled her arm.

Sarah turned her body, but she kept her focus back on Wilbur. After a couple of steps, she stopped.

"How dangerous is it, really?" she questioned Mr. Smith.

Wilbur mustered up a big spit wad and spat into a bucket behind the counter.

"Well, missy," he replied. "Got out of there pretty fast. Never seen rats as big as they have there. I mean real rats, not people. There are crooks everywhere, and whores, and mountain men. But the Aussies, they'd soon kill you as look at you."

Wilbur was quiet for just a moment, and then he started up again. "You going there?" he asked.

The reverend wasn't hesitant.

"We certainly are," he countered. "And we're not scared. We're going there to help."

Wilbur wasn't impressed.

"Help, my ass," he answered. "Probably get robbed or killed up there."

CHAPTER 30

SAN FRANCISCO

There was a lot of tension in the air when Sores Aguilar called the meeting with his partners. Min Cho Fat was not happy. It was his opinion that he didn't get a fair deal when the opium was brought back from Hong Kong by Cyrus Welch and Suk Too. Sores had already made arrangements to sell the opium in San Francisco. He had spelled it out to Fat when the deal was first arranged. However, it turned out that Min Cho Fat was never satisfied with any business deal. He always felt that he was being taken advantage of by his partners. He was making his displeasure well known to everyone who would listen.

Cyrus Welch was not in good graces with Sores either. He had agreed not to bring any of the captured sailors back to San Francisco. Sores viewed them as a threat to the operation. If just one of them got to the law, everyone would be in jeopardy. And that was before Sores got in- volved with the Vigilance Committee. But Sores didn't make the trip to Hong Kong. He didn't know or understand how to deal with captured slave labor. Cyrus Welch did know. He had learned the hard way. He worked with them every day and night. He found out that after they were captured, it was better to treat them like the rest of the sailors. Guarding them all day and all night was not practical. Cyrus figured out early on to tell them they would not only be released on the return to San Francisco, but they would also be paid just like the other sailors. That was the way Cyrus liked doing his business. If the captured sailor wouldn't oblige, he would be thrown off the ship.

Billy Lambert, one of the captured sailors, was a very good hand. He was the only captured sailor who was allowed to survive the trip. The others were thrown overboard. Welch had spoken to Lambert about working full time, but that was not in Sores Aguilar's plan. It was causing considerable trouble between Welch and Sores, and it was going to have to be addressed. In the meantime, Lambert was back on the ship, chained to the inner bowels of the vessel.

Suk Too was the only member of the four partners who didn't have a beef with one of the others. He just wanted his money. He was ready to find the prostitute of his choice and do his business. The business arrangement was good for him, but it divided Sores and Min Cho Fat even more. Fat viewed Suk Too as his man. Sores had made Suk Too an even partner. It was just another source of friction.

The meeting was held at the Lonely Sailor at three o'clock in the after- noon. Just the day before, Big Jim Stuart had been hung from the second- floor window of the warehouse on Market Street, and the Melba Lee had arrived back in the bay. Sores gathered everyone around the table before he locked the doors to the bar.

Min Cho Fat wouldn't wait on Sores to start the meeting.

"Need more money from deal," he said sharply. "Used my contacts. No deal without me. Need more money."

Suk Too sat next to Fat and did not say a word. Cyrus Welch looked at Sores who had already briefed Welch on how difficult it was to deal with Fat.

Without changing expressions, Sores confronted the situation.

"We appreciate your view," he told Fat. "But we had a deal. We were to split the money four ways."

Fat became even more enraged.

"No deal. Need more money. No more contact if I don't get more money."

Sores stared Min Cho Fat down. Finally, he spoke.

"Okay," he said. "How much more money do you want?" Fat never flinched. "Split five ways. I get two pieces."

Cyrus Welch started to stand up and confront Fat, but Sores gently grabbed his arm and settled him back into his seat. There was a pause at the table for about two minutes. Sores looked at Suk Too. He received no expression at all back from the giant Chinaman. He looked at Cyrus Welch. It was obvious that Welch was fit to be tied, but he kept his cool. It was Sores who took the initiative.

"I propose that we give Fat what he wants. What do you say, Suk Too?" Too nodded his head. Sores took his answer as a yes. Cyrus Welch spoke up.

"I'll agree on one condition, mate," he said loudly. "I don't want to be in the room with him again."

Obviously, he was referring to Min Cho Fat.

"Done," said Sores Aguilar. "I need time to make my connections and sell the goods. Let's meet back here at the same time in two days. I will have your money then."

Sores stood up to shake hands with Fat and Suk Too. Cyrus Welch got up and left the table. He was in no mood to be gracious to anyone. Min Cho Fat and Suk Too made their way to the door. Before he left, Fat couldn't resist one more shot at Sores Aguilar.

"Two days all you have," he said sarcastically. "Have money here at next meeting."

Before Sores could respond, Fat bolted out the door.

After Fat and Suk Too were out of sight, Sores walked over to the bar. "Come on over," he ordered Welch. "I'll buy you a drink."

Welch reluctantly walked to the bar. He took the whiskey Sores handed him and drank it in one gulp.

"Why you agree to that?" he asked. "You know we don't need him any- more, mate."

Sores took his whiskey glass and swirled the liquor around in a circle. "Tell me more about this Billy Lambert," he asked.

Welch explained the difficulties of the trip to Hong Kong. He went into detail about his views on how to handle the labor. Lambert, he explained, was very much like the two of them. He was looking for an opportunity, and he would do what it took to get a job done.

Sores listened carefully. It was pushing five o'clock in the afternoon, and the fog had rolled in from the bay.

"Bring Lambert here tomorrow morning at eight o'clock. I want to meet him. If he is everything you say, maybe we can use him," he said.

Welch smiled. "Thanks, mate," he said. "Will be here bright and early." By changing the subject to Billy Lambert, Sores dodged Cyrus Welch's question.

Sores Aguilar never did anything without a plan. Things didn't always go perfectly for him, but it wasn't because he didn't know what he was doing. The situation he was currently dealing with was no exception. He decided to test Suk Too's loyalty. Even though Suk Too left the Lonely Sailor with Min Cho Fat, Sores knew the giant Chinaman would be in contact with Cyrus Welch before the end of the evening. The question was simple. Would Suk Too show up with Welch at the morning meeting involving Billy Lambert? If he did, it would give Sores one answer. If he didn't, there would be a different answer. That was how Sores saw it. It was simple.

Sores was restless all night. He only slept an hour or two. He was on edge about a lot of things. He didn't trust Min Cho Fat, and the Billy Lambert issue was bothering him. Sores was up and out of bed at four o'clock in the morning. He went up to the second floor, lit a lantern, and made some coffee. He then sat down and started reviewing everything. Promptly at eight o'clock, there was a knock at the door. Sores walked <over and peered out the window. Standing on the stairwell was Cyrus Welch, Suk Too, and Billy Lambert. Sores opened the door and then turned his back on the three men. He walked over to his place at the table without saying a word. Cyrus and Suk Too rambled over and took their seats. As he was instructed to do by Cyrus Welch, Billy Lambert stood at the door like a bodyguard. He didn't join the other three men at the table. Welch knew Sores would like that.

Sores poured Cyrus and Suk Too a cup of coffee. The three men sat in silence for a couple of minutes. Finally, Cyrus spoke up.

"You remember Billy Lambert," he asked.

Sores took a drink of his coffee before standing up and focusing on Lambert. Cyrus Welch and Suk Too stood up too. Lambert was holding a hat in his hands. He had not shaved in three months. He smelled terrible. Welch encouraged him to come over and meet Sores. Reluctantly, he did as Cyrus asked. Sores was cool but respectful. He did not offer his hand for a handshake.

Lambert looked at Sores Aguilar like he was some kind of a king. Sores remembered all the details of the night he had kidnapped him in the Lonely Sailor. Lambert was surprisingly calm and unassuming. He didn't seem bitter. It was more like he was interested in a job. Sores finally spoke.

"Billy," he said. "Would you and Cyrus mind be giving me and Suk Too a few minutes of privacy?"

Cyrus Welch didn't know what to say. However, he trusted Sores and knew it was probably in his best interest that he obliges. "Sure, mate," Cyrus responded. "We'll be down in front of the bar."

Welch and Lambert walked out the door and down the stairs. Sores started softly with Suk Too as they sat down at the table. "Who has your loyalty?" he asked the giant Chinese man. "What you mean?" Suk Too responded.

Sores peered into his eyes and said, "Who has your loyalty? Is it me or Fat?"

Suk Too didn't understand at first. Sores had to press him.

"If you had to choose between me and Fat, who would you choose to work for?"

Suk Too thought to himself quietly.

"You," he finally said.

Sores needed to confirm the commitment.

"Do you understand what I am asking?" he asked Suk Too. It suddenly dawned on Suk Too what Aguilar meant. "I never owe him," Suk Too answered. "I do business with you." Of course, that was exactly what Sores wanted to hear. He decided it was time to tell Suk Too about some details.

"Fat will never be satisfied with our business arrangement. He will al- ways want more and more from us. You told the people in Hong Kong that we would be back in three months with more gold, didn't you?" Suk Too nodded his head.

"You can find them again, can't you?" Sores continued.

Suk Too nodded again.

"Good," Sores replied.

A few awkward moments passed before Sores spoke again. "Then we don't need Fat anymore. Do you agree?"

Sores looked him in the eye. Suk Too stared back at Sores.

After about thirty seconds, he nodded his head again.

Sores got up out of his chair and walked to the door. He opened it and motioned Cyrus Welch back up the stairs. The four men sat down at the table. Sores started the conversation.

"I hear you are worth your weight," he said to Billy Lambert.

"I have a proposition for you."

Lambert was on edge. He squirmed in his seat, but he said nothing. Sores continued.

"I have a job for you. If you do it well, you will not be a partner, but you will be well paid for all your services on and off the ship."

Lambert shrugged his shoulders.

"What if I don't want to do this job?" he asked.

All three men, Sores Aguilar, Cyrus Welch, and Suk Too, stared at him. None of them said a word. It was obvious that if he refused the job, the consequences were not going to be good. Lambert looked down at his boots and nodded his head. He wondered to himself if he had just made a deal with the devil. When he looked up at Sores, he was ready to ask the question.

"What's the job?" he asked.

Sores looked him in the eye and responded.

"All of you meet me here tonight at six p.m.," he said.

Then he turned to look at Cyrus Welch and Suk Too.

"We will meet again tomorrow at the time agreed to split the money," he said. "But there will only be three of us. Fat won't be at the meeting." Sores didn't want to talk any more. He needed to be alone. There was no way he was going to jeopardize his drug contacts. He changed into his alternate look to dispel anyone from recognizing him. He changed to a much broader brimmed hat and wore a long overcoat with big pockets. Someone had left the coat at the bar. He kept the opium in his coat pockets. He had bought a scarf down at the docks that he could bunch up around his neck and jawline. It made it very difficult to see his face. He made his way down to the docks first. He needed to get rid of Big Jim Stuart's little finger. He discreetly dropped it into the water as he walked through the docks.

The transactions had been planned in advance for weeks. Sores would only be paid in gold. There was too much counterfeit money on the streets to take a chance on currency. He had educated himself on how to tell if gold was real or fake. In less than three hours, Sores returned to the Lonely Sailor. He was now a very wealthy man.

Sores Aguilar knew that Min Cho Fat would rise promptly at 6:00 a.m. He walked to a local store about a half mile from his residence on Jackson Street. Sores had been stalking him for months. He knew Fat's daily schedule. He knew where he liked to spend his time. He knew about his protection. He knew about his vulnerability.

Along the way to the store, Fat would pass by an alley that seemed to be innocent. However, it was a perfect place for an ambush. Sores would be near the alley, pushing a food cart that he had bought a month ago. He had completely changed the way he looked from the night before. Any- one who paid attention to him would think he was an Indian. He had also taught his partners on how to change their appearance.

The bottom shelf on the cart had plenty of room to store Fat's body. Sores had carefully calculated exactly how to fold it. Cyrus Welch had a very important job on the mission. If any trouble broke out during the at- tack, he would cover for Lambert and Sores. He would pull his gun and challenge anyone who was a threat. Suk Too would be waiting back at the Melba Lee prepared to take care of the carnage.

The plan was in place. The four men awoke from bed at two in the morning. They changed into their attire and took their places. There they waited for Min Cho Fat. Sure enough, Fat woke and started his trip to the local store in the Chinese section of San Francisco. He was looking for- ward to the meeting at the Lonely Sailor that afternoon. Nothing made Fat happier than accumulating wealth. He reached the alley at about the halfway point of his journey to the market. Suddenly from behind a stack of crates, a man jumped out in front of him. Min Cho Fat's eyes widened and his jaw dropped. There he stood face-to-face with Billy Lambert.

CHAPTER 31

The four hundred miles from Los Angeles to San Francisco was the easiest part of the journey for Sawyer Crenshaw's stagecoach. There was actually a road that had been tracked by wagons and horses. The coach followed both the road and the other travelers who were heading to the same destination. The tracks led more inland than anyone thought they would or should, but nobody complained.

All along, Crenshaw planned on traveling fifty miles per day on aver- age. The coach had not made that kind of time up to this point. But now, with a more sophisticated road, fifty miles a day was easily attainable. John McLemore didn't make the journey to San Francisco. He stayed back in Los Angeles. Crenshaw waited two full days so everyone could go to Mara's funeral. Ray Andrews waited at the cemetery with McLemore after everyone else had left. He wanted to make sure the grave was proper. Ray argued with the cemetery workers when he knew they had only dug down five feet. He was so upset that he asked McLemore for help to move Mara's casket. Then he grabbed a shovel and dug the grave out correctly. He and McLemore finally left after securing the burial and preparing a rock headstone for Mara.

Once again, Ray brought up the subject of the brooch, but that angered John McLemore.

"I don't want it back," he bellowed at Ray. "And I wouldn't get too attached to it if I were you. Everybody who does seems to die." Ray was taken aback by McLemore's comments.

"What do you mean?" he asked.

Ray noticed that McLemore turned away for a minute. Ray didn't hesitate. He walked right around and faced him eyeball to eyeball. He needed to get some things straight about the brooch.

"What do you mean everyone seems to die?" he asked.

John McLemore gathered himself and wiped the snot off his nose with his shirt sleeve.

"We bought it for my daughter's wedding present," he answered. "She loved it, but she died three months after we gave it to her. Mara asked me if she could have it, so I gave it back to her. A couple of months later, Mara got sick. We tried to get her out here to California so she could get well, but we ran out of money. I had to sell the brooch to Fields to pay Crenshaw the fare for the trip."

McLemore was all but crying now, but he continued with his story.

"I told her that I packed it. I was hoping she wouldn't miss it, but I was wrong. She wanted to see it. Of course, I had sold it. When she figured out that we didn't have it anymore, she just gave up. I feel like such a coward."

McLemore looked up at Ray.

"It's valuable. Don't just take anything for it. Make sure you get it ap- praised by somebody who knows what he's talking about, you hear me. Just keep it away from me."

One of the reasons Crenshaw justified staying in Los Angeles was that he wanted to find a couple of new people to take the two open spots on the coach. He was unsuccessful, so there were only four passengers left on the trip. The four included Ben Fields, Junior Hoskins, and John and Lovie Kitchens. The cook, Willie Foster, still rode on the bench driver's seat with Crenshaw while Ray and Henry scouted from their horses.

With fewer people and less luggage, the coach could travel quicker. Water was plentiful, but there was little sophistication and few townships. However, one thing motivated the group. Everyone knew that they were just a week out from their destination, San Francisco.

On the third night of the trip, Ray finally mustered up enough courage to bring up the brooch at supper. Ben Fields and Junior Hoskins were playing cards like they did almost every night. Ray sat down with them by the fire and started asking questions.

"Will you guys tell me what the heck happened back in Yuma?" he asked.

Fields looked at Junior, but she never even looked up from her cards. Ray had been trying to figure out their relationship since the first day of the trip. They were certainly a very odd pair. Fields was slick and good looking. Junior was rough and crude. She was anything but attractive outside of being occasionally entertaining.

Ray continued his questioning.

"You two were about to kill each other. Then, all of a sudden, every- thing was okay. I need to know. Were you just using me?"

It was quiet for a moment, and then Junior spoke up.

"Yea, I guess we used ya, Andrews," she said. "We knew you would look out for us. We had seen ya in action.

We paid you good though. That brooch is worth a lot of money."

Ben Fields finally spoke.

"You see Ray," he said. "We didn't know that country. You can't ever tell how people will react when they lose money. We figured you might not go along with us if we told you what we were doing."

Ray looked at Fields, and then he looked at Junior. "That's just it," he said. "What were you doing?"

"Damn, boy," Junior Hoskins chimed in. "I sure worry 'bout you in San Francisco. We worked together on a card game. You satisfied? We beat that rancher and that banker. And I couldn't believe how easy that dealer was to fool. We paid that other feller, Benny Hicks, a hundred dollars to help us. There were people watching us. We needed you to guard the money."

Ray leaned back and took a deep breath. Finally, he understood what had happened. He still had a question though.

"But you two were at each other's throats after we left Yuma. What was that about?"

Fields flipped his cards into the pile of chips by the fire.

"Better to be safe than sorry, Ray. What's that you always say? Use your best judgment. We used our best judgment. We needed to get pretty far away from Yuma before we relaxed," Fields said.

Ray looked at the both of them. By now, everybody else in the camp had joined in listening to the conversation.

"So, you mean I participated in a cheating scheme? "Ray asked. Ben Fields stood up and stretched.

"I wouldn't look at it like that, Ray," he said. "I don't think we cheated. I see it as we were just smarter than those other fellows. Cheating is a harsh word, don't you think, Junior?"

Ray gripped his hands together behind his neck.

"I don't know what to think," he answered. "I guess I just broke the law that I swore to defend back in Texas."

Junior Hoskins had heard enough.

"No, you didn't," she scoffed at Ray. "You were working for a livin', and now you have a brooch that's worth some good money."

Ray pulled his hands down.

"Maybe I'll just give it away," he said sarcastically.

Junior was ready to pounce on him.

"Maybe you should give it to that girl and her old man to start a church in San Francisco. Whatever you do, you need to get rid of it. It's bad luck."

Junior's idea gave Ray a spiritual lift. He picked up a rock, turned around, and fired it straight overhand at a tree thirty yards away. When he looked back around at the rest of the camp, he couldn't help himself. "Okay," he said. "Which one of you is going to help me write a letter?"

CHAPTER 32

LOS ANGELES

*T*he road had been long for Sarah Thomas and her father, Reverend William. The reverend had planned all along on passing right on through Los Angeles. However, he knew Sarah would be expecting a letter there.

It took Sarah almost two hours to find her way down to Temple Square on Spring Street. There she finally found the post office. The same old, grubby looking man worked as the clerk at the desk. He hadn't taken a bath since Ray Andrews came through two weeks ago. Sarah worked her way to the front of the line. She used her most ladylike, polite demeanor when she approached the clerk.

"Sir," she asked. "Would there be a letter here addressed to a Sarah Thomas?"

The clerk mustered up a grin. He had been waiting for her. Exchanging the letters between the two young lovebirds was the best entertainment he had enjoyed in a long time.

"Let me see here," the old clerk teased.

He fumbled through some papers for a couple of minutes.

"No," he said. "I don't see anything here for a Sarah Johnson." Sarah snapped at him. "Sarah Thomas not Sarah Johnson."

The clerk looked up at her. She was very tall for a woman. "Still don't see anything for a Sarah Jones," he answered. Sarah was livid by now, which was exactly what the old clerk wanted.

"t-h-o-m-a-s!" She all but screamed.

The clerk pulled out a letter and handed it to Sarah. She smiled and shook her head as if the problem had been solved. However, when she looked down at the envelope, her facial expression turned to an ugly scowl. The letter was addressed to a Sarah Bingham.

"This is really important to me," Sarah told the clerk. "Let's try again." She placed the letter on the counter. "Is there a letter here for a Sarah Thomas? That'st-h-o-m-a-s." Once again, the clerk fumbled through a stack of mail.

"No, I don't see it," he deadpanned. "I just don't think there is a letter here with that name on it."

Sarah was devastated. She turned around and was ready to leave, but the old clerk had almost enjoyed enough fun for the day. "Young lady!" the clerk yelled at her.

Sarah stopped and turned around.

"Was the letter left by a good-looking, young man with a really smooth face?" he asked.

Sarah nodded her head yes as she started walking back to the counter. "Was he about six foot tall?" the clerk asked again.

Sarah smiled at him.

"Was there also a letter addressed to him here at the post office?" he continued.

"Yes," Sarah all but screamed. "That's him," she said.

The old clerk smiled at her. Then he said, "Well, I don't know anybody like that."

Sarah Thomas all but climbed over the counter and choked the old clerk. Finally, the clerk laughed and laughed as loud as he could laugh. He walked over to the special little mail slot where he had been saving Ray's letter for her. He pulled it out of the slot and started waving it at her. Sarah walked around the counter and grabbed the letter. Without saying anything, she headed for the door. As soon as the sun hit her face, she stopped and looked back at the clerk. Their eyes met, and they smiled at each other.

"Thank you," Sarah Thomas said.

"You're welcome, missy," the old clerk answered. "Hope I didn't tease you too bad. I was just having me some fun."

Sarah started walking back to the wagon. The reverend was there waiting for her. She wanted to stop and read Ray's letter, but she knew she needed to get back to her father. She put the letter in her back pocket and started walking as fast as she could. She had been gone a long time, and she knew the reverend would be worried.

As she turned the corner at Elm and Twentieth Street, an old man stepped in front of her. Sarah slammed into him and knocked him down to the ground. She couldn't believe what she had done.

"I'm so sorry!" she said over and over again. As she helped the man to his feet, she noticed that a walking cane was lying on the ground. She picked up the cane and handed it to him. He was short and burly with a white beard. His hat was sitting on his head sideways. He looked absolutely harmless. It took him a couple of minutes to stabilize himself with the cane.

Once again, Sarah apologized.

"Are you all right?" she asked him.

He seemed a little shaken. Finally, he spoke, "It's okay, darling. I think I can make it. You were walking pretty fast. I couldn't get out of the way." Sarah continued to apologize.

"Can I help you with anything?" she asked.

"No," he answered. "I'm just trying to make it back down to the road." The old man started trying to walk, but he could barely move.

Sarah watched him, feeling a tremendous sense of guilt.

She stayed with him as they both walked in the same direction. "Name's Oscar," he said. "Oscar Sellers."

Sarah didn't think twice about introducing herself.

"I'm Sarah Thomas," she said. "I feel so bad that I knocked you down." The old man grimaced.

"You sure are pretty," he told her. "What's a gal like you doing here in downtown?"

Sarah decided to walk with Oscar to the road. She started explaining the reason that she went to the post office. Her enthusiasm engulfed her. She was so excited about the letter that she had to tell someone. Oscar focused on every word. After Sarah rambled on for five minutes, he spoke. "That is so interesting. I hope everything works out for you, darling. Where are you heading?" he asked her.

"My father is waiting for me back at the main road," she answered. Oscar smiled.

"That's where I'm heading," he responded. "Can I walk with you?"

Sarah was in a hurry, but she couldn't be rude to Oscar. It was against her nature. She walked with him at a very slow pace. Her patience was running thin, but she didn't have the heart to leave him.

"When are you going to read your letter?" he asked her.

She thought about it a minute, then she answered, "I'll read it when Pop and I get on our way. It will be a good way to pass the time."

Oscar was impressed.

"Good idea," he told her. "Good idea."

The two of them walked all the way to the main road and talked just like old friends.

It took them about an hour to get back to the reverend and the wagon. He was obviously glad to see Sarah. He was not glad to see Oscar. Sarah introduced him anyway.

"Pop, this is a new friend of mine. His name is Oscar Sellers." The two men shook hands and exchanged greetings.

"I accidently ran over Oscar back in town," Sarah explained.

"It turned out all right, didn't it, Oscar. Now we're friends." Oscar looked around to see who was watching. He noticed that it was pretty much just the three of them. The next wagon close to them was a quarter mile away.

"Well," Oscar said. "It was really nice to meet you. Now I have a re- quest."

Sarah did a double take toward him with a perplexed look on her face. "What's your request?" she asked.

"Well," he answered. "I need your money."

Sarah seemed to feel sorry for him.

"Oscar, we don't have much money or I would be glad to help you," she answered.

Oscar looked at the reverend.

"You don't understand," he said. "This is a holdup. I need your money."

Sarah was dumbfounded. Oscar wasn't capable of a holdup.

She wondered if he was just joking like the clerk. Sarah talked like she was a nurse speaking to a sick patient.

"Oscar," she said. "We can't give you any money."

Suddenly, Oscar hooked Sarah around the neck with his right arm. He slammed her to the ground and pounced on top of her. He pulled a knife with his left hand and stuck it in Sarah's cheek. Oscar went from a sickly old man to a savage animal.

"Give me everything you have, or I'll cut off her nose," Oscar sneered at the reverend.

Sarah was speechless. Oscar had her tied in a knot. She couldn't move, and she was afraid to talk. The reverend started emptying his pockets right in front of them. All he had was a few coins and a few bills in his pockets. He removed his watch and dropped it on the ground. He ran to the wagon and grabbed his suitcase. Frantically, he pulled out a small bag and ran back over to Oscar and Sarah.

"Here," he said as he threw the bag down by the rest of his valuables. "I swear that's all we have. Please, sir, please let her go." Slowly, Oscar re- leased his grip on Sarah. She rolled away from him, and he picked up the watch, the coins, bills, and the small bag.

Then he turned to Sarah and said, "You're lucky you're with your old man, darling," he said. "Normally, there would've been a little more for you to pay."

Oscar turned and started walking away. Sarah was quiet. She reached into her right pocket and took out the rock she carried every day. She scrambled to her feet and fired the rock straight at Oscar Sellers. It hit him square in the back of the head just above the brim of his hat. He dropped face down into the street. Sarah didn't waste any time. She bolted toward him.

"Sarah!" the reverend yelled at her.

She reached Oscar and kicked him right up under the ribcage. Then she dropped to her right knee and punched him hard in the face. She grabbed the small bag first. Then she wrestled the bills and coins out of his hands. Oscar squirmed on the road. By now, her confidence was soaring. She couldn't resist kicking him in the groin. The knife he used to terrorize her was lying on the ground. It was easy to reach down and grab it.

Sarah walked back over to the wagon. The reverend was waiting for her in the bench seat. He was ready to make a run for it. But Sarah Thomas took her time. She climbed up on the seat next to her father and looked back at Oscar. He was still on the ground, writhing in pain. She checked to make sure the letter was still in her back pocket. A couple, maybe in their thirties, walked up to the wagon.

"Is everything all right?" the man asked.

Sarah looked down at them.

"Just a little skirmish between friends," she said. "That's all." The reverend snapped the reigns and the horses took off at a quick pace.

Sarah waited until her father had them safely out of the sight of Oscar Sellers. She took a deep breath and reached into her pocket for the letter. Once again, the handwriting on the envelope was beautiful. Sarah knew that Ray didn't write it. Hopefully though, he was the one who spoke it. She opened the letter carefully. The reverend waited patiently. He allowed Sarah to read it in its entirety before he stuck his nose into her business. Finally, he broke the silence.

"Well, daughter, what does it say?" Sarah took a deep breath before she began to read.

"Dear Sarah," she said. "I hope your journey is going well. We are making good time on the stagecoach. We hope to make our destination very soon. I do not know if I will be able to get you another letter. I will be looking for you at the San Francisco post office. Come there when you get to town. I will leave you a letter there. Tell the reverend hello for me. I re- ally look forward to seeing you. The people here in California are really nice. I have a good feeling about them. I feel that I can trust them. Sincerely, Ray Andrews."

Sarah looked back at the city of Los Angeles. It was beautiful. She could feel the ocean. The air was light, and it was cool. The reverend couldn't help but to giggle.

"Daughter," he said. "You sure showed ole Oscar, didn't you? What in the world got into you?"

Sarah laughed a little herself. "I don't know," she answered. "I just wasn't gonna take it, I guess."

The reverend changed expressions and said, "Well, the Lord helped us on that one. I appreciate what you did. I don't know what we would have done if he would have got away, but please don't ever do that again."

Sarah focused straight ahead. She saw other travelers on the road up in front of them. The reverend kept talking.

"Well, what do you think about Mr. Andrews?"

Sarah shrugged her shoulders and pulled out Oscar's knife. She tried to open it, but she couldn't. She figured there was some trick to it. Finally, she answered.

"Well, I told you, Pop," she said. "I just don't think he's very smart, and I know he isn't a very good judge of people."

CHAPTER 33

SAN FRANCISCO

*B*illy Lambert had been walking the city all day long. He was on a scouting mission. He was ordered to walk the docks and the streets, looking for just the right man. His two new bosses, Sores Aguilar and Cyrus Welch, had been good to him. They had provided a room for him to stay at night. For the first time in his life, he had some money in his pocket.

Sores and Welch kept him busy. There was always something to do. Only once had they asked him to execute a crime. That was the incident with Min Cho Fat. Other than that, Billy's work had been very interesting. He had never been involved with the brain's side of a business be- fore, and he was enjoying it.

The men that walked the streets of San Francisco could be very deceiving. Sores and Welch were stubborn about identifying a prospect. They followed one for a few days before making an approach. The prospect had some requirements. He had to be big. He had to be strong. He had to be healthy. Those characteristics were not so hard to observe. But there were other characteristics that were tougher to measure. They didn't want a prospect who might lead others. A more dumbfounded type would be better. Mutiny on the ship was always a concern. Welch wanted a softhearted, not so smart, friendly, spirited young man. He would be much easier to brainwash.

Billy knew of some men that qualified. Only six more sailors were needed for the trip to Hong Kong. The last six would not be paid. They would be slaves. Sores had convinced Cyrus Welch to plan, plan, and plan more. The Melba Lee would not leave San Francisco without being totally prepared for the next trip. There was just too much to lose.

This particular piece of the plan was pretty simple. Billy would walk the streets and look for the right man. If the situation warranted, he would approach him, and then he would talk to him a bit. If he really liked an individual, he would hand him a piece of paper. The paper was an advertisement for the Lonely Sailor. There was an address and directions on the page. It was simply a step to get a prospect over to the saloon so Cyrus Welch and Sores could get a look at him. If the situation was right, there would be further steps taken.

Billy was about ready to call it a day. It was a calm, clear evening in San Francisco. The brilliant setting sun enhanced one of the most beautiful places in the world. The chill in the air forced Billy to put on his coat. As he was doing so, he noticed a funny looking carriage being pulled by four horses. It was slowly moving toward him. The burnt reddish-brown color of the carriage was shining from the reflection of the sun. Billy had never seen such a vehicle.

He watched the carriage go right by him. He noticed the two cowboys that were riding on each side. There were people inside. Billy's fascination encouraged him to follow it. He walked a safe distance behind. The old man at the reigns turned the wrong way down a side street and got blocked into an alley. It was obvious that he didn't know where he was going.

Billy decided that it was in his best interest to intervene. He walked up behind the carriage and spoke to one of the cowboys on horseback.

"You fellas look lost," he said to Stuttering Henry Jones.

Henry just looked at him. He was totally exhausted. His age had caught up to him. Henry didn't like to talk, but he was especially quiet when he was really tired. He nodded toward Ray. The gesture told Billy Lambert that he was talking to the wrong person.

Ray didn't hesitate to answer from the other side of the coach.

"We are a little bit lost. We're looking for a hotel. Some place to settle for a while."

By now, Billy knew the city well.

"I can help you," he said. "What kind of price range you want?" Ray got down off his horse as Henry helped navigate Crenshaw's stagecoach out of the alley.

"We got two women," Ray explained. "Really, one-and-a-half women, I reckon. One of them is the same as a man. We just need a place to rest for a while. We'll all decide what we're gonna do then."

Billy introduced himself and started telling Ray about the city. After Henry and Crenshaw got the stagecoach headed back into the street, Billy shook hands and eyeballed everyone. He asked all about the stagecoach and the trip. It was amazing to him that he had never seen or heard about one before. It didn't take long for Billy to befriend every one of them. "Why don't I just lead the way through town," Billy explained. "When you see something, you like, we'll just stop. I think you should get away from this part of town though. You have women in your group."

Stuttering Henry was watching Billy Lambert closely. Ray had insisted the night before that he and Henry inventory their guns and ammunition for the arrival into town. Henry had a Colt Navy revolver tucked into a gunny sack. The sack was in his saddlebag. He also had a loaded Navy on his belt. That was twelve shots ready to fire. One of his shotguns was also loaded. It was tied down on his horse.

Ray was armed the exact same way with the exact same inventory of shots. Ray and Henry always liked to match firepower because it helped them when they worked together. They would have a feel for how aggressive each one should be in dispensing shots.

Billy got out in front of the coach and led the travelers into one of the nicest parts of town. There were some nice hotels that were far away from Aussie town. He didn't want this group close to that area. Crenshaw finally stopped at a hotel in the downtown area called The Barnes Inn. Everybody got out of the coach and made it into the building. Ben Fields and Junior Hoskins hit the bar as soon as they walked in the door. The Kitchens wanted a room. Sawyer and Willie Foster, the cook, were exhausted. They checked into a room they would share and asked the clerk where they could get a good deal on whiskey. Henry and Ray just stayed out in front of the hotel. They wanted to wait things out a bit.

Billy Lambert kept the conversation going strong. Finally, he got to the root of his motivation. He liked both of these men. One of the men, the older one, looked pale and gaunt. Billy didn't think he would last through the voyage to China. The other man seemed like a perfect fit. "Are you men looking for a job?" Billy Lambert asked.

That got Ray's attention.

"We haven't really talked about some things," Ray answered. "It's been a long trip. I might be interested though." Henry's eyes darted toward Ray. The subject had yet to come up be- tween the two of them. Both had been thinking about it, but neither had the courage to mention it. But now they had accomplished their mission. They had made it to San Francisco.

What was next?

Billy pulled the flyers out of his coat pocket. He handed one of the papers to Ray.

"Here," he said. "Come over around eight o'clock in the evening on a Wednesday or a Thursday. That's when we interview men. Don't be scared of the place now. It's just a saloon. My bosses will want to meet you. We pay good wages and treat people fair."

Ray took the flyer and put it in his pocket. He was interested. All he could think about was finding Sarah Thomas and maybe looking for a job. Crenshaw was heading back to Austin. Everybody on the trip knew that. He would try to pick up some travelers that wanted to go back. It had never been mentioned about what would happen if Ray or Henry wanted to stay in San Francisco.

Suddenly, Sawyer Crenshaw walked up to Ray.

"Here's your room key. You and Henry have a room together. I honor my word. I will pay for two nights here in town. You are free to do as you please. After that, we're heading back to Texas. There's a stable round back for the horses."

Crenshaw turned around and walked back into the hotel.

Ray looked at Stuttering Henry. He didn't know what to say. Billy Lambert decided it was time to go.

"Well," he said. "You have my address. It's a great opportunity. I hope you will come down and check on it. Remember, Wednesday or Thursday nights at eight o'clock. If you come down, I'll vouch for you." Billy walked away.

It was dark now, and the air was chilly. Ray and Henry started walking to the stable. Not a word was spoken. Neither of them knew what to say.

CHAPTER 34

*E*verybody on the coach was too tired to do much on the first night they were in San Francisco. However, everyone was up and going early the next morning. San Francisco was a fascinating place. After the long, hot trip they had taken, the weather in Northern California was wonderful. John and Lovie Kitchens started looking for a place to live. Ben Fields and Junior Hoskins disappeared. Nobody could find either one of them. Crenshaw and Willie Foster took care of their business and commenced to drinking.

Ray Andrews had one thing on his mind. He was going to get the brooch appraised. He remembered how Junior had pawned it at the card game. Ray thought he knew the rules. It was obvious to him that the brooch was valuable, and it was also obvious to him that there would be people who would try to take advantage of him. He awoke early and started collecting his thoughts.

Henry wouldn't have breakfast at the hotel. The price was too high. Ray followed him down the street to a street vendor who was selling hotdogs. That was where Ray decided to share his plan.

"Henry, I need to see how much this brooch is worth," he stated with confidence.

Henry just looked at him.

"Will you go with me?" Ray asked. "I would feel a lot more comfortable if you would."

Ray knew Henry would do anything he asked him to do, so the two of them started walking the streets. Ray figured that he would go to at least three different parts of town and see what the brooch was worth. That way, he could be objective and wouldn't get tricked.

They had walked only two blocks before a place jumped out at Ray. It seemed clean and honest. There was a sign on the door that read Green's Jewelry. In smaller, darker print under the store name, the words We Buy Gold and Silver was easy to see. Ray looked at Henry and decided to go in the store. But first, he had to get some things straight.

"Okay Henry," he started. "You stand over to my right. You're the guard. Don't take your eyes off the brooch. I want them to think that it's really valuable."

Henry looked up at the sky for a minute. He never said a word. He wasn't in the mood to talk.

Ray waltzed in the front door of Green's Jewelry. A heavyset man, may- be Mr. Green, was behind the counter. He wore a white shirt with a dark- brown vest. His black tie seemed to fit a little too tight around his neck. He had long sideburns and oily hair. He was not friendly.

"How ya doing?" asked Ray.

The jewelry salesman looked at Ray but didn't answer. Ray pulled the brooch out of his pocket. Henry scurried around to Ray's right. He was in good position, and he did not take his eyes off the brooch.

"I'm in the mood to sell this fine piece of jewelry," Ray said to the salesman.

He put the brooch down on the counter. The salesman picked it up and put his left hand over his left eye. He looked at the brooch closely.

Finally, he handed it back to Ray.

"Piece of junk," he said to Ray. "Ain't worth nothing."

Ray was a little in shock. This exchange hadn't gone the way he thought it would, but he continued on course.

"Sir, I know that brooch is worth at least $700," he scolded the salesman.

But the salesman was not impressed.

"Nope, I'll give ya five dollars for the jewelry, but the diamond is a fake."

Ray was about to argue some more, but Stuttering Henry had seen enough.

"C-C-Come on, Ray," he said as he scooped up the brooch from the counter. "Let's go."

Ray watched Henry put the brooch in his pocket and followed him out the door. He didn't know what to say. Henry decided to talk.

"D-d-d-don't like him," he stuttered. "Let's keep going."

Ray didn't say anything. He just followed Henry. They headed toward the sun. That's what they had been doing most on this trip anyway. The scenery began to change. There were fewer buildings. It seemed brighter. Henry noticed a big sign down at the end of the street. It read Gold and Silver. Henry headed for the front door.

This time, the sales clerk was a woman. Both Henry and Ray were enamored with her beauty. She was average in height with long, curly, blonde hair. She had a beautiful face, and her dress jumped out at them. It was red and very well fitted to show off her gorgeous figure. Unlike the salesman at Green's Jewelry, she was very friendly.

"Hello, boys," she said. "My name's Georgia Tipps." She held out her hand to Henry first. He took it and kissed it. Ray had to smirk at the sight for just a second. He had never seen Henry do any- thing like that before. Georgia turned and offered her hand to Ray. He shook it just as if it were a man.

"What's your business today?" Georgia asked them.

Ray looked at Henry, but Henry's eyes were fixated on Georgia. Finally, Ray spoke, "Henry, show her the brooch."

Henry pulled out the brooch and shined it on his shirt. Then he gave it to Georgia. She took it and placed it on the counter. She pulled a smooth handkerchief from under the table and really gave it a going-over. After she was finished, it glistened like brand new.

Ray noticed her pulling out one of those small one-eyed goggles. She got right down on top of the brooch and examined it. Henry and Ray were more interested in watching Georgia than they were watching the brooch. Suddenly, Ray snapped out of it and got back to business.

"I witnessed it being sold in Yuma for $700," he said.

"Is that where you bought it?" Georgia asked.

Ray was ready for that question.

"No, ma'am," he said. "I acquired it as my pay for work as a guard." The fact that Ray just could not lie had gotten him into trouble several times in his life. The thought hit him that this might just be another time. Georgia leaned over the counter and looked up at Henry and Ray. Her dress was low cut, and Henry was awestruck by her cleavage. Ray was impressed too, but he kept his focus on the brooch. Georgia decided to make an offer.

"I want it, boys, but I'm going to have to have the right price. I can make you an offer, or we can break it up and measure the gold and the diamond. What do you want to do?"

Ray thought for a moment.

"Well," he said. "I don't want to break the piece of jewelry down. I want to keep it intact. What will you give me for it?"

Georgia looked at it really closely. She knew Ray had just broken the basic rule of negotiating when he asked her to name the starting price.

"I can give you $200 if you just want to sell it as jewelry. That's a fair of- fer."

Ray's education about jewelry was developing fast. Henry decided that he wanted to talk.

"Look really close, Miss Georgia. Do you see that gold trim around the diamond? It's real gold, not fake," Henry said it without the slightest stutter. "That's a real diamond too."

Georgia was impressed.

"Well, honey, I think you're right, but I would have to break it down be- fore I could say for sure."

Ray had practiced this next part.

"Georgia, would you give me $500?" he asked.

Georgia put the brooch on her chest and walked over to a mirror behind the counter. The same thought hit Ray and Henry at the same time. That brooch had been the center of attention for weeks, but the thought of someone actually wearing it had never been brought up in conversation. Georgia came back to the counter to face Ray and Henry.

"I will give you $250. That's all I can do. I would really like to have it. You can go look somewhere else if you want. If you get a better deal, then sell it. But if the other guy's offer is close to mine, bring it back. We can talk some more."

Ray was now interested in measuring the gold and silver. "Georgia," he asked. "Do you think we should break it down?" Georgia looked at the brooch again. She was slowly falling in love with it.

"That's a good question," she answered. "You see, it has a lot of value as a piece of jewelry. It's beautiful. But we don't know what it is really worth until we measure it. That makes it kind of a mystery piece."

Things were starting to get too complicated. Ray knew Henry was un- der tremendous pressure to decide whether or not he would go back to Texas. Ray had already made up his mind. He was going to stay and wait for Sarah Thomas. There was not a doubt about it. Now he was learning about all these issues with the brooch. Georgia couldn't help but to add some more information. Normally, she looked for every advantage with a customer. However, she liked Ray and Henry.

"You see, boys," she told them. "We don't know what this piece of jewelry is worth. That could be good or bad. But I will tell you one thing. In these parts, you want to deal in gold if you can. You deal with silver if you have to, but I would watch out for paper money. A lot of paper money here is fake, and it's hard to carry if you have a bunch of it. This brooch is a smart way to carry a lot of money without taking up much space."

Ray was ready to go, but he had to be polite. "Georgia, it was a pleasure to meet you. We'll take you up on your offer and come back if you're appraisal is comparable to the others. We might come back anyway if you don't mind."

Georgia laughed out loud. "Boys, it would be great to see you any time. I'll see you around."

Ray and Henry left the Gold and Silver. It had been a delightful experience.

They started walking again. They walked a long way through town. The hills made both of them tired. Along the way, they saw all kinds of different sights. Both of them were surprised at how the town would transition from wealthy neighborhoods to slums in just a few blocks. It was the people that really got their attention. There were a lot of Chinese folks. There were also a lot of Aussies. Ray was determined to get at least one more appraisal. He wasn't in the mood to sell the brooch today; he just wanted to get an idea of how much it was worth. He wanted Sarah to see it be- fore he sold it.

Ray and Henry made their way down to Market Street. There was plenty of business going on in that part of town. Henry noticed a place that had a sign on the front. The sign said Delany's Pawn. It looked decent. It was clean and seemed to have nice goods inside. When they entered the door, an argument was going on between two people at the counter. It was loud and awkward. Ray walked up closer so he could hear.

"A deal's a deal," said the man behind the counter.

"You took advantage of me, Delany," the other man yelled. Delany didn't waiver a bit.

"I didn't take advantage of anybody. I gave you the best price I could for that ring. I'll sell it back to you if you want it."

The customer who felt betrayed by Delany was livid.

"Okay, I'll buy it back for what I sold it to you for," he said. "No," Delany said. "You can buy it back at my price, fifty dollars."

The customer was really upset.

"I sold it to you for twenty-five dollars," he said.

"That's right," Delany answered, "and I want fifty for it now." The customer was furious.

"You're a crook!" he screamed at Delany.

Delany decided that he had heard enough.

"Get out of here, your varmint!" he yelled at the customer. That triggered the next event. The customer jumped right up on the counter like a cat. He dove right into Delany, leading with his hands. He had Delany up against the back wall as he tried to choke him to death.

Both Ray and Henry knew exactly what to do. Back in Texas, they had been in this situation many times. They both broke for the back of the counter. Ray grabbed the customer, and Henry went for Delany. Ray had the customer secured in a few seconds, but he noticed that Henry seemed to have his hands full with Delany.

Ray wrestled the customer out the front door.

"Get on out of here," he told the customer. "You can come back when you calm down."

It suddenly occurred to Ray that he was sure taking Delany's integrity for granted. He might really be a crook.

The customer called Ray a few names and backed away from the front door. He raised his arm in defiance. Ray turned and walked back into the pawn shop. It was quiet. There was no scuffle. He figured that Henry had things under control.

Ray didn't see anyone in the store. He walked around to the side of the counter. There he saw Delany kneeling down on his knees. He had Henry's head in his lap. Delany reached over Henry's body and pushed hard just under Henry's rib cage. He was trying to stop the bleeding. He had used a switchblade to stab Henry up and under the torso. He hadn't realized that Henry was actually trying the help him.

Ray jumped down on the floor. It was too late. Blood was gushing from one of Henry's vital organs. The two former Texas Rangers locked eyes. "S-s-sorry, R-ray," apologized Stuttering Henry Jones. "D-didn't s-see that knife."

Henry looked out the front door of the pawnshop. His eyes settled. He was gone.

CHAPTER 35

The Life. Both her mother and father said it every day. But she had the Lord will provide." Sarah Thomas had heard that slogan all always been a skeptic. Maybe it was her exceptionally high intelligence. Maybe it was a generational issue. Maybe she just didn't want to buy into the theory. Whatever it was, riding into the south side of San Francisco brought her doubts to another level. She was worrying so much she couldn't sleep at night. Her stomach was tied up in knots, and it was difficult for her to eat.

All along, the plan was to get to San Francisco and find a specific Meth- odist Church. From there, her father would begin his mission. His instincts had told him to come and help fight the debauchery of the town. It was where he was supposed to be. Sarah, on the other hand, was supposed to be in school at the new Baptist College in Waco. The reverend knew all along that it would be hard to get her to stay in Texas when he was heading to California. The fragmenting of the Thomas family would be too much. After all, Sarah and the reverend had just lost their dear mother and wife, Abigail.

Money and supplies were almost gone. Neither Sarah nor the reverend was quite sure where to go or what to do. They had gotten used to sleeping in the bed of the wagon every night. Sarah had figured out how to actually make it comfortable. However, Northern California was cold during the night. The reverend was not a young man. Something was going to have to give.

As their wagon pulled into town, both Sarah and the reverend were awestruck by the beauty. The fact that their long journey was over gave them both a sense of accomplishment. Things were tough though. Things were also very unpredictable. However, there was one glimmer of hope for Sarah. Hopefully, she would finally reunite with Ray Andrews.

Sarah held the reigns as the wagon made its way into town. A makeshift road had been dug out by the other travelers. The bay area landscape escorted all travelers the same direction. There were many people staking out the entrance to town, looking for possible customers or victims. The people who already lived in San Francisco knew about them. The people who were just arriving would learn later. One of the scouts that hung around the entrance to town was none other than Billy Lambert.

Lambert had learned that one of the best ways to find easy marks was to catch them entering town. After all, people needed to work. They didn't know where to look, so why not catch them as they arrived in town. Sores Aguilar and Cyrus Welch were putting more and more pressure on Lambert to find some prospective sailors. The Melba Lee would be sailing back to Hong Kong in just a few days.

Lambert didn't pay any attention to Sarah and the reverend until their wagon rolled right past him. That was when he spotted Sarah. He was a young man himself, and he appreciated the beauty of a young woman. He didn't get to see one very often. Even though Sarah had her hair up and under her hat, she couldn't escape Billy Lambert's eye. It was his lucky day, he thought. And he better seize the opportunity to get to know her.

Lambert started following the wagon. Finally, he decided to walk as fast as he could and get up ahead of it.

"Hey there," he said to Sarah. "Where are you folks going?"

Sarah pretended not to even notice him. The reverend was not interest- ed in talking either, but Billy wouldn't give up. He ran around to the other side of the wagon and tried to speak to the reverend.

"Sir," he said. "Can I help you find your way? I know the town well." It took Lambert a half a mile to get the reverend's attention. Finally, the wagon came to a stop. The reverend didn't know where he was going, and he did need help. After the experience with Oscar Sellers, he and Sa- rah were very leery of anyone. However, he knew he had to do what he had to do to find his way.

"I thought you would never stop," Lambert said as he caught his breath. "Where are you going?"

The reverend pulled out a piece of paper from his shirt pocket.

"There is an outreach center at 580th Capp Street," he answered. "It is close to Van Ness Avenue. Do you know where that is?"

Lambert was a little dumbfounded. He had never heard of an outreach center, but he answered anyway.

"Don't know about no outreach center, but I know Van Ness Avenue. Follow me. I'll take you there."

Lambert felt like he might have impressed the girl on the bench seat of the wagon.

The reverend nodded his head, and Billy took off, walking. He led them downtown. Every now and then, he would try to stop and talk, but the hills wore him out. He was huffing and puffing the entire way. Sarah was watching him closely. He was quite a good-looking young man. He was tall with long, black hair. He had a beard that hid his facial features. Sa- rah didn't like facial hair. She preferred clean-shaven men, but she did think Lambert was quite handsome.

After about an hour, Lambert came to a stop.

"This is it," he said. "Van Ness. What was that address?"

The reverend looked the town over. It was about what he had pictured. "It's 580th Capp Street," he answered.

Billy walked over to a saloon across the street.

"What is the address here," he asked.

The old codger who stood at the door answered, "This is the three hundred blocks."

Billy walked back to the wagon and gave them the news. "We have a way to go," he said.

Lambert turned southbound and started walking down Van Ness Avenue. After two more stops for directions, Lambert finally found Capp Street. Finally, the wagon made it to the destination. Rev. William Thom- as slowly got down off the bench of the wagon. The church was in terrible disrepair. The building was abandoned. There was no one to be found. The front door was lying out in the street. Both of the front windows had been smashed to pieces. There was nothing to mark the place as an outreach center or anything else. It was just a condemned property. Billy Lambert knew he was running late. Sores Aguilar and Cyrus Welch would not be happy if he arrived late at the Lonely Sailor. "I have to go," Lambert said to the reverend.

Then he walked over to Sarah and handed her a flyer from the Lonely Sailor.

"I will come back soon," he said. "Maybe I could buy you supper?"

She gave him a weak smile.

"Thank you for your help. It means a lot," she answered.

The reverend walked over to a business about thirty yards to the north. A blacksmith was working on a huge piece of iron. The reverend was very polite.

"Sir," he asked. "What is this address?"

The blacksmith pulled off his gloves and looked at the reverend. "This is 581th Capp Street," he answered.

The reverend knew they had found the right place. He smiled and greeted the blacksmith.

"My name is William Thomas. I understand that property is available," the reverend said.

The blacksmith looked at the reverend like he was crazy.

"That's where the bums sleep at night," he said. "I wouldn't give you two cents for the place. I wish they would tear it down.

The reverend William Thomas didn't flinch. He turned around and faced Sarah. She couldn't help but notice the big smile on his face. The reverend walked toward her. He looked up to the sky. Finally, he focused on Sarah.

"This is perfect for us," he said.

CHAPTER 36

Sores Aguilar continued to move forward with his business ventures.

To around quickly about his connection with the Vigilance Committee. It was a great insurance policy for him against the Aussies who wanted to bully and extort him. Once again, he had outsmarted them all.

The first run to Hong Kong had been very lucrative. It was a risky ad- venture, no doubt. But Sores had a different attitude about the second trip. He was much more conservative this time. The first trip was a gamble on house money. The windfall he had obtained from the payroll robbery in West Texas had financed the plan. This time, it was earned money that would be put up for risk.

Min Cho Fat was out of the picture this time, but Cyrus Welch and Suk Too were not. They were both eager for more. However, complacency had set in on the both of them, especially Suk Too. Cyrus Welch never stayed on land for very long. He was ready to get back out to sea. His crew was also ready. Cyrus only needed six more men than he had al- ready sewn up for the crew. Sores didn't want to pay for any more men. That would cut into the profits. He wanted to go a different route for la- bor. But Cyrus was the captain of the ship. It was he who would have to deal with these men out in the Pacific Ocean. Sores only had to put up the gold it took to buy the opium. Then he could run the Lonely Sailor and attend to his business. After that, he only had to wait on the Melba Lee to return to San Francisco. In

Cyrus Welch's mind, Sores had the easiest part of the arrangement.

Sores also had the power, and he handled it well. He had formed a bond with both Cyrus and Suk Too that would be very difficult to break. He realized that he had to obtain both their trust and their friendship. Not a day went by that he didn't work on both of them. He would buy them gifts. Cyrus's face was extremely weather-beaten from all the years on the sea. Sores bought him an expensive new hat that would shield him from the sun. He also gave him Tom Jenkins's gun and gun belt.

The gift of the gun was a strategic move. Sores wanted to make sure that Cyrus had the firepower he needed in case of a mutiny or some other problem on the trip. The two of them, Sores Aguilar and Cyrus Welch, had an odd relationship. There was a strong mutual respect for one another. However, they were as different as night and day. Sores was calculating, scheming, and always thinking ahead. Cyrus worked off the top of his head. He was extremely impulsive. Though he had been in many a fight, he had never had much to do with any firearm. Sores had to teach him how to use the Colt Navy revolver. Cyrus Welch, however, never paid much attention to Sores when he demonstrated how to load it. He figured if he ever got into a fix, he would just use his knife.

Suk Too was a different type of person altogether. He rarely spoke. When he did, he used rough, broken English to explain himself. He would use hand signals when he could. If that didn't work, it was up to whomever he was trying to communicate with to figure out what he was saying. Sores studied Suk Too closely. Every time he thought Suk Too might find a lady friend on his own, Sores would interrupt the relationship and take control. He knew of Suk Too's weakness for women. If he could control Suk Too's women, he could control Suk Too. He was doing a good job of it too. Suk Too was becoming very spoiled. Sores was beginning to worry how he would handle being away from San Francisco and the women for the two months it would take to make the trip.

Even with his concerns, Sores felt that he had a good handle on Cyrus and Suk Too. He wasn't near as confident about Billy Lambert. There had always been something about Lambert that worried Sores. Lambert was younger than him. He was also very smart. Sores noticed immediately how Lambert could manipulate Cyrus Welch. He both admired Lambert and feared him. Sores was still undecided on what Lambert's fate would be in the long run. He had prepared two different plans on how to deal with him.

A meeting was called at the Lonely Sailor by the boss, Sores Aguilar. It was time to get serious about the next trip to Hong Kong. Four men were present. They were Sores Aguilar, Cyrus Welch, Suk Too, and Billy Lambert. Sores ran everybody else out of the bar.

The meeting started with Sores making a quick observation.

"We need more opium," he said. "We can sell it in a heartbeat. The law doesn't even monitor it."

He looked at Cyrus Welch.

"When will you be ready to make the next trip?" he asked. "The Melba Lee be ready, mate," he answered. "Just need a few more men. Been wondering how ye want to handle that problem." Every one of the four men knew exactly what he was talking about. Sores wanted to use captured slave labor on the ship for sailors. He had two reasons. First, he didn't want to extend the payroll. That would cut into the profits. Paying sailors to make a trip like the one to Hong Kong was expensive. The second reason was even more important. Sores wanted as few people as possible to know about the opium. He had his reasons for that. If the law knew of the kind of money drug smugglers were making, it would lead to a lot of trouble. The law itself was also a concern. Even though they seemed not to care about the drugs now, there was no guarantee they wouldn't care later.

There was another concern for Sores. He did not want to take a chance on anyone from the Vigilance Committee finding out about what he was doing. Strangely enough, right now, he was a respected businessman in San Francisco. Nobody knew about his past, and he planned to keep it that way.

The meeting continued.

"How many days do you think it will take this time to make the trip?" Sores asked Cyrus.

Welch rubbed his chin and thought for a moment.

"Well, mate," he began. "I think we can make it over and back in forty to fifty days this time."

Sores liked what he heard. He looked at Suk Too.

"Are you ready for such a trip?" he asked.

Suk Too frowned as he ground his teeth. Finally, he shook his head. He was ready.

Billy Lambert was not ready. Sores finally turned to him.

There was no question in Sores Aguilar's mind about Lambert's role. He was going on the trip. That was just part of the deal.

"We still need some more men for the trip," he said. "It's your job to find them. That's what I'm paying you for."

Lambert looked down at the floor. He had thought about leaving town. He could do it. There were not enough men available to track him for Sores. It wasn't hard for Lambert to remember the nightmare of being kidnapped and turned into a slave. There was still tremendous bitterness. However, he loved San Francisco. It was his home now, and Sores was paying him extremely well. He had never had such a good job. Then there was the preacher's girl. What about her?

"Is there any way I can stay here and not make the trip?" Lambert asked.

All he received in return was a long, blank stare from Sores Aguilar. Finally, Lambert got a verbal answer.

"No," answered Sores. "You're going."

The two men locked eyes. Both saw hate in the other man.

CHAPTER 37

The San Francisco Post Office was down at what they called Union square. was right in middle of town. everywhere.

They knew businessmen often came there, and it was a good place to beg. Ray Andrews went there every day. Even though he had money in his pocket, he slept on the streets. The cold night air of the bay area made him so lonely he would cry. His two best friends, Tom Jenkins and Stuttering Henry Jones, were dead. Ray had inherited everything Henry owned, but that only made him suffer more.

Henry had been buried over on the west side of town. Ray found the proper place after a couple of days looking. There were other deceased people there, and it didn't cost anything to bury him there. Sawyer Crenshaw had immediately rejected any idea of carrying Henry's body back to Texas on the stagecoach. Ray couldn't blame him for that.

Ray dug the grave himself and put Henry to rest. Everyone on the trip attended the burial, even Ben Fields and Junior Hoskins. Lovie Kitchens cried through the whole event. Ray almost asked her to be quiet once, but he couldn't muster up the strength to do it.

The trip had taken a great toll on everyone. Sawyer Crenshaw asked Ray to go back to Texas with him and Willie Foster, but Ray declined. There was too much unfinished business in California.

Ray inherited ninety-two dollars from Henry, which included his pay from Crenshaw. He also inherited all of Henry's weapons. That included two Navy revolvers and two shotguns. Ray also obtained Henry's knives and his horse, Buster. The inheritance actually made Ray a wealthy man in town. He was wealthy only in material value though. On the inside, he was a broken man.

Ray sat on the post office steps one Saturday morning. The bums were driving him crazy. He was bored, and his patience was running thin. He was having trouble sleeping out in the open air. He sat down and leaned against the wall in front of the building. There he fell asleep. An hour later, someone shook his shoulder.

"Ray, wake up, wake up," a voice said to him.

He thought he was dreaming. A smile crossed his lips, and he fell back to sleep. But once again the voice woke him.

"Ray, wake up. It's me, Sarah!"

Suddenly, Ray shook his head and looked up. Sarah Thomas was crouched down and looking him straight in the face. The awkwardness of the situation startled him. He gathered his thoughts and made it to his feet.

Neither of them knew what to do next, so Ray did what he always did around ladies. He tipped his hat and smiled.

"How long have you been here?" Sarah asked him.

Ray was doing everything he could to wake up and clear the cobwebs out of his head.

"I dunno," he answered. "Maybe a couple of hours."

It didn't take but a few minutes for the conversation to start flowing. They talked like they had known each other for years. After a while, the talk got around to Stuttering Henry.

"Where is the man who did all the work on our wagon?" she asked.

For the past few weeks, all Ray had thought about was Henry. Meeting up with Sarah had gotten his mind off the nightmare for just a while. Sarah's question brought it all back.

"He's dead," answered Ray. "We lost him in a stupid knife fight. We were both just trying to break it up. The man who killed him didn't know he was just trying to help."

Sarah seemed a little shaken, but she continued to pry. "Where are all the rest of your friends?" she asked.

Ray looked around at the people at Union Square. Finally, he answered. "They're gone, I guess," he said. "Last time I saw any of 'em was at Stut's funeral. I know the stagecoach is already headed back to Texas." It dawned on Sarah that Ray had been waiting for her all by himself. He looked pitiful.

"Come on," she ordered him. "Come with me."

The two of them walked the five miles to 580th Capp Street. They talked all the way like two long-lost friends. When they arrived, the reverend was waiting. He had been there all day, surveying the property.

The reverend was really glad to see Ray, and he showed it. He walked straight to him and gave him a bear hug. Sarah hadn't even got to hug Ray yet. She had been too shy. The reverend didn't just give Ray a token hug. He hugged on him like family. It made Ray feel really good, so he hugged the reverend back.

"What are you doing here?" Ray asked him. "Where are we?" The Reverend smiled.

"We are trying to figure that out ourselves," he answered.

"You see, Ray, this is the address I was told to find from the people of our church back in Mississippi. Crazy, isn't it? It's just an abandoned building. The bums sleep here at night. Sarah and I have enough money to stay at the boarding house around the corner for a few more nights. We would like to move in here. I went down to the courthouse yesterday. I can purchase the deed for $600. Don't have that kind of money. I'm just trying to figure this out."

Ray looked at the building and started getting really interested. He kicked around inside for a few minutes. Sarah and the reverend just watched him. After examining the entire place, he walked back to them. A big smile crossed his lips and he spoke.

"I think I can help you with that," he said.

"What do you mean?" Sarah asked.

Ray continued to walk around and survey the property. "Well," he answered. "I have this piece of jewelry. I need to get it appraised and sold. I don't want to keep it. I think it is worth between $400 and $700."

Both Sarah and the reverend were stunned.

"We can't let you do that," blurted out the reverend. "That's your money, not ours."

Ray looked at both of them. He wondered if it would be worth the effort to explain the story about the brooch. He certainly didn't want to relive it again. Finally, though, he decided they needed to hear the truth.

It took him almost an hour to tell the whole sordid tale about the card game and John McLemore's pitiful situation. He told them the story about the saloon incident in Los Angeles. Finally, he got to the knife fight at the Delany's Jewelry where Henry was killed.

It was hard to reenact everything, but he did a great job. Sarah and the reverend watched and listened to Ray. It was painful, but it did give Ray a sense of closure.

"I want the money from that brooch to do something positive. It's brought a run of bad luck to everyone who's had much to do with it. I want to sell it and get that deed for you, Reverend. That would make me feel good for Mrs. McLemore and Henry. I believe in you, and this town needs a place like this."

Both Sarah and the reverend were awestruck. Neither knew what to say, but the opportunity to obtain the deed and start the mission brought both of them a euphoric feeling. The reverend had to ask Ray about the whole plan again to ease his anxiety.

"Now, Ray," he started. "Are you sure about this? We are not here to make any profits. We just want to have a house for God. I heard about the debauchery all the way back in Mississippi. I felt the Lord telling me to come here. I just want to make sure you won't have any regrets."

Ray shook his head and looked out at the hills and the breathtaking view of San Francisco.

"Well, Reverend," he said. "I was gonna ask you for one small thing." Reverend Thomas was quick to reply, "Anything, Ray, what do you want?"

"Well," answered Ray, "I was hoping you would let me sleep on the floor for a few nights."

Reverend Thomas couldn't help but to burst out in laughter. "Of course you can sleep on the floor," he almost yelled.

It was time for Sarah to join in on the conversation.

"Well, let's get to work," she said. Her joy and enthusiasm made both Ray and the reverend feel really good. For the first time in months, she felt a sense of confidence and home. The conversation flowed from the three of them. But then suddenly, a voice rang out from a man walking down the street toward them.

"How are you folks doing today?"

The voice came from the man they had met a couple days earlier. It was the voice of Billy Lambert.

Lambert's presence put a damper on the enthusiasm. It was obvious to the reverend that he was smitten with Sarah. Ray had already met Lambert when the stagecoach rolled into town. There was only one entrance into the south side of the city. Lambert scouted it daily to find potential sailors. He had immediately noticed Ray.

"I remember you," Lambert said to Ray. "I've been waiting for you to come talk about a job."

Ray was in a great mood, but he was savvy enough to sense that he had a little competition for Sarah's affections. However, he didn't show it. "I've been busy getting settled," Ray told him with confidence. "Pretty soon I'll be ready to talk to you about it."

Lambert was insistent.

"We're filling up fast," he said. "You need to get on down there and hear all about it. It's a fine opportunity, and you would be a great prospect."

Sarah didn't trust Billy Lambert. He was just a little too slick for her. However, she was willing to reserve judgment for a while. After all, he did seem like a nice fellow, and Ray was gonna need a job. Lambert turned to her and tried to gain her attention.

"Have you had any luck on settling?" he asked her.

Sarah didn't want to share the day's news with him. She was happy with just spending time with Ray and her father. Lambert's mere presence was making things crowded.

"We're still trying to figure it all out," she answered politely.

Lambert could tell that he was an outsider. He had walked all the way down to Capp Street to see Sarah. He hadn't been interested in Ray or the old man. However, Billy Lambert was competitive. There were very few women in San Francisco. The town sure didn't have many women like Sarah Thomas. Lambert's jealous side was beginning to show.

"I was going to see if you were interested in me taking you to supper," Lambert said to Sarah.

It was obvious he wanted Ray to go on the defensive. Either that or maybe Ray would just go away. However, Sarah was not about to let anything get in between her and Ray Andrews, especially on this night.

"Thank you so much," she answered. "But I can't. My father and I have Kother plans tonight."

The words blistered Billy Lambert. He was no dummy. He knew he wasn't welcome. He also knew it was because of Ray Andrews.

"Well, maybe another time," he answered politely to Sarah. Lambert turned and focused on Ray.

"I would really like to see you come down and check out this opportunity. You are the kind of man we need."

Lambert dug into his pocket and pulled out a flyer. But Ray already had one.

"Are you still meeting on Wednesday and Thursday nights at eight o'clock?" Ray asked.

Lambert seemed impressed. "Why, yes," he answered. "Do you still have the paper I gave you?"

Ray pulled the flyer out of his own back pocket and gently waved it.

Billy Lambert walked over to Ray and offered his hand. "Name's Lambert, Billy Lambert," he said.

"Ray Andrews is my name. Glad to meet you."

The two men shook hands. Lambert continued to sell Ray on coming to check on the job.

"I will tell my boss to be looking for you, Ray Andrews," he said.

Lambert quickly refocused on Sarah and the reverend. He made sure they knew his name. He did not offer them a flyer this time like he did the first time they met. He knew one thing for sure. If he was to have a chance to gain Sarah's affections, the last thing he wanted was for her to find out about what was going on at the Lonely Sailor.

CHAPTER 38

The following morning, a Wednesday, Ray Andrews awoke from his hotel room fresh and ready to go. He had decided to celebrate his good fortune of meeting up with Sarah Thomas by getting himself a room. Usually, he simply found a street corner and built himself a bed. Hopefully, tonight, he would sleep on the floor of the mission on Capp Street.

Ray was so excited about the future. This morning, he would go to the boarding house where Sarah and her father, the reverend, were staying. He would buy the two of them breakfast. Then he and Sarah would go about their business of trying to sell the brooch.

Everything was going according to plan. At breakfast, the reverend once again quizzed Ray if he wanted to use the money made from the sale of the brooch to finance the mission. Of course, Ray had already made up his mind to do so.

After Ray assured the reverend of his intentions, it was time to change the subject.

"Reverend," Ray asked. "If you don't mind me asking, what are you gonna call the place?"

The reverend was trying to wipe the scrambled eggs he had just spilled off of his pants. He looked at Sarah, and then he turned to Ray.

"I would like to call it Grace Methodist Mission Church of San Francisco."

Ray was impressed, but he still wondered about the name. "Why do you want to call it Grace Mission Church?" he asked. The reverend was impressed with Ray's interest.

"Well, Ray," he answered. "I just think we are all here because of the grace of God. I think that grace is fitting."

That was a good enough answer for Ray. He had just never understood what grace meant.

Ray asked the reverend if he wanted to go with them to sell the brooch, but he wasn't interested.

"No, if you don't mind, I thought I would go back to the mission. I want to spend my time there."

Ray nodded to the reverend and got up to pay the bill. As he walked to the counter, a sense of family came over him, and it made him feel a little uneasy. He wasn't really sure how to handle it.

Sarah and Ray started walking northeast. The reverend went back west to the mission. On the way to the first store, Sarah told Ray the story about Oscar Sellers in Los Angeles. Ray was impressed with her courage and physical strength. Sarah reached into her pocket and pulled out the knife she had picked up off the ground.

"I guess I stole this knife from him," she said. "I hope the Lord forgives me, but I thought it was warranted."

She tried to open it, but she was unsuccessful. She pulled on it. Then she pressed on it, but she couldn't open it. Ray gently laughed at her but not in a disrespectful way.

"Here," he said. "Let me see it."

He took the knife and popped it open. He had seen a similar knife before. All it took was to simply raise a side blade with his fingertip, and the blade opened immediately. Sarah was impressed.

"How did you do that?" she asked.

Ray explained, and then he demonstrated it for her. The young couple walked three more blocks. Sarah practiced opening and closing the knife all the way.

Ray had decided that, if possible, he wanted to do business with Georgia Tipps at the Gold and Silver. He felt good about her, but her price was a little low. However, she only wanted to buy the brooch as a piece of jewelry. She didn't want to break it down. He was willing to throw his own money into the mission if need be. That was how much it meant to him. But first, he felt that he needed to hit at least three more exchange stores.

Gold was actually plentiful in San Francisco. Miners brought it in from the hills every day. It was just that not very many individuals had a lot of it. Storing gold or silver was difficult in the city because of all the Aussies. They would steal anyone blind if the opportunity presented itself. Pawn- shops and gold and silver traders quickly sold any of the metals they bought to other merchants. It was too dangerous to keep much on hand. That was just how the business of gold and silver exchange was done. The going rate of exchange was 1 percent of the price of the metals. Down in Southern California, word was that a miner could get 2 percent, but he would have to travel to get it. It wasn't worth the trip.

The first exchange shop today was an old-fashioned general store. There was only a small sign above the front door. It read Gold Exchange. Ray liked the looks of the place. It was clean and seemed relatively safe. He started to walk in the door when Sarah gently grabbed his arm.

"I know you're from Texas," she said. "But you need to learn a few things about women."

Ray had no idea what she was talking about. Sarah smiled at his naïve nature. The challenge of taming this rough character had a tremendous appeal to her.

"I don't know what you mean," Ray responded.

Sarah walked up in front of him. "You need to let me go first," she said. "And hold the door open for me."

Of course, Ray did exactly as she said. As he grabbed the door, it was obvious he was a little embarrassed. Sarah walked in and Ray followed her. Ray walked right up to the clerk and started the conversation. After all, he had a little experience now. He also wanted Sarah to think he knew what he was doing.

Ray stuck out his hand as he addressed the clerk behind the counter. "My name's Ray Andrews," he said. "How are you doing today?" The clerk did not offer his hand to Ray. He seemed a little put off. Ray pressed on.

"I have this brooch I would like to sell."

The clerk smoothed his handlebar mustache on both sides. His bald head reminded Ray of a cue ball. After the clerk fixed his mustache, he tightened his bowtie. Finally, he responded.

"I don't buy jewelry," he said. "I only buy gold or silver."

That wasn't what Ray wanted to hear, but he kept the conversation going anyway.

"Would you mind at least taking a look at it?" he asked.

The clerk nodded his head, so Ray pulled the brooch out of his pocket. The clerk pulled out his funny little one-eyed goggles. He peered in at the brooch. Nothing was said for a couple of minutes.

Finally, the clerk spoke, "This is a fine piece of jewelry. I would say the diamond is worth about $150. The gold is probably worth about twenty- five. I'll give you $175."

Ray Andrews wasn't a brilliant man, but he wasn't a fool either. He had already been around the block a time or two in dealing with this brooch.

"I thought you said you didn't buy jewelry," he shot back.

"I'll make an exception here," the clerk said as he looked up at Ray. "My anniversary is coming up. This would be a good present for my wife." Ray looked at Sarah, and then he turned back to the clerk.

"You will have to break it down and measure it first, right?" he asked. The clerk realized that he couldn't fool Ray.

"That's what I will give you for the jewelry," he said.

"Usually, I don't buy this kind of stuff, but I would like to have this piece."

Ray reached onto the counter and picked up the brooch. "Think I'll keep looking around," he answered.

He turned and walked back to the front entrance. He opened the door for Sarah to leave the store. As they walked out, the clerk hollered, "I'll go to $200!" Sarah kept walking. Ray watched her walk out the door. He made sure he stayed behind her.

The awkwardness of Ray Andrews trying to be a gentleman amused Sa- rah. Ray was a good ten yards behind her.

"Get on up here with me, just don't walk out in front," she teased him. "Okay, okay," he replied.

Sarah's competitive energy was running fast.

"That was fun," she said. "Where are we going next?"

Ray was thoroughly enjoying himself, but he realized that he had made a commitment to coming up with $600. He had to get a good deal on the brooch.

After walking another four blocks, Ray spotted a store that had a sign on the front advertising gold and silver exchange. As they got closer, Ray and Sarah noticed a sign on the front that said Horacio's Metals and Jewelry. The building was old, but it seemed reputable. Ray opened the door, and Sarah walked in. There was an old man behind the counter. He was wearing a suit and tie. His hair was combed, and he looked as if he had just bathed. He was probably around sixty years old.

"Hello, friends, I'm Horatio," he said in a high-pitched voice. "Welcome to my store. What can I do for you today?"

Sarah was impressed with his friendly personality, but she said nothing. Ray pulled the brooch out of his pocket.

"I would like your opinion on this piece of jewelry," he told Horatio. "Of course, of course," Horatio replied. "Let me take a look."

Once again, he pulled out one of those one-eyed goggles and started examining the brooch.

"Oh, very nice," he fawned over the piece of jewelry. "I really like it. Where did you get such a piece?"

Ray wasn't in the mood to tell the story again. He just stood there in silence. Finally, he spoke, "It's just something I inherited."

Horatio was already interested in talking business.

"I'll give you $350," he said.

The news took Ray and Sarah a little by surprise.

"Do you want to break the piece down to appraise the gold and silver?" Ray asked.

"No, I like it just as it is," Horatio replied. "I would like to have it."

"Five hundred," Ray answered. "Five hundred, and it's yours." Horatio started looking at the brooch through the one-eyed goggles again.

"I might be able to go to $400," he responded. "I don't think I can go any higher than that."

Ray knew that if he could get $500 for the brooch, he could add his own money and have the $600 needed for the deed to the mission.

"I have to get $500," he answered.

Horatio seemed like he knew what he was doing. He studied Ray closely.

"I would really like to have it, but right now I can go to $375. I'm afraid that's all I can do."

Ray frowned and picked the brooch up off the counter. However, Horatio wasn't finished.

"I'm interested in where you obtained this piece of jewelry. Can you tell me more about that?"

Ray just was not in the mood to tell the story about the brooch again. He was already getting tired of the process.

"I'll tell you what, Horatio," he said. "I'm gonna go to a couple of more places. If you are close to the price of the best offer, I might come back and sell it to you. Is that a deal?"

Horatio looked at Ray.

"I can't make you any promises, sir. My business is run from deal to deal. I invite you back anytime, but I can't make any standing offer. I think the brooch is worth $375. That's a fair offer. I would like to hear a little more history on how you acquired the piece. That might make a difference to me."

Ray was confused, but his mind was racing. It was time to regroup and think a little.

"Why is it so important to you to hear about how I acquired this jewelry?" he asked.

Suddenly, Horatio became tired of the negotiation. His tone turned to being a little course.

"My offer is $375. I can pay you cash money right now."

Ray tipped his hat to Horatio and led Sarah back toward the door. On the way out, he mumbled under his breath. Sarah asked him what he said.

"Why is he so interested in where I got the brooch?" he asked her.

The two of them walked across the street to a general store. There was a bench there for them to sit down and reevaluate the situation. It had dawned on Ray that some of the buyers only wanted to buy the brooch as a piece of jewelry. They weren't interested so much in the metals. He couldn't make sense of it.

"There's something we're missing," he stated to Sarah.

She was enjoying the process. Spending time with her new boyfriend in a beautiful place like San Francisco had captured the main focus of her attention. For sure, she had never experienced the negotiation of a particular item like that. The whole experience to her was surreal.

She realized that Ray was confused, and she wanted to help him. Suddenly, she snapped out of being infatuated with her new life and focused on the situation.

"Can I see the brooch?" she asked Ray.

He pulled it out of his pocket and handed it to her.

"Be careful with it," he said. "It's bad luck."

Sarah looked it over closely. It was about the size of a clenched fist.

There was some kind of rough-designed metal that formed a beautiful base. In the middle of the metal sat an oval-shaped piece of ivory carved with the face of a woman wearing a diamond earring. The oval-shaped piece of ivory was framed in gold. The question was how valuable was the diamond and how valuable was the gold.

Suddenly, Sarah sat up straight and pushed the brooch right up to her eye. That caught Ray's attention. He leaned over and looked closely at the brooch himself.

"What is it?" he asked.

Sarah moved the brooch close to his face so he could see it better.

"Look right here." She showed him.

Sarah was holding the brooch with her left hand. She took her right fin- ger and pointed to the side of the ivory. There was a very small slit that was open between the ivory and the metal base. The gold frame stopped and started around the slit. It was necessary to look really close to see it. "That little opening doesn't look right," Sarah said as she continued to examine the brooch. "What do you think?"

Ray's eyesight made it difficult to make a distinction. He leaned back on the bench and rubbed his eyes with his hands.

"I don't know," he said. "But I know where to find out."

CHAPTER 39

*R*ay was a little impatient as he walked with Sarah back down to the Gold and Silver on Market Street. After all, he was supposed to walk behind Sarah. Even though she could walk fast, she couldn't walk as fast as him. His mind was racing. He wanted to talk to Georgia Tipps. After dealing with the traders of San Francisco, he had decided with whom he wanted to do business.

Ray and Sarah turned the corner and saw the store.

"Okay," he said to Sarah. "I like the lady trader in here. I am gonna ask her for $500. If she wants to buy it for that, we sell it. But if she won't buy it, we ask her to break it down and measure the gold and silver." Sarah was confused, but she was careful.

"Are you sure this is the best way to go?" she asked him.

Ray thought just for a second, and then he responded, "That's my best judgment. It's a gamble. If we break the brooch apart, I doubt if we can put it back together again. We might not get anything for it. On the other hand, I wonder if the gold and silver isn't more valuable than we think." Sarah had a perplexed look on her face. She looked at the sign, which read Gold and Silver, and then she looked at Ray.

"Okay," she responded. "Let's go."

They walked across the street and into the store. Georgia was talking to another customer over in the corner. Sarah was stunned to see such a beautiful woman in San Francisco. Georgia immediately recognized Ray. She slowly separated herself from the customer and walked toward him. "Well, hello, Ray," she said. "Glad to see you again."

Sarah couldn't help but to be a little jealous. She had on no makeup, and her hair was tucked up under her hat. In this state of appearance, she was no match for Georgia Tipps.

But Georgia was a savvy businesswoman. She knew immediately that if Ray brought this girl with him, she was special. Georgia was at least ten years older than Ray. Even though she was very attracted to him, she realized that she had better stick to business. After all, she had been thinking about what a mistake it was to let that brooch get out of her store. She turned to Sarah and held out her hand, "Georgia Tipps," she introduced herself.

"You hit the jackpot with this fellow here, didn't you?"

Sarah was very intimidated. She couldn't speak, so Georgia kept the conversation going for her.

"What's your name darling?" she asked.

Sarah finally answered, "I'm sorry, ma'am. My name is Sarah Thomas." Georgia knew that if she was going to get the brooch, she needed to win over Sarah, so she kept her at the center of attention. "It is so nice to meet you. I have some tea brewing in the back. Would you like some? I don't get to talk to ladies very often. This is quite a treat."

Georgia's hospitality and charm won Sarah over quickly. "Do you think that would be okay, Ray?" Sarah asked.

Ray looked at Georgia. Georgia winked back at him.

"Sure," he said. "We're not in a hurry."

Georgia took Sarah by the hand and escorted her behind the counter and into a backroom. They stayed back there for about ten minutes. When they emerged, Sarah was sipping from a hot, smoking cup. The two of them were talking like sisters.

Ray had been looking around inside the store. There were all kinds of goods. It was mostly jewelry and fine linens, stuff that women were interested in buying. Over in the corner though, a very huge man peered at Ray. He was obviously some kind of a guard.

Georgia walked back around the counter.

"So, Ray, do you still have that brooch?" she asked him. "Yes, ma'am," he answered. "I still have it." Georgia couldn't help but show her enthusiasm.

"Well, bring it over here. I want to see it again."

Ray looked at Sarah. Slowly, he moved to the counter. He pulled the brooch out and handed it to Georgia. She already had her one-eyed goggles in her hand, and she immediately started inspecting it.

"So where are we right now?" Georgia asked him.

Ray felt comfortable, but he didn't want to move too fast. He couldn't help but to look at Georgia's beautiful figure. He had already fallen in love with Sarah, but Georgia was a striking woman. It was only natural to watch her. Finally, he gathered his thoughts and spoke.

"Georgia," he said. "I'm gonna just shoot you straight, okay?"

The sentence was part statement and part question. Georgia smiled. She knew she had him just where she wanted him. Ray continued.

"I need $500 for this brooch. I don't know if we should break down the metals or keep it as a piece of jewelry. What do you think?"

Georgia bit her lower lip with her teeth. It was something she always did when she got down to business.

"Can't go that high, Ray," she said. "I just can't go that high." Georgia and Ray stared at each other.

Sarah was watching closely. She walked up to the counter. There was a stalemate going on in the negotiation. Sarah reached into her pocket and pulled out the knife that she took from Oscar Sellers. With the knife in her right hand, she clipped the switch and the blade opened. She took a quick look at both Ray and Georgia. She reached down to the counter and pulled the brooch toward her. She took the knife and placed the tip of the blade into the little slit on the side of the ivory. With one little turn of the knife, the ivory popped open. There was a huge diamond inside the brooch. All three of them stared at it in disbelief.

It took almost an hour for Georgia to weigh and measure the gold. There were two diamonds to appraise too. Georgia got down to business. "Ray," she said. "There is no reason to mess around. I will give you $1,500 for the brooch and the diamond."

Ray looked into her eyes.

"Is that a fair deal?" he asked her.

Georgia was as serious as she had ever been in her life. "It's a very good deal. We can both make some money.

Dealing with diamonds is a professional job. We need to get that diamond out of here right now. I don't want it in the shop. Let's close this deal now."

Ray made the deal. Georgia went into the back room and opened her safe. She came back with $1,500. If Georgia Tipps would have taken the deal Ray had offered for $500, she would have made the deal of her life. But it was not to be. However, she still made a healthy profit. She couldn't help but to give Ray a big hug and a kiss on the lips before she closed the doors. She turned to Sarah.

"You take care of my man now you hear."

Georgia Tipps smiled. She couldn't help but to grab Sarah and give her a hug too.

"Now, listen you two," she said before leaving. "If you find anything else to sell, you know where I am."

With that, she and her guard took off down the street.

It was now late in the afternoon on a Wednesday. There was no time for the reverend to go to the courthouse to obtain the deed today. That would have to be done tomorrow. Tonight, they would celebrate. Ray took Sarah and the reverend to dinner. He wanted a beer, but he was scared of the reverend. It was Sarah who ordered one for him.

Ray kept the money on his body. There would be no funny business until the deal with the city was done. The next morning, the three of them made their way down to the courthouse. Ray paid the city $600 in cash himself. The clerk asked what would be the name to put on the paper. Ray turned to the reverend.

"I will let you take it from here," he said.

Rev. William Thomas walked to the counter. He had tears in his eyes. "I would like it to say Grace Methodist Mission Church of San Francis- co," he told the clerk.

The reverend turned back to look at Ray and Sarah. It was quite an emotional moment for all of them.

After the paperwork was finished, the three of them started walking back to the mission. First, however, Ray wanted to stop at a bank. He had never been in one before, but he figured it was time. Inside the bank, he told the teller to open an account for Grace Methodist Church of San Francisco. After establishing the account, he deposited $500.

Sarah, the reverend, and Ray went by the hotel and the boardinghouse to collect their personal items. From there, it was on to the mission. When they arrived, Ray noticed that the place looked a lot different. The front door was back in place. The floors had been swept, and the mission actually looked clean. The reverend had done a very good job.

Ray found a corner in the back of the building to establish his bed for the night. He secured two gunny sacks in a closet. One of the sacks was his and the other had belonged to Stuttering Henry Jones. Inside the sacks was a strong collection of weapons. It was an arsenal that could outfit a small army.

Ray walked around the corner. From there, he watched Sarah and the reverend. They were obviously enamored with their new home. Ray didn't want to interrupt them, but it was five thirty on Thursday evening. He was in a hurry and had things to do.

"I'll be back later," Ray said softly.

He wasn't quite comfortable with his new domestic surroundings. Sa- rah walked over to him.

"Where are you going?" she asked.

Ray wasn't hesitant in his response.

"Well," he said. "I guess it's time for me to find a job. I think I will go down and see what that Lambert fella has to offer." Sarah smiled at him. The reverend walked over and joined the conversation.

"Ray," he said. "I just can't thank you enough."

He couldn't help himself. He had to give Ray a bear hug. Ray walked out the front door and started heading down the street. He had never been happier. Things had come together after all. It was just too good to be true. Suddenly, he heard Sarah call after him.

"Ray wait!" she yelled.

He turned around, and she came running up to him. It was then that Sa- rah Thomas did something that she had never done before. Instinctively, she grabbed Ray and awkwardly kissed him right on the lips. With the exception of her father, it was the first time in her life that she had ever kissed a man. It was a very clumsy kiss. It took her a second to find Ray's lips. Finally, she got the job done. Awkwardly, Ray hugged her and kissed her back. It was quite an odd sight in the middle of Capp Street.

The two of them finally left each other's clutches. Ray backpedaled down the street as he looked at Sarah. Finally, he turned and walked away.

"I need to get a job." He laughed. "I need to make something out of myself."

Sarah watched him walk away.

"Be careful!" she screamed at him.

Ray had a feeling of invincibility. He looked back at her. "Don't worry about me," he answered. "Nothing can hurt me tonight!"

Part III

CHAPTER 40

*R*ay Andrews couldn't ask for a more beautiful view on his walk from Capp Street to the corner of Montgomery and Filbert. It was a picturesque day in San Francisco. He was fortunate to enjoy one of the sunniest days of the year. There was a slight wind, but there was no fog.

He headed straight north up Van Ness before veering right onto Market Street. That led him to the northeast. Market Street was the busiest street in town. All types of buildings lined the street. The dirt road had been packed down so tight that it all but repelled rain. Rumor was that the city was about to pave the road. It was badly needed.

Eventually, Ray made his way to Montgomery Street and headed north. Billy Lambert's directions were very precise. It was not possible to get lost if they were followed.

Ray had never ventured up Montgomery Street. He had heard about it though. Saloons of all types littered the road. Montgomery Street was not as well kept by the city as Market Street. The smell of stale alcohol and trash dominated the atmosphere. Bums were everywhere. Ray hated bums. He had learned to walk right past them. However, that didn't stop them from begging.

Ray had heard about the opium dens on Montgomery Street. They were lined up in the 600th block. Most of the shacks were about to collapse. Asian people seemed to dominate the block. Ray didn't think much of it.

Chinatown was only a couple of blocks away.

As Ray came up on the 500th block of Montgomery Street, he saw a different type of house. That was where the women of pleasure lived. Ray remembered they were called whorehouses in Texas. There just seemed to be a lot more of them here in San Francisco.

Different kinds of businesses lined the street. All of them were involved in vice. Barkers were out in front, trying to lure patrons inside their establishments. Sometimes the barkers bothered people more than the bums. Ray stopped at the 300 block and looked at his flyer. He was only two blocks away from the Lonely Sailor. He looked around the street. Every- one seemed to be having a great time, so he took a few minutes to think about all that had happened to him in the past few months.

He had experienced winning the Colt Navy revolver shooting contest. He had lived through the robbery of the payroll wagon on Rosary Hill. The result was the death of five men, including his best friend, Tom Jen- kins. It also caused his exit from the Rangers.

He had been rescued by another Ranger, Stuttering Henry Jones. He had become a guard for a stagecoach and met all the characters on the trip. He and Henry had conquered both Indians and outlaws on the way. He had met a girl, Sarah Thomas, that he knew he loved.

The experience with the brooch had been both excruciating with the loss of Henry but exciting with the finding that it was so much more valuable than he thought. It had all gone by so fast. His life was so different now. It was time to find a job. He was trying to figure out how to ask Sa- rah if she wanted to get married. There was no way he was going to ask her until he had a steady job.

Ray started walking down Montgomery Street to the 100 block. It only took a few minutes until he saw the two-story building at the corner. He stood on the other side of the street and studied the Lonely Sailor. There wasn't much business there tonight. People were walking up and down the street, exploring the city. It was probably a little early for the serious drinking to start.

Ray didn't have a watch, but he knew it was about ten or fifteen minutes 'til eight o'clock. He decided to go on into the bar. He looked up on the top floor and saw the sign that read Enter Here. He walked up the stairs and entered the saloon.

As he suspected, there were only ten men in the building. There were a few women there. He looked over at the bar. There he saw Billy Lambert who was working as the bartender. Ray's lack of a mean demeanor had been a problem for him in the past. Even though he viewed Lambert as a threat for the affections of Sarah, he didn't dislike him personally.

Ray walked up to the bar. Lambert didn't notice that it was Ray until he looked him straight in the face. When he did notice him, it was obvious that he was glad to see him.

"Well, hello," Lambert said to Ray. "Thanks for coming!"

Lambert started shuffling glasses and bottles. He walked around the bar and shook hands with Ray.

"Come on over here to a table and sit down. Let me get you a beer," Lambert said with enthusiasm.

Ray sat down at a table and relaxed. He surveyed the room. There was a card game going on in the corner. There were two miners standing at the bar. Four older men were sitting at a table, arguing about something. Lambert came walking back over to Ray, holding a large mug of beer.

"Here," he said to Ray. "Enjoy this beer while I run these people out of the bar. The boss is down below. I'll tell him you're here. It'll only take a few minutes for me to get things ready to talk."

Lambert quietly went to the two tables and informed the men they would have to leave.

"Please finish your drinks," he said politely. "Then we are closing for the night."

He said the same thing to the miners at the bar and the old men at the other table. The women had already disappeared.

Lambert left through a door behind the bar. He was only gone for about five minutes. In the meantime, Ray was drinking the beer that Lambert gave him. He was really enjoying it. Finally, he was beginning to relax a little bit.

Suddenly, the door behind the bar opened, and Lambert reappeared. Once again, he urged the patrons to leave the bar. He was very patient with them. As the last one of the customers walked out the door, another man walked in. He wore a fine hat. His vest had some kind of shiny metal beads on it, and he wore a big knife on his belt. He walked right over to Ray and offered his hand.

"Name's Cyrus Welch, mate," he said to Ray. "Glad to meet ya!"

Ray tried to stand up to shake hands, but he lost his balance. He dropped his beer on the floor because he had to use both hands to catch his fall.

Ray was embarrassed.

"I'm sorry!" he said.

Billy Lambert ran over with a towel.

"No problem," he said. "I'll get you another one."

Cyrus Welch liked what he saw.

"Sit down, mate," he told Ray. "Tell me 'bout yourself." Lambert was right back at the table with large beers for both Ray and Cyrus. They were cold too. Ray had never tasted better beer.

"I-I-I'm from Tex-x-x-as," Ray said to Cyrus Welch.

"Well then, mate," Welch replied. "Let's drink to Texas!"

Cyrus held his own beer up to toast with Ray. Ray responded and took a big gulp.

Ray couldn't get his eyes to focus. He leaned back in his chair and al- most fell over. Cyrus Welch peered over the table.

"Keep talking, mate," he said. "I want to hear all about you." Ray continued.

"I was a Ranger-r," he said with a slur.

Cyrus was very interested.

"A Ranger," he answered. "Me heard of the Rangers."

Ray's head was spinning. Billy Lambert was now behind the bar. "Come on over here," Lambert urged Cyrus and Ray. "I have the map." Cyrus got up and helped Ray get out of the chair. The two of them walked to the bar. Cyrus took Ray's arm and guided him to a spot, standing directly across the bar from Billy Lambert. Lambert took the beer he was drinking and held it up to Ray for a toast.

"Thanks for coming," Lambert exclaimed.

All three of the men took big drinks from the mugs. Suddenly, the door behind the bar opened, and another man entered the room. This time, though, neither Billy Lambert nor Cyrus Welch said anything to him. He had long, black hair and dark skin. His clothes were all black.

"Ray," Lambert said.

Ray looked back at Billy Lambert, but he couldn't focus his eyes. He was about to pass out. The man dressed in black walked behind the bar and stood beside Billy Lambert. Ray tried to focus on him, but it was a struggle. Then Ray noticed something very odd. It shocked him, and he gathered his focus. The man with the long hair and dark skin that was dressed in all black had a red feather woven into his hair just below the jawline. Ray looked closer. "Empty Heart!" he mumbled.

Once again, Ray lost his focus. Everything seemed to be moving slowly. Billy Lambert proposed a toast.

"To business!" he proclaimed loudly.

Ray didn't know that he was standing on top of a trapdoor. He was so drunk from the opium-spiked beer that he was almost unconscious. Sores Aguilar pulled a lever, and the trapdoor opened. Ray Andrews fell twelve feet and crashed on the first floor.

It got worse. Suk Too was waiting for Ray. He stabbed him under the rib cage with a dull knife called a Slung Shot. Then Suk Too picked Ray up by the shirt collar with his left hand. He leaned him back and then pulverized him with a punch from his right hand.

Ray Andrews lay flat on his back on the bottom floor of the Lonely Sail- or Saloon on Montgomery Street. He was now completely unconscious and injured. By this time tomorrow, he would be on a ship in the Pacific Ocean called the Melba Lee. He was headed for Hong Kong.

CHAPTER 41

"Wake up," said a voice. "Wake up, man," the voice said again.

"Ray Andrews slowly opened his eyes. He had a splitting head ache. His right knee was throbbing in pain, and his left side was aching. "Wake up," the voice sounded even louder this time.

It took all the energy Ray could muster to raise his head and face the man who was trying to get his attention. He tried hard, but the headache he was dealing with made it next to impossible to focus. Finally, the man trying to get Ray's attention lost his patience.

"I thought you were dead," the man said. "I'm glad you finally woke up."

As Ray pulled himself up into a sitting position, he noticed the shackle that was chained to his left wrist. He looked at it in disbelief. The talkative man sitting next to him kept on jabbering away.

"Can you believe this?" he asked.

Ray didn't know what to say. He was still in shock. He looked around the rest of the room. There were seven other men chained to the walls just like him. Three of the men were awake, and four of the men were asleep. All seven of them had one hand chained to the wall. They were in the car- go deck of a clipper ship. The smell of oats and tea leaves was over- whelming.

"Name's Wilbur Hill," the man next to Ray said. "What's your name?"

Ray leaned back against the wall still trying to compose himself. "Ray Andrews is my name," he answered.

Wilbur Hill kept talking. "I can't believe I was so stupid!" He all but screamed.

Ray did a double take. He looked at Wilbur Hill and asked him a question, "What did just happen?"

Hill bellowed back at Ray, "We all got kidnapped!"

Ray reached down and rubbed his right knee. It was swollen, and its really hurt. He had no idea how he had injured it. The shackle on his left wrist had a long chain connected to it. There was a wooden toilet in the middle of the room. Ray slowly made his way to his feet. The chain al- lowed him to make it to the toilet, but he didn't need to use it. He only wanted to stand up for a while. All of a sudden, the ship rocked, and Ray fell back down on the floor. He landed right on top of Wilbur Hill. Hill shoved him away.

"We're not that good of friends yet," he barked at Ray. "Get off of me." Ray took a deep breath. Suddenly, the memory of seeing who he thought was Empty Heart crossed his mind. Could it be? he wondered. His next thought was of falling through the trapdoor. His mind was racing now. Even though his head was pounding, he was trying to get a grip on his bearings. Where was he and what was he going to do? Those were the questions he wondered. The answers were that he was on a ship in the Pacific Ocean, and he couldn't do a thing about it. He was chained to the wall of the cargo deck.

Suddenly, the door at the top of the staircase opened. Someone started making his way down the stairs. A huge Chinaman walked to each of the prisoners and opened the shackle on their wrist. All the prisoners starred at him, including Ray. When the last man was unshackled, the large Chi- naman finally spoke.

"Follow," he yelled in a broken accent.

The large Chinaman walked back up the stairs. The prisoners followed him.

Daylight hit the men right in the eyes. A brisk wind was blowing. Ray Andrews had never been out on the sea. He looked all around. Suddenly, he was sick to his stomach. It was his first experience being seasick. He turned to his left and vomited. After composing himself, he looked around. All he could see was water.

The group of prisoners all lined up side by side. Three men walked out in front of them. One of the men, the youngest, started talking.

"My name is Bill Lambert," he said.

Hearing the name stunned Ray. All of a sudden, a tremendous bitter- ness came over him. It was not until then that Ray realized Lambert had tricked him.

Lambert continued, "You are on a ship named the Melba Lee. This ship is headed for Hong Kong."

Ray looked over at Wilber Hill. Hill looked back at Ray before he spat down on the ground.

"We should be there in approximately forty days," Lambert said. "You will be part of the crew on this ship. If you cooperate and do a good job on this journey, you should make it back to San Francisco alive. We're even prepared to pay you for your work when we get back."

Lambert walked up close to the men and inspected all of them.

"However," he continued. "If you decide to cause trouble, you will be shot on sight and thrown overboard."

Lambert was now behind the men. He was obviously trying to intimidate them, and he was doing a very good job of it.

Lambert made his way back around in front of the men.

"Do you understand?" he asked loudly.

All the men shook their heads. What else could they do? Lambert wasn't finished. He walked over to the big Chinaman.

"This man's name is Suk Too. He is in charge of guarding you on this voyage. Should you get out of line, you will deal with him." It was obvious that Suk Too could barely understand what Lambert was saying. He didn't smile or even change expressions.

Then Lambert walked over to the other man.

"This is the captain of the ship," he exclaimed. "His name is Cyrus Welch. He is an expert sailor who will lead us on our voyage. Whatever he tells you to do, you are expected to do it. Do you understand?" All seven of the prisoners nodded.

Lambert didn't ask if anyone had a question. "Mr. Welch," he said. "I yield to you."

Cyrus Welch took a few steps toward the men. Lambert had showed power and a mean nature. Welch did not.

"Men," he started. "We don't want to harm ye." He then paused for a moment. "But don't think for a minute that we won't." Welch reached down and pulled a gun out of his belt. Ray immediately recognized it. It was a Colt Navy revolver. After the kidnapping, Sores had claimed Ray's gun and belt.

There weren't that many of those guns around, especially in California. He knew it was Tom Jenkins's gun. The whole thing came together for him. Ray started shaking his head. It made sense to him now. The man dressed in black with the long, dark hair and the red feather was Empty Heart. He had stolen three of the Colt Navy revolvers during the raid on Rosary Hill. Since leaving Texas, Ray hadn't seen one of the guns on any- one but himself or Stuttering Henry Jones.

"I'll shoot ye right in the noggin," continued Cyrus Welch.

"Better yet, I might just have Suk Too throw ye to the sharks. That al- ways makes it interesting."

Welch started laughing. He obviously thought he was very funny.

"But now, boys," he rambled on. "I don't want to do that. Just do what ye are told and all will be well."

Welch stepped back. The thought hit him that once again he had direct orders from the boss, Sores Aguilar, to throw one of the prisoners overboard on the first day. Sores was convinced that the terror of seeing the execution of a man would deter the rest of the prisoners. That, Sores believed, would eliminate any possibility of a mutiny.

Cyrus Welch, however, was against it. He was a hard man, a man capable of killing or even murder at the drop of a hat. However, he didn't agree with just killing to show force. Also, he had argued, it would be a long voyage, and every man was valuable. Deep down inside, Cyrus Welch had a conscience. On top of all that, he was very irritated that Sores would make such an order. Sores had never captained a clipper ship. It had been a source of friction between Cyrus Welch and Sores Aguilar all along.

Cyrus scanned the seven prisoners. He was wondering which of them would have to go. It needed to be the weakest, most vulnerable man. Any man who could do the physical labor would be given the benefit of the doubt.

Suddenly, Lambert reappeared. He was dragging a box. He started pulling a heavy fabric. It was obviously a sail. He spread the sail out on the deck. Welch started talking again.

"This is why ye are here," he said. "Ye men are the crew of this ship. Look up there."

Welch pointed up at the sails on the ship. There seemed to be a ton of them. When we have little wind, we need more sails. If it gets windy, we take some of them down. That be your job, mates."

Billy Lambert took over for the next thirty minutes. Over and over again, he demonstrated to the prisoners how to furl and unfurl the sail. He was very careful that they understood. Ray noticed that he was a very good teacher.

"You will have to do this up on the mast," he preached. "Be careful. If you fall off the mast, it will probably kill you."

Lambert pointed to Ray.

"You, Andrews," he yelled. "Get over here!"

Ray limped over to him. Everyone noticed that he was injured, but no- body seemed to care.

"Get up on the mast and see if you can unfurl that sail." Lambert point- ed to a sail about fifteen feet high. Ray was scared of heights, but he re- fused to show it. He started climbing up the mast. His right knee was killing him. It took him about ten minutes to climb up and unfurl the sail. Then he climbed back down.

Cyrus Welch was impressed. "Very good, mate!" he exclaimed. "If all of ye are that good, this be an easy voyage."

Lambert then pointed to Wilbur Hill. "Get up there, Hill, and furl it back into place."

Hill was not near as physically gifted as Ray Andrews. He struggled up the mast. It took him thirty minutes just to get organized. He couldn't get the sail furled. Finally, Lambert and Welch lost patience and ordered him down. On his way down, Welch couldn't help himself.

"Ye better learn how to crew, mate, or ye be some good shark bait." Cyrus Welch howled and howled.

All the men had to climb the mast and demonstrate their skills. Billy Lambert was disappointed in all of them but one. The other men seemed to be weak physically. Lambert had not done a very good job of gauging physical fitness or strength. He and Welch knew it immediately. There was only one man out of the seven prisoners who could really crew. His name was Ray Andrews.

Cyrus Welch's mood changed from being a jokester. Suddenly, he be- came very serious. He and Billy Lambert huddled for a moment. Cyrus then walked over and consulted with Suk Too. Ray didn't see any other Colt Navy revolvers anywhere. Just as he had always done as a Ranger captain and a stagecoach guard, he was already taking a weapon inventory.

Cyrus Welch walked back to the prisoners.

"Okay, Billy," he said loudly. "One of these mates has to go. Which one will it be?"

Suddenly, even more terror spread through the seven prisoners. Lambert walked to the front. He examined every man. He had secretly hoped that it would be Ray Andrews who would be the weakest. That way he would be gone, and his competition for Sarah Thomas would be eliminated. However, it turned out that Ray was by far the best man of the seven captured slave sailors. He would have to be spared. Lambert was not stupid. He knew the Melba Lee would need Ray Andrews.

Lambert stopped in front of Wilbur Hill. The rattlebox Hill started to panic.

"I can crew!" he yelled. "I'm a good laborer. Please, please!" Lambert didn't want to hear it.

"Shut up!" Lambert yelled at him.

Suk Too stepped forward. Cyrus Welch had already given him the order to take Wilbur Hill. Suk Too grabbed Hill and started dragging him to the edge of the ship. He was smiling all the way. Suk Too, it seemed, did not have a guilty conscience. He seemed to enjoy killing.

Hill squirmed and fought all the way. That warranted Suk Too to stop and smash him in the side of the head with his fist. The blow knocked Wilbur Hill unconscious. Suk Too picked him up and threw him to the front of the ship.

"Stop!" one of the men yelled. "Don't do it!"

Everyone on board looked back to see who it was that had spoken up in Hill's defense.

"Don't do it," said Ray Andrews once again.

This time he didn't raise his voice quite as much.

"I'll teach him. I take the responsibility. I will teach all these men. Just don't throw him overboard."

Ray dropped his head down and looked at the floor of the ship. He knew that he might be the one who would be thrown overboard now. He just couldn't take any more senseless murder. He had reacted instinctively and probably very stupidly. He just couldn't stop himself.

Suk Too had stopped in his tracks. It was something about the tone of Ray's voice. It just commanded respect. Suk Too dropped Wilbur Hill on the deck. It was an odd scene. It was as if Ray Andrews was suddenly in command, so Suk Too simply waited for an order.

Lambert and Cyrus Welch looked at each other. Welch walked over to Ray Andrews. He pulled the Colt Navy out of his belt again. He cocked the trigger and pointed the gun into Ray's face. Then he took the barrel and stuck it into Ray's forehead.

Ray had never had a gun pointed at his head before. He was scared, but he was also bitter.

Right now, Ray thought to himself. It might not be so bad if he did kill me.

At least then it would all be over. He peered into the barrel and up through the revolver. All of a sudden, Welch turned and took a step to- ward Suk Too. When he did, Ray noticed something odd. The Colt Navy wasn't loaded correctly. There were no percussion caps attached to the bullets. If Welch pulled the trigger, the Colt Navy wouldn't fire.

There was an awkward moment of silence that seemed like an eternity. Finally, Cyrus Welch spoke.

"Okay Mate," he said. "I like your spunk. I will take ye up on ye offer. Ye in charge to teach these mates to crew now."

Welch focused his eyes.

"I'll tell ye what though," he added. "I be watching ye close, Andrews. Ye don't perform, ye a dead man. Understand?"

On the other side of the deck, Billy Lambert watched.

What did all this mean to him? he wondered.

He had never seen a man stand up to Cyrus Welch like that. He certainly had never tried it himself.

CHAPTER 42

*S*arah Thomas was heartbroken. She didn't know what to think. Everything had been going so well. All of sudden, it had been fallen apart. It had been four days since Ray had walked away down Capp Street. But he never came back. Where was he? What had happened to him? Did he find someone else? Had something happened to him? She didn't know. She had always had a nervous stomach. Now her stomach was causing excruciating pain to her.

The reverend was upset too. He had stayed busy trying to organize the Grace Methodist Mission Church the best he could. He kept a strong up- per lip, but he was worried that something really bad had happened to Ray. He was just as confused and disappointed as his daughter.

All the while, Sarah and the reverend had refused to openly talk to each other about the situation. They had both just hoped Ray would walk in the door at any minute. The two of them had more than landed on their feet. The reverend's belief in God had been proven true to Sarah. It was mindboggling how things had worked out. Not only did they have a church and a place to live, but they had money in a bank. It was all be- cause of the grace of God and a "rough around the edges" Texas Ranger named Ray Andrews.

Early on a Tuesday morning, they were trying to build something that would resemble a choir loft in the back of the building. Sarah was trying to leverage a long board into place with her knee. The board was sup- posed to be a bench seat. Finally, she broke down. She dropped the board, causing a loud crash. She fell to her knees and started sobbing. The reverend knew why she was crying. He was crying inside too.

He walked over to her and tried to give her some comfort. Years and years of experience told him what to do, which was usually nothing. He just sat there with her and let her get it out of her system. When she calmed down, he opened the conversation.

"Tell me what you think might have happened to Ray," he asked her. She looked up at him. Tears streamed down her face. She was scared to say what she really thought. The reverend was a master at helping in this type of situation.

"Everybody deserves time to grieve," he said. "You are such a strong woman, but you must air your feelings when needed."

He took his arm and placed it around Sarah's shoulder. He was not an affectionate man. He never had been. However, he made an exception to- day. He had not hugged Sarah this tight since his wife and her mother, Abigail, had died.

"I don't know where he is," Sarah sobbed. "I'm scared something has happened to him. I can feel it."

The reverend had the same fear, but he tried to be positive.

"I know, I know," he said. "But I can tell you one thing, daughter. Ray Andrews is one of the smartest men I have ever met. We have to believe that he will find his way back."

The reverend's comment brought Sarah out of her funk.

"You think he is smart?" she asked. "I always thought he was a little slow, you know."

The reverend shook his head.

"You always underestimate people," he answered.

"I've heard you say that before. I have never understood why you think that,"

The reverend's comment that he thought Ray was smart had taken an edge off of Sarah's grief and the guilt that went along with it.

"You really think he is a smart man?" she asked her father again. The reverend didn't change expressions.

"Yes, I do," he responded. "I have great confidence in him." The two of them sat in the future choir area for a little while longer before anything else was said. Finally, the reverend brought up the question that both of them were wondering.

"What about Lambert?" he asked.

The reverend could see the scowl on Sarah's face when he asked the question.

"I never liked him!" she answered. "I bet he is part of this somehow." Again, the reverend was thinking the same thing as his daughter. He thought for a moment and then asked Sarah a question.

"Do you still have that flyer Lambert gave you?"

CHAPTER 43

Sores Aguilar continued to expand his empire in the community of San Francisco. He was close to being able to move his residence from the Lonely Sailor on Montgomery Street into a nicer, more sophisticated neighborhood five streets to the west past Kearney Street. After all, he was now a wealthy man. The noise of Aussie Town was loud at night. He was ready to settle down a little more and find a quieter place to live. The Lonely Sailor would be his business residence, not his home.

A lady friend had also come into the picture. Her name was Josephine Park. She was a beautiful woman from Los Angeles. Her reputation was a bit of a mystery. She didn't offer much information to Sores, and he didn't ask too many questions. He had met her at a luncheon that both of them had attended with some of Sores's Vigilance Committee friends. Sores and Josephine were a bit of an odd couple, but neither of them thought anything of it. Sores adjusted to being a sophisticated man with the help of Josephine. However, business was his first responsibility.

Sores looked down upon any man who would commit extortion. His experience with both his father and Big Jim Stuart had soured his attitude on that sort of crime. He also had other reasons not to get involved with physical intimidation. It was he who had brought Big Jim's exploits to the attention of the Vigilance Committee. Therefore, Sores knew not to be that kind of a hypocrite. It would be bad for business in the long run.

Sores had specialized in selling alcohol at the Lonely Sailor. Business was consistent and healthy. He hated wasting any type of resource, and he was known to be very frugal. Though he didn't drink much himself, he studied those who did. Therefore, he always seemed to know when to open for business and what kind of enticements to offer his customers. There were other side business ventures in the works too. Sores had started a small pawn business in the corner of the saloon. He was a very shrewd negotiator for goods. He would only do business if he saw a healthy profit. Land acquisition had become one of his favorite ventures. His experiences in the purchase of the Lonely Sailor had tipped him off on how easy and cheap it was to obtain property. He had also learned the ropes on how to bribe city clerks to get inside deals.

Sores took great pride in dealing on the right side of the law. However, there was a lot more money to be made in the opium business. His first foray into the drug trade with Cyrus Welch had been his biggest profit yet. There was a lot more at stake on this second trip to Hong Kong. Sores's plan was to buy as much opium on this trip as he possibly could buy.

Cyrus Welch couldn't get the ship out of the docks and on the way to Hong Kong fast enough. Tensions between himself and Sores had gotten a little frayed. Sores's attention to detail and planning were getting old to Cyrus. Sores would calculate everything down to the hour if possible. Any issue that came up might halt the start of the trip for days because Sores would study it long and hard before making any decision. Finally, with the capture of Ray Andrews, there were enough men to leave San Francisco.

Sores wanted to study things for a couple of more days. Welch, completely out of patience, finally influenced him to let them take off for Hong Kong.

There was no communication once the ship sailed. It was all about trust. Sores knew that if Cyrus Welch decided to break off on his own, he would never see the Melba Lee again. There could be a mutiny by the prisoners that led to disaster. Something could go wrong in China. A storm could capsize the ship. There were all kinds of bad things that could happen.

All along, Sores Aguilar knew to establish leverage with everyone in- volved on the voyage. Suk Too knew Sores would always take care of his sexual desires by supplying prostitutes. Billy Lambert knew he would never find another job with the income opportunity that Sores provided. Cyrus Welch had many reasons not to cross Sores. Who would find the drug contacts in Hong Kong? Who would sell the opium on the streets of San Francisco? Cyrus detested that side of the business. Also, he knew of no one else who could fund his voyages on the Melba Lee. To Cyrus Welch, the thrill of sailing the seas was everything.

Sores had also started to gather more and more people into his organization. He kept his distance from them, but he needed their protection. The best man he had to help him organize his small army was Billy Lambert, but there was never much trust between the two of them. It is hard to trust a man who once kidnapped you. Sores felt that Lambert was a wild card. He would tolerate him until he could replace him. When it was time to replace him, Lambert would never know what hit him. That was how Sores Aguilar did business.

Early in the evening of Thursday night, Sores was trying to get away from the Lonely Sailor. It was important to him to be on time for his dinner date with Josephine Park. They both enjoyed the seafood at an upscale restaurant about six blocks away. Of course, Sores had to escort Josephine because of the seedy characters that roamed the streets at night. To protect him and Josephine, Sores carried one of the Colt Navy revolvers. If anyone tried anything against him, he better have some fire- power. Sores could fire off six shots without reloading, so he felt safe.

Sores counted the petty cash that would be needed for the saloon cash- box that night. He made sure the bartenders, bouncers, and card dealers were in place. He had hired two of the best-looking women in town as waitresses. The Lonely Sailor was one of the hottest nightspots in the city. Sores rarely left the saloon at night, but he was really looking forward to an evening with Josephine.

Finally, around seven o'clock in the evening, he started making his way down the staircase on the outside steps of the Lonely Sailor. A gusty wind had whipped up suddenly, and it was very chilly. Sores wrapped his coat tight around his body and pulled his hat down tight. He had just shaven and combed his long, black hair into place. He wanted to look his best. It had occurred to him that Josephine might not appreciate the red feather that he always had woven into his hair. He asked himself the question if it might not be time to remove it. After some thought, he decided not to do it. "Maybe someday," he said to himself. "But not now." As Sores walked down the staircase, he did the same thing he had done all his life when he left any building. He chased the area. His hat covered his eyes, but he was looking at every person on the street. He focused his eyes through windows to see if there was any sign of trouble. He never took anything for granted.

After making his way to the bottom of the staircase, he stopped in his tracks. He looked to the street corner of Filbert and Montgomery. There he saw two tall men standing in odd-looking overcoats. Both had hats on that were tipped forward to conceal their faces. One of the men was stocky. The other was very thin. It was dark, windy, and cold, but Sores focused on them as he walked across the street. He didn't want them to know that he saw them.

Sores had developed the habit of using cigarettes. He didn't smoke them. He just liked to put them on his lips. He enjoyed the taste but not the smoke. He pulled out a cigarette as he stood up against the wall. All the while, he kept his eyes on the two men. He didn't like the looks of them.

Sores Aguilar never did anything he didn't think through, so he stood there and thought about his next move. They could just be two men that have no concern for my business, he thought. Then again, I better get up as close to them as possible. I need to see their faces in case I meet up with them again.

Sores flicked the cigarette down to the ground and turned toward the two men. Underneath his coat, he grabbed the handle of the Colt Navy. If anything happened, he could kill them both easily though he didn't think that would happen out in the middle of the street.

He started walking down the street toward the two men. He got to within fifty yards of them before they suddenly started walking south back down Montgomery

Street. Sores realized his instincts were correct. They were stalking him. He walked faster trying to catch up with them, but they had a big lead. He couldn't catch them.

Finally, Sores decided to stop. Whoever the men were, they knew he was on to them. He would make sure that all of his men knew about this incident. It was a concern for him. The two men looked dangerous. He wondered if they might be carrying weapons under their coats. He didn't take his eyes off them as they disappeared down Montgomery Street.

CHAPTER 44

"That's all the information we have," said Sarah Thomas.

The look of concern on her face was obvious. "There is something going on down there, I just know it," she continued. The woman she was addressing, Georgia Tipps, wanted to help.

"Let me get this straight," she answered. "You say this man walked to- ward you like he knew you were watching him? But then again, you really weren't watching him. You were just watching a saloon? I'm a bit con- fused, honey. Did you know who the man was?"

Sarah was embarrassed about the confusion.

"No, ma'am," she responded. "We didn't know him. We still don't know him. My father and I thought we were some kind of detectives or something, I guess."

It was obvious that Sarah was very uncomfortable being in the Gold and Silver. It was just that she felt she could trust Georgia Tipps. After all, she had nowhere else to go. She knew of no other person in the city who might be able to help her get information on what might be going on at the Lonely Sailor.

Georgia scratched the back of her head, and then she rubbed her eyes. She reached down below the counter and pulled out a map of San Fran- cisco. She unfolded it on the counter. She pulled out a magnifying glass and looked closely at the map.

"Yeah," she said. "That's right on the edge of Aussie Town, the Barbary Coast."

Sarah and the reverend were a little dumbfounded. "What do you mean Aussie Town and the Barbary Coast?" Sarah asked. Georgia looked up at her. "Well, honey," she answered. "The Australians are thick in that part of town. Most of them are outlaws. That's why they call it Aussie Town. They call it the Barbary Coast too. The area reminded some big shot about a place in Africa. That name just stuck. Anything goes down there. You'll hear it called both names. I stay away from there, but I know people who can help us get some information.

The reverend had been standing in the back of the room, trying not to be noticed, but Georgia finally spoke to him.

"I don't bite, sir," she said to him sarcastically. "I have my faults, but I won't hurt you."

It was very obvious that the reverend was uncomfortable. He had never been in a pawnshop before. Finally, he walked toward the counter and held out his hand.

"Name's William Thomas, ma'am. I'm sorry if I was rude. I just am a little nervous."

Georgia smiled. All she wanted was to meet the reverend.

"I understand," she responded with a smile. "This is a mean town, mean people. I'll see what I can find out for you."

Quickly Sarah spoke up.

"We'll pay you for the information," she said.

Georgia's eyes lit up immediately.

"Well, I'll take you up on that. I was thinking ten dollars.

For that, I will work 'til you are satisfied with the information I provide."

Sarah was ready to make the deal.

"Done," she said. "When do you want us to pay you?"

Georgia Tipps wasn't used to dealing with people of integrity. She usually had to force people to pay.

"Half now, half when the job is finished," she answered.

The reverend stepped forward.

"I will be back in a couple of hours, Miss Tipps. I don't have that much cash on hand."

Georgia giggled at his honesty.

"Don't worry, honey. I trust you."

She looked at Sarah.

"I just hope we can come up with some good news for you." Georgia walked around the counter.

"You know," she continued, "I don't promise that we will report good news, honey. There are some bad people in Aussie Town." Georgia obviously saw the despair in Sarah's face.

"You better prepare yourself for some tough news," she said to Sarah. It was quiet for a few minutes. Finally, Georgia broke the silence.

"If I was just a few years younger, you would have had some competition for Ray," she said. "He was a keeper. I liked Henry too. Couldn't sleep for a week after I found out what happened to him."

It got quiet again.

"We'll get to the truth, honey. I just don't know what the truth will be."

CHAPTER 45

*T*he fog from the Pacific Ocean had been playing games with Ray Andrews's mind. He hated how it masked anything that could be seen. He had been counting the days since Billy Lambert first told the prisoners that it would take approximately forty days to get to Hong Kong. It was day thirty-two since Ray had started counting. He knew they must be close.

Cyrus Welch and Billy Lambert rotated the two sets of crewmen. There were eight men per crew, and each crew had five paid sailors and three slave sailors. One group would work all night and the other group would work all day. The men were fed as they rotated, twice per day. The food was terrible. It was mainly just slop. Rice, beans, and oatmeal were the staples on the trip. That was what was served every single meal. The men hated the food, but they ate it anyway. It was foggy almost all the time. The cloudlike days made it virtually impossible to figure out the time. On rare sunny days, Ray could calculate the time pretty well. On foggy days, life seemed to be a haze just like the air.

It was on the tenth day of the voyage that Ray noticed that the men seemed to start figuring out how to sail. That was the day that the Melba Lee really took off and covered a great deal of distance. Cyrus Welch himself was singing and dancing on the deck of the ship. He exclaimed that on that day, the Melba Lee had never clipped the seas so quickly.

Ray had worked with all the other men. Cyrus rotated him between the two groups. Over and over, again and again, he taught them how to furl and trim the sails. He worked with the men as a group, and he worked with them individually. Every one of them had become a very competent crew member, even Wilbur Hill.

But when the weather got tough, and the job was really difficult, it was always Ray who drew the toughest job. One night, he climbed all the way to the top of the mast in a driving rainstorm. His crew had both paid and slave sailors. Every one of them followed him. The wind was blowing at twenty knots. If he didn't get the sails furled from the top down, the ship might spin out of control. If he slipped and fell off the mast, he would be a dead man. But he made it look like he had done it a million times. When he got down, Cyrus Welch commented that he had never seen such fine work. Had Ray not acted quickly to get the sails down, the ship very well could have wrecked into the sea.

It was amazing how well Ray seemed to take to sailing, but he seemed to take to any type of a job he had ever attempted. Sailing was different though. He knew that if he didn't succeed, he would be thrown over- board. He focused with all his might on not only getting the job done but also making sure the other prisoners knew what to do. He realized that he had to make himself irreplaceable.

On the thirty-second morning that Ray had counted on the trip, he was working the day shift. He had eaten the sloppy, watery oatmeal for breakfast and then taken his place on the deck. Working as a crewman was actually a strange job. When he was busy, he worked nonstop all day or all night. However, if the weather was right and the sails were set properly, the crew members could just sit and enjoy the voyage. They literally didn't have to do anything unless

Cyrus Welch was in a bad mood. If he was in a bad mood, the crew would probably be scrubbing the deck.

This day, the wind was blowing at ten knots. The fog seemed to be lifting. Ray was on the third yard of the mast tightening a sail when the fog cleared. From his perch about fifty feet in the air, he was the first to see the city of Hong Kong. It was a beautiful sight. Water surrounded the entire city. A mountainous terrain provided a beautiful landscape. There were buildings that seemed to stretch into the sky.

Ray stabilized his body on the mast. His knee was feeling much better. The pain was still there, but the swelling was gone. He didn't think about it much unless he made a sharp turn and it popped out of socket. When it did dislocate, he had learned how to put it back together.

He could only enjoy the scene for a little while. Cyrus Welch had spotted the city too.

"Andrews, get back down here, ye hear!" he shouted.

Ray slowly climbed back down to the deck. Welch was waiting at his feet.

"We well ahead of schedule, mate," he said. "Should be able to get back even quicker."

Welch walked to the front of the ship. Billy Lambert had surfaced, so had Suk Too. Everyone on the ship was in a grand mood.

It only took three hours to reach the city. By then, it was close to noon. Cyrus stopped the ship and dropped anchor about a mile from the city's docks. He ordered all the slave labor down below. There they were chained to the wall. All the slave prisoners wondered what would happen next.

Two days passed. The prisoners remained chained to the walls of the cargo deck. They ate twice per day. The chains were long enough for them to move to the head. They had all gotten used to the stench and pathetic indignity of using the toilet in front of each other.

On the third night, the hatch opened. Billy Lambert and Suk Too walked down the staircase. Suk Too was carrying a shotgun. Lambert un- locked Ray's shackles first.

"Get upstairs—now!" he screamed in a vicious tone.

Ray got up and did what he was told. Next, he unlocked the shackles of the biggest of the prisoners. His name was Ed Blake. Blake was a quiet man and had caused no trouble. He was well over six feet tall and weighed two hundred pounds. Blake scurried up the stairs. Lambert then unshackled two other men. Their names were James Meredith and Har- Kold McWade. Both were normal-sized men.

Lambert followed the men up the stairs. Wilbur Hill wanted to know what was happening. He just couldn't keep his mouth shut.

"Where are you going?" he asked. "Take me. I want to get out of here." The door slammed before he could say anything else.

Lambert led the four men to another staircase on the other side of the ship. There they climbed down into another cargo deck. Lambert pointed to two large boxes with straps on each side.

"Andrews, you and McWade take that one. Blake, you and Meredith take that one. Let's go!" Lambert said.

The four men carried the two huge boxes up to the deck.

Cyrus Welch was waiting for them. He looked over his men. There were seven men that included the four prisoners, himself, Billy Lambert, and Suk Too.

"Men," he said. "We going on a little mission. Don't get any ideas. Ye sure don't want to be left in Hong Kong. Do as ye told, and everything be fine."

But things were not fine. Ray had already counted the weapons. Suk Too had a shotgun that could be fired once. Billy Lambert was carrying an old one-shot handgun. Ray had seen the model before. It was useless unless it was fired at target less than twenty feet away. Cyrus Welch was packing the Colt Navy. Ray knew it was loaded incorrectly. It wouldn't fire. Cyrus never bothered to attach percussion caps. If they got into a gunfight, they were all dead men.

It was at that time that Ray Andrews had to make a split-second decision. Did he say something or just keep his mouth shut? He knew one thing for sure. He did not want to get stuck in Hong Kong. How in the world would he ever get back home if he did? That was when he decided to speak.

Ray had never spoken directly to Cyrus Welch. He was a prisoner, and prisoners didn't speak to the captain of the ship. That was made clear early on the voyage, but this was not the time to be timid.

"Mr. Welch," Ray said with humility but with confidence. "May I have permission to speak?"

Billy Lambert went into a rage.

"I ought to kill you right now, Andrews. Who do you think you are?" he said.

Lambert pointed his gun right at Ray's forehead. Cyrus Welch walked over and put his hand on Lambert's shoulder. It got deathly quiet in the dark, cold air. Finally, Cyrus Welch spoke.

"It better be 'portant, mate," he said to Ray Andrews.

Ray swallowed and cleared his throat.

"Have you ever fired that revolver, sir?" he asked.

Cyrus took the Colt Navy out of his belt. He pointed it at Ray's temple. Now there were two guns pointed at his head. "Why you ask, mate?" he answered.

"It's loaded incorrectly, Mr. Welch," Ray responded. "You will have nothing if you try to fire it. If we get into a fight, we will have only two shots. Let me reload it. That one gun can kill six men if used properly." Both Welch and Lambert had seen enough of Ray Andrews to know he was telling the truth. Welch removed his gun belt and sat Ray down on the ground. Suk Too held the shotgun to the back of his head while Ray disassembled the Colt Navy. He cleaned it the best he could. Then he reassembled and loaded it using the percussion caps that were stored in the gun belt. This all took place under the stars on the deck of the Melba Lee. Ray completed the entire task in less than twenty minutes.

Not a word was said as the seven men ventured into the city. Suk Too led the way. He was from Hong Kong and knew the way. Ray and Blake followed close behind him, carrying the large case. Meredith and McWade carried the other case. Lambert and Cyrus Welch brought up the rear.

They walked for over two hours. Suk Too stopped twice. It seemed to the rest of the men that he was lost. However, he gathered his wits both times and moved along. Suddenly, Cyrus Welch started getting talkative. "Isn't this it, mate?" he asked Suk Too.

Lambert started asking questions too. When Suk Too turned a corner, Welch and Lambert knew they had reached their destination.

The four prisoners were not comfortable. They were unarmed. The situation reeked of trouble. It was dark, cold, and scary. Suk Too knocked on the door of the same small house they had visited before. This time, however, the little old Asian lady didn't answer. It was an Asian man. Suk Too and the man talked in Chinese for a few minutes. The other six men had no idea what was being said.

Suddenly, the door opened. Suk Too waved all of the men to come into the small house. Once inside, Suk Too disappeared behind the same curtain as he did the last time. Finally, he surfaced and waved Lambert and Cyrus Welch to join him. The four prisoners stood outside the curtain holding the cases. It was James Meredith who broke the silence.

"Let's make a run for it," he said. "It's now or never." Ray wasn't so sure.

"How will we get back to America?" he asked. "We need to stay put." Meredith was about to let go of the case and run, but Cyrus Welch walked out from around the curtain.

"Bring the cases back here, mates," he said.

The men did what he told them to do.

The four prisoners knew what was in the cases. They weren't stupid. When Billy Lambert unlocked the padlock and opened the first case, it came as no surprise. Several articles of clothing were on top, but Lambert pulled everything away. There were gold bars hidden at the bottom of the cases.

The exchange was made in about an hour. Welch and Lambert simply took the gold out and put the opium back in the two cases. Then they neatly packed the clothing back on top. The deal was done. There was no shaking of hands. Cyrus Welch was ready to go. The men picked up the cases and proceeded to leave the small house. The opium was much lighter than the gold.

But things were just going too smooth. As soon as the men walked out the front door, they were face-to-face with a small mob of Chinese men. It was a set up. Both sides stared each other down. Ray counted seven men on the other side. Cyrus Welch was standing just behind Ray. Billy Lambert was standing next to Cyrus.

"Mr. Welch," Ray said. "If you want to get out of here alive, you better hand me that gun."

Cyrus Welch was proud, but he wasn't stupid. He pulled the Colt Navy out of his belt and handed it to Ray. Nobody on either side saw the ex- change except Billy Lambert.

Ray didn't turn his head, but he spoke, "Mr. Lambert, take the one on the far right. I have the rest of them."

Lambert was not happy about the situation, but he nodded his head.

Suk Too was the wild card. Ray didn't care what he did as long as he didn't turn on him and the other men. There were some yelling and threatening messages exchanged. For a second, Ray thought they might be able to talk their way out of it. Cyrus was doing the talking, which was a problem. The Chinese bandits didn't care for an Aussie. All of a sudden, one of the Chinese men raised his gun and aimed it at Ed Blake. There was a short moment of silence.

The first shot was fired by Billy Lambert. He dropped the Chinese man on the right just like Ray told him to do. That started it. Suk Too fired the shotgun into the gang of men, but the gun seemed to misfire. The shot was useless. The Chinese men started firing away. Ed Blake went down. Cyrus Welch was hit in the arm. Ray dove to his right and secured a position. There wasn't a man on planet Earth who could fire the Colt Navy revolver like him. One of the Chinese men charged Cyrus Welch with a long knife. Ray shot him in the head. There were still two other Chinese men standing, trying to get to their knives. Ray shot both of them down. Both men were hit directly in the torso.

Obviously, the Chinese gang had never seen a revolver that could shoot multiple shots. There were still three other men on the other side. Ray had three bullets left in the chamber. He couldn't waste a shot. It got qui- et again for just a second. Finally, the Chinese men leaped out from be- hind their cover. Before any of them could get off a shot, Ray dropped them to the ground. He hit one man with a shot to the head. Another man was sprawling on the ground after being hit in the shoulder. The last man tried to run, but Ray shot him in the back of his right leg.

Cyrus Welch, Billy Lambert, and Suk Too watched in awe as Ray ran over to Ed Blake. He could find no pulse. Blake was dead. Ray handed the Colt Navy to Cyrus Welch. He motioned to Suk Too to pick up Blake. "Leave him," Billy Lambert yelled.

Ray glared back at Lambert.

"I'll carry him if I have too," Ray whispered. "We can't leave him here." Lambert had a hateful look on his face. Finally, he gave in to Ray. He motioned for Suk Too to pick up Blake's body. Lambert grabbed the handle of the case opposite of Ray Andrews. Cyrus Welch was bleeding, but he was not hurt badly. Ray looked around at the other men.

"Let's get out of here!" he whispered.

CHAPTER 46

Georgia Tipps loved to make money. She was especially enthralled with making money outside of her pawnshop. It was a challenge for her to do something new. She had her contacts in town. She also had her bodyguard, who she always paid handsomely, to help her. It only took her a week to get a good deal of information.

Right on time, Sarah and the reverend showed up at the Gold and Sil- ver. The three of them had agreed to meet again one week later. Even though Georgia had warned about bad news, Sarah was hoping for something good.

Georgia welcomed them and immediately started talking business.

"The owner of the saloon at Fourteenth Montgomery Street is a man named Sores Aguilar. He has quite a reputation down in Aussie Town. Turns out he is the man who led the Vigilance Committee to Big Jim Stu- art."

Sarah and the reverend had never heard of Big Jim Stuart, so Georgia had to tell them the whole sordid story.

"Big Jim was an Aussie who was extorting people left and right. Some- thing had to be done. The Vigilance Committee was a bunch of men who took the law into their own hands. They sought justice without waiting on the law. Aguilar led them straight to him. They hung Big Jim down on Market Street out of a second-floor window. Aguilar is kind of a hero to a lot of people." Georgia cleared her throat and continued.

"He's got a lot of connections, and he makes a lot of money, big money."

Sarah and the reverend were confused.

"How does he make so much money?" the reverend asked. Georgia looked around the room to make sure that nobody else was eavesdrop- ping on the conversation. They were not. "Well," she said. "Word on the street is that he can produce opium. You know that's a big deal in town, don't you? Nobody is sure whether it is illegal or not. The law has enough to enforce around here without getting into vice."

"What is vice?" Sarah asked.

Georgia smiled.

"Honey," she said. "Vice is all things bad that people enjoy." Sarah and the reverend were completely ignorant about drugs and crime.

Sarah looked at her father. Then she looked back at Georgia. "Go on," she said.

"One of my contacts found out that he has a big shipment coming in soon," Georgia continued.

Sarah and the reverend didn't know what to do with the information. "What do you think this has to do with Ray?" Sarah asked. "I found out a little information that is pretty upsetting, darling," Georgia answered. The look on Georgia's face caused Sarah's heart to drop. Their eyes met. Georgia continued, "This next piece of information has got to stay with the three of us. I don't want it to get around that I know about it." Sarah and the reverend both nodded.

"Word is that Aguilar has been kidnapping sailors in his saloon. I bet that's what happened to Ray. It makes sense. He goes there one night, and then you don't hear from him again. I bet he is on a ship out in the ocean. There's no telling what has happened to him."

Sarah's stomach was churning. She felt that she was going to vomit. The problems with her stomach had intensified in the past few weeks. This bit of news from Georgia made things worse.

The reverend stepped up to the counter.

"You're right," he said. "It does make sense. That is the first logical ex- planation of things I have heard of this episode yet."

The news was bad, but it at least gave the reverend some hard facts to pray about. He actually felt better about the situation.

"Do you have anything else we need to know?" he asked Georgia.

"Just some information about Aguilar himself," she responded. "He is some kind of a half breed. Nobody can figure him out. He is a real out- cast. He wears a red feather in his hair. Must be some kind of an Indian. Very smart, travels with bodyguards unless he is going to see his lady friend. Then he travels alone."

"How do you know that?" Sarah asked.

Georgia winked and answered, "Because I know her."

Sarah was astonished. "You know her!" Sarah responded. The disbelief in her voice was obvious.

"We're not good friends or anything," Georgia calmly responded. "I met her a couple of months back at a party up on Nob Hill. Her name is Josephine Park. I think she is a kept woman."

The reverend stepped forward.

"What do you mean, a kept woman?" he asked.

Georgia had a big smile on her face.

"I'm not sure about that, but it means that she is a high-class prostitute," she said.

The reverend raised his eyebrows.

"Oh, I understand." He said it like he knew all about it.

Georgia tore off a piece of paper from a notebook and scribbled an ad- dress on it. She handed the paper to Sarah.

"I would try tracking him again from Miss Park's boardinghouse. He will come around to see her, I guarantee it. Do a better job of hiding this time. Be more discreet. I bet you can find out some information if you follow him."

Sarah spoke up quickly, "I'm not sure I would recognize him, Georgia." Georgia smiled again.

"You'll recognize him. I haven't seen anyone who looks anything like him around here. He is big and tall with long, black hair. He wears a red feather in his hair. Always dresses in black. If you don't recognize him, you will recognize Josephine. She is tall with black hair. Probably the most beautiful woman in the city, except maybe you, Honey."

Sarah looked at the address. She didn't recognize it. Georgia could tell by Sarah's body language that she was unsure of herself, so she took an- other piece of scratch paper to draw a map. The map was directions to the boardinghouse where Josephine Park lived.

Sarah and the reverend turned to walk out the front door. Georgia Tipps couldn't help but follow them.

"I'm gonna keep working on this. I haven't lived up to my wages yet. I will see what I can still find out for you,"

Georgia said. Sarah and the reverend didn't say anything. They both looked at Georgia who began to look worried.

"Now you two don't do anything stupid, you hear. Let me try to get some more information. Whatever you do, make sure you're careful," Georgia warned.

Sarah thanked her for her trouble. She and her father started their walk back to the mission. Both of them said nothing. Sarah's stomach was churning. She felt queasy. The reverend was trying to figure out how to talk her out of pursuing this, Josephine Park. Both of them were scared to death.

CHAPTER 47

*T*he trip back to America was going well for Cyrus Welch. The crew knew what to do to sail the ship. The Melba Lee was making great time. One of the slave sailors died during the first ten days of the return voyage. Malnutrition was a problem, but the real reason was that he had just given up hope. Cyrus Welch simply ordered him buried at sea. Ray Andrews handled the duties. He had developed his own system since he took care of Ed Blake.

Ray wrapped the body in sails that had been torn and were of no use. He stuffed every spare part he could find into the pockets of his clothes for weight. Cyrus even allowed him to use chain links that were lying around on the deck. He got an honorable funeral. Ray took off his hat and had a moment of silence. He didn't know much about praying. After that, Ray stated his name and simply pushed him overboard. It was Ray's new custom to not allow anyone to speak until the body completely disappeared into the water.

Cyrus Welch was doing some serious soul searching. He had some real problems on his hands. He didn't know what to think about what had happened with the drug connection. Suk Too wasn't worried at all. The men who tried to rob them were dead. Suk Too swore the family who supplied the opium wouldn't betray him. They were lifelong friends. Cyrus Welch wasn't so sure. Suk Too didn't care even if they had betrayed him.

"Just walk down street," he said. "Find plenty dope."

Cyrus didn't know exactly how he would handle the next drug deal. He did know he wouldn't go back into Hong Kong without immense firepower.

The other problem that really bothered Cyrus was how he would deal with the slave labor. It was a long, arduous duty to capture, hold, train, and then kill the sailors. In his opinion, it wasn't worth it. He had learned the hard way. It also really bothered him that Sores Aguilar was trying to manage his business on the Melba Lee. Cyrus Welch didn't mind following orders on how to manage a drug deal. He didn't mind sharing the wealth with the partner who financed the voyage, but he didn't like someone telling him what to do on his own vessel. He was fed up with that, and he had decided that he was going to tell Sores about it.

As a matter of fact, he had already decided that he would only throw a sailor overboard if he became useless or a threat. He would keep his sailors chained below in the cargo deck. He wanted to feed them better on the next voyage. He also wanted to hire Ray Andrews just like he and Sores had hired Billy Lambert. It was a dangerous idea, but Welch never lacked the self-confidence that he could handle Ray Andrews if it came down to it. He would simply shoot Ray in the head and throw him overboard if he didn't cooperate.

Sores Aguilar had many responsibilities in the opium smuggling operation. First, he planned it. Next, he recruited the men to execute it. Third, he financed it. Fourth, he sold the opium in San Francisco. Then he supposedly split the money between the partners.

However, there were some other more subtle duties. It was his responsibility to ensure a safe docking spot for the Melba Lee when the ship returned. Cyrus wanted the opium off the ship as quickly as possible. There was no time to waste. That issue was one of the only things Sores had not thought of the first voyage. This time, a place would already be secured. Cyrus would only have to launch the small tender boat on the side of the Melba Lee and paddle into town one time. He would find Sores. The docking position would already be in place. Cyrus would then simply row back out after meeting Sores and bring the Melba Lee into dock. The first voyage was a learning experience. It was hard to predict anything. This time, Sores Aguilar and Cyrus Welch had a good idea what to expect.

Sores made his way down to the docks every other day. He wanted a good place to dock the Melba Lee, but he didn't want to be front and center either. He had found the perfect spot. It was just south of the busiest part of the dock. It would be far enough away not to gather much attention, but it wouldn't be too isolated. The Melba Lee would be back very soon.

Sores enjoyed the walk over to Nob Hill to visit Josephine Park. It was always the highlight of his day. He would court her and often take her to dinner. After dinner, the two of them would often retire to her room for a while. After he left the boardinghouse on Wilson Street, he would make his way down to scout a place to dock the Melba Lee. He knew that he would need to pay the fee to secure a spot in a day or so. There was no reason to take a chance on losing the position.

Josephine Park was guilty of altering Sores Aguilar's focus. He really was smitten with her beauty and charm. His walk to her boardinghouse was never a dangerous one. At least that was what he thought. But for the first time in his life, Sores Aguilar was taking things a little too casually.

It was Friday night. Sores had made his usual trek down to Nob Hill. He knocked on the boardinghouse door and entered. Across the street, sitting in the parlor of another boardinghouse was Sarah Thomas and Rev. William Thomas. The owner of the house let them sit quietly in the foyer as long as they paid to drink coffee and tea. The window treatments blocked any view Sores might have from the other side of the street. There they waited.

Sores reappeared twenty minutes later. This time, he was escorting a woman. Sarah couldn't help but to comment.

"She really is the most beautiful woman in town," she whispered.

The reverend thought about arguing with her. He thought Georgia Tipps was actually more attractive than Josephine. However, his instincts told him not to comment. He figured he shouldn't be making comments about such things. Sarah and the reverend knew they didn't need to follow Sores. He would be back later. Then they would follow him anywhere but back to Aussie Town.

Three hours later, Sores and Josephine returned. They went into the boardinghouse for about an hour. Then Sores left the house alone. He started walking back to the east. Sarah and the reverend were much more careful this time as they followed him. At first, they figured he was heading straight back to the Lonely Sailor. However, he was much further south, and quickly, it became obvious that he was headed elsewhere. They followed well behind him. He made his way to the docks. It was easy for them to hide behind buildings and not be seen. They watched him as he stood in front of an empty place in the docking area next to the water.

The reverend got excited.

"That's it," he whispered to Sarah. "That is where his ship will come in. I know it."

Sores took out a cigarette, but he didn't light it. He was enjoying the evening. He had a beautiful woman. He had security. He had money. Very soon he would pull off a huge drug score.

Finally, he turned and started walking. Sarah and the reverend followed until they realized that he was headed home. They broke off and headed back to Capp Street and the Grace Methodist Mission Church.

Sarah and the reverend followed the same process two more times. Both times, Sores followed almost the exact same schedule. After seeing Sores walk to the same place at the docks three times, they decided they didn't need to follow him anymore. They needed to stake out the dock. When a ship docked in that spot, hopefully they would find Ray Andrews on board.

CHAPTER 48

On the twenty-ninth day of the return voyage, Cyrus Welch saw the beautiful coastline of the San Francisco Bay Area. It was late in the afternoon on a clear day when it appeared. Cyrus calculated that the Melba Lee had been averaging 250 miles per day to travel the 7,000 miles from Hong Kong. There had been very little trouble. This crew was the best he had ever used. He didn't want to lose them. His dilemma was how he would keep slave labor fed, quiet, and alive while the clipper was docked. He was determined to figure it out.

The sailors saw the city too. They were all so weak from not eating that it was hard for any of them to be rebellious. Ray had considered a mutiny, but he and the other men were just in no mood to pull it off. It took every ounce of energy each one of them had just to get through the day.

Cyrus needed the men to get the Melba Lee into position to dock into the San Francisco Bay. It would be tricky to stop the ship and secure the men down below without a scene. He decided it was time to talk to the men.

Cyrus ordered the ship to a halt about five miles from the entrance to the bay. He had Billy Lambert call the slave labor up in front. He looked them over before he spoke.

"You, mates, the best crew me ever had," he said. "Know it's been bad. Couldn't take chances though. Things be different now. Me would like to keep ye alive. Have to work with me in order to do it. Me boss is stubborn, mates.

Me want to talk to him. Try to convince him to let ye live. Think me can do it."

The sailors looked at Cyrus Welch like he was crazy. He had just told them the truth about their fate. At least he didn't lie about it.

"Aye think aye can talk him into it," he continued. "Ask that ye give me a chance."

The sailors were in disbelief at Welch's nonchalant attitude about their lives. It was funny though. They trusted him. It crossed Ray's mind that probably their best chance was to let Cyrus Welch plead for their case.

Cyrus walked over to Ray.

"Andrews," he said. "I offer ye a job. Come work for me as a full-time crewman. Pay good wages. Need a good mate like ye."

Ray was dumbstruck. Now Cyrus Welch had offered him a job.

Welch continued on his rant.

"Now, mates, we gonna dock the Melba Lee. Only need four of ye to do the job. We gonna drop anchor here about a mile or so out from the city. We go find where we to dock. Then we come back and get the clipper into the city."

That was the plan. Billy Lambert and Suk Too escorted the men back down into the cargo area and chained them back to the wall. It was simple, and there was no resistance. Food deprivation worked on slave labor. Cyrus Welch knew that and gauged it very well. His goal was to get the most out of the men on the least amount of food he could feed them. They would be exhausted and depressed to a point they would not be riled up against the captain. It was a good plan, and it worked well.

Suk Too stayed back with the ship. Cyrus Welch and Billy Lambert lowered the bounty boat and rowed their way into town. They got off the boat and headed straight for the Lonely Sailor. By then, it was two o'clock in the afternoon. They made their way to Fourteenth Montgomery Street, but they had to wait on Sores Aguilar. He was having a late lunch with Josephine Park. Finally, he arrived at ten minutes until six in the evening. Cyrus Welch and Billy Lambert were sitting on the front steps of the Lonely Sailor when he arrived.

Obviously, Sores was glad to see them.

"How did the exchange go?" he asked.

Both of them were a little peeved that he didn't even bother to say hello or good to see you before he started talking business. "Had some trouble, mate," barked Cyrus Welch. "Had a shoot 'em up."

Billy Lambert knew to stay out of the conversation.

"What happened?" Sores asked.

Cyrus Welch stood up and walked over to him.

"One of the sailors shot our way out of it," he answered. "Need to get him on the payroll. He one of the best hands me ever saw." Sores had learned from experience. Even though he didn't like Billy Lambert, he did know the value he had brought to the organization. It didn't surprise him that Cyrus Welch had another man he wanted to hire.

"What about the rest of the men?" Sores asked.

Cyrus Welch was ready for a confrontation.

"They be chained to the bottom of the storage room on the clipper. Most still alive."

Cyrus was surprised not to get a tongue-lashing from Sores.

The reaction he received was surprising, but Sores had been studying the situation. He had come to the same realization as Cyrus. If they could keep the men alive, another trip could immediately be planned to go back to Hong Kong.

"Good," Sores answered. "What about the cargo? Is it on the ship?"

Cyrus Welch had been considering a renegotiation of his part of the deal. However, he decided against it. He was very tired himself, and he knew Sores would provide a tremendous payday in only a few hours after the ship docked. He decided to stay with the plan.

"Cargo is on board," Welch said. "Want to get it off soon as we dock. Can ye be ready by noon tomorrow?"

Sores nodded his head.

"Everything is arranged. Let's walk back to the docks. I will show you where to come in tomorrow. I will have the contacts ready with their money around midnight tomorrow night. We can get it done in a day."

Sores Aguilar, Cyrus Welch, and Billy Lambert walked back down to the docks. Sores and Cyrus talked all the way. Billy Lambert never said a word. The plans were set as they walked toward the dock position that Sores had already rented. The three men stood at the waterfront and looked out onto the bay. After only one more day, Sores, Cyrus Welch, and Suk Too would be very wealthy men. Billy Lambert would also be extremely well paid.

Across the street, hiding behind the corner of a storage building stood two people disguised as dockworkers. Sarah Thomas and her father, Rev. William Thomas, were wearing worn men's clothes and hats. They had salvaged them from the discards people had brought to the mission. They were very discreet, and it was very difficult for anyone to detect them. Sores Aguilar, Cyrus Welch, and Billy Lambert didn't realize that they were being watched.

CHAPTER 49

*T*he following day, Cyrus Welch brought the Melba Lee into the docking space almost exactly at dusk. He planned it perfectly. The crew of sailors guided the clipper right into the harbor. About a half mile out, Suk Too ordered the captured crewmen at gunpoint back downstairs to the cargo room. There he chained them back to the wall. Cyrus Welch and Billy Lambert easily guided the ship into position and tied it off on the dock. The paid crew was dismissed. They took off in different directions into the city.

Sarah and the reverend were watching from a distance. They didn't know what to do. They could only see a few sailors on board of the ship. Sarah couldn't help but to start crying. Her stomach was killing her. She hadn't eaten a good meal in three days. She thought she was going to pass out. The reverend jolted her shoulder.

"Sarah, get a hold of yourself," he chastised her. "This is not the time to be weak."

Normally, the reverend wouldn't be so hard on his daughter.

However, he knew that they had progressed into very dangerous territory. His survival instincts had kicked in. If they were to survive this situation and just maybe rescue Ray Andrews, it would take every ounce of concentration they had in their souls. Sarah slowly rebounded. The reverend pulled an apple out of his pocket. He handed it to Sarah. She gladly ate it. Earlier in the day, she had refused it several times.

The two of them watched the clipper for the rest of the evening. Nothing was happening. As midnight approached, the reverend was getting really tired.

"It is time to leave for the night, daughter," he said.

Just when he said it, the action started on the Melba Lee. Four men suddenly appeared and joined Sores, Cyrus Welch, Suk Too, and Billy Lambert. There was a brief meeting. Suk Too and Billy Lambert then led the four men onto the Melba Lee on the long plank-like board that they had lowered upon arrival.

Sarah and the reverend could see that something was happening. Twenty minutes after walking up the plank, the four men came back down. They were led by Billy Lambert. The four men were carrying two large cases. Suk Too raised the plank from the dock of the ship. He then climbed down over the side of the ship to the dock. He used an attached rope to keep his balance. Sarah watched how he did it very closely. Though he was over three hundred pounds, Suk Too seemed to be quite agile. He was down off the ship in a couple of minutes.

All the men left the ship and headed downtown. Sarah and the reverend watched them walk down the street. When they were out of sight, Sarah Thomas decided that she would not ask her father for permission to go to the ship. She unbuttoned her coat and dropped it on the ground. Before the reverend could say anything, she was gone. She sprinted to the ship and grabbed the line. Although she wasn't as adept as Suk Too, she made it onto the ship in a couple of minutes. She vaulted her torso over the rail and landed on her back. She was on the deck of the ship. As she disappeared from sight, the reverend was praying as hard as he could pray.

Sarah saw no men. It was dark and cold, but she was dressed appropriately if she just kept moving. She walked all over the ship, looking for any human being. She saw none.

She ran back to the front of the bow to look for the men. They were gone. She waved at her father. When he saw her, he frantically started waving for her to come back to him. However, she was not finished searching.

She walked the ship again. This time, she looked for ways to get down below. She walked the entire length of the ship but saw nothing. She decided to head back to the front of the ship to check if the men were returning.

She was walking very fast. Suddenly, she tripped and fell to the deck. The fall caused a loud thud. Directly underneath the noise, Ray Andrews awoke from a dazed state. He was barely alive. Cyrus Welch had ordered not to feed the men for the past two days. He needed to keep them very weak. That way, they wouldn't have the energy to rebel.

Sarah climbed back to her feet. She had torn her shirt and skinned both of her elbows badly.

"Damnation!" she yelled. It was the first time in her life she had ever cussed. Her frustration had peaked. Her anger had boiled over, and her patience had broken.

However, the sound of her voice awoke Ray Andrews. He was jolted by a surge of adrenaline. "Could it be?" he whispered to himself. He scrambled to his feet and made his way as close as possible to where he heard the sound.

"Who's out there?" he yelled as loud as he could into the ceiling of the cargo department.

He started pounding the roof with the palm of his hands.

Sarah froze in her tracks. She was stunned. It didn't register with her that it was Ray down below. She only hoped it was him. She got down on her hands and knees.

"Ray Andrews!" she screamed. "I'm looking for Ray Andrews!" Ray started laughing. It was his instinctive reaction.

"Sarah!" he yelled. "Is that you? I'm down here!"

At that moment, Sarah Thomas felt the biggest rush of excitement that she would ever experience in her life. She started crying again. She couldn't help herself.

"Ray, I'm here!" she screamed downward.

There wasn't time for small talk. Ray immediately went into leader mode.

"Do you see anything to knock the lock off the door?" he screamed upward.

Sarah jumped to her feet and frantically started looking for something to use. However, Cyrus Welch would never leave any kind of tool unsecured. Everything was locked up tight. There was not as much as a wrench available. After looking all over the deck for something to use, Sarah returned to the cargo area.

"I can't find anything!" she screamed. "Everything is locked up." She started pulling on the lock. It wouldn't budge. By then, all the other men were wide awake. They all
sensed an escape.

"Sarah, stop!" Ray screamed.

As much as he wanted out from the cargo area, he realized he would have to be patient.

"You're gonna have to come back tomorrow night!" he yelled upward. "Can you hear me?"

Sarah got back down on her knees.

"Yes, I can hear you!" she yelled back to him.

Ray got his face right up to the ceiling.

"Listen closely, Sarah!" he screamed. "Come back at the same time tomorrow night. Don't come on the ship unless everybody is gone. Bring the biggest axe you can find."

Sarah's mind was racing.

"Where do I get an axe?" she asked.

Ray was a little frustrated by her question.

"I don't know," he answered.

He wasn't screaming as loud now. She could hear him fine.

"The blacksmith next door to the mission, he'll have one. Come back with an axe," Ray said.

It got quiet for just a few seconds. Ray was thinking. Suddenly, a thought hit him.

"Sarah," he said. "Do you still have all my belongings? There is a burlap sack. Bring it with you."

Sarah was already thinking about her return trip. She wondered how she would carry an axe and the burlap sack onto the ship.

Ray wasn't finished.

"And Sarah," he yelled again. "Bring three five-dollar bills." Sarah was perplexed.

"Why do you need money?" she asked him.

Ray didn't waste any time answering.

"Just bring them. Now get out of here. Come back tomorrow night."

Sarah was getting a little worried. She hated to leave, but she knew she needed to get off the ship. There was no telling when the men would be back.

She took a couple of steps to the bow. Then she stopped and went back to the cargo compartment. She dropped back down to her knees.

"Ray," she yelled.

Ray looked up to the roof.

"Yea, I'm here," he yelled back to her. Sarah tried to figure out what to say.

"I'm sure glad I found you!" she said.

Ray smiled. "Me too!" he answered.

Sarah waited for about ten seconds; then she repeated herself, "I'm really glad I found you!"

Ray looked at the other men. James Meredith whispered something to him. Ray couldn't understand what he said. Meredith whispered a little louder, "Tell her thank you."

Suddenly, Ray got the hint. He looked back up at the ceiling.

"Sarah!" he yelled. "Thank you!"

A big smile covered Sarah's face. For just a brief moment, her stomach stopped hurting. She got up and dusted herself off. Before she left, she yelled down below one more time.

"You're welcome. I promise. I'll be back tomorrow night."

CHAPTER 50

*S*ores executed the opium exchanges flawlessly. Before he and his four soldiers made the deals, he left Cyrus Welch, Suk Too and Billy Lambert at the Lonely Sailor. He would not take them with him. That was part of the deal. There was no need for Sores to give up that kind of leverage. If they met the contacts, it would erode his power. Neither Cyrus nor Suk Too cared though. They had done enough. The voyage had been exhausting. They were fine with Sores taking care of the San Francisco end of the deal.

Sores treated the men to all the beer and whiskey they wanted that night at the Lonely Sailor. He put Billy Lambert in charge. Sores also had arranged for Suk Too to meet up with his favorite prostitute that very evening.

By daybreak, the opium deals were done. Sores arrived back at the Lonely Sailor around 7:00 a.m. Cyrus and Billy Lambert had gone downstairs and found a place to sleep in Sores's old quarters.

As he had done on the first deal, Sores took a cut off the top.

He took advantage of getting the men drunk and the early morning hours. Before he awoke the men, he separated some of the gold and dropped it off with Josephine Park. He figured he skimmed about a fourth of the gold that had been exchanged. He knew they would never know the difference.

It didn't even matter to Cyrus Welch and Suk Too. They were paid handsomely. Their trust in him made them weak in Sores's eyes. It wasn't until noon that the three men met upstairs at the Lonely Sailor. Sores had been to the gold exchange and paid the men in cash. Billy Lambert was paid well too. However, he was not a partner.

"Don't blow all your money," Sores lectured Cyrus and Suk Too. "Put most of it away. We worked too hard for it."

Cyrus just smiled. "I be fine, mate. Ye need to mind ye own business."

Suk Too and Billy Lambert said nothing.

Sores was ready to start talking about another trip to Hong Kong. "When do you sail again?" he asked.

Though he had been unknowingly cheated out of a good deal of money by Sores Aguilar, Cyrus Welch was still astonished by his payday. He had never had this much money in his life. He only needed a few days to recover, and he would be ready to hit the sea again.

"Let me think, mate," he answered. "Maybe in two weeks."

Billy Lambert rolled his eyes. He was not going on another trip to Hong Kong. Suk Too, on the other hand, was a follower. He was ready to do as he was told.

Cyrus got up out of his chair and put on his hat.

"Need to go check on the clipper," he said. "Come on, Billy. Need to feed the men."

Billy Lambert grabbed his hat and coat and followed Cyrus out the door.

Ray Andrews and the rest of the slaves were literally on a deathwatch. Their eyes had sunken back into their heads. They were gaunt and weak, almost dead. However, now they had hope.

Cyrus Welch and Billy Lambert arrived at two o'clock in the afternoon. They had picked up some bread from the street corner bakery. They would feed the men a better meal today though it was still a very poor one. Oatmeal and bread were the menu. The men would only be fed once this day. Cyrus had no idea that an escape was planned for tonight.

There wasn't much to do after feeding the men. Welch and Lambert left after walking around the docks for an hour or so. It would be another night of heavy drinking for both of them. There was no need to guard the men. They were too weak to cause any trouble. The waterfront noise would drown out any attempt to scream for help, and they were chained to the walls for security.

The reverend was there when they arrived at the docks. He watched the Melba Lee all day while Sarah prepared herself for the night. It was the reverend now whose stomach was churning. However, he realized he couldn't stop her. He might as well try to help her.

For Ray, Sarah, the reverend, and the rest of the prisoners, it was the longest day of their lives. The time crept along. They were gearing up for the most important night of their lives. The chances for problems would be high. Many things could go wrong. All they could do was wait.

That evening, Sores Aguilar planned on taking his lady friend, Josephine Park, to a nice dinner. Cyrus Welch would be ready to start drinking by three or four o'clock. Billy Lambert was thinking about heading down to 580th Capp Street to see if Sarah Thomas wanted to go to dinner before he started drinking. Suk Too had another date with the same prostitute he had courted the night before.

Sarah Thomas had walked over to the blacksmith just like Ray had told her to do. It took twenty minutes to muster up enough courage to ask him if she could borrow his axe. She was surprised when he offered it to her without any hesitation. She had also gone to the bank and withdrawn the three five-dollar bills. It finally dawned on her why Ray wanted the money. The men wouldn't be a whole lot better off free in the city without money. Five dollars would be plenty of money for them to pay for food and find a place to stay.

It was the burlap sack that bothered her the most. She wasn't a fool. She knew what it contained. She opened Ray's closet. He had hidden the sack in the corner. It was covered with his saddle. Sarah opened the sack and pulled out one of the Colt Navy revolvers. She thought it was loaded, but she wasn't sure. Ray had a backup gun belt in his belongings. It was the first one he had ever owned back when he was just a kid. Sarah strapped it around her waist. She pulled it tight. Then she realized how much she hated guns. She quickly unbuckled it and put it back in the sack.

She decided to walk around the neighborhood to ease her anxiety. She wandered into a hardware store. She wanted to look at some locks. She would have to break one open tonight. Suddenly, she spotted what looked like the exact lock she had seen on the deck of the ship. She asked the storekeeper about it. He informed her that it was very common. It was used on ships. One universal key would open it. If the lock on the deck was indeed the same lock she saw in the hardware store, she knew she could open it. She purchased the lock and the key for fifteen cents.

The reverend had been standing watch all day at the docks. Sarah arrived at midnight. She had found a big bag with a shoulder strap to haul the axe and the burlap sack. By then, the reverend was exhausted and hungry, but adrenaline had taken over the evening. He would stay through the entire escapade. After the escape, the three of them would make their way back to the mission as quickly as possible.

Sarah took a step toward the ship. Her father called her back. "Sarah," he said in a loud whisper. "Come back here."

She walked back to him. They embraced. The reverend clutched his daughter like he had never done before. Not a word was spoken. There was nothing to be said. Finally, the reverend broke the ice.

"They left at two o'clock this afternoon, daughter," he said. "I haven't seen them since. Make this a quick trip. Get off that ship as quick as you can."

Sarah broke away and started running toward the ship. She never looked back. It was quiet on the docks. There was no one to be seen. Sarah made it to the Melba Lee. She grabbed the rope and climbed up on the deck. She made it over the top easily and slid on her knees to the cargo area. There she began banging on the deck with the axe.

"Ray!" she yelled. "Do you hear me?"

Down below, the men were barely conscious. They had eaten a better meal today than normal, but it was not close to enough nutrition to sustain a grown man. The cool, damp weather didn't help the situation either. Two of the men had developed a recurring cough problem. Of course, Cyrus Welch didn't think about outfitting the men with warm clothes. All of them were so weak they could barely stand. However, they had been waiting all day. The noise from above gave them energy.

Ray rose from his crouched position and moved to the hatch. "We're here!" he screamed. "Did you bring the axe?"

Sarah smiled and looked around for any sign of trouble. "I've got it!" she shouted back at Ray. "First, let me see if I can open this lock."

She pulled the key out of her pocket. It only surprised her a little when the key easily turned and opened the lock. She pitched the lock aside and started pulling the door open. Ray was close to the hatch, but he was not close enough to help her open it. She pulled and pulled, but she wasn't big enough to get it open. The door raised up about a foot, then it slammed back down as she let go of the handle. Sarah was starting to panic.

Ray calmed her down.

"How did you get that lock to open?" he asked her.

"I have a key," she responded.

Ray was impressed. He wasn't sure, but he thought the lock on his chained cuffs was the same lock as on the hatch door.

"Just drop the key down in here," he yelled to Sarah.

She opened the hatch door about six inches and pushed the key down into the cargo room. It fell to the floor close to Ray. He picked it up and opened the lock that had cuffed him to the wall. The exhilaration he felt was unbelievable. However, he didn't scream or jump for joy. He simply started opening the locks that shackled the other men. James Meredith was first. As soon as he was free, Meredith started climbing the steps out of the cargo area. He put his back against the hatch door and pushed. He was too weak to open it. One of the prisoners got up and started pushing Meredith's chest. Suddenly, the door opened and slammed as it turned over and hit the topside of the deck. The men stumbled clumsily out of the hatch. Ray stayed below until everyone else was on deck.

Sarah was stunned by what she saw. The men were emaciated. They looked like they were walking dead. The smell of their body odor hit her. It was the worst odor she had ever experienced. The filth was beyond imagination.

Sarah stepped away from the men and held her hand over her face. The men didn't run away. They waited for Ray Andrews to walk up the steps. Finally, he climbed his way out of the cargo area. He was the last man up the stairs. His face was covered with a rough beard. His hair was so long that Sarah barely recognized him. He had lost almost fifty pounds.

Sarah stepped forward. She was carrying the huge bag.

"Ray," she said shyly. Like all the other men, he had to shield his eyes from the starlight even though it was the middle of the night. Finally, he got himself together. He looked at Sarah. She was the prettiest thing he had ever seen.

"Thank you so much," he said to her.

Immediately, the rest of the men joined in thanking her.

There was no hugging or carrying on between them. Ray was too much of a mess for that. Sarah simply walked over and handed him the gunny sack. He knelt down and opened it. He started examining what it contained. He placed the two Colt Navy revolvers on the deck. He pulled out a pouch. It was wrapped in some kind of paper. He struggled to get it open. Finally, he tore the paper. It was beef jerky. Ray started tearing off pieces and handed them to the men. All of the men struggled with the first protein they had eaten in weeks, but just a little bit of food made a huge difference for them physically.

"Don't we need to hurry?" Sarah asked Ray.

He looked up at her. Then he picked up one of the Colt Navy revolvers.

"No," he said. "We're in control now."

The other men were watching and listening to every word he said.

"Did you bring the money?" he asked Sarah.

She pulled it out of her pocket.

"Give each man a five-dollar bill," Ray instructed her.

She did as she was instructed.

Finally, it was time to go. Ray thought for a moment to wait on Cyrus Welch, Suk Too, and Billy Lambert. He could kill them all if he just waited on them to come back to the ship. He had two guns and twelve shots. This nightmare could be avenged easily. However, even though he was a very bitter man, he was not a murderer. It was time to leave the ship.

Ray looked at the men and raised his right fist into the air. "Until we meet again!" he yelled at the top of his voice.

He obviously wanted someone, maybe Cyrus Welch, to hear him. The other men raised their fists and responded.

"Till we meet again!" they said almost in unison.

Sarah took off for the bow of the ship. She climbed down the rope and swung herself to the ground. The other men followed. As soon as each man hit the ground, he took off running. They seemed to go in different directions. Ray was the last man down. He and Sarah looked at each other.

"Let's go!" she ordered him.

He nodded his head. They had escaped from the Melba Lee without as much as a hint of violence.

CHAPTER 51

*C*yrus Welch awoke at ten o'clock the next morning, which was a Saturday. He had hit three bars the night before in San Francisco. He started his night out at Rose's Tavern on Market Street where he drank the house black whiskey. He got bored there and wandered down to a bar called The Aussie Escape on lower Montgomery Street. There he drank the house beer. He finished his evening across the street from the Lonely Sailor at a bar called The Shark's Den. He liked The Shark's Den better than the Lonely Sailor for drinking.

Cyrus curtailed his drinking a little at The Shark's Den. He had been noticing all night the signs of opium out on the streets. Sores had warned him not to try it even once. However, he knew the signs of the drug. The dazed look on the face of people was a sure sign they were high. The damage of the drug was becoming very obvious to Cyrus. He finally ate some dinner late in the night around midnight. The Shark's Den had a pretty good Australian menu. After he ate, he stumbled across the street to the Lonely Sailor. Sores Aguilar was always good to him, and he was allowed to sleep downstairs on Sores's couch. He was not allowed to sleep in Sores's bed.

Sores had left for his other residence much earlier in the evening. Cyrus just knew not to sleep in the bed. He had a splitting headache from the drinking the night before. After stumbling across the room, he had enough composure to make some coffee. He then choked down some stale biscuits that had been left out from the night before.

Thirty minutes later, Sores walked in the front door. He was already tired of Cyrus Welch loitering in his old quarters. However, he held his tongue and didn't say anything. Sores was anxious to get Cyrus back out on the Pacific Ocean headed to Hong Kong for another opium haul.

Sores newfound sophistication was making Cyrus Welch a little uncomfortable. He decided to tell Sores about it. He was still drunk from the night before, so he didn't worry about mixing words.

"You getting a little high an' mighty, aren't ye, mate?" Cyrus said.

Cyrus stumbled back to the couch, spilling some coffee along the way. He sat down and continued.

"Ye making me nervous," he said. "Lot on the line ye know."

Sores gathered his composure. He wasn't mad. Cyrus was right, and he knew it. Sores enjoyed the good life. As a matter of fact, he probably enjoyed it a little too much. He had already thought of that himself. It was just that domestication had its advantages, and Sores was enjoying them.

"You're right," he told Cyrus. "I'm probably getting a little too comfortable."

He was wearing new clothes that he and Josephine had picked out yesterday.

"I'll take care of it,"

Sores poured a cup of coffee and took a sip. He grimaced as he swallowed. The coffee was terrible. Cyrus had made it really strong like they drank it back in Australia.

Sores sat down in a chair across from Cyrus. After a few more moments of silence, he spoke.

"We need to make another run as soon as possible," he said. "The time is right. I have more customers on the other side than I can supply. If I can't get them what they need now, they will go to someone else."

Cyrus was waking up now. He gave Sores a hard look.

"Ye don't understand, mate. Ye job is easy. Me is the one who has the tough duty. Takes two months to get over and back. Love to sail but has its limits."

Cyrus continued on his rant.

"The men we captured are all good sailors," he said.

"Least the ones still alive. Hard to keep 'em down, mate. They loble to die tonight. Need to treat 'em better, but that's risky. They could mutiny me."

Cyrus struggled to his feet.

"Worried 'bout Billy too. He a good sailor, but he hates it. Probably will run off soon."

Sores Aguilar's biggest fears were alive and well. He had trusted the sailing part of the business to Cyrus Welch. Now Welch was showing real weakness. It could jeopardize the operation. Sores knew not to come down on Cyrus though. He was already well aware of everything he had just been told. Secretly, he had wondered why Cyrus had waited so long to start complaining.

"I understand," Sores responded. "You're right. We need to talk about some things. We need to look at the big picture."

Sores Aguilar was one of the greatest liars of all time.

"I care about you," he continued. "We need to make it right." Sores wanted to take a look at the slave labor situation, but he realized that he needed to focus on Cyrus Welch right now. "Let's go to the docks and check on the men. I will help you feed them," he said.

Cyrus poured himself another cup of coffee. "Sure, mate," he answered. "Let me get myself together first."

The two of them made their way to the docks. It wasn't a long walk. It took forty-five minutes to get there. Cyrus stopped on the docks and looked at the Melba Lee. The lines that secured her to the dock didn't look right. They were loose. Cyrus didn't think much of it. He grabbed one of the lines and hoisted himself up and over the rail. Sores was right behind him.

Cyrus Welch was still in a bit of a drunken state. He walked over to the cargo hatch. The lock was missing. At first, it didn't register with him. Suddenly, it hit him. Something was very odd. Sores Aguilar walked up behind him.

"What's the matter?" he asked.

Cyrus Welch reached down and grabbed the handle of the hatch. Unlike Sarah Thomas, he pulled it open easily. Down below were chained cuffs lying on the floor of the cargo room. Everyone was gone. Cyrus Welch was stunned. He couldn't believe it. Sores shook him.

"Cyrus," he said. "Wake up! What's the matter?"

Cyrus Welch came to his senses.

"We been robbed, mate!" he screamed. "We been robbed!"

CHAPTER 52

$\mathscr{R}$ay Andrews had to take three baths before Sarah Thomas was satisfied with the way he smelled. Ray not only shaved his beard, but he shaved all the hair off his body including his head. Sarah was afraid that he might have lice.

It took three days for Ray to get his strength back up to an acceptable level. Sarah and the reverend gave him his own room in the back of the mission. He slept for hours at a time. Ray didn't say much. Sarah would check on him often, but she didn't pry about what had happened to him on the voyage. Having a man other than her father around was a new experience for her. She was trying to get used to it.

Ray didn't venture out much except to walk up and down Capp Street. He was thinking about what he would do next. Although he was not a hard man by nature, he was extremely bitter toward the men who had captured and enslaved him.

Ray finally made his way out to the main lobby of the mission. Sarah was there cleaning the room. She had been mopping the floors. She had this thing about cleanliness. The mission was spotless. Keeping the church in great condition kept her mind and body busy. She had been the janitor of every church her family had been involved with since she was a young girl.

Ray sat down in one of the pews and watched her. She noticed him, but she kept right on working. She was too shy to say anything, so Ray broke the silence.

"Sarah," he said. "Please come over here and sit down." Sarah kept mopping the floor.

"I'll be done soon," she answered.

But she kept mopping the floor for thirty minutes. She was stalling for time because she was scared. She was also trying to get the floor clean to her specifications. It was the first time that Ray realized that she had extreme standards about such things. He had thought her reaction to his personal cleanliness was a little odd, but he didn't give it that much thought. It was okay with him though. It gave him more time to admire her beauty. She was tall and thin with a great body. Her long, black hair was in a ponytail. Her facial features made her look like a queen.

When she was ready, Sarah put the mop away and got herself together. She walked over to the bench where Ray sat. She stood for several minutes. Ray finally had to ask her to sit down. She was really nervous. Ray took her hand and held it like a gentleman.

"It's okay," he told her. "I'm nervous too."

The two of them started talking. It only took a couple of minutes before the conversation started flowing. They were already best friends. Ray focused on Sarah. He wanted to know everything about her because they had never really had much time to talk. Eventually, the conversation got around to how she figured out he was on the Melba Lee. She told him every detail. He was particularly interested in hearing about Sores Aguilar.

Finally, the conversation got around to him. Ray really wasn't interested in telling stories. He was interested in what he was going to do next. He still hadn't figured it out yet.

"Tell me what you know about this Sores Aguilar," he asked her.

She gave him all the information she knew.

Sarah looked him in the eyes.

"You're not telling me everything," she said. "Don't keep any secret from me. I won't stand for it."

Ray sensed that she might hit him if he didn't start being more descriptive. She was, after all, almost six feet tall, and she had already proven her physical strength and skills.

"There's just too much evidence," he finally said.

Sarah had no idea what he was talking about.

"What evidence?" she asked.

Ray was holding the feather he had picked up at the site of the payroll robbery. It was the feather he found when the coach made its way back through Rosary Hill.

"If this feather matches the feather Aguilar is wearing, I will know without a doubt that it's him," he said. "I think it will be enough evidence back in Texas."

Sarah didn't understand.

"You're gonna have to do better than that," she said.

Ray told her about the shooting contest, the guard duty, the robbery, and William T. Nelson. It hurt him deep into his soul to tell the story. When he got to the part about finding his best friend, Tom Jenkins, he started crying. Sarah was stunned.

"We called him Empty Heart because we didn't know his name," Ray said. "He cut a body part off of everybody he killed. It was usually a finger or an arm. He tried to chop Tom's foot off at the ankle, but I guess he didn't have time to finish the job. We had information that he wore a red feather. Right before I blacked out, I saw a man behind the bar. He looked like an Indian. He was wearing a red feather that looked just like this one."

Ray gathered his composure. After a couple of minutes, he continued, "Then Cyrus Welch pulled out a Colt Navy revolver on the ship. I recognized it as soon as I saw it. There are only a few of those guns in Texas. There can't be any of them out here. Empty Heart stole three of them during the robbery."

Ray leaned back in the pew.

"It's him. Sores Aguilar is Empty Heart. I know it in my gut. He killed five men and robbed the payroll. Now he's out here kidnapping men. There's no telling what else he's up to. He's got to be brought to justice."

Sarah chimed right in on the subject.

"How in the world are you going to do that?" she asked him. "Are you going to take him back to Texas?"

Ray Andrews wasn't thinking in those terms. He didn't want to go back to Texas.

"I don't know," he answered. "I have to figure it out."

Sarah walked back over to her mop and bucket. She started working again. Ray sat in the pew and watched her. After about five minutes, he got up and started walking away.

"Where are you going?" Sarah asked him.

Ray turned around.

"I've got to get dressed," he said. "I need to get to work."

CHAPTER 53

*B*illy Lambert had thought long and hard about just walking away. They would never find him. Everyone was too busy. But in the end, he decided he had too good of a deal in San Francisco. He loved it there, and he was very well paid. The money was the deciding factor in his decision to stay. He figured if he stayed with Sores Aguilar, he was going to make his fortune.

He walked up the staircase and entered the Lonely Sailor. Sores Aguilar was sitting at a table by himself. Billy walked over to him. Sores looked up at him.

"The sailors are gone," Sores said. "We should have been guarding them."

Billy Lambert couldn't believe it.

"Gone," Billy said in a panic. "What do you mean gone? They were chained to the wall."

Sores rolled his eyes.

"Someone unlocked the chains," he said. "They got away without having to fight."

It didn't take Billy Lambert any time to react. "Andrews," he said with a smirk. "It had to be him." Sores Aguilar rose out of his chair.

"What do you mean, Andrews?" he asked.

Billy Lambert looked Sores in the eye.

"He was the only one who could have figured out how to get away."

Cyrus Welch never bothered to tell Sores about Ray Andrews, so Billy Lambert did.

"He's dangerous. I don't think we would have made it out of Hong Kong alive without him. He told Cyrus that gun wasn't loaded right before we went into town. He sat right there on the deck of the ship and reloaded it with a shotgun pointed at his head. We walked right into a trap after we made the deal. Cyrus handed him the gun. I fired first, and then Andrews shot our way out of there."

Sores Aguilar was all ears now.

"What gun are you talking about?" he asked.

Lambert looked at Sores.

"That revolver you gave Cyrus. Andrews told us he knew that gun better than anybody. He was right. I've never seen anybody shoot like that. It was dark too."

"Did Andrews ever mention the Rangers?" Sores asked.

Lambert was beginning to put things together himself. "Yeah, he did," Billy Lambert answered. "He said he used to work for them back in Texas."

All of a sudden, Sores Aguilar figured out the identity of Ray Andrews. His heart sank. His mind immediately raced back to the payroll robbery. He didn't have time to dismember the body of the Ranger who was staked into the hill with the arrow. He never separated the spirit from the man. The gunfire was too close. He had to get away. That spirit had followed him to San Francisco. That spirit was Ray Andrews.

Sores sat quietly for a moment. Billy Lambert broke the silence.

"I bet I can find him," he said. Sores looked up at Lambert.

"Where?" he asked.

Billy Lambert gathered himself. He realized that for the first time he had leverage with Sores Aguilar. Suddenly, things were awkward as Lambert tried to figure out what to say next. He had become a shrewd businessman. He had become just like Sores Aguilar. The value he brought to the organization had just escalated. Delivering Ray Andrews was possible, but he had concerns.

"Now look, Mr. Aguilar," Billy said. "We better be careful here. If we get into it with Andrews, we better be ready. I'm not so sure about this."

Sores Aguilar rose up out of his chair and stepped toward him. He put his hand on Lambert's shoulder.

"Don't worry, Billy," Sores said. "I will make it worth it to you if you can find him."

That was what Lambert wanted to hear.

"So, if I find Andrews, will there be a finder's fee?" he asked. Sores was used to everyone in the organization positioning him for a payday.

"Yes," he responded. "One hundred dollars if you can tell me where he is located. After we know where he is, we can plan our next move. Are you sure this Ray Andrews was the man who planned the escape?"

Billy Lambert was sure, but he hedged his bet.

"Ask Cyrus," he answered. "I'll bet you that he will tell you the same thing."

Sores left Billy Lambert at the Lonely Sailor. Of course, Lambert knew that Ray Andrews was probably staying close to the Grace Methodist Mission Church down on Capp Street. It was obvious that he and Sarah Thomas had something going on together. Lambert's pride and jealousy were sneaking into the new dynamics of the situation. He knew that if he led Sores Aguilar down to the church, serious trouble was likely. Eliminating Ray Andrews from the picture was in his best interests.

CHAPTER 54

*R*ev. William Thomas had been doing his homework since he had heard Ray Andrews's story of being kidnapped. He decided that he would do his own detective work. He walked down to the San Francisco County Sheriff's office. It took him about an hour to gather up enough confidence to approach the receptionist.

"Ma'am," he asked the old lady who worked behind the desk. "What do I have to do to speak to the county sheriff?"

The old lady behind the desk never looked up at him. However, she did answer his question.

"Colonel Hays is not taking any walk-in visitors," she said as she concentrated on her paperwork. "Fill out this form, and we will try to schedule you into his day It will probably take a week or two."

Without looking at him, she handed him the form. The reverend filled it out and handed it back to her. He tried to get her attention again.

"Ma'am," he said. "I'm not sure this can wait a week or two.

I really need to see someone who can help me now. This situation is very serious."

The old lady was not impressed.

"Colonel Hays has a very busy schedule. You must wait your turn to speak to him."

The reverend didn't know what to do. He walked over and looked at a framed picture of Col. John Coffee Hays. He looked like a sophisticated man. He didn't look like the other lawmen that the reverend had known. With the pressure off the reverend about his initial approach to the situation, he gained more confidence. He decided to people watch for a while. The workers in the office seemed busy but disorganized. He decided to be more aggressive. A refined man was standing in the corner reading a local newspaper, The San Francisco Evening Journal. He was smoking a pipe. The reverend saw fit to approach him. He walked over and started up a conversation.

"That Colonel Hays is really a character," the reverend complained to the man. "I would have thought he would be friendlier."

The refined man rolled his eyes.

"You mean you actually got to talk to him?" he answered. "He usually dodges anybody who has a real problem. He is much too interested in politics to worry about enforcing the law."

The reverend was taken aback.

"Name's William Thomas," the reverend said. "Reverend William Thomas. I just started a church down on Capp Street."

The reverend held out his hand to shake. The refined man changed his pipe into his left hand. He was now holding both his newspaper and his pipe in his left hand. He extended his right arm to shake the reverend's hand.

"Russell Snipes is my name," he said. "Pleasure to meet you. I'm a plaintiff attorney."

Snipes immediately produced a small piece of paper. On the paper, he had carefully written his name and address.

"You need any help with the law, I'm available," he said.

"Seems a bit unorganized around here to me," the reverend commented. "I need some help with a problem. I don't feel too confident that I'm gonna get it here."

Russell Snipes had seen it before. Hanging around the sheriff's office was part of his normal daily routine.

"This place moves at a snail's pace," he said. "Don't count on any help from these people. This is a political office not a law enforcement office."

The reverend squinted his eyes.

"What do you mean a political office?" he asked.

Snipes wasn't impressed.

"Colonel Hays is an old Texas Ranger. Did you know that?" he asked the reverend.

The reverend shook his head. He had never heard of John Coffee Hays until this day.

"He did some great things in the past," Snipes continued.

"But he is a politician now. I don't think he is much interested in law enforcement any more. He has his hands full with the Vigilance Committee."

The reverend was interested in the Vigilance Committee, so he asked about them. It took Snipes fifteen minutes to tell the reverend about how they operated.

It was obvious to the reverend that Russell Snipes didn't like Colonel Hays, the current sheriff of San Francisco County, so he decided to keep pressing the issue.

"I need information about pressing charges of kidnapping. How do I go about doing it?"

Russell Snipes eyes perked up. He looked directly at the reverend.

"Who are you going to press charges against?" he asked the reverend.

The reverend wasn't ready to give Snipes that kind of information. He was just on a fact-finding mission today. There was no reason to get into details.

"I have an eyewitness to a terrible crime," the reverend said. "I am concerned about what might happen if something isn't done by the law."

Russell Snipes laughed at the reverend.

"You want strong law enforcement in San Francisco?" he bellowed. "Listen, Reverend, you are better off to take things into your own hands. The law enforcement in this town works more toward the aggressor than it does for the victims."

However, Russell Snipes was always looking for a way to make money.

"Maybe I can help you for a small fee," he said to the reverend. "I have a lot of connections here in town. Maybe we can work out a deal."

The reverend didn't trust Russell Snipes for a minute.

"So, you don't think I will get much out of Colonel Hays?" he asked.

Snipes smiled again. "Nope," he said. "I don't. Who kidnapped whom?"

Before the reverend could answer, a huge crowd came walking into the foyer outside the courthouse. It was very noisy. It was Col. John Coffee Hays and his entourage. People followed him all the way into the building.

Questions were being asked. Nonsense was being said. Colonel Hays walked right by the reverend and into his office. The door slammed behind him.

The reverend looked at Russell Snipes.

"See what I mean?" the lawyer said. "He doesn't have time to be the sheriff. He wants to be mayor. Besides, there isn't any money for a real organized law enforcement program. That's why this town is going to hell in a handbasket. There is no law. I'm convinced that Hays would go out there and arrest people himself if he had the power, but he doesn't. This isn't Texas."

The reverend looked at Snipes. He didn't know what to think. Finally, he asked, "So if we produce evidence of a crime, we may not get any help from the authorities?"

Snipes nodded his head. "Hate to admit it," he answered. "But that's the truth. Hays doesn't have the manpower yet. He's trying though. Maybe someday things will be different but not now."

"What can you tell me about Aussie Town?" the reverend blurted out to Snipes.

The lawyer snapped his eyes toward the door. A criminal was being walked into the courthouse by a mob of people. Snipes spotted a prospective client.

"Stay away from there," he warned the reverend. "They're the worst of the worst. That's what I can tell you. If you are smart, you won't confront them."

With that, Russell Snipes scampered away to the chained man who obviously needed representation. Rev. William Thomas watched the entire scene. He was very upset. He took his hands and rubbed his eyes. He feared a violent end to this affair was coming in the near future. It was becoming very clear to him that Ray would be forced to fight fire with fire.

The reverend's scouting mission didn't stop at the courthouse. He was interested in the Colt Navy. Up and down-Market Street he walked looking for any gun place, pawnshop, or hardware store that might have one. He found nothing. Most of the business owners had never even heard of it. The reverend trusted Ray when he told him there weren't many of the Colt Navy revolvers around anywhere including Texas. He just needed to see for himself. Now he knew without any doubt. There was at least one down at the Lonely Sailor. Ray insisted that there were four. Down at the mission on Capp Street, Ray Andrews had three. That was twenty-four shots for the bad guys and eighteen shots for the good guys. It was easy for the reverend to do the math.

The reverend took a deep breath as he stood on the north side of Market Street. He decided to sit down on the bench seat to take a break and think for a while. It was only a few minutes until he found himself in prayer. He prayed for wisdom, and he prayed for guidance.

Suddenly, the reverend stood up and started walking. He was forty-six years old, but he was in great physical condition. He exercised every day by walking, and he had never given in to alcohol or tobacco in his life. He was actually a young man in comparison to others his age.

He covered a mile very quickly. He turned north on Montgomery Street and picked up the pace. He was walking uphill to what they called the Telegraph at the top. Just below the apparatus that the US Army had set up to attempt to telegraph incoming and outgoing ships stood what the people in town called Aussie Town. On the north end of

Aussie Town was a small two-story bar called the Lonely Sailor. It was easy to see.

The reverend made his move to the staircase on the north side of the building. He walked up the stairs and stepped into the bar. There were several people there. It was obvious that business was very good. It was a Friday afternoon, and the Aussies were already drinking. The reverend was careful to stay away from the bar. He noticed that rugs had been placed all the way around it.

Nobody will be kidnapped while I am here, he thought to himself.

He sat at a table in the corner of the bar all by himself. A fine-looking young woman eventually made her way over to him.

"What you having, cutie?" she asked.

Rev. William Thomas had never been called cutie in his life, not even by his wife. He played along anyway.

"Bring me a beer," he answered her.

It was obvious that the waitress was in a hurry. She had other patrons to serve.

"Light or dark?" she asked.

That caught the reverend off guard.

"What do you mean light or dark?" he responded.

The waitress looked at him with a little bit of disdain. "Listen, honey," she said. "You want light or dark? That's all we have."

The reverend looked around the room. Finally, he answered her, "Just bring me something I can see through. I don't like that dark beer. I don't know what's in it."

The waitress turned away and came back with the new house brew in only five minutes.

"Want to run a tab?" she asked.

Once again, the reverend didn't know what she was talking about. He didn't know what running a tab meant.

"Sure," he said as he pulled out his wallet. By the time he got it out of his pocket, the waitress was gone.

The reverend dabbed his tongue into the beer, but that was all he tasted. He was just curious. He had never had one before. He refocused his attention on the bar. He wanted to see for himself where men were being captured and enslaved. The opium dens had started taking over the town. He saw the damage they did every day. He needed to see where it was coming from. His instincts told him that he was sitting in the building that was the number one source of the drug for the city. Of course, he was correct in his assessment.

Behind the bar, a man was wiping glasses dry. The reverend focused on him. There seemed to be nothing really out of the ordinary going on in the place. The reverend knew he needed to be patient, so he waited for over an hour. The waitress checked on him every ten minutes. He didn't want to look suspicious. He was tucked into the back of the bar. The floor was a total mess. He decided to pour a bit of his beer out underneath the table. That way, it would look like he was drinking.

Just after seven o'clock, the reverend reached into his pocket and pulled out his timepiece. He didn't want to stay much longer. It was then that he heard a door open behind the bar. His eyes were glued to the man who walked in the door. It was him. It was Empty Heart, Sores Aguilar.

The reverend bounced back and forth between thinking about the situation and praying for help. He never had doubted anything that Ray Andrews had ever told him. That wasn't why he went on this reconnaissance mission. It was just that he had to be totally sure of the facts himself. If he was going to be involved in a deadly battle with other men, he had to be sure of the facts.

Sores Aguilar was a big man dressed all in black. His hair was very long, down on his shoulders. His skin was dark but with a reddish tone. The reverend had never seen anyone before with that type of appearance.

It was dark and not easy to see. The reverend got up and moved to the bar. He wasn't afraid. He walked right to Empty Heart. When he reached the bar, he looked down at the rugs placed over the floor. He gripped the bar with both hands. If the floor opened, he would have to hold on tight.

"I need to pay my bill!" he said loudly.

Empty Heart turned to face him.

"What did you have to drink?" he asked the reverend. William Thomas glared at him.

"I had one beer," he responded.

Sores walked right up to him. Only the bar separated the two men. They stared directly into each other's eyes. The reverend looked down and noticed a red feather dangling onto Sores's chest. It was tied to the bottom strands of his hair. The reverend was positive it was the same feather Ray had in his possession back at the mission.

"That one's on the house," Sores said to the reverend. "Come back and visit us again someday."

The reverend didn't know what to say or how to act. He simply nodded his head. He turned and walked to the door. Before he left the building, the reverend turned back to take another look. What he saw stunned him. Empty Heart was standing at the bar with his arms folded. He was glaring right back at him.

PART IV

CHAPTER 55

Sores Aguilar had gone through a tough week. Somehow, the sailors that he had worked so hard to capture had escaped. He was conflicted about it. He had ordered Cyrus Welch to kill all of them before returning to San Francisco. However, things change in the black-market drug business. Cyrus decided to keep them instead of having to capture a new crew. That infuriated Sores at first. But after thinking it through, he had adjusted his thoughts. It was true that Cyrus, Suk Too, and Billy Lambert were ready to make another run to Hong Kong very soon if the enslaved sailors were still alive. Cyrus's plan had grown on him. Then, all of a sudden, the rug was pulled out from underneath him when the slaves escaped the ship.

But that wasn't the worst part of his week. Sores didn't expect worse news, but he got it. The next evening, he headed down to the boardinghouse up on Nob Hill like he had done many times before. He was not in a good mood, and he was looking for some companionship. He made it to the house where his girlfriend and companion, Miss Josephine Park, lived. When he asked the doorman to call for her, he got a strange response.

"Mr. Aguilar," the doorman said. "Miss Park has checked out of the house."

At first, Sores didn't realize the situation. He had a cigarette on his lips. Of course, it wasn't lit. Suddenly, the news hit him.

"What do you mean?" he scolded the doorman.

The doorman could only look at him with a desperate expression on his face.

"She left yesterday," he answered.

Sores lost his composure. He grabbed the doorman by the lapels of his coat and shook him.

"What do you mean she left yesterday?" he asked in a vicious tone.

The doorman was scared to death. Sores slung him away. He knew exactly where Josephine's room was located. Up the stairs he ran. When he reached room 205, the door wouldn't open. It was locked, so he busted through it, leading with his shoulder. He knocked the door handle completely through the trim. However, when he entered the room, nobody was there. There was no luggage or sign of any renter.

Sores had been taken again. Josephine Park, the upscale call girl, had run off with the gold Sores had asked her to keep. She had gotten away with close to $1,000 worth of treasure. Sores's humiliation was evident. He rushed back downstairs and confronted the doorman. "Where did she go?" he asked him. The look on the doorman's face was framed in terror.

"I don't know, Mr. Aguilar," he answered. "I didn't ask her. She left yesterday around noon."

Sores gathered himself and sat down in the lobby of the boardinghouse. He took off his hat. Then he looked up at the doorman. He took a deep breath. His anger was obvious. Most of it was towards Cyrus Welch and Josephine Park. But Sores Aguilar was a very smart man. He knew that the real person he should be mad at was himself. He had gone against everything he had relied on throughout his life. He had never trusted anyone since his mother died. He had always planned and calculated everything. He questioned himself. Why in the world did he let Cyrus Welch get that much control? Why in the world did he trust a woman with that much money?

Sores stood up and walked back to the doorman. He pulled a dollar out of his wallet and gave it to him. "Thanks for your trouble," he told him. Sores knew if Josephine Park was still in town he would find her. That was why he knew she was gone. He could try to chase after her. However, he knew she would be smart enough to hide the money where he couldn't find it.

He wondered to himself if chasing $1,000 and a disloyal woman was worth it. In the end, he decided it wasn't.

As he walked back to the Lonely Sailor, he began to collect his thoughts. It was time to go back to the basics. It was time to plan. It was time to do what was necessary. It was time to deal with Ray Andrews.

Two days passed. Cyrus Welch was in a worse mood. He had been totally humiliated by the escape of the slaves. He had worked hard to gain Sores's trust and respect. He had earned it too. But he took a big step backward when he failed to guard the Melba Lee. He had been spending most of his days back on the ship since he and Sores discovered the slaves were gone. He had taken it upon himself to clean the ship and tighten down any problem. The ship was back in prime condition, and he was itching to sail again to redeem himself.

Cyrus had been drunk and chased enough women for a while. Now it was time to get back to work. He walked the streets at night looking for Ray Andrews or any of the other men. Sometimes Suk Too went along with him. However, he didn't see any sign of any of them.

Billy Lambert was keeping his information to himself. He was waiting for the perfect time to cash in. Lambert didn't want things to look obvious. He wanted to make it look like he had worked to get the knowledge. He disappeared for a couple of days as he spied on the Grace Methodist Mission Church on Capp Street. Ray Andrews finally appeared one evening. He and Sarah Thomas went out for a walk. Lambert followed at a safe distance. He was extremely jealous.

When the young couple made their way back to the mission, Lambert headed back to the Lonely Sailor. It was time to tell Sores of Ray Andrews's whereabouts. He would make it look like he had roamed the streets to find him. Lambert had already decided to attempt to get an extra one hundred dollars out of Sores for the information. He didn't know exactly how he would do it. He just knew he was going to try.

Billy Lambert was sure about one thing. Ray Andrews had to go. Pride had gotten involved. Ray had earned his hatred. Then there was the money. Lambert was getting ready to have a big payday for finding Ray Andrews. To top it off, there was the girl, Sarah Thomas. With Andrews around, Billy Lambert had no chance with her.

It just so happened that when Lambert walked into the bar that night, all three of the partners were there. They had already discussed the situation. Sores was tending bar.

Cyrus was drinking whiskey, and Suk Too was hanging around waiting to be told what to do.

All three of them knew Lambert had inside information on Ray Andrews. As soon as he walked in the door, they all started congregating around him. Finally, Sores called for a meeting to be held downstairs. The four men sat around a table in the kitchen. Sores poured everyone a cup of coffee. Then he got right down to business.

"Where's Andrews?" he asked as he looked directly into Lambert's eyes. "We know you know where he is."

Billy Lambert tried not to squirm in his seat. He looked at each of the men.

"We had a deal about a finder's fee," he said.

Sores took a big gulp of coffee. He reached into his pocket and pulled out a chunk of gold. Casually, he pitched it on the table in front of Lambert.

"That will cover your fee," he told Lambert.

It was obvious to everyone in the room that Sores had quite a bit of disdain for Billy Lambert.

Lambert sat forward and put his elbows on the table. He looked directly at Sores.

"He is staying at a church down in the mission district—580th Capp Street is the address," Lambert said. "It's an old church. A Methodist preacher and his daughter are running the place."

None of the men in the room questioned Lambert on how he got his information. They were just interested in finding Ray Andrews.

Sores hadn't put it together that the preacher Lambert was talking about was the same man who he had given a free beer the night before.

"Go on," Sores said. "What other information do you have for us?"

Lambert was ready to spill the beans.

"Obviously, they helped him escape," he said. "I met them when they first came into town. I was scouting for some sailors at the south end of the city. I never trusted the old man. I was just interested in the girl. I went back to see her. Somehow, Andrews knew them. He was there. I had already been trying to get him to the saloon."

Lambert put both hands around his cup of coffee. He sipped a long drink, and then he continued, "They're starting up a church down in that part of town. That's where the bums go for food."

Sores kept prying. "How much firepower does he have?" Lambert didn't know the answer.

"Not sure," he said. "I just wouldn't underestimate him. He's really dangerous."

"Any more information?" Sores asked.

Lambert shook his head no. "That's all I know," he said.

It was enough. Sores turned his back to the men and slowly started pacing. Finally, he spoke.

"It's too dangerous not to deal with him now," he said. "He threatens our operation. If he gets to the right authorities or to the Vigilance Committee, he could bring us down. Right now, he is probably trying to figure out his next move. We need to beat him to the punch."

It got quiet. Sores was trying to figure out a plan. He walked back over to the table.

"Meet back here in two days at the same time. I will have a plan by then. Nobody says a word about this. If you come across Andrews, play it straight. Avoid him for now. We have to be careful."

Neither Cyrus Welch nor Suk Too had said a word during the meeting. They both got up to leave. Billy Lambert rose out of his chair, but Sores Aguilar wanted to speak to him alone. Cyrus and Suk Too didn't even look back as they walked out the door. Before Lambert could make it out of his seat, Sores called out to him.

"Billy," he said. "I need to speak to you alone."

The thought hit Billy Lambert that he might not make it out of the Lonely Sailor alive. He turned and faced Sores.

"Sit down," Sores ordered.

Billy did as he was told. Sores walked over to the cabinet and pulled out a bottle of whiskey. He grabbed two glasses. He sat down and poured two drinks. Lambert waited for Sores to drink first. That way he knew he wouldn't be poisoned. After a couple of excruciating minutes, Sores finally spoke.

"We've never really got to know each other, have we?" Sores asked.

Lambert knew exactly what he meant, but he played dumb. "What do you mean?" he asked.

Sores was quick with an answer.

"I didn't like you too much when I first met you. It wasn't anything personal, it was just business. But you've really impressed me." Sores took another drink. "I think it's time to make an agreement," he said.

Lambert was cool on the outside, but he was terrified on the inside.

"What kind of an agreement?" he asked.

Sores looked him directly in the eye.

"You probably realize that the chunk of gold I gave you is worth a lot more than one hundred dollars," he said. "It's way more than what you asked to find Andrews."

Lambert had thought the gold was way too large to be worth only one hundred dollars, but he hadn't said anything.

Sores leaned forward and put his elbows on the table.

"Here's the agreement, Billy," he said. "I'm gonna put you in position to kill Andrews.

If you do it, we'll make you an even partner in our organization."

It got really quiet. After about a minute, Sores continued.

"Now you have already accepted the gold. You don't want to give it back, do you?"

CHAPTER 56

*S*ince the night of the escape, Ray Andrews had been sleeping in the utility room of the church. The day he got there; Sarah Thomas started telling him he had to find his own place. She didn't like the fact that guns were in the church. She was also very concerned about what the neighbors and the patrons of the church would think about them. After all, they were not married.

One morning, the two of them started walking east to look for a place for Ray to live. They ventured up to an area called Potrero Hill. It was a forty-five-minute walk from the mission. It was located at one of the highest places in town. The view from the top was fabulous. They could look down on the entire city. Ray immediately noticed that he could see the mission from the top of the hill. Somehow, Potrero Hill escaped the fog and dampness that the rest of the city had to suffer on a daily basis. Both of them fell in love with it. Ray knocked on the door of the Thompson Boardinghouse and asked to see a room. The place would be quite adequate for the price. He moved in that afternoon.

The next day, Ray made his way down to Market Street. He stepped into the Gold and Silver to see his friend Georgia Tipps. Of course, Georgia was glad to see him. He told her that he only had limited money to spend on a ring, but he would be very grateful if she would sell him one. She played along that she was really disappointed that he was off the market, but she would be glad to help. She made him a great deal on one of her personal favorites. Georgia put the ring in a nice little box for Ray, but he wouldn't buy it, not yet anyway. He wasn't sure Sarah would say yes, and he for sure wasn't sure she would like the ring. He wanted to think about it some more.

Georgia assured him she would keep it in a safe place.

"Come back when you want it, honey," she told him. "I'll keep it right here."

Ray was set to ask Sarah to marry him. He wasn't sure how he was going to do it, but he had made up his mind. There was one problem. He still didn't have a job. He had been asking around town about what was available. There was plenty of work, but he wanted to be sure of what he was doing.

There was one job he was pretty sure he could get. He could go to work as a policeman. The city was desperate for lawmen. They would hire almost anyone. The problem was that the pay was terrible. The fire department was set up the same way. Ray knew that if he really needed a job, he could go to either one. However, he wanted something that paid better.

However, going to work for the local police would have its advantages. Ray was trying to figure out how to deal with Sores Aguilar and his gang. He had to bring them all to justice. All this had to be done before he could get serious about proposing marriage to Sarah, at least he thought.

Billy Lambert wasn't aware that Ray had moved to Potrero Hill. He thought Ray was staying in the mission. Once again, Ray was one step ahead of Lambert. Sores Aguilar was hunkered down at his house, working on a plan. Of course, he also had no idea that Ray had moved to Potrero Hill.

Sarah Thomas was going about her daily chores. The reverend and Ray both argued with her that she worried way too much.

However, Sarah was smart enough to know the people who had captured Ray were not going to be happy. She also knew that Ray was a very bitter man, and that would lead to trouble.

The Grace Methodist Mission Church was in very good shape financially thanks to Ray Andrews and Reverend Thomas. Ray had produced the upfront money, thanks to Mara McLemore's brooch. However, the reverend had already produced a small but steady income flow for the church. He had reached out to local leaders and citizens. Although he was a good preacher, the reverend's real strength had always been organization and fundraising. He had always excelled in those areas. He prided himself as a preacher of the word. He would get a little bit chippy when people explained to him that he was a better fundraiser than a speaker. It had always been an underlying issue that motivated him to move west. His view of serving was saving souls, not raising money. However, the truth was that any church he worked with would eventually be financially solvent.

There was another issue that was really bothering Sarah. She didn't like guns, but she had let Ray talk her into keeping a loaded Colt Navy inside the church for protection. He had trained her to fire it even though she never actually pulled the trigger. Sarah would have none of it. She was a good student. If it was ever necessary to use the Colt Navy, she would be ready. The reverend didn't seem to mind that the gun was in the mission. That surprised Sarah.

The morning after he moved to Potrero Hill, Ray made his way back down to the mission. There he found the reverend and Sarah doing a little housecleaning. A fresh pot of coffee was brewing, and the three of them sat down at a table in the kitchen. It only took a few minutes for the conversation to turn to the obvious.

"Are you going to go after Sores Aguilar?" the reverend asked Ray.

Ray wasn't in the mood to talk about it. However, he had too much respect for the reverend just to ignore the question. After a couple of minutes, he responded.

"Yes," Ray said. "He has to be brought to justice. He is the main source of opium in the city. People are dying on the streets because of him. He killed five men in Texas, and he also stole $3,000 from the state."

The reverend and Sarah already knew all of that.

"How are you going to bring him to justice, Ray?" the reverend asked.

Sarah started asking a question before Ray could answer.

"Are you sure you have enough evidence to convict him in Texas?" she asked.

Ray started to comment on the fact that he had been involved in the conviction of many outlaws with a lot less evidence than he had against Sores Aguilar, but he decided against answering. Sarah didn't stop.

"You have a red feather, that's it," she said. "You don't have any witness that can identify him. Ray, you can't take him back to Texas. It isn't worth it!"

Ray didn't seem a bit fazed. He simply looked at the both of them. Finally, he asked, "Well, what do you think I should do with him?"

A dumbfounded look took over both the faces of the reverend and Sarah. Neither of them had put any thought into that. They had both been focused on convincing Ray on what not to do.

"I know what I am going to do," Ray said calmly. "I've been watching their saloon."

Now Sarah and the reverend were really confused. They both began wondering how and when he had been watching. They didn't realize that Ray had been leaving the mission at night to scout.

"This won't be over until Empty Heart is dead," Ray said very seriously. "I don't like taking another man's life. It really bothers me, but I have to deal with him. If I don't, he will kill me and probably you too."

Neither Sarah nor the reverend had ever heard anyone say anything like that before. They had lived their lives on the right side of the moral law. Ray had lived most of his life fighting people who lived on the wrong side. Sarah took her hands and covered her eyes. She knew that Ray was right.

Ray wanted to take the conversation in a different direction. "Reverend," he said. "I want to ask you a question."

The reverend looked up at Ray.

"Of course, son," he answered.

Ray stood up and pulled his shoulders back.

"What would you think if Sarah and me got married?" he asked.

After about thirty seconds, Sarah comprehended what he had just asked. She leaned over to him and slapped him hard on his left arm.

"What are you talking about?" she scolded him.

Ray smiled. "I picked out a ring down at Georgia Tipps's place. I think you'll really like it."

He was almost teasing her. The reverend didn't smile, but he was pleased. He just wanted to be serious.

"That's quite a question," he said to Ray.

It got quiet again. The reverend glanced over to Sarah. He could tell by the look on her face that she was ecstatic. She was not doing a very good job of acting like she was mad at Ray.

"I guess it would be all right," the reverend said. "But only on one condition."

The answer surprised Ray.

"What condition?" he asked.

The reverend stood up and poured himself some more coffee.

"Violence will win you some battles, but it will never win the war." Ray understood exactly what the reverend meant.

"But, Ray," the reverend continued, "you put a collar around your neck and you can stop this debauchery in San Francisco. It's a moral issue. If it isn't stopped, it will spread through the territory and into the rest of the country. The church will get the job done."

Ray looked at Sarah. The reverend smiled and continued talking.

"But, sir," he said. "I would be honored to welcome you into our family."

Just then, Sarah Thomas stood up and spoke.

"Well, are you two just going to decide my future?" she asked. If she was really mad, she would have made a much bigger scene. However, the truth was that she was very happy.

"You can't tell me what to do," she scolded Ray. "I have my own ambitions."

Ray nodded his head.

"And I keep a clean house," she added. "If you don't like it, that's too bad. You can leave."

She started looking around the mission. It was as if she was searching for something.

Finally, she looked back at Ray.

"I'm not putting up with any nonsense. No drinking or smoking or carrying on, you hear?"

Ray again nodded his head. All Sarah knew to do was to nod her head back to him. Then she asked a question. "Well, are you going to go get the ring?"

CHAPTER 57

*R*ay immediately headed north on Van Ness Boulevard. He would turn east on Market Street. If he hurried, he could make it to the Gold and Silver before it closed. Sarah Thomas didn't show much emotion. She just told him to go get the ring. Ray took that as a yes to his clumsy marriage proposal.

It was 7:00 p.m., and it was dark. Ray was walking faster than most people could run. He was on an emotional high and couldn't wait to get that ring in his hands. He knew Georgia Tipps closed the Gold and Silver at 8:00 p.m.

He turned right onto Market Street. It was a bustling Thursday night. Ray slowed down and took a look at the core of the city. Naturally, he started looking around. He looked over to the other side of the muddy street. Someone caught his eye. It was a big man dressed in black. Ray watched him as he got closer. He focused his eyes for a better look. Suddenly, he instinctively crossed the street where he could come face-to-face with this man dressed in black.

After walking fifty yards, Ray stopped. The man dressed in black was walking directly to him. Ray waited until he was about thirty yards away.

"Sores Aguilar!" Ray barked. "Is that you?"

But Sores Aguilar had been waiting for Ray Andrews all day long. The two men stopped and faced each other. People walked right on by the both of them as they stared each other down. The rest of the public didn't seem to be interested in their feud.

Finally, Sores answered, "I'm Sores Aguilar."

Ray went right into Ranger mode.

"You're responsible for killing five Texas Rangers and stealing $3,000 from the state of Texas. I'm going to bring you to justice!" Sores stared at Ray. He didn't look like an outlaw. He looked more like a sophisticated man. After a few seconds, he answered, "The hell you are. You got nothing on me."

Sores turned to other bystanders who had stopped to watch. "Did you hear that man threaten me?" he exclaimed. "I don't feel safe around him. He is threatening me. Please, can you help me? I am an unarmed man. This outlaw is a threat to all of you." Ray was caught totally off guard. A big crowd had now gathered around Sores, and he was doing his best sales job. "This man has been extorting me!" he cried. "He is the kind of man we have to deal with to secure our city."

Right on cue, Billy Lambert appeared out of nowhere.

"That man has also threatened me!" Lambert yelled. "We finally have him cornered. Let's take him to trial right now before he runs away! This is why the Vigilance Committee was established!"

Ray Andrews was absolutely stunned. He knew nothing about the Vigilance Committee or what they did. Before he knew it, he was swarmed by angry men. Several of them ganged up on him and secured his arms. They took possession of his gun. Then the march to the meatpacking warehouse at the end of Market Street began.

Sores Aguilar had planned everything perfectly. He had been waiting for Ray to walk down Market Street. If he spotted Ray, he would approach him. Sores had positioned Billy Lambert perfectly to confirm his story. That way, there would be two witnesses who would lie about evidence against Ray Andrews and not just one. Cyrus and Suk Too watched from different vantage points to help identify Ray. They couldn't be a part of the mob of the Vigilance Committee. There was no way an Aussie or a Chinaman would ever be accepted into their ranks.

The crowd reached the meatpacking warehouse and hurried Ray upstairs. A new man was in charge of the Vigilance Committee tonight by the name of Carlton Smith. Sores had already told him they would probably arrive tonight with a well–known thug. Smith got right down to business.

"What is the charge against this man?" he asked.

Billy Lambert stepped forward. "This man has been threatening me. He demands money, or he says he will kill me!"

Ray spoke up in his own defense.

"I have never threatened anyone in my life!" he said loudly. "This is all a setup!"

Carlton Smith walked over to Ray and looked him in the eye. "What's your name?" he asked.

Ray stared back at him.

"Ray Andrews is my name, and I deny all these charges." Smith wasn't patient.

"Sit down," he ordered Ray. "I need ten volunteers for a jury. I'll be the judge."

It only took a few minutes for ten people to volunteer. They were ready for blood.

Smith slammed his fist on the table.

"Who makes a charge against this man?"

Billy Lambert stepped forward.

"Bill Lambert is my name. This man has been threatening me. He says that if I don't give him money, he will kill me."

The crowd hissed at Ray.

"How many times has he threatened you?" Smith asked Lambert.

"Five times," Lambert answered.

Smith looked out into the crowd.

"Does anyone else want to testify against this man?" he asked. Sores Aguilar calmly stepped forward.

"I want to testify. That man has also threatened me. I have had to run from him three times. Each time he says I have to pay him, or he will kill me."

"Have you ever paid him money?" Smith asked. Sores was quick with a lie.

"Of course," he said. "I have had to pay him twice." Smith looked over to Billy Lambert.

"I have had to pay him four times!" Lambert added.

Carlton Smith turned to Ray Andrews. It was obvious that he wasn't convinced of the crime. Ray was standing next to the jury. His hands were tied behind his back.

"What do you have to say in your defense?" Smith asked. Ray was very calm considering the situation.

"That man right there, Sores Aguilar, is guilty of killing five Texas Rangers and stealing $3,000 from the state of Texas. I was on the payroll detail for the Rangers when he committed the crime."

Before Ray could get to the part about Sores Aguilar and Billy Lambert kidnapping him and using him as slave labor, a voice broke in from the back of the room.

"Texas Rangers!" someone yelled. "You were a Texas Ranger!"

Suddenly, a sophisticated man came walking up from the back of the room. It was Colonel Jack Hays.

"How do I know you were a Ranger?" Hays asked Ray.

Ray's heart was racing.

"I was a Ranger for almost eight years. Look at my gun. That's a Colt Navy revolver.

There are only a few of them in circulation. That gun was made for the Rangers. Aguilar stole three of them during the payroll robbery, and he stole one from me when I was kidnapped. He killed five good men."

Sores Aguilar didn't plan on the county sheriff and former Texas Ranger, Colonel Jack Hays, showing up at the trial. Hays had been both fighting and working with the Vigilance Committee. It was all he could do to keep them under some kind of control. Hays looked at Sores and said, "What do you have to say about that Mr. Aguilar?"

Sores stared at the colonel.

"I have no idea what he is talking about, Colonel," he answered. "He has me mistaken for someone else."

Colonel Hays walked over to Ray.

"I am taking this prisoner into custody," he said as he took Ray by the arm. "I want to investigate these charges myself." Hays walked Ray right past Sores Aguilar on his way out the door. Ray and Sores locked eyes for a second, but the feather draped onto Sores's shoulder caught Ray's attention. The thought hit him that Sores's didn't realize it was the feather that provided the strongest evidence against him.

The colonel walked Ray right down to the courthouse and placed him in a jail cell. The Vigilance Committee broke up and dispersed throughout the city. It wasn't the first time that Colonel Jack Hays had upstaged them. For the moment, Sores Aguilar's plan had been foiled, but he had come so close. Had Colonel Hays not seen the mob scene and followed them to the meatpacking warehouse, Ray Andrews would have been hung right out of the second-floor window.

Colonel Hays put Ray into jail without any paperwork at all. He left for a few minutes, but he returned with a key to Ray's cell. He opened the cell and walked Ray to a room upstairs. There, Hays interrogated him for over two hours about the robbery on Rosary Hill. He asked questions he knew only a Ranger could answer. Ray quickly convinced him of his sincerity. It wasn't hard to do. Besides, Hays had already heard stories about Sores Aguilar.

After the interrogation, the colonel released Ray.

"Son," the colonel said to Ray. "I am sending word to Texas for someone to come get Aguilar and take him back."

The colonel chomped on his cigar.

"He's probably gonna try to kill you."

The colonel stared at Ray.

"If we get him back to Austin, you will have to go back and testify against him."

Ray already knew that. In the meantime, Colonel Hays had to figure out how to arrest and hold Sores Aguilar.

It was now three o'clock in the morning. Ray headed back to Potrero Hill. He was very careful that nobody was following him. He needed to get back and inventory his weapons and ammunition. He already knew what he had. It was just a process that made him feel comfortable.

CHAPTER 58

*R*ay slept for a few hours. After he awoke, he started planning. The hours passed. He didn't think it was wise to go down to the mission before dark. It was too dangerous. He might be spotted, and it would put Sarah and the reverend at risk.

Right at 5:30 p.m., darkness fell. Ray was starting his walk down to the mission to talk to Sarah and the reverend when he saw the first fire. It was about a mile north of the mission up toward Market Street. About a hundred yards to the south, another fire started. The high ground of Potrero Hill provided a great view. Suddenly, another fire started close to the other two. It wasn't odd for San Francisco to have fires. They happened all the time. However, these fires looked suspicious to Ray.

Sores Aguilar had gone back to his old plan. He figured that his strategy of placing four gunmen at specific stations and creating a crossfire would be the end of Ray Andrews. Only this time, he would use fire as the distraction, not arrows. As soon as Ray Andrews walked out the front door of the mission, either himself, Billy Lambert, Suk Too, or Cyrus Welch would shoot him down. Then they would all scramble back to the Lonely Sailor. Lambert would be placed closest to the mission. If things went according to plan, he would be the one who would kill Ray Andrews.

Ray was standing on Potrero Hill, observing the scene. It was Suk Too that gave the plan away. Ray could see him easily because Suk Too was so big. Every time the fire flamed, there was plenty of light to identify the giant Chinaman. He was taking the flank opposite of Billy Lambert down close to the mission. Ray's instincts reminded him of the attack on Rosary Hill. He started looking for the other gunmen. It only took him a few minutes to see Lambert hiding behind a water barrel. He couldn't see either Sores Aguilar or Cyrus Welch, but he visualized almost the exact spot of their locations.

Sores Aguilar had gone back to what he knew. The plan of attacking from four sides had always worked for him before. However, there were two big differences this time around. First, Ray had thought long and hard about how to defend such an attack. Second, Sores had no idea that Ray Andrews had the high ground and had spotted them before the attack.

Ray knew he had to be very careful about the angles of the gunfire coming from four directions. He slipped down the hill and headed for the biggest threat of the four men. That would be Billy Lambert. Ray knew that Suk Too and Cyrus were both poor shooters. He wasn't sure about Sores Aguilar. In only fifteen minutes, Ray had Lambert in his bearings. He could take him out easily with one shot. However, Ray Andrews was not a cold-blooded killer. He didn't like shooting anyone under any circumstance.

Ray gradually worked his way down the hill toward the mission. As he closed within fifteen yards, he saw a couple of buckets. He grabbed the buckets and threw one of them at Billy Lambert's shooting perch. When the bucket bounced off the water barrel, Lambert panicked. He came out from behind the barrel and fired a wild shot. Ray was on him in an instant. He threw the other bucket as hard as he could throw it. It hit Lambert in the head and knocked him down. Lambert fumbled his revolver onto the ground. He was propped up against the barrel when Ray Andrews fired a shot. The bullet pierced the barrel six inches away from Lambert's left ear. Water began pouring out in a perfect flow. Ray was on him in a second. He pointed the Colt Navy directly at Billy Lambert's forehead.

Their eyes met.

"Get out of town, Billy," Ray told him. "If I see you again, I'll kill you."

Suddenly, Billy Lambert scrambled to his feet and took off running north on Capp Street. Ray watched him until he ran out of sight. Ray hid the Colt Navy underneath the water barrel. His next target would be Suk Too.

The fire was raging by now. The sound of the gunfire mixed in with all the other noise. Across the street, Suk Too and Cyrus didn't even hear it. Sores Aguilar did hear it, and it worried him. Sarah and the reverend noticed it from inside the building. The mission was in danger. The reverend poked his head out the front door. As soon as he did, a shot rang out. A bullet bounced off the roofline. Suk Too had taken the shot. The reverend jumped back inside and grabbed Sarah. They both fled to the back of the building and got down on the floor for cover. After a couple of minutes, Sarah ran to a nearby closet. She grabbed a box and scrambled back to the reverend. Inside the box was a loaded Colt Navy.

Ray snuck all the way around the back of the mission to get an angle on Suk Too. It was easy to do. Suk Too was a great warrior in hand-to-hand combat. However, he knew nothing about guns. Ray got to within ten yards of him. Suk Too never knew he was there. Ironically, the fires that were burning had become an advantage for Ray.

"Suk Too!" Ray yelled. "If you try to shoot, I'll kill you!" Suk Too slowly turned his head toward Ray.

"Drop the gun!" Ray yelled.

Suk Too did as he was told.

"Kick it toward me," Ray continued.

Suk Too kicked the gun with his boots about three yards. He looked at Ray with a blank expression on his face.

"This is your chance," Ray said. "Leave now and don't come back. Head west and Sores will never know what happened. If I see you again, I will shoot you on sight."

The fires were burning all around them. Suk Too scowled at Ray, but on the inside, he was grateful. He knew Ray had spared him. He scrambled on all fours out of sight.

He headed west.

Ray worked his way north. He instinctively knew where the next shooter would be. He just didn't know who it would be. The light from the fires made it very bright even though it was night. All of a sudden, Ray saw a hat peek out from behind the corner of a building. Ray carefully moved toward it. He waited patiently. Suddenly, Cyrus Welch tried bolting to the other side of the street. He never saw Ray. Cyrus stopped and got down on all fours behind a water trough. He was a sitting duck if Ray wanted to shoot him. Ray was hidden from Cyrus's view, so he sounded like a ghost when he yelled, "Cyrus! I don't want to hurt you, but I will if I have too."

Cyrus Welch was in shock. He squirmed around and looked for Ray.

"I always liked you," Ray yelled. "But it's over. I'm giving you a chance to get away. Drop your gun and take off north."

Cyrus finally figured out where Ray was hiding. He smiled and turned in that direction. He pitched the Colt Navy on the ground.

"All right, mate," Cyrus said. "Ye win!"

Ray stayed low, but he stepped into sight from around the corner. The two men looked at each other.

"Leave town!" Ray yelled at him. "If I ever see you again, I'll have you arrested!"

Cyrus Welch knew Ray was telling him the truth. It was time for him to go. Very gradually, he slipped away and out of sight.

Ray knew there was a small chance the three kidnappers could meet up and come back against him. But he let them go anyway. He didn't care. There was only one more villain to apprehend tonight.

It wasn't hard to find him. Sores Aguilar always had a master criminal mind. However, he wasn't a master criminal himself. He always got other people to do the dirty work for him. The only exceptions were made when it came to collecting money. He always liked to handle that chore himself. He knew he could never beat Ray Andrews in a fair fight.

Things seemed to settle down a bit. People were afraid of the gunfire, but they were even more scared of the fires. Slowly, there was some success in putting the flames down. Again, Ray slipped around to the back of the area. He was looking for Sores's shooting position. It was only a few minutes before he found it. Sores was hiding behind a table that he had propped up on the street.

That was when Ray Andrews did something that was a little odd. He stepped right out into Capp Street and started walking toward Sores Aguilar. Sarah and the reverend were watching from the window of the mission.

Ray was trying to draw a shot from Sores. It was obvious. He was ready to start firing if he saw any sign of a gun. But Sores was too smart for that. He watched Ray walking toward him. Even if he stood up and got off the first shot, he knew his odds were not good.

Sores chose to do something else. He pitched the Colt Navy out in the street. Then he stood up behind the table.

"You're not going to shoot an unarmed man, are you, Andrews?" Sores asked Ray.

Sarah Thomas opened the front door of the mission, but neither Ray nor Sores noticed. They were totally focused on each other.

Once again, Sores Aguilar had been thinking on another level. "I don't have a gun, but I have a knife," Sores said.

Suddenly, he pulled a Bowie knife with his left hand. Ray wasn't surprised. Sores knew Ray wouldn't shoot him if he wasn't armed with a gun.

"Why don't you fight like a man, Andrews?" Sores asked as he slowly crept toward Ray.

"Why do you need to hide behind a gun?" Sores continued to chastise him.

"Throw your gun down and let's settle this man to man," he yelled.

So, Ray accommodated him even though he hated knife fights. The two men were standing fifteen yards from each other. The fires had calmed down. People were watching from buildings all around them. Ray dropped his gun and pulled his knife. It was nothing like what Sores was holding. It was just a simple hunting knife that he had owned for years.

Sores Aguilar smiled and started moving forward. Ray didn't move. When Sores got within ten yards, he suddenly raised his right arm. He was holding a Derringer pistol. He pointed it straight at Ray. Suddenly, a shot rang out, and Sores Aguilar fell to the ground. He was shot right in the chest. Ray looked to his right. Standing there, holding a Colt Navy revolver was Sarah Thomas. She had fired the shot.

Ray kicked the Derringer and the Bowie knife away. It wasn't necessary though. Ray knelt down. Sores was gasping for air. He looked up at Ray and was desperately trying to get control of himself. All of a sudden, he stopped struggling. The two men locked eyes. Ray could barely hear Sores whisper, "I'm glad it's over."

Sores Aguilar died right there on Capp Street. Ray noticed that the shot had gone through Sores's coat. It had torn the pocket open. Inside the pocket was a small pouch. Ray got down on his knees and opened it. Inside the pouch were six blood–stained feathers of the Summer Tanager, the native bird in Southwest Texas.

CHAPTER 59

There were never any charges filed on the shooting at Capp Street. The fires were a lot more important news. The area which was now becoming known as the Mission District was lucky. Smart firefighting by the locals stopped a disaster. There was some damage, but it wasn't substantial.

Sores Aguilar was laid to rest in an area on the northwest side of town. Ray Andrews had decided against the burial being too close to Stuttering Henry Jones. They were still laid to rest two miles apart. Ray gave Sores a nice burial. He dug the gravesite seven feet deep. He didn't want any animals to get to the body.

There were only three people who showed up at the funeral. The reverend conducted the service. Ray did the labor. Sarah helped with the details. She had never killed anyone before. It was bothering her, but she would get through it fine.

Cyrus Welch, Suk Too, and Billy Lambert met up with the crew at the Melba Lee. They got on the clipper and took off early the next morning. The three men separated in Southern California. All three of them had plenty of money in their pocket Their business ventures with Sores Aguilar had been very successful.

Ray took a job in the sheriff's office and worked all over the county. Sarah continued to work in the mission with her father. Ray and Sarah married and had a son whom they named after the city. They lived in the Potrero Hill area the rest of their lives. Neither one of them ever fired a gun again. That was a little odd considering that Ray was a deputized man. He always found a way not to use his firearms, but he certainly did make some threats.

The reverend took ill a couple years after the shooting on Capp Street. He was gone in just a few weeks after he started a bad cough. Before he died, he made sure that everyone knew he was a very happy man.

"My job here is complete," he said many times. "I know Sarah and Ray will continue the good fight. I leave with a smile on my face."

He was buried on the grounds of the mission.

The mission itself continued to grow. Ray finally retired and helped Sarah full time at the church. Several other churches of different denominations started springing up in the area, and the rest of the city continued to flourish.

The town boomed throughout the 1850s. When the Civil War began, it was hard for the locals to really say they were involved. It was so far away. Eventually, its roots did creep into California, but it was the search for gold that kept most of the people's attention.

John and Lovie Kitchens settled in San Francisco and lived a happy life. Ben Fields and Junior Hoskins continued to work together for a couple more years before splitting up and going their separate ways. Fields opened a saloon and gambling hall south of the city and lived into his sixties. Junior traveled her entire life. She earned income as a sharpshooter in gun shows. She also played a lot of poker. She died in Austin in 1859. She was shot after getting into an argument about a card game.

Sawyer Crenshaw made it back to Austin, but he never made the trip to California again. He bought a hardware store in Austin and lived to be an old man. He always provided a job for his buddy, Willie Foster. The Overland Stagecoach Line began operations in 1857. The business of transporting passengers to California changed. The independent coach operator was all but out of business.

Georgia Tipps made a small fortune as a gold and silver trader and pawnshop owner. One day, she was trying to cross Market Street when she was trampled by a runaway horse and buggy. She was sixty-two years old and was wearing Mara McLemore's brooch at the time of her death. Georgia's niece sold the brooch at an estate sale for fifteen dollars in 1892 to a young lady from Sacramento, California.

The Vigilance Committee continued on its mission for years. Finally, Colonel Jack Hays and some other politicians seized control and the hangings stopped. The Aussies continued to invade the city, and the problem with opium continued.

Jack Coffee Hays became the land surveyor of San Francisco County in 1853. He never served as a law enforcement officer again. His interest in politics led him to several posts. Eventually, he became a very wealthy man by investing in real estate.

The Lonely Sailor never opened its doors again. At first, people just thought the bar had closed down for a few days. Then people started to ask questions. The doors were locked when Sores Aguilar left for the last time. It became abandoned property and burned in a fire on April 10 of 1854. The gold that Sores hid under each light fixture was never retrieved. It's still there, buried under the property.

Between the three of them, Ray Andrews, Henry Jones, and Sores Aguilar had transported seven Colt Navy revolvers into the city. Ray's guns had only been fired a few times. Sores's guns were passed around between different men and fired many times. There had always been a problem though. Nobody in Sores's crew ever learned how to load a Colt Navy correctly.

Ray kept all seven of the guns close to him for a few months. Finally, he decided to give all but two of them to the sheriff 's office. He always enjoyed training young law enforcement officers how to use them. One of the guns Ray kept was the Colt Navy that Sarah used to shoot Sores Aguilar. He marked it so it could always be identified. Sarah wanted nothing to do with it, so Ray stored it at the sheriff 's office under lock and key.

Ray Andrews made sure he kept possession of that particular Colt Navy for years. When he became an old man, he donated the gun to the San Francisco Historical Society. When he told Sarah about what he had done, she just shook her head. They hadn't talked about the incident in years.

CHAPTER 60

San Francisco, April 1917

*S*unday morning was always Francis Andrews's favorite part of the week. His mother and father had always made Sundays very enjoyable for him. It was always a day for them to celebrate and spend time together. Naturally, Fran gravitated toward the ministry. He took over the Grace Methodist Mission Church when he was twenty-five years old. Now in his sixties, he was one of the spiritual leaders of the entire city.

However, this day was not just any ordinary day in San Francisco. Thirty-six preachers in the city had banded together. They had all agreed to focus their sermon on putting an end to the seedy, red-light district in town that many referred to as Aussie Town. That part of town stretched from Montgomery and Kearny Streets down through Pacific Avenue. It had become well known throughout the western part of the United States. It was famous for its "anything goes" reputation.

However, the fight to shut it down had grown too strong of an opponent. Most of the Aussies who had established the area were gone. When the gold rush in Australia ended, so did the migration of the Australian outlaws to America. San Francisco was still the Wild West, but sophistication was definitely showing its strength.

The religious organization of the town had gone to extremes. They placed barricades to block the streets of Aussie Town. That infuriated the saloon keepers, brothel owners, and opium den tenants, but it also made quite an impression on anyone else who noticed. One of the main preachers to make a stand was Francis Andrews.

He was excited but nervous about his sermon that morning. He would be strong but not mean-spirited. He had gotten to know many of the people who frequented Aussie Town. He loved the first service of the day at nine o'clock in the morning. That had always been his favorite.

Reverend Fran had run out of things to do before the service, so he decided to grab a broom. He still had an hour before church. Quietly, he swept and prayed at the same time. That was when Vivian Johnson and her two children walked in the front door. Fran welcomed them.

"Well, hello, Vivian," he said with a smile. "Thanks for coming!"

Vivian had on her finest dress. It had a plunging neckline, and it also showed off her beautiful legs. She wasn't in a good mood, and she didn't seem to have much to say. Her two children, Willie who was ten and Jane who was eight, were happy to be there. However, they knew not to say a word. They feared that their mother might slap them if they did.

Reverend Fran beat them to the punch. "Willie, it's great to see you," he said. Reverend Fran knelt down to face Jane. "How are you, Jane?" he asked.

She couldn't help but to smile. Vivian grabbed both of their hands and pulled them back.

"You know why we're here," she scolded the reverend.

But Fran had been waiting not only for Vivian and her children but also several other broken families that day.

"Of course, Vivian," he answered. "Come on back to the kitchen."

The four of them made their way back to the small dining room in the back of the church. Reverend Fran had prepared a feast of a breakfast to anyone who wanted to eat. He had pancakes with butter and bacon with the special seasoning that he loved. There were plenty of scrambled eggs. When the children hit the door, their entire demeanor changed. Jane couldn't help herself.

"Reverend Fran, you made my favorite pancakes!" Jane said.

Willie grabbed a plate and took his place at the front of the line like he had done many times before. The reverend served up the breakfast. At first, Vivian wouldn't eat, but it only took a few minutes before she couldn't help herself. She always had enjoyed the reverend's cooking.

Reverend Fran poured himself and Vivian a cup of coffee. They all sat down at the table. They looked into each other's eyes. Neither said anything. Finally, Vivian broke the silence.

"You know you're gonna get what you want," she said between taking bites of her breakfast. She took a big gulp of coffee.

"How am I going to feed these kids?" she asked him sharply. "I don't have any other way to make any money. We'll starve."

She rubbed her eyes and tried to wipe the tears away.

"I've lived here all my life," she said. "I have no place to go." Reverend Fran knew every angle of the dilemma that he and the other preachers in town had created.

Softly, he answered her. "Vivian," he said. "We're fighting for a minimum wage law. That will help you if you will be patient. I will help you get a job; I promise."

But that wasn't good enough for Vivian Johnson. She was a veteran of the oldest profession, prostitution. She knew that the odds of someone giving her a job were small.

Reverend Fran's heart was heavy. He loved her and her kids. There were literally hundreds more just like them in the city, and the reverend knew most of them too.

"I'm gonna have to leave the city," Vivian said. "I don't know where I will go."

Tears streamed down her face. Willie and Jane had finished their breakfast and were playing on the floor of the kitchen. Willie was teasing Jane and had made her scream.

Vivian jumped out of her chair and grabbed Willie. She raised her arm. Before she whacked him, she looked at the reverend. He didn't say anything. She held back her fury and scolded her son.

"That's enough, young man," she screamed. "You act right when you are in this church."

Vivian looked at the reverend and managed a smile. She let go of Willie's arm. The two kids started playing again. Reverend Fran couldn't help but to compliment her.

"You're such a good mother," he said. "You don't have to hit them to make them mind you."

Vivian went back to her breakfast. Finally, the reverend spoke, "It's over, Vivian."

She looked up at him. "I know," she said. "I know."

Fran looked deep into her eyes. He could see the damage that years and years of opium abuse had caused.

Vivian finished her breakfast and got up to leave.

"We're going up to Central Methodist," she said. "A bunch of us are taking our kids. We're gonna sit on the front row. Maybe the church will back off and leave us alone."

She knew that wasn't going to happen though. The end had come for Aussie Town.

"Come on, children!" Vivian scolded Willie and Jane. "It's time to go!"

The three of them started toward the door. Before they got to the exit, Willie stopped and turned around.

"When do we eat again, Reverend Fran?" he asked.

Francis Andrews was quick with an answer.

"Tuesday night at six o'clock," he said. "I'm making meatballs." Willie jumped up in the air.

"I love it when you make meatballs!" he screamed.

Fran followed the family out the door and watched them walk away. After about thirty yards, Vivian stopped and turned around. "Thank you, Reverend," she said. "Probably see you Tuesday." She said it like she was asking for his permission.

"See you Tuesday!" the reverend answered with enthusiasm. Other people started filing into the church. Almost all of them were down on their luck. Reverend Fran knew he had about twenty minutes to feed some people before the service started. He always kept the first service short, because he knew how many people counted on him to get something in their stomachs on Sunday morning.

He started to make his way back to the kitchen. However, for some reason, he turned and walked to the window. He looked out at the small cemetery in the back of the church grounds. There lay his mother and father along with his grandfather. He folded his hands together and put them up to his chin. He knew he had made them proud.

ABOUT THE AUTHOR

*G*erald **Brence** has written three novels. **Ox in the Culvert** is historical fiction about a disgraced Texas Ranger who guards a stagecoach on a treacherous journey to San Francisco during the California Gold Rush. **Agent 49** is also a historical fiction story about one of the greatest crimes in American history. The book chronicles the illegal passing of the Atomic Bomb blueprint from the United States to the Soviet Union. **Old Money** is a tale about three young boys who take on the town bully. As they grow older, the paths they take put a strain on their relationships. What was fun and games as kids become life and death as adults. Brence is a former English teacher and coach. He also is the author of a non-fiction book about high school football titled **The 70-30 Split.**